THE
RAVEN
AND THE PIG

THE CELWYN SERIES BOOK 3

THE RAVEN AND THE PIG

LOU KEMP

4 Horsemen
Publications, Inc.

4 Horsemen Publications, Inc.
1497 Main St. Suite 169
Dunedin, FL 34698
4horsemenpublications.com
info@4horsemenpublications.com

Cover by J.Kotick
Typesetting by Autumn Skye
Edited by Joseph Mistretta

Library of Congress Control Number: 2022949207

Paperback ISBN-13: 978-1-64450-705-6
Hardcover ISBN-13: 978-1-64450-706-3
Audiobook ISBN-13: 978-1-64450-708-7
Ebook ISBN-13: 978-1-64450-707-0

Table of Contents

Acknowledgements:

MANY THANKS AND LOVE TO MY daughter Charmaine who supports me no matter what I dream up. Thank you to friends Nikki, Debbie, Peggy, and Karen for their support and advice. Authors, who are also friends, have improved my work beyond simple mistakes and to think as I write: Anita Dickason, Bejamin X. Wretlind, Bob Van Laerhoven. I am grateful to John Helfers of Stonehenge Editorial for his patience and expertise in the initial editing of the Celwyn series.

Cast of Characters:

Jonas Celwyn: immortal magician, tea lover, and provocateur

Professor Xiau Kang: automat, doctor, academic, and scientist

Bartholomew: Brave, superstitious engineer, widower from Juba

Pelaez: Celwyn's immortal and immoral magician brother

Annabelle Pearse Edmunds: heiress and ward to Uncle Celwyn

Captain Patrick Swayne: fiancé of Annabelle, friend to Celwyn

Mrs. Elizabeth Kang: tolerant & beautiful wife of Professor Kang

Qing: mechanical bird and lover of all things shiny & wonderful

Zander: an orphan rescued on the way to Prague

Otto: an orphan who joined them on their journey to Singapore

The Elizabeth: their magically-enhanced vintage train

Tara McFein: good witch and good vampire

Simone Redifer: good vampire

Valentine Soriano: vampire and uncle to Tara & Simone

Thales: ancient healer of immortals

Wolfgang Augustus Griffin: Celwyn and Pelaez's father

Lorimar Duncan: malevolent wizard working with the Mafioso

Captain Nemo: skipper of the *Nautilus*

Jules Verne: author

Prologue

1877
The rolling hills near Odessa,
north of Constantinople

FOR EACH STEP HE TOOK, PROFESSOR Xiau Kang sensed the intensity and importance of what he would find. Above all, he felt the weight of his sadness. He had done his best to ignore that there was no guarantee Captain Nemo had located Thales. If Nemo failed to find him, Jonas Celwyn would be dead within a matter of days, perhaps hours.

A long time ago, as new friends they sailed westward across the Pacific on *The Zelda*, and when under strain, the magician had doubted a mechanical man could feel emotions. So wrong. Right now, Kang stopped walking until he regained his control. The automat knew real sorrow—a wrenching grief that they would lose Jonas. He swallowed hard and walked faster, climbing to the top of the berm.

There she was! The long black submarine lay still in the water. A single sailor stood on patrol and another perched in the cage up top with a spyglass. With the low hills surrounding them, they would not have been able to see *Elizabeth's* smokestacks where she sat miles away.

Kang called, "I'll bring Mr. Celwyn. Please let the Captain know we're here."

Halfway back, Conductor Smith joined him as they ran towards the hired coach. The others had seen them and began unloading the magician onto the stretcher that Kang had fashioned for this moment. He skidded to a stop and grabbed Celwyn's hand.

"The *Nautilus* is here. It isn't far."

In the distance, a low hum reached them; the sound sputtered and grew stronger.

The magician's eyes opened slowly, like a thread from his memory had raised his lids, compelling him to look as if he knew what was to come. Everyone gazed upward.

The noise grew louder, and a bright yellow flying machine crested the low hills, heading toward the estuary.

"Yes!" Kang shouted, raising his fist in triumph. Mrs. Elizabeth Kang grasped her husband's arm and kissed him.

The plane swerved to the north, banked, and then flew toward them again in a wide arc.

"Oh, my God, it's Bartholomew!" Elizabeth exclaimed.

Bartholomew wore a broad smile and his scarf fluttered in the breeze as he sailed over them. He waved at them in pure elation. As he banked, the engine revved and he turned, descending for another pass. Celwyn raised himself onto an elbow to wave back.

"Hurry," Kang said. "Bartholomew is going to land. We must get Jonas onto the ship."

<hr/>

Captain Nemo led the way to his study and lifted the magician's legs onto the sofa himself. As the automat tucked blankets around him, Nemo placed more pillows under Jonas's head. The magician's eyes closed again. Just moving him had depleted him further.

"As you can see, the situation is dire." Kang faced Captain Nemo. "Did you find the healer?"

From his position at the foot of the sofa, Jules Verne's eyes bounced between Nemo and the automat. Before Nemo could answer, Phileas Fogg arrived, joining the gathering in front of the magician.

Fogg's demeanor bothered the automat; it showed in the shiftiness narrowing the man's eyes and the assessing looks he aimed at both Captain Nemo and Kang. Before today, he had exhibited a measure of respect for Captain Nemo. Now, he didn't seem to have any at all, brushing by him with a haughty glare.

Across the room, a collection of silvery fish swarmed the glass of the ship's aquatic window as if they too could see inside.

When Bartholomew appeared in the doorway, he filled the study with infectious exuberance. Then he saw the magician.

"Oh, Jonas..." The big man dropped to a knee and smoothed the hair off Celwyn's forehead. In a whisper, he asked, "What happened?" The magician's eyes remained closed, his breathing shallow.

"He was already sick when we were attacked in Prague." The automat swallowed hard and looked directly at Bartholomew, and then at Captain Nemo. "I think he is dying."

"That is why Professor Kang asked me to find the healer. It is the only chance your friend has." Captain Nemo turned to the automat. "Thales exists, but it will take several days to travel to him."

"Jonas..." Bartholomew walked away, his shoulders shaking as he held his head in his hands and wept.

"We need to leave now," Kang said. "He has so little time left."

As Captain Nemo started to speak, Phileas Fogg stepped in front of him to gaze down at Celwyn. With a voice as controlled as a machine, he said, "That is not possible. We will take the flying machine south to Morocco as planned."

"No." Captain Nemo squared off in front of him.

Fogg bristled. "It is *my* money."

Nemo's voice turned as hard as the sides of the submarine. "I am the Captain of the *Nautilus*, and we go—"

"Perhaps I can resolve this." Fogg's smile sent chills up Kang's back, and his premonition came too late.

Fogg removed a pistol from his coat and aimed it at the magician.

"No!" Bartholomew dove in front of Celwyn as Fogg fired.

The bullet hovered before Celwyn's chest, then it crystalized and shattered—the magician's final act. Bartholomew tackled Fogg. As the revolver fell from Fogg's hand, they rolled across the floor, and the big man squeezed the life out of him.

The magician sighed and closed his eyes.

Into the violence, Celwyn's music began.

Softly, from within the air, as if they too struggled to breathe, the same five notes played so delicately they could barely be heard. The notes faded and stopped. Melancholy overwhelmed them as Qing flew overhead, cawing forlornly.

Time stilled, and the grieving began.

The violins returned in force, marching in harmony, strong and pure, with the five notes reverberating the air. From the shadows beyond the bookcases, the strange man that the automat had last seen at the café in Singapore, who enjoyed manipulating fish with pig faces, sauntered toward them.

He bowed and regarded Kang as if he was a particularly useful chess piece.

"So nice to see you again, Professor. Allow me." He knelt beside the magician and put a hand over his chest. In another second, a sigh escaped the magician's lips.

The man leaned forward and whispered in Celwyn's ear, loud enough for them all to hear.

"It wouldn't be seemly for you to die on me, Brother."

Pelaez's eyes gleamed as Celwyn groaned. The music strengthened, and he began breathing again.

"We have so much to talk about, wouldn't you say?"

With an infuriated growl, Bartholomew flung Fogg's lifeless body at Captain Nemo's feet.

Chapter 1

A S THE ETHEREAL VIOLINS WANED, the stranger backed away to allow Professor Xiau Kang access to Celwyn, lying as still as death. The automat placed his fingers on the magician's pulse, nodded, and checked his eyes.

"He is stronger and his breathing regular," Kang's voice shook as he straightened and faced the much taller visitor. "I suspect that he breathes again because of you."

"That is correct."

Captain Nemo approached the crewman stationed by the hallway door. Seconds later he ended a murmured conversation with, "...as quickly as possible. South 110 degrees."

Before he returned to stand beside the magician, the lights in the study of the submarine dimmed twice and then brightened again.

1

"Heavens! I must tell the others—" the automat bolted down the corridor and scampered up the spiral staircase. When he emerged, he saw their livery driver Edward as he paced on the estuary bank. Like an unexpected foot massage, the metal stairs under Kang's feet vibrated as the *Nautilus'* engines commenced.

"Tell Elizabeth I love her! We need to save Jonas, and Bartholomew is going with us!" Kang had warned his wife this might happen. He called out, "Take everyone back to Prague—"

"Sir, what—" Edward shouted.

A wave of frigid water sloshed across the nose of the ship just as Kang felt a tug on his leg and heard Bartholomew. "Get in here. They are diving!"

"I must go—" The automat scrambled inside the hatch, shouting, "Tell her I love her!"

As Kang tumbled down the ladder into Bartholomew, the hatch closed above them with a loud clang. He immediately felt the submarine moving and heard the faint rush of water overhead, or imagined he did. With a half-smile, he wondered what Edward would think of the sight.

"Come," Bartholomew said, leading him back up the corridor.

They entered the study to find Jonas's brother relaxed in a chair, watching the fish and greenery through the aquatic window as the *Nautilus* moved forward, gaining speed. The man smoked one of Nemo's cigars and sipped a whiskey, completely at home, as if the situation wasn't urgent.

Why is he here? Kang glared as he crossed the room. The magician still lay on the sofa, his eyes closed and face slack, but his color seemed better. Kang knelt beside him.

"My friend." The automat brushed hair off Celwyn's brow and noticed Qing had snuggled onto the magician's pillow, resting his beak next to the magician's ear. The mechanical bird blinked at Celwyn; his glittering eyes diminished. "He will be fine, Qing." Even the Professor's own words did not ring as sure as he had hoped.

The automat monitored Celwyn's breathing a moment more and then stood as Bartholomew approached the stranger. At over seven feet tall, the big man appeared formidable, even more so as he clenched his fists—probably controlling an urge to violently confront this outsider. Whereas Jonas was nearly as tall and strong as Bartholomew, his brother appeared to be no more than six feet tall with a compact frame, like a circus acrobat. Bartholomew could toss the interloper across the room if he could catch him, and Kang wished he would.

The man had watched their approach in the window's reflection. When they arrived, he swiveled, leaning back to study Bartholomew's face above him, then switched his regard to Kang's much shorter stance.

"Perhaps, I can guess. You are angry, but do not know why. And the reason Mr. Bartholomew hasn't tried to throttle me is because you suspect I am the only way to keep Jonas alive." He eyed them with nonchalance and then smirked. "You are also a bit afraid." Kang held Bartholomew's arm to stop him from grabbing the bastard.

Now that things weren't as dire, the automat had time to note how the man's voice sounded as cold and unsettling as any he had ever heard, and Kang had existed a very long time. Close up, Pelaez displayed little similarity to Celwyn; he had much darker skin, a spare and chiseled face, and eyes like a gathering storm. In comparison, Jonas's emerald-green gaze radiated mischief and good nature.

Bartholomew inhaled and held his breath until he calmed down, then pulled chairs closer to the table. When they were seated, Kang noticed Jules Verne by the bookshelves, watching them without any sign of embarrassment. If Jonas were conscious, he would bully his friend into being circumspect; the author had a history of gossiping and using what he heard and saw in his books. Kang didn't want Celwyn's last days to appear in one of them.

"Who are you?" Bartholomew asked the stranger.

The man shrugged. "Your first question should be, am I able to keep Jonas alive? The answer is yes, with magic. But only temporarily."

"Wonderful. Another magician." The automat threw up his hands. He had known it when he first saw this interloper, but ignored it.

"How temporarily?" Bartholomew demanded.

As if he'd learned the art of the nonchalant French shrug from Verne, the man lifted his shoulders and let them drop again. "I must be nearby, and I can only do so much because I do not have Jonas's ability in this area. I can keep him breathing. That is all."

The automat remembered the strange encounter in Singapore.

"Are you Ratzel, or Pelaez?"

"Both." A satisfied smile covered the man's face. "You have heard of me from Jonas." He raised an expectant brow, ready to hear more.

Bartholomew did not disappoint him. "Jonas said you were a stronger magician."

"But of course."

"Only in some ways."

Captain Nemo entered the room and drew closer to the stranger. He paced in front of the glass, oblivious to the assorted sea life and exquisite colors prisming through the water. Kang glanced at the sofa; Celwyn's eyes remained closed, but his chest rose and fell, keeping time with the ticking of the wall clock. It was at this point the automat noticed Fogg's body had been removed. Good.

With a most interested expression, Verne tracked Nemo's progress as he went to the bar, fixed a drink, and detoured to sit across from Celwyn on the other sofa. Over a period of minutes, the room darkened as they traveled deeper, and the water turned muddy and black. In response, the wall sconces brightened.

"Sir, where are we?" The Professor asked as Nemo popped up again and resumed pacing, evidence of his inner turmoil. Nemo continued to the window and back.

"Captain?" The automat repeated.

"Excuse me?" He stopped and frowned. "Sorry. We've entered the Danube Delta. The water will be like this for the next hour or so."

5

"And then?"

"We'll continue to the Cape Verde Islands off the west coast of north Africa. Near the Senegal province."

Kang would ask more later. He turned to the man who had called Celwyn "Brother." There was something most unsettling about Pelaez, as if anyone watching could only see the very top of the glass that he swam in.

"Are you a colleague of the Captain? How did you get here?"

"Jonas is my half-brother." The man nodded at Celwyn with the kind of casualness that suggested his condition was nothing but a toothache. "Why wouldn't I agree to assist if asked?"

"I want to know what is happening at once!" Bartholomew leaned forward; his melon-sized hands balled into fists.

The man did not answer, instead substituting a smile that made Kang want to avert his eyes. "Instead, perhaps the Professor and I can discuss his flying machine." The bastard raised a knowing brow at the automat. "I believe he works with Democritus's theories. Tsk, tsk. Such destructive possibilities."

Kang gasped. How could Jonas be *related* to this man? He thought fast and kept his face blank. The effrontery! The automat realized the most worrying aspect was that Pelaez knew of his work with atoms, not just about a machine that flew. Jonas had said Pelaez could not read minds. No matter—Kang would hide his work before the man found it. He'd only brought two bags aboard, including the one containing his papers.

Captain Nemo cleared his throat and glanced at Verne. "Jules, please leave us."

Without the usual dithering that Verne handed Celwyn when they wanted him out of the way, the author arose, bowed, and walked out. Except for the unconscious magician and the guard outside the door, they were alone.

"I cannot speak for this gentleman's activities before he arrived." Nemo nodded at Pelaez. "As we prepared to leave Singapore to travel here, he lobbied us, saying he was Mr. Celwyn's brother and could help."

The automat glared. "How did he know we needed help?" Kang looked over his shoulder and met the bastard's smirk, whose eyes danced with amusement.

"Out of thin air, he volunteered?" Bartholomew growled under his breath. "It doesn't make sense."

Pelaez continued to drink and, by now, had brought the whiskey bottle to his side without getting up. Apparently, a fraternal habit.

Captain Nemo looked at Bartholomew. "Yes. He knew you were in Prague, and he knew of Mr. Celwyn's condition. He volunteered to help while we journey to Thales. If there had not been an urgency to arrive here, we would have investigated more." Nemo sent Pelaez a hooded glance.

From the sofa came a muted groan. Immediately, Kang went to the magician's side and felt his pulse. After a moment, he returned.

"He is very weak."

Pelaez spoke up, "Perhaps, to save unnecessary worry, you should think of my brother as being suspended inside a bubble. He is comfortable, except for his thoughts, which are probably disturbing."

Nemo's glare indicated a desire to fling Pelaez onto the next rock the submarine sailed by. He stood. "I must get back to the bridge." He stared through the murky water to the muddy walls threaded with plants and tree roots. Nemo jerked his head at Pelaez. "He boarded the *Nautilus* just before we left Singapore and remained in his cabin until we got here. We were in a desperate hurry, per your request. Mr. Bartholomew—and most of the crew—did not know he was aboard." A series of gongs resounded from below. "I know no more."

Bartholomew's scowl at Pelaez didn't change.

Perhaps anticipating the next question, Nemo added, "Mr. Pelaez said he would keep his brother alive as needed, and for that, I am grateful. It is only a few days until we reach Thales."

With his hands on his hips, the automat confronted Pelaez. "What do you expect from this journey?" His anger rose with his voice, and if he had been Jonas, by now, the glassware at the bar would be shaking.

Pelaez got to his feet slowly and faced the aquatic window. In the reflection, his face appeared benign. The countenances of many snakes could also, the automat reminded himself. The stranger said, "I hope to be introduced to Thales. That is payment enough."

8

The Professor suspected him. If Jonas had been awake and healthy, he could verify what the automat observed; Pelaez exuded a confident air, full of arrogance and innate assurance that he had nothing to fear. At the moment, Kang would love to know what Celwyn thought about the situation. He peeked at the sofa, but there was no change in his friend, just a reminder of the wrenching melancholy that Kang couldn't shake.

Bartholomew didn't believe Pelaez, and his tight-lipped look at the automat said so.

"Is there anything more, gentlemen?" Captain Nemo turned toward the door. "I am needed elsewhere."

Bartholomew caught his sleeve. "The flying machine?"

"It will be sent by barge to another location until..." he nodded at Celwyn, "...things are resolved."

Chapter 2

KANG SETTLED AT THE CHESS TABLE and checked his pocket watch; a Waltham, and a most handsome gift from Elizabeth.

It was only one in the afternoon, and he sighed from hunger ... or from a sense of unease. As the automat watched the crew set up the luncheon table in front of the aquatic window, he remembered the last time he had eaten in here; the ship had been floating in a volcanic lake when she was slammed broadside by a pair of battling sea monsters.[1] Things seemed calmer now as the *Nautilus* traveled through water sullied with mud from the Tyllhul River and toward the Black Sea.

Wild, strong rivers returning to the sea always reminded Kang of the cycle of life. Infinite life that never stopped. Jonas was part of that. Once Captain

---

[1]   See *Music Shall Untune the Sky*, book 2 of the Celwyn series.

Nemo finished his duties on the bridge, the automat planned to consult him about the details of their westward journey. If it took too long, Jonas could die.

The big man must have thought the same. When the table had been set, Bartholomew settled in one of the chairs across from Verne and asked, "What do you know about our destination?"

Verne put his napkin in his lap, licked his lips, and eyed the soup tureen. "Nothing." A crewman stood behind him, waiting for the Captain to arrive before ladling the soup. "So far, the Captain has not shared that information with me." He gave a slight nod to his left, where Pelaez held a spoon up to the light to admire his reflection.

Kang happened to be sitting directly across from the man and could think of better dinner companions. On his other side, Bartholomew regarded the interloper with a controlled fury that nearly vibrated the table. The automat's initial impression had been correct; none of Jonas's good nature existed in his brother. In its place, fierce intelligence lit up the man's sleepy eyes, along with a good dose of conceit.

Over Pelaez's shoulder, the Professor had a direct view of the sofa where Celwyn lay; he couldn't detect a change in his friend, and it remained so even after the Captain arrived. Nemo greeted everyone and tasted the wine. When he approved, the soup course began.

"Perhaps you can answer this." The automat eyed Pelaez. "Jonas was hardly eating at all before our arrival. I worry if he can last much longer without nutrients. Is there something you can do?"

While Kang spoke, Pelaez had no trouble sampling his soup. As he continued to sip without a response, Bartholomew's annoyance grew until Kang tapped his shin, a signal to wait for the bastard to honor them with an answer. Pelaez fed on irritation.

"Professor, when I said I suspended my brother in a figurative bubble, that is exactly what it is. He will not waste away any further until we meet the elusive Thales."

What if he is wrong? Kang couldn't help but worry, nor could he bring himself to thank the man. Bartholomew had another idea.

"We appreciate your efforts." As Bartholomew smiled, the automat recognized the big man's attempt at subterfuge when he added, "Do you know anything about Thales?"

Pelaez shook his head. "Not yet. Unlike my brother, I cannot read thoughts." His expression changed, sending a cold shiver up Kang's spine. "I have other talents."

For several minutes, they ate in silence while the automat and Bartholomew took turns keeping an eye on Celwyn and fretting. With a bright, diamond-like gaze, Qing maintained his vigil perched next to Celwyn's head, hardly blinking or moving. The seawater outside once more ran clear, and the ship had risen nearly to the surface, swimming through filtered sunlight that pierced the water.

With his manner as smooth as melted butter, Bartholomew addressed Pelaez. "Please, tell us about yourself."

The man enjoyed a sip of wine before he answered. "Apparently, my dear brother hasn't said very much about me."

"Just where he had last seen you."

"Ah, Fotheringhay Castle." Pelaez's expression did not show any dismay at what the location represented. "An event where Lady Jane lost her pretty head."

"He wasn't sure you still existed." As Kang studied the man's mannerisms and speech patterns, he couldn't determine Pelaez's country of origin and knew he didn't sound like Jonas or anyone else the Professor could compare him to.

"Well, it was a memorable afternoon. I believe I still have my invitation to the event somewhere." He regarded them with an insolent lift of his brow that made the automat want to shake him. "It was considered a social coup to be invited. After the beheading—which, by the way, wasn't done particularly well—I traveled to Africa's southern tip, to what will be known as Johannesburg, and then over to Sao Paulo. The journey took a while. Eventually, I ended up on the Falkland Islands near Antarctica." He hugged himself at the memory. "I get chilled just thinking about it."

Verne had been listening to the exchange with the same careful attention as when he wanted to remember and use what was said. The author probably wished he had pen and paper since material for a new book appeared ready to fall into his lap. The big man saw him, too.

"I remember your promise." Bartholomew eyed Verne.

Kang said, "I know Jonas would be very disappointed if you did not keep our confidence."

Pelaez watched the exchange with apt amusement.

"But—"

"No. You promised," Kang's voice rose.

Pelaez turned toward the author like an alligator after an unlucky bird who mistook the reptile for a log and landed on it.

"I don't believe we were properly introduced." The stranger's stare intensified, and Verne shrank back. "I am Pelaez, lately of London and Tehran." A halo of fire crackled as it surrounded his face. "And you, sir?"

Verne licked his lips several times, and his color faded to gray, matching his little suit.

"Jules Verne ... I write novels."

Pelaez snapped his fingers. "Ah! I have read your book about the big balloon racing around the world. Why are you here?"

The automat rather enjoyed watching Verne squirm. From beside him, the big man looked like he did too, to a point—but he would have rather sat on Pelaez. Nemo frowned at Pelaez, then went back to his soup.

"Captain Nemo is a dear friend." The author knocked over his water. "So is Jonas."

Pelaez stared, and the liquid evaporated. A full glass again sat in front of the author, and Verne gulped air like a fish finding itself out of water. Pelaez switched to Bartholomew, "You are black, and your diction indicates you are from eastern Africa. How did you come to be a part of my brother's entourage?"

The Professor detected curiosity, not prejudice, in the question. From his expression, so did Bartholomew as he answered him, "We met last year. I respect your brother very much."

"I don't know why." Pelaez studied his fingernails with affected boredom.

With a growl, Bartholomew's patience snapped. "We *respect* each other. By the way, Jonas didn't know much about you."

Pelaez ignored him and turned a malevolent smile on Verne. The author dropped his fork. Satisfied with the reaction, Pelaez regarded the Professor. "I know about some of Jonas's activities, and I was surprised to learn that you..." he nodded to Bartholomew also, "...were friends. You both seem a bit, ah ... tame—to associate with him."

"Oh?" Kang thought things were plenty exciting with Jonas, perhaps too exciting most of the time. Right now, he was glad Pelaez couldn't read minds; he felt a certain reluctance in letting him know of Elizabeth and the other occupants at Tellyhouse.

"Why do you describe their relationship with Mr. Celwyn as 'tame'?" Captain Nemo asked. "And I would appreciate you not trying to scare my guests."

Pelaez pretended he did not hear the request. "My brother loves adventure. Neither of them fits that description."

Nemo finished another bite. "I see." He kept his eyes down and thoughts to himself. As Kang watched him, he suspected that the Captain planned every move he made and every word he spoke. He'd probably had allowed the bastard's rudeness during dinner to study him. Nothing would be disclosed to Pelaez unless Nemo felt it necessary.

By the time their desserts arrived, Verne had appeared calmer; it might have had something to do with his decision to scoot his chair closer to Bartholomew. As he spooned fruit ice, the author pointed a curious nose at Pelaez, who in turn studied the automat with the fascination of a gold miner who had just found a fat nugget in his pan.

"I have followed your activities for years, Professor," Pelaez said with deliberate innocence. "Would you believe that I met your wife in San Francisco?"

Kang's world stopped. Bartholomew reached across the table and laid a heavy hand on his arm.

"Please, no need for alarm." Pelaez held his spoon like a small shield between them and then dipped it into his fruit ice. "Mrs. Kang was not harmed. Such a beautiful woman. I congratulate you, Professor."

If Captain Nemo hadn't begun talking at that moment, there was no telling what the automat would have done. Knowing Pelaez kept Jonas alive was the only thing that restrained him.

"Gentlemen, would you care to hear about our current journey?" Nemo leaned back and waited while the crewman poured coffee. When he withdrew again, the Captain said, "If all goes well, we'll arrive in the Cape Verde Islands in about four days." He sniffed his coffee and drank.

"This is good news." Bartholomew added cream and stirred, but his eyes stayed on Pelaez. "I do not know anything about Thales."

"There is a distinction between the Thales we seek and the much earlier mathematician, the Thales that the Greeks knew." Minutes went by until Nemo spoke again. During the silence, the automat did his best to let his fear and anger at Pelaez go. It wouldn't help Jonas if he couldn't think straight.

Kang said, "Agreed, the Thales we seek pre-dates the Greek and Chinese civilizations. That would make him very old."

"Jules, everything about Thales and our journey is not for discussion with others." Captain Nemo eyed Verne. "Someday, perhaps."

If only Jonas could see Verne now. Kang enjoyed the next moment as the author's eyes shifted, and he squirmed with frustration, proving he had been planning to do something he shouldn't. Captain Nemo knew Verne very well indeed to demand his obedience without dangling him over a roaring waterfall, as Celwyn had resorted to.

"It is said that in the earliest times our civilizations were visited, and their cities enhanced, by visitors that were not of this Earth. These visitors' descendants were gifted in many ways." As Professor Kang spoke, he imagined what the interactions would have been like. *What would they have done and said, and in what language?*

"Please provide an example?" Bartholomew asked.

"There is Eridu Genesis. Or the attributes of the Greek gods themselves." Nemo tossed out a few more names as if they were part of everyday culture.

Bartholomew's shock mirrored Kang's. "The myths were real?"

"I'd suspected some of them were." The automat grew quiet, lost in thought. *What if the glowing tabernacles in the desert were true? What if Moses had help when he raised the Dead Sea?* These thoughts led to wondering about other flying craft.

When the Professor focused again, he discovered Pelaez regarding them like specimens in an experiment—captivated, superior, and detached. The automat noticed the man rarely engaged in conversations with them, only watching, always watching.

Bartholomew found his voice. "The Hesiod myths have always fascinated me."

Silence reigned until Captain Nemo said, "Immortals such as Mr. Celwyn are the grandchildren and great-grandchildren of this crossbreeding, as it were. Some of them have had children of their own over the years."

"Jonas does not have any." The automat raised a skeptical brow at Pelaez. "Do you?"

"Not yet, but I will in a few years."

Bartholomew's head jerked up, and his eyes widened.

The automat stared. "So, one of your talents is knowing the future?"

Pelaez tested his coffee and added a few drops of cream. "Is this from a sea cow?" When Captain Nemo nodded, Pelaez continued, "The future? Not exactly. To be precise, in some instances, I know my future, which tells me about the future around me." A teasing smile went with that.

Minutes later, dinner concluded, and they left the table to settle in chairs beside Celwyn. Kang checked his patient and patted his hand before sitting down.

"From Thales's background, we learned it would be logical to assume that a few of the original demi-gods exist because they are immortal, and their children's children are immortal also," Captain Nemo said. "On occasion, though, something goes wrong."

"When it does, they would need someone to heal them, such as Thales." Bartholomew loosened his tie. This promised to be an interesting discussion.

Pelaez shrugged but didn't speak.

The automat whirled and skated away. "Captain, do you believe Thales can save Jonas?" If he hadn't glanced at Celwyn at that moment, he wouldn't have seen the magician's finger move. Kang swallowed and held up his index finger, then lowered it again. As he did so, Celwyn's right eye opened just a fraction, and Kang saw a glimmer from within.

The automat started to speak but stopped; if he interpreted what he just saw correctly, Celwyn didn't want him to react, just to know that he listened. Kang stole a glance at him again, but the magician's eyes had closed.

Meanwhile, Captain Nemo continued, "Yes. From what I know of Thales, he can be of use to us."

Kang liked that he used the word "us."

"I will do everything I can to save Mr. Celwyn." Nemo locked eyes with Pelaez.

Qing chose that moment to fly the short distance to the Captain and sit at his feet. He squawked. Nemo ignored him. Qing jumped onto his chair arm and complained louder.

The Captain leaned in so close that the bird could have bitten his nose. Qing blinked slowly. Nemo did the same.

Pelaez clapped with sarcasm. "How adorable."

Chapter 3

J ONAS, MY DEAR BROTHER, COULDN'T place restrictions upon me in his present condition. Perhaps now would be an optimal time to explore and stir up the inmates on this glorified tin boat.

By mid-afternoon, we still traveled just below the surface, judging from the degree of lightness in the endless green water. As we went by, occasional schools of fish scattered as if a small bomb had gone off underneath them. Before leaving the study, Captain Nemo had mentioned his intention to reach a remote section of the Amuri River late this evening.

To pass the time, I consulted the detailed map on the wall between the sea window and Nemo's book collection. The appointed spot where Nemo expected to spend the night lay about ten miles off the coast of Constanta. *Hmm.* The topography of the island indicated a few mountains. Maybe the

Captain would send out a hunting party. Venison steak would be nice. I already tire of fish, fish, and more fish.

Behind where I sat, the large black man, Bartholomew, still remained beside Jonas. He appeared to be worrying, judging by his melancholy expression. For some reason, he and the mechanical man took turns sitting vigil, thinking they guarded Jonas from me. How heroic! However, like it or not, it was time that I had a few minutes alone with my dear brother. To talk, of course.

I sent a petite fire to the end of the ship's main corridor, mostly consisting of smoke and confusion. When the alarm sounded, the black man rushed out to investigate, and I waved a hand, closing and locking the study door.

For a moment, I stood over Jonas, reminiscing. He looked more like his mother than our father. Perhaps it was the deceptive handsomeness. I had no such affliction, being what women termed "interesting" and men called "strong-featured." At the moment, no one would find him attractive. Jonas looked awful, wasting away to nothing. I would bet his mind was as sharp and suspicious as ever, though.

I gave him more oxygen and adrenalin.

His eyes popped open.

"Lay back." I pushed on his chest until he subsided. At the sight of me, a surprising flare shone in his eyes. "How are you?"

After a dramatic wheeze, he said, "Sick."

He had sounded just as melodramatic as a child, too. "How much of what has been said did you hear?"

His eyes became hooded, and he looked to the left.

Someone tried the door from the corridor.

"Open the door—" Bartholomew bellowed, pounding on the frame.

I was ready to quiet him when Jonas grabbed my wrist. "They are my *friends*," he said in a croak.

The pounding stopped.

Jonas smiled.

Oh drat.

A second more, and a muffled noise came from behind the library shelves. The little Professor ran into the room with Bartholomew on his heels. I shook off my brother's grip and clapped.

"Well done, considering your condition, Jonas," I said admiringly. "You managed to send them a silent message. I'd forgotten your talent for that." I turned to the automat. "Where is the door you used?"

Bartholomew advanced, wearing a glower intended to frighten me. I blocked his progress, and he roared like an enraged bull.

Jonas managed a hiss, and the block disappeared. The big man reached me. In seconds, I dangled inches above the floor in a most undignified manner.

"Tell him to release me, or I will be sure that he does so," I said.

Bartholomew pushed me back into my chair while the Professor studied Jonas. Probably checking for injuries. How distrustful!

"What is going on?" Kang confronted me as if he, too, was ready to dangle me by the throat.

Such overacting. "I revived him sufficiently for a conversation. A private one." I shrugged.

"He needs to rest." The Professor advanced, clearly outmatched against my remarkable abilities, but game nonetheless.

"We'll talk another time." I passed a hand across Jonas's face, and once again, his eyes closed. I studied the others for a moment. "There must be a strong bond between the three of you. Why, I don't understand."

Bartholomew took a step closer. "There is." He looked at Jonas. "If you hurt him—"

I patted the air. "It would never cross my mind." Little did he know that I could do so faster than he could blink. Not that I would, of course. My expression must have been easy to read because the Professor spoke up.

"How do we know that you wouldn't?"

The automat was just full of logic. Ha, ha. I bet Jonas found that tiresome. "You'll have to take my word for it." I smiled a warning at him.

When the big man moved toward me again, Kang grabbed his arm.

"Bartholomew, I don't think we'll have a problem." The Professor stared into my eyes, and I could almost see the gears inside his head working. "Pelaez here wants to know about the flying machine. He'll have to do it the old-fashioned way, since he can't search minds like Jonas can."

Bartholomew laughed. "Now, isn't that interesting?"

Chapter 4

JONAS COUGHED AND STOPPED breathing.

Pelaez pushed Bartholomew out of the way and put both hands on his brother's chest.

"Don't die on us, Jonas." Bartholomew hovered over them.

Pelaez sat back again. "Don't be silly. He won't." Pelaez gestured at his brother. "He breathes again." As Kang verified it was true, Pelaez yawned and stretched, reverting to his unconcerned presence. "I'll leave you for a bit, so you can discuss me in private."

Kang watched him saunter from the room, waiting a moment before crossing to the doorway and watching until the man reached the end of the corridor and entered the room next to the bridge.

As the automat settled beside Celwyn's feet, he called a request to the big man, "Pour me one too, please." When Bartholomew and his whiskey arrived, he lowered his voice. "We may not have much time until that bastard returns."

Bartholomew scooted his chair closer, putting Celwyn between them. "Go ahead."

"Jonas is sometimes conscious, and I hope he can hear us." Kang turned to him. "Would Pelaez kill you?"

Bartholomew's eyes widened, and he held his breath as they watched the magician. A minute went by, then another before they heard Jonas, even though his eyes remained closed and his lips did not move. He sounded so weak; Kang debated whether to stop this for now.

"No ... but he would cause ... pain to get what he ... wants."

Kang tapped his hand. "Thank you. Rest. We will always guard you. He will not get near you again. We are on our way to see the healer, Thales."

So soft, they could barely hear it, came a weak whisper, "Tea ... please."

A broad smile of relief spread across Bartholomew's face for the first time in days. "I will ask for some, my friend. Even if all you do is smell it." He headed toward the door, and then the automat heard him say in a very different voice, "Oh, I see you're back."

Pelaez strolled across the room again, wearing a knowing smile.

That evening, they dined under the smaller aquatic window in the Captain's dining room. The white tablecloth seemed to glow in the candlelight, making everything in the dining room cozy and yet feeling unreal to the automat. It would take a bit of time to become used to the sea.

Verne had chosen to remain in his cabin to write, probably because of Pelaez. Bartholomew sat opposite the Captain, leaving the Professor to face Jonas's devious brother. Since they had met him, the man never seemed to sit still; his hands or eyes were always moving, or sometimes both, yet tonight, he sat as quiet as a nun at prayer. Pelaez also avoided Kang's scrutiny, never quite meeting his gaze. However, the most suspicious aspect was that tonight the bastard hardly moved at all.

After the crewman began to serve bowls of fat clams in a steamy garlic broth, Captain Nemo sniffed the aroma and appeared to relax. "We are well on our way to Thales, gentlemen." He thanked the crewman and waited to eat until the others were served. "We will pass through the Bosporus Strait late tomorrow."

"Isn't that the spot where the Byzantine soldiers stretched an iron chain across the water to stop Suleman's attack?" Bartholomew asked.

"Yes. Parts of the chain still exist, by the way. If we had more time, I would send an escort with you into the city to see it."

Kang shuddered, remembering the siege. He lowered his voice with reverence. "When the Sultan took the city, thousands of women and children were killed during the rampage." He shook his head

27

in sympathy. "Most of the men defending the walls of the city jumped to their deaths."

Everyone ate in silence for a few minutes. It was at that point Kang noticed Pelaez hadn't really swallowed any food. A horrible suspicion clutched at Kang's throat. He sent Bartholomew a look and then addressed the table.

"Please excuse me. I must visit my lavatory." Kang arose. "I am sorry—" He rushed out.

Instead of trotting left down the hallway to the cabins, Kang detoured as quietly as possible into the study. As he feared, he found Pelaez standing over Celwyn; and he was also sitting at the Captain's dinner table. He knew the man in front of him was the real one because Pelaez had Celwyn's arm in a vise-like grip. His voice was too low to hear anything except the menace in it. Kang saw the pain on Jonas's face and his wide-open eyes.

"Leave him alone!" Kang cried. "Get away from him!" The automat flew at Pelaez, who laughed and backed up, literally into the air. Qing squawked from atop the library shelves.

Celwyn's face relaxed, and he whispered, "Don't ... let him hurt Qing," before closing his eyes.

Bartholomew arrived with the Captain close behind. Nemo's face darkened when he saw the tableau. "What is going on?" he barked as he stalked into the room.

A half-dozen crewmen thudded to a stop behind him.

Like a feather descending an air draft, Pelaez drifted to the floor. "Nothing."

"He was twisting Jonas's arm when I came in!" Kang shouted.

Bartholomew lowered his head and took a step toward Pelaez. All of a sudden, a wall of flames surrounded him.

"*Not on my ship!*" Captain Nemo gestured to his crew, and they drew their side arms.

The flames disappeared, and Pelaez executed an exaggerated courtly bow. "Please, this is a simple misunderstanding." He leaned against the sofa and treated them to a yawn.

"No—*it is not*," Kang ground out. Despite the threat of flames or worse, he came within inches of Pelaez. "I know what you want." He tapped the bastard's chest. "In case you need an incentive to leave Jonas alone, you should know you won't get anything from us if you hurt him. And nothing anyhow; Bartholomew has made half of the flying machine so far and keeps everything in his memory—without a written copy. There is nothing to steal." Kang pointed at his forehead. "I have the rest of it, and we will only give it to the Captain."

Bartholomew glared at Pelaez.

"I am not after your information." Pelaez's smile sent a cold hand up Kang's back.

"Yes, you are!" Bartholomew's outrage rattled the bottles on the bar.

"How can you abuse Nemo's hospitality in this manner?" Kang stomped to the aquatic window and back, sparking with anger. He glanced to the area in front of the bar where the guard Nemo had left on duty had gotten to his feet and shook his head, seeming unaware of what had happened.

Captain Nemo still clutched a dinner napkin in his hand. With a wave, he dismissed his crew and eyed Pelaez. In a voice full of certainty, he said, "If you weren't keeping Mr. Celwyn alive, you would be expendable, Sir."

Pelaez opened his hands in supplication. "Again, this is a misunderstanding..."

Captain Nemo glared at him.

Bartholomew had been watching the exchange and sighed. "It seems we're all dependent upon each other."

There appeared to be no limit to Pelaez's boldness, as in seconds, he went from provocateur to questioning them as if nothing had just happened. "What do you receive from this besides the flying machine, Captain?" His voice sounded casual, raising another suspicious flag in Kang.

"I am repaying a debt. And I, too, respect Mr. Celwyn."

The automat assumed that if they saved Jonas, Celwyn would have no problem dealing with his brother and his malicious magic. As they filed out of the room to return to the dining room as if it didn't matter, Pelaez asked Kang, "How did you know I wasn't actually with you?"

The automat nearly laughed. *Let him wonder.*

He would remember to tell both Nemo and Bartholomew later what he'd surmised; Pelaez could disable the *Nautilus* just as easily as Celwyn or he could do other things. He was playing with them now, pretending to behave. There must be something he wanted, and the Professor would bet it had just as much to do with Thales as the flying machine.

When they resumed their dinner, both the real and unreal Pelaez were absent from the table. Kang took advantage of the situation and, in a whisper, told them why he had suspected Pelaez.

"That was it?" Bartholomew raised both brows and whispered back, "Because he hadn't eaten?"

"Also, this version of him sat too still compared to his usual jittery mannerisms." Kang nodded thanks as the crewman poured more wine. "From now on, I suggest we have our meals next to Jonas or have many more guards for him."

Captain Nemo finished a bite of sea bass and replaced his fork on his plate with care. "We'll do both. This situation is my responsibility. I did not know what to expect from that man, and I decided his promise to help Mr. Celwyn was worth taking him on this journey." His head snapped up, and he gazed at them with barely concealed anger. "This behavior was unexpected."

"I do not trust him." Bartholomew stabbed a piece of lettuce.

"Concur." The automat couldn't help checking the door. "I also agree that we're all dependent upon each other."

"We don't know the extent of his powers, and it is highly unsettling to be in his presence." Bartholomew pushed his plate away. "We need to know more."

Kang motioned them closer and lowered his whisper still further. "There's only one person who can tell us about Pelaez besides the man himself."

"Jonas."

As they awaited dessert, talk turned to the Bosporus Strait and the cisterns of water located in the hippodrome there. Nemo informed them that all eastern churches stored fresh water from holy springs. This became important when Constantinople fell, later becoming the Muslim city of Istanbul.

"A most colorful area. After we pass by the strait, we travel due west?" the big man asked.

"Yes, at a fairly deep level. There is something I want to show you along the way." Captain Nemo's eyes twinkled in anticipation, his irritation at Pelaez forgotten. For the moment.

Chapter 5

UNLIKE MY DEAR BROTHER, I MAY not be able to read a man's thoughts, but my hearing is excellent. One might even say extraordinary. As I passed by the closed dining-room door, I had no problem hearing Professor Kang and the others discussing me; perhaps it was time they received an artful demonstration of my talents and abilities.

I backed out of the way to allow the crewman into the room with their desserts. After the door closed behind the cart, it couldn't have been a moment more before Bartholomew squealed, and a chair fell. Heavens! He must have found tiny trout bravely swimming through the thick cream on his berries. I whistled as I continued down the hall and into the study.

Jonas lay still. From across the room, I verified he still breathed and took a seat on the opposite sofa.

All the while, the twin guards the Captain had left behind kept me under observation from their posts beside the sea window.

"Dear Brother, pay attention." I watched him, noting a barely perceptible movement of his hand, which seemed more of an involuntary twitch than a reaction to my voice. I resisted tickling his foot since it would only annoy his protectors. When we were boys, he would climb any available tree to escape me until one day, the tree's branches embraced him, and I bit his ear. He soon learned how to manipulate the trees as well.

"You should be proud," I told him. "Your friends are dedicated to you and even willing to attack me to protect you." As I tugged down my cuffs, I told him, "By the way, I took the liberty of borrowing this jacket from your trunk. It is a beautiful velvet." I smiled at him and ran my hand down the front of it. "No use wasting it while you lay there."

The door to the hall opened, and Professor Kang led the way into the room. I waved.

A crewman followed him in with a coffee service. The Captain and the squat little author came next, then the oversized black man, holding open the door for the two guards who had been dismissed. As everyone settled next to Jonas, Nemo stood beside me, never taking his eyes off mine.

I asked, "Did you enjoy your desserts?"

Bartholomew's mouth opened and snapped shut. The Professor just sighed. I'd bet my brother found that tiresome when he performed praise-worthy magic.

Captain Nemo ignored my question and asked one. "What should we know about Thales?"

"You asked this before," I said.

I could almost hear the Captain's teeth grinding as he said, "Humor us, please."

How far could I push him? My, my. Look at that stiff upper lip ... so much decorum and military correctness.

Verne took out a notebook and settled at the chess table a few feet away. Before continuing, I waited for him to uncap his pen. Despite what is said, I am a considerate person. Not patient, but considerate.

"Again, everything I know about Thales is hearsay, but reliable hearsay, from our father." I flipped a hand. "He heard about Thales from various individuals in his early years."

Kang asked, "Does Jonas know any of this?"

"When we spoke of it, he was much younger than I. He may not remember." I gave Jonas a playful poke in the leg. "It is unfortunate that you aren't awake."

"I hope he can hear you," Bartholomew grumbled.

"And Thales?" Captain Nemo prompted me.

I shrugged. "It is said that Thales is the offspring of the demi-god Gaia from ancient times. If true, we are not far from his birthplace. It is in Greece, on Mount Ossa."

None of them could help but gaze through the window as the ship silently slid through the immense black void of water that seemed like an abyss filled with the timeless mystery of everything that had come before. Captain Nemo noted Bartholomew's

35

nervous expression and said, "We'll surface for the night soon. The ship requires a secluded place for maintenance several times a week."

Bartholomew let out an audible breath. One could almost see his anxiety lift like fluffy clouds blown across a blue sky, causing me to wonder why my brother chose such a superstitious person as a companion.

"Will you send out a hunting party as before?" Verne asked Nemo. "I would love some fresh meat or bird eggs."

"Perhaps. We arrive in approximately five hours."

I crossed my legs, sipped, and savored. "To go on ... I do not think that anyone knows how many descendants of Gaia exist, let alone how many children there are from the other gods. What they all must have in common is immortality, wouldn't you say?" I tapped my lips with a finger, remembering what I'd heard. "They may appear to be very normal otherwise and, of course, have innate differences. Or both, like Jonas and myself."

"You don't seem as fond of music as he is," the Professor observed.

I smiled at him until he dropped his speculative gaze.

With a glance over the top of Bartholomew's head, I caused the ornate organ in the corner to play a tinkling baroque ballad. "I enjoy music, at times." When I lifted my chin, the speed increased until it became a blur of sound. Kang covered his ears.

"However, music isn't what my magic is tied to." I noticed Verne writing as fast as he could in his little notebook. In the next second, his pen faded away until he held nothing. There are certain things the man didn't need to repeat. To entertain him, I deposited a gelatinous blood-red frog on the table next to his hand. The creature emitted a guttural noise, causing Jonas's bird to stick its head up, on alert. Verne reared back, and the bird hopped on the back of the sofa. More squawking. The frog answered, and between them, they made another version of music, causing the desired outcome; Nemo's annoyance grew, and his brows lowered.

"Did your father meet Thales? What is he like?" Bartholomew asked. From the other side of the sofa, the mechanical bird approached him with his diamond-like eye focused on the big man's ring.

"Unknown. He only said that Thales could 'fix a problem' or something similar."

The Professor gulped his drink, tilting his head to the side. "Did he try to save your father?"

I laughed. "Whyever for? The old bastard is still around. I don't know exactly where, though."

Jonas stirred, and a low moan escaped his lips.

Chapter 6

IT WAS NEARING THREE IN THE AFTER-
noon the next day when a series of gongs resounded
from the belly of the submarine, sounding much like
discordant bells from a haunted church.

The dark green water remained clear. As they
passed logs, undulating tendrils of foliage tickled
the sleek tuna swimming toward their lights before
zipping away again. For the last hour, Kang observed
that the *Nautilus* traveled deep, more than fifty feet
below the surface. Clouds of small white fish with
bulbous faces scattered before the ship, and a long
Mako shark with prehistoric eyes swerved toward
the glass, disappearing below the submarine.

The automat jumped as they passed over a
cluster of bubbling steam vents that disturbed the
water like a series of boiling kettles. He had not been
expecting the phenomena until he realized there
must be many volcanic tubes under the seafloor

nearby. The *Nautilus* turned slightly, following the path of the vents.

"I've not seen something like that before."

Bartholomew made the comment from his position opposite Kang as they played chess and took turns gazing through the glass. The Professor tried to sip tea. Not his first choice, but the smell of it heightened his empathy for Jonas in his fragile state. He had positioned the teapot, minus its lid, beside the magician, his offering of comfort. They sat close enough that Celwyn could hear them converse, even if he couldn't smile and twist the ends of his mustache while he talked or teased them with magic. The magician still breathed, but nothing more.

At that moment, Pelaez was out of the room, "napping." Kang doubted the man did so, especially since he could never sit still and twitched like a dog covered in fleas.

"I say, do you hear those gongs?" Verne trotted in with his notebook under his arm. He pulled out a chair and joined them.

"We do," Bartholomew said. "I'm sure the Captain will let us know what they mean." He moved a rook toward the automat before turning a deceptively bored look upon the bookshelves.

Kang noted the move before glancing out the window. What *was* that? He left his chair to get as close as possible to the glass; Qing saw him and flew to the ledge below.

"Do you see this?" The automat pointed at the endless depths.

The big man squinted and, in one fluid movement, reached the window, pressing his face close. "It looks like..." He gulped.

Kang couldn't stop staring. From no further away than the length of the ship, one by one, dozens of towering ivory columns appeared, their color a glowing alabaster. They became more distinct as the ship drew closer, and he noticed the pillars supported the tiled roofs that depicted carvings of goats, deer, and other animals. A few seconds more and a structure with massive doors came into view. Kang's curiosity grew. As the ship silently glided by the buildings, the gongs inside the *Nautilus* subsided.

Walkways connected courtyards, their paths strewn with piles of broken pottery. Many of the buildings appeared habitable, while others seemed like little more than a mountain of debris. An even larger structure loomed closer. Fractures as wide as a man dissected the walls, causing the automat to squint into the interior that extended deep into the shadows.

"Look—there are big carts." Verne vibrated with excitement. "See the block wheels?"

"Of a sudden, this display seems much older than I thought." Bartholomew nodded to himself.

"Look at the mounds of bones next to them. I think that is an ox skull or similar." The Professor squinted. "Maybe ... a horse skull." Feet more, they came upon a multitude of white bones poking out of the sand. The area looked enormous, like a graveyard of carcasses.

Captain Nemo had joined them, watching the undersea scene as they passed by dozens more buildings. The glow from the *Nautilus's* lamps illuminated the ruins, then dissipated when the inky water enveloped everything again. The submarine slowed in front of a procession of grand marble stairs leading upward and a mirrored set of steps leading to a dark chasm below.

"That was the main temple," Captain Nemo announced. An enormous ivory building materialized out of the dark water. "I'm not sure what this is."

Kang tried his best to see further into the water but failed. "Sir, I would love to use your diving apparatus to explore here."

From beside him, Verne's eyes bounced like excited fireflies. "What *is* all of this?"

Nemo hesitated and stared at the author as though deciding if he should tell him.

Pelaez had arrived without using the door or walking across the room. He just appeared. After enjoying Bartholomew's gasp, the man had no reservations about describing the scene. "It has to be Atlantis. Nothing else would be this big or advanced." Pelaez leaned toward the glass. "My, my... just as I imagined it." He examined the landscape for another moment. "Though I do not see a great deal of destruction, considering."

Odd. The Professor stared. He didn't detect any bones from human corpses, just from animals. *How decidedly peculiar.* Pelaez had referred to the sudden disappearance of Atlantis, one minute a thriving metropolis full of culture and wonderment, the next, gone, as if it never existed. *Where were the people?*

Thousands of bubbles erupted from under the ship as they passed over another steam vent, this one much larger than the others. As the submarine's shadow covered the vent, Bartholomew stared into the roiling water and said, "There's no destruction here at all. Do you know what happened, Captain?"

Nemo's glance at the author probably included a wish that Celwyn was healthy enough to put a block on what Verne saw and heard. Or sit on him. Pelaez might be able to do something similar, but he couldn't be trusted.

With a shrug, Nemo said, "There are many theories. Plato wrote a great deal about Atlantis, as did Mikonisis."

"Yet, this looks like neither one," Bartholomew speculated. "There are differences in what we see here compared to the long-standing descriptions from Plato and others." He pointed to the building in front of them. "Such as the sculptures carved into the buildings. I wonder ... that last steam vent was huge. As wide as this ship. I ... I think we're passing over an active volcanic cap."

"Perhaps. The field of ruins here is enormous. Doesn't it seem more likely this city just sank beneath the waves?" the Professor asked. "However, I see no volcanic ash or sludge on the buildings. Why? The lava would have hardened when it met the water."

As they talked, the *Nautilus* gradually ascended, keeping her distance as the seafloor rose underneath her. Soon, the reflection from streaks of brighter water painted their faces. Bartholomew pointed to the buildings. "Is it that simple? That the sea levels rose and covered everything?"

Pelaez had watched the last of the buildings and houses go by with a special kind of illumination behind his disturbing eyes. He asked a question intended to make things even more puzzling.

"Gentlemen, what if they built the city underwater in the first place?"

———

For the next several days, Jonas slept as the *Nautilus* traveled steadily west through the Aegean.

Their journey became a historical parade of shipwrecks. Everything from warships, barques, Roman naves longae, carracks, and debris from more recent three-masters lay across the expanse of sand below them. Many of the ships appeared the same as the day they sank; their hulls complete from bow to stern and decorated with skeletons, pieces of clothing, metal barrels, and an occasional view inside the hold of a ship that had been punctuated by a volley of cannon balls. As they cruised by a six-masted carrack split in two, an undulating current caused one of the skeletons buried in the sand to raise its arm, seeming to signal to them as they passed.

Kang whipped around and stared at Pelaez, who sat beside the bookshelves reading. "Did you do that?"

Pelaez turned, saw the skeleton, and waved back with amusement dancing across his face.

The automat tightened his lips but said nothing more about it. If he'd found Jonas a tad annoying at times, he could not compare to his brother. Worse, while Jonas had an erratic temper, he had common sense, too. He wouldn't endanger them, at least not on purpose. Kang glared at Pelaez, knowing that he couldn't say the same about this bastard.

The automat checked Jonas's forehead for fever and then his breathing. As he bent close, the magician whispered, "Xiau..." his voice so weak, Kang barely heard him, "...do not agree to evil ... to save me."

It took a moment, then the automat understood. "You mean Pelaez or Thales?"

"Both."

It was just a breath, but Kang understood. He patted him on the shoulder.

Celwyn sighed deeply, as if his life had depended on delivering the message.

"Rest, my friend," Kang whispered. He squeezed Jonas's hand and turned to regard his brother, who seemed engrossed in a book about sea flora he held under his beak of a nose.

"Is it your understanding that we'll reach our destination early this evening?" Kang asked him.

Pelaez finished a page, taking his time before responding. "Yes. However, Cape Verde consists of many islands scattered across a hundred or so miles. I doubt we will see Thales until tomorrow."

Kang thought for a moment. "We need to make arrangements for transporting Jonas." The Professor bustled out of the room and ran into Bartholomew coming in. He smelled of aftershave and good cheer.

The automat tugged on the big man's sleeve, and they stepped into the map room. After he closed the door, Kang grabbed a pen, dipped it in ink, and wrote.

Pelaez can hear long distances and through closed doors.
Jonas woke up long enough to request that we do not "agree to evil," as he put it, to save him. Pelaez may have heard him. I do not care if he did.

Bartholomew grabbed the pen, and after a moment, handed the paper back.

I would do anything to save him. We need to confer.

"I agree," Kang said aloud. "We are probably meeting Thales tomorrow. Do you know if the Captain has a plan to transport Jonas? Or what the conditions are once we're on the island?"

"No." Bartholomew bowed Kang out of the room. "Let's go ask him."

Chapter 7

A S THE *NAUTILUS* FLOATED OVER AN
expanse of water under the noonday sun,
everyone in the study looked east through the top
half of the aquatic window. Qing squawked his
opinion from his perch on the magician's pillow.

Beyond the mist, in the distance, a forbidding island of towering cliffs and high mountains
rose above the water, only to be obscured and then
appear again as a restless sea sloshed against the ship's
window. To Kang's eye, the island measured at least
five miles long, maybe more, and fog shrouded its
highest peaks. The *Nautilus* moved nearer, closing
the distance.

From beside the automat, Captain Nemo
addressed the room. "I surfaced so that you could see
Antigo Island as we approached. Except for Thales,
it is uninhabited."

"Why?" Bartholomew asked.

"Because..." Nemo watched the waves increase, slapping the glass in a slow rhythm as the ship moved closer, "...none of the residents from the other islands will come near here. My report does not say why."

Bartholomew shaded his eyes and studied the higher peaks of the island. "This could be as dangerous as we feared."

Kang faced Nemo. "Is Thales expecting us?"

"No, but we will be prepared. He may attack if he feels threatened."

"Absurd." Pelaez inserted himself into the conversation, standing so close to the big man he could have straightened his tie. "Thales will probably enjoy our company."

The automat ignored him. "Let's get Jonas ready." He exchanged a significant look with Bartholomew. In a series of notes, they'd made plans to protect the magician from Pelaez and enlisted Captain Nemo's help.

⁓

During the trips topside, while they prepared to go ashore, Kang noticed the island appeared to be asleep. No birds flew overhead, no animals ran through the brush, and the only sounds were the steps of their party crossing the *Nautilus's* floating pier and onto an expanse of white sand. Groves of short trees that the wind had twisted into grotesque monsters led the way inland through acres of low brush. Within twenty feet, the land began to ascend toward the lush mountains that lay in the center of Antigo Island like the spine of an enormous corpse.

From his position in front of the stretcher, Bartholomew raised his head and sniffed the air. "I smell lemons, but do not see any lemon trees." His coat billowed in the breeze as he inhaled again, scanning the terrain. "It is a most agreeable scent combined with the sea."

Kang fussed over the blankets tucked around the magician. Again, he bent over to verify Jonas still breathed. The magician's pallor had been paler the last few days, and the automat could barely see his chest rising and falling. Whether Pelaez's magic was failing or purposely withheld, Kang didn't know; they just needed to get him to Thales.

"This wind may become a problem." At his side, Captain Nemo turned a frown upon the bay and pointed to the white-capped water surrounding the ship. "If it grows stronger, the crew will move the ship further offshore to deeper water."

Nemo glanced at Pelaez, who had sauntered to the far end of the beach they'd selected and stood underneath high cliffs scrutinizing the sheer sandstone walls. Captain Nemo murmured to the Professor and Bartholomew, "It is my understanding Thales can be found in the caves straight ahead." He brought a glass to his eye to study the area about a quarter mile away.

Bartholomew did so, also. While they looked, Kang glanced again at the sea as the gathering wind whipped the waves into a field of white lace that danced merrily across the bay. Miles away to the west, the outline of two more islands could be seen.

"There are several cave entrances at various levels on the rock face." The big man squinted at the mountain. "We couldn't climb up there with Jonas."

"Never fear," Pelaez called from fifty yards down the beach, proving he eavesdropped and the power of his hearing, "I will elevate my brother as needed."

Nemo studied Pelaez a moment before saying, "All right, then. Let's get on with it."

The Professor stared at the rock wall in the distance, certain he could spy a shadowy entrance at ground level. Hoping he could. Kang said nothing, not sure if he had seen someone there or if it was his imagination manifesting his desire to find something, anything, to save Jonas.

Their trek through the brush began with the Captain in the lead, then Bartholomew and the crewmen bearing Celwyn's stretcher. Kang followed them while Pelaez brought up the rear in front of the guards from the ship. Verne and Qing had been left behind, each for a different reason.

The wind increased, the gusts strong enough to blow Kang's hat away. He chased it under the brush, but when he reached for it, it rolled away again. "God-damned Pelaez," Kang grunted when he finally had the hat in hand. As he jammed it back onto his head, he noted tracks in the dirt from unidentified animals, at a guess, rodents and some kind of large cat.

It took another half hour to reach the base of the mountain. Captain Nemo and Bartholomew stood and conferred. Mist rose from a broad and furious river that rushed by in front of them, daring them to cross to the other side.

"Allow me," Pelaez said with a bow. When he straightened again, an arched stone bridge, no wider than a carriage, lay above the surface of the water, reaching to the far side.

Wordlessly, the Professor took the lead, as he should; Kang considered himself the least superstitious of their party, not the bravest, and he suspected this trait would soon be put to the test. He had also been exposed to the habits and abilities of warlocks, witches, and magicians more than the others. Nothing surprised him. It would also be best that he didn't mention it would be geographically unlikely for a river of this strength and breadth to exist on a five-mile-long island. A possible explanation could be a powerful underground spring, but Kang didn't believe it. More likely, this was Thales's form of defense, and only someone versed in magic or similar could cross.

As Pelaez fell into step with him, the automat asked, "Do you have enough energy for both this and keeping Jonas alive?"

"Certainly. I could even provide a procession of jugglers and acrobats to lead the way, or other accompaniment, and still be able to transport us and support my brother. Shall I demonstrate?" Almost as he finished speaking, a herd of mouse-sized goats with extraordinarily long ears appeared before them, bleating in a falsetto appropriate to their size and leading the way forward.

At this point, Kang spied a rather large pig awaiting them on the other side of the bridge. Bartholomew and Captain Nemo saw it too. Bartholomew drew a pistol from his waistband. In contrast to Kang, he was unwillingly familiar with magicians; and in case this happened to be something—or someone—else, he prepared himself.

They reached the other side, stepped onto the dirt again, and approached the pig.

"Weapons won't be necessary," Pelaez told them and patted the pig's head as if it were a family pet. Kang raised an inquiring brow at the big man, who shrugged.

"Shall we?" Pelaez asked and started forward again, the pig waddling along behind him.

When the last guard had stepped off the track and into the brush, the bridge dissolved as if it had never been there.

Too late. Kang's anxiety rose. He cursed silently. *What if Pelaez wasn't with them when they left again?* Pelaez stood too close for the automat to pass along his conclusion that unless Celwyn recovered, they would have to depend on Pelaez's goodwill to return to the ship. From the Captain's lowered brows, Nemo may have thought the same as he rubbed the handle of the pistol strapped to his side.

Celwyn groaned, and they moved forward again.

When they reached the mountain, everyone stopped to gaze at a granite wall rising five hundred

51

feet or more above them. Like a celestial hand had cut through the rock, deep gouges and sharp crevices dozens of feet wide covered the area between smooth expanses of rock. With a shiver, Kang recalled the origin of who they expected to find inside and decided his fanciful supposition about the rock face was not all that fantastic.

Bartholomew studied the eight-by-eight-foot irregular gap in the rock in front of them. "Does anyone else think it odd that there is a cave entrance right here, so convenient for visitors?"

Pelaez shrugged. "I didn't do it."

The pig sat in the dirt beside him, not even winded after it had waddled faster than Kang thought possible to keep up with them. Although the automat didn't want to, he looked directly at the pig to confirm what he'd tried to ignore—yes; the pig had fisheyes. He couldn't help another shiver before he addressed Nemo.

"What do you suggest, Captain?"

Nemo motioned to his men. They saluted and marched forward, disappearing into the cave. No more than a minute transpired before they returned, and one of them murmured in the Captain's ear. Nemo nodded and addressed the others.

"Gentlemen. Beyond the opening is a flat empty area that branches off toward the center of the mountain."

Pelaez swept a hand toward them, and a collection of lanterns appeared at their feet.

Kang gazed at Celwyn. "Let us hurry."

Chapter 8

AS PROMISED, THEY FOUND A WIDE passageway leading inward. Bartholomew had to stoop slightly, making the ceiling a bit less than seven feet tall. As they moved forward, at times, the stretcher barely fit between the walls, and twice Pelaez had to use magic to get it around sharp corners as the shaft twisted and turned its way ahead, always ascending.

Kang tripped, composed himself, and started forward again, inhaling the sharp freshness of lemons that Bartholomew had noted earlier. The further they went, the stronger the perfume became. A sea breeze whistled by, vanishing ahead into the tunnel. Again, Captain Nemo led the way as the passage climbed steeply, and Bartholomew's muscles strained to lift the stretcher higher.

Nemo gestured for them to halt. Several corridors split off from where they stood, and after they conferred, Bartholomew retraced their steps before pushing ahead once more. Like they had a talisman, Pelaez's pig snorted as it waddled along behind them.

They reached a level area just big enough for everyone. The guard by Kang blinked rapidly and shivered.

Bartholomew asked, "Do you hear that?" Perspiration dripped off his face, and the automat suspected it came from nervousness as much as exertion.

As Kang listened, he detected what sounded like the beating of wings. Thousands of them. The *whup-whup-whup* echoed many times over, multiplying until it became a cacophony of noise. The others turned inquiring faces in different directions. As they moved ahead again, the wind shrilled, whipping around them and bringing more of the heavy sweetness of lemons, along with an impending sense of danger Kang couldn't ignore. He checked the others, finding most of them felt it too in their furtive looks to the rear and beyond where they walked.

The Captain motioned for them to stop; Bartholomew placed the stretcher on the ground and withdrew his pistol. Three steps led Nemo to a rock wall blocking the light and what lay beyond it. As he approached, he handed off his lantern to a crewman and withdrew his pistol. The wind erupted past him, first taking his pistol, then the man himself over the wall.

Bartholomew rushed forward with Kang close behind. They found Captain Nemo on the ground and helped him up.

Kang could only gawk, and his breath caught in his throat.

They stood before a wide ledge, gazing across a cavernous vortex. From many stories below, the wind swirled round and round, ascending into a widening maelstrom. Nemo recovered first and gestured at the others to join them. As a group, they walked across the ledge to where it intersected the wall of an enormous amphitheater crowned with a domed ceiling that glittered with thousands of stars, yet it was daytime. To Kang's educated eye, the positions of the stars did not appear random ... they reminded him of Galileo's studies of the planets ... and they looked so real he again reminded himself it was the middle of a sunny day.

Within the churning wind at the bottom of the vortex, thousands of white opalescent birds no bigger than a hand beat their wings furiously through broad streamers of light. It seemed as if they blocked what existed above from what churned in constant movement and turmoil below. Flocks of even smaller red birds flew above them and dived back into the vortex.

Kang glanced to the right, seeing only more towering walls of the amphitheater. Far below, an expanse of water glimmered back to him in the low light. He pulled on Bartholomew's arm and pointed; on the edge of the vortex, the automat saw something he couldn't believe. Within the whirling turbulence, skeletons rode the wind like horses, waving imaginary hats and crashing against the walls before bouncing back and racing forward again. Above it all, the scent of lemons became overpowering.

In front of them, graduated steps led downward along a path to a wide, flat shelf of rock built into the wall. It measured roughly half as long as the *Nautilus*. Beyond it, rounded windowless structures backed up to the wall. When Kang turned back, a thick layer of mist had risen from the water below, hovering as if waiting. The automat could have sworn he saw movement before the buildings, but when he squinted, he saw nothing there.

They needed to get closer.

Bartholomew must have thought the same, for he retreated to the tunnel, and when he and the guards emerged again, they brought the stretcher. Kang checked Celwyn's eyes and breathing, walking with his hand on the stretcher until the path narrowed dangerously and started down the rough-hewn stairs. The pig trailed Pelaez, who seemed subdued, except for his eyes, which darted from the sparkling dome to the whirlwind below, and back again.

Above their party, the flapping of wings became louder as the birds rushed upward into a molten cloud; their formation widened as more birds arrived, and the cloud became tighter and denser. Suddenly, a hush fell over the amphitheater, silencing the birds and everything in the abyss. Their world softened to a dead quiet except for the roar of a waterfall far below.

With a shudder, Kang realized something; the stage had finally been set, and he was part of the chorus. It was not surprising at all. Celwyn and Pelaez had an innate tendency toward the theatrical, and he wondered if all immortals were so dramatic.

Captain Nemo waited for them where the path leveled. When they had all gathered, he started forward once more. So quietly from the maelstrom below the automat wasn't sure he heard it, came the music from a single violin riding the wind upward, becoming louder and more distinguishable the further into the mist they walked. *Was this Celwyn's doing?* Kang wondered. Hearing the violin after so much time with Celwyn wasn't surprising, but a glance at the magician showed that he still lay unconscious, his mouth open and slack. Moreover, Pelaez had said that he did not use music.

Who provided the violin?

Something caused Kang to gaze upward. He gasped when he saw the gilded dome above them shimmer, change translucency, and then disappear as extraordinary, unnatural brightness bloomed overhead. They shielded their eyes, and when they looked again, the mist covering the amphitheater had dissolved.

About twenty feet away, a robed man sat on the ground, cross-legged, staring into the vortex.

Waiting.

By previous agreement, Bartholomew remained beside Jonas as protection. Pelaez, his pig, and the guards gathered on the other side of the stretcher. Captain Nemo and Professor Kang approached the man and stopped ten paces off. Somehow, the automat knew it wasn't wise to get too close.

The man in front of them was no bigger than a young child, yet his wrinkled features appeared the same as any man. His ear lobes hung so low they brushed the collar of his robe, its color reminding the automat of a deep blue mountain lake. The man was shoeless and hairless, with an impossibly round head. Opaque eyes watched them without expression.

Scores of horns and harps joined the lone violin, and the unseen music multiplied tenfold while the concert rose and fell, repeating in slow rhythm like the tides of the sea. Kang shuddered and tried to control his growing fear as the music segued into something familiar—the five notes Celwyn played in times of extreme magic. Yet, they were not exactly the same. And Jonas was in no condition to make them occur. It was not comforting. The automat snuck glances at the others, seeing similar reactions. He filed his observation for later when things were not as dire.

Kang preferred that Nemo speak, and after a long, tense moment, he did.

"I am Captain Nemo of the *Nautilus*." He gestured around him. "These are my associates, Professor Xiau Kang —"

"Stop."

Although the man appeared tiny, his voice resounded like the endless abyss, hollow and sonorous.

"I know who you are." The man stood and faced them. "I know what you want."

In the extremely bright light, Kang watched the man's colorless eyes for a clue and wondered if he was blind. The man turned fully toward them.

"Bring the magician."

Bartholomew licked his lips and summoned his courage. He and the guards brought the stretcher forward. In one fluid move, they set Celwyn on the ground in front of the man and backed away to join the others. Without being invited, Pelaez drew near the stretcher. The old man swiveled and stared. When Pelaez kept coming, he lifted a hand, flinging him against the wall. Pelaez rolled into a crouch and waited, his eyes glittering like a panther's.

Kang started forward, all at once afraid for Jonas, but Captain Nemo laid a restraining hand on his arm.

Thales dropped to a knee and hovered over Jonas, saying nothing while the music of the violins—so like, but unlike, Celwyn's—cavorted with the wind around them. As Kang watched, a faint golden glow emanated from the center of the man, growing more distinct until it covered him as he leaned over Celwyn. He gathered the magician into his arms, holding him close like he embraced a loved one after a long absence.

Carefully, as if he would shatter, Thales lay the magician down again. Long minutes went by so slowly that Kang's hope for his friend was crushed. Celwyn's eyes remained closed as the silence turned sorrowful and heavy.

Kang glanced at Bartholomew and saw tears rolling down his cheeks. The automat understood; he had hoped for so long that Jonas would live.

As the seconds ticked by, and Jonas did not move, Kang's hope began to fade. His sense of melancholy returned, smothering him. He looked down, grief overwhelming him, and he remembered how he loved to tease Jonas, their joking, and relieving their grief when Telly died. Remembering Celwyn's joy when they floated above the train and scared Verne—

A cough. Another, and Celwyn's hand moved. His eyes flickered open.

"Yes!" Bartholomew yelled and raised both fists in the air.

"Jonas!" Kang started forward, but once again, Captain Nemo held him back.

Celwyn turned his head and saw them. When Kang spied the familiar gleam in his eyes, he breathed again. The automat tried to smile for him, but at best, his lips trembled.

The tiny man lingered over Celwyn, running his hands over the magician's face and his heart. When he got to the sword wound, Celwyn winced and then relaxed, breathing deeply.

In a low voice, Kang told Nemo, "I cannot thank you enough for helping us bring him here."

With a grave half-nod, Captain Nemo murmured, "It isn't over yet."

Many minutes passed before the tiny man sat back on his heels. The golden glow began to fade and, in seconds, had disappeared. The magician propped himself on his elbows, then swung his torso upright. He inhaled deeply several times.

Celwyn's voice sounded like the croak of a large, green-eyed frog. "Thank you." He tried to shake Thales' hand and stopped as the man moved out of reach.

Thales spoke in measured tones. "You will live ... a very long time ... if you can refrain ... from ill-conceived ... actions."

"I'm sure I would." Celwyn nearly smiled. "Are you Thales?"

The man studied him as if memorizing him or remembering him and nodded.

"I didn't know you existed," the magician said.

"Very few visit me here." Thales's voice echoed many times over as it traveled downward inside the vortex.

Celwyn regarded the swirl of skeletons that moved below and above them, colliding and clattering together. "Were those visitors?"

It sounded like Thales coughed. His shoulders shook, and then Kang realized he was laughing.

"No."

Celwyn nodded. "I am grateful to you. Beholden. May I do something for you?"

The automat winced, although he tried to hide it. He had been dreading this moment. Yet Jonas appeared serene, if a bit disheveled, with his crumpled shirt and flattened hair. Even his mustache drooped like decimated mice tails.

Pelaez rose and sauntered closer, but not too close. Thales half-turned toward him, saying nothing and studying him with disdain. "Your brother is very much unlike you."

The ever-logical Professor Kang wondered why Thales knew so much about them.

"Thankfully, we are different." Celwyn shot Pelaez an unreadable glance. "However, I would be dead if not for him."

Thales got to his feet carefully, a telling sign of his true age. To Celwyn, he said, "You may stand."

Kang couldn't wait any longer and bounded forward to help Jonas up. "Xiau." The magician swayed and then leaned on him. By then, Bartholomew had arrived on his other side.

The big man rumbled, "I have missed you, Jonas."

Celwyn patted his shoulder. "And I, you, my friend." He pointed his chin at Nemo. "Now, it is I who am in your debt again, Captain."

Thales said, "This is all very touching. However, I wish to answer your question."

Kang felt his earlier premonition solidify into dread as the magician steadied himself and bowed. "What can I do for you?"

Thales's eyes glowed with an inner fire that scared the hell out of Kang. The word *otherworldly* sprang to mind. There wasn't anger in the man's reaction, but the automat would bet it had something to do with revenge or impish glee. When Thales began to speak, the traveling skeletons increased their speed, racing along like they swam through water, up and down the walls, their bones rattling loudly.

"Go to the catacombs in Palermo. Your father is there." Thales's commanding voice grew louder, echoing across the amphitheater. "Convince him to come here."

Pelaez reared back, astounded, and not hiding it.

Celwyn paled, and Kang caught him as he fainted.

Chapter 9

CELWYN AWOKE TO FIND Bartholomew holding him in his arms like a child holding a doll and the automat fussing with him, checking his pulse and lifting his lids to check his eyes. For the first time in weeks, Celwyn felt like himself. Past Kang's shoulder, he saw the tiny hairless man he now knew as Thales. Then, he remembered the last thing Thales had said, and he shuddered, suddenly cold and enveloped in a kind of worry he didn't want to describe.

Kang tried to check his pulse again. The magician stopped him. "I am fine, Xiau. Really," Celwyn said gently and eyed Bartholomew. "I imagine I weigh less than the last time you carried me."

"It is true," the big man grumbled as he helped him to stand again.

Celwyn slowly approached Captain Nemo and bowed. "Like I said, I owe you so much."

"It is nothing." Nemo shook his head. "My reward is seeing you restored to health."

Pelaez eyed Thales, then Celwyn, before drawling, "I believe the proverbial ball is in your court, Brother."

A pair of skeletons crashed into the wall above Pelaez, dropping a leg bone in front of him, then resumed racing around the amphitheater. Celwyn inhaled several times before turning to the tiny man, who once more sat cross-legged on the ground in front of the vortex. Thales stared into it with the kind of concentration that made the magician wonder if he could see. He glanced that question at the automat, who shrugged.

"I haven't seen my father in hundreds of years." Celwyn hesitated. "However, I do not ignore a debt." He steadied his nerves, remembering terrible things he had purposely forgotten for so long. "I will do as you ask."

Before they entered the tunnel again, Celwyn stopped and squared off in front of Pelaez. The others gathered around them, either to prevent bloodshed or out of curiosity.

"I do not know your game, but I know your tricks. We will talk more once we are out of here," Celwyn ground out.

Pelaez's eyes danced a jig. "I look forward to it."

"Fine."

With Pelaez's pig in the lead, and Bartholomew holding Celwyn's arm with every step they took, the scent of lemons accompanied them as they entered the tunnel. Once outside and breathing clean salty air, Celwyn stopped, gathered his strength, and rested several times more as their party picked their way through the brush to the river. They stood so near to the water the mist bathed them.

When the clouds parted, the sudden intense sunlight caused Bartholomew to squint as he studied Celwyn. "If you are tired, I can carry you the rest of the way."

"The offer is appreciated." The magician stood as tall and straight as he could. "It feels so good to touch a breeze again. However, my most pressing need is to reach the ship, to drink some tea, pat Qing on his little brain, and food." He included Kang and Nemo in his short speech before saying, "You should all know that Thales did more than save my life. We will talk of it when we are on the ship."

As Captain Nemo clapped him on the back, the sun deserted them, and the air became colder. "Let's get you to the *Nautilus,* then." He stared at the roaring river. "Everything else can wait."

Kang walked onto the loose dirt at the edge of the waterway and tottered backward as the bank gave way. He sent the river a dirty look and returned to the others. "We had help from your brother to cross over the first time. You should conserve your energy." He turned to Pelaez. "If you don't mind?"

"But of course." Pelaez swept a hand, and the stone bridge appeared again.

With a critical eye, Celwyn regarded it. "I suppose it will do."

Pelaez's voice grew louder, "You *suppose?*"

Celwyn maintained his grip on Bartholomew's arm as he pivoted to face the man that he had hated for three hundred years. "*Why* are you here?"

As a hint, Kang and Captain Nemo stepped onto the bridge, and the automat signaled to Bartholomew. The big man tried to steer Celwyn forward, but he resisted, glaring at Pelaez.

"You are still an ungrateful bastard, Jonas." Pelaez brushed by him and the others, calling over his shoulder, "Hurry up."

As the big man helped the cursing magician onto the bridge, the wind whipped Celwyn's face, and gales pushed a bank of dark clouds toward them. Between the river and the sea lay another expanse of brush and then more sand before a picturesque bay. "Where are we?"

Bartholomew said, "Cape Verde Islands. This island is Thales' home."

The magician squinted to the right and pointed. "There appears to be someone watching us from those trees. Probably someone from another island." With Bartholomew's help, he began walking across the bridge.

Kang waited for them, studying the trees, not seeing anyone as he walked on Celwyn's other side. The magician looped an arm across his shoulder, and once again, the three of them strode forward. Friends reunited.

"I was more worried about you than I can say," Bartholomew told him.

Kang said, "We both were."

When they caught up to Nemo, Celwyn asked, "Sir, where did you find Pelaez? I could have made us a dog if we needed a pet."

"He found us." Nemo's lips twitched as he matched his gait to the still-frail magician. "Suspiciously so, just as your condition worsened." He gazed upward. "The storm is almost here, and I must speak with my crew. Excuse me." He bowed and marched ahead at full speed.

"This experience is interesting, is it not?" Kang asked, as he, like Bartholomew, maintained a grip on Celwyn's elbow, just in case he took a turn.

Captain Nemo awaited them at the far end of the bridge, conferring with the crew who flanked him wearing unreadable expressions. Nemo turned and called out, "Quickly, please! The storm is almost upon us. I don't want my ship any closer to the rocks."

"I understand—" Celwyn shouted. "If my keepers don't mind, I'll supplement what I can do."

With magic, he propelled himself forward feet above the bridge, and the others broke into a run behind him. By the time they made it to the other side, the river seemed ready to lick their ankles. The bridge dissolved behind them as they ran, and in minutes, they sprinted across the sand as the first raindrops fell.

The *Nautilus* surfaced, floating toward them.

Chapter 10

BY THE TIME THEY'D BOARDED THE submarine and filed down the corridor, the internal gongs competed against each other, and the vibration of the engines increased. Celwyn had missed the clanging commotion and braced himself for the familiar dip from the ship as she began to descend. As she dived, he entered the study in time to see the clouds of bubbles against the aquatic window and a thin strip of the setting sun above the waterline.

Qing squawked as loud as he could and flew to him in a blur. They rubbed beaks and noses and cuddled before the bird burrowed into his jacket. "Ah, Qing." The magician blinked his emotions. "I am so happy to see you."

Bartholomew had tears in his eyes, too. "He missed you as much as we did. And he never left your side."

The magician felt the same emotions, thankful to be alive and to see everyone. The colors, the smells—everything looked different now, much dearer. Clearer.

Several crewmen followed Pelaez into the room and began setting up the table where they would dine. The magician moved out of the way, standing by the bar to better see everything and inhaling the wonderful sense of cheating death. It felt good. He snuggled Qing again.

"Here you go, Jonas." Kang thanked another crewman for a tea tray. He poured and handed over the cup. "As you once said, you'd miss Earl Grey very much if you died. Thankfully, that has not happened."

His brother watched them from his position by the bookshelves. Celwyn noted that Pelaez's face held no expression at all, but his eyes bounced just as restlessly as the magician remembered. His brother moved to the aquatic window, turning his back on them, and drumming his fingers against the glass, not playing an internal piano but attacking something as he thought.

Pelaez had changed little. Perhaps a touch grayer at the temples, and his eyes set a bit deeper under the same straight brows, but he still dressed like a fussy undertaker, even sporting a wilted rose in the pocket of his fancy vest. It had been hundreds of years ... Celwyn wondered where Pelaez had gone after Fotheringhay Castle and what he'd done over the decades since then.

"Did you marry?" Celwyn asked.

Kang and Bartholomew had been passing out whiskies while keeping an eye on Celwyn. They froze and proceeded to demonstrate their version of stealth; one of them watched Celwyn while the other dropped a book as a distraction. When the magician raised a sardonic brow at them, the automat grinned and approached to hand him another cup of tea. Meanwhile, dining preparations continued as a crewman arranged the silverware while another filled the ice bucket. Although he saw all of this, everything became muted and inconsequential as Celwyn gazed at his brother.

"Not yet," Pelaez replied.

Celwyn recalled one of Pelaez's talents, seeing future events. "Have you met her yet?"

"Well, well. Aren't you nosy?" Pelaez's brows went up in annoyance. "I will meet her in London in another fifty years or so."

Captain Nemo walked in, noted the tableau, put his head down, and went straight to the bar. After pouring a healthy portion of whiskey, he joined Bartholomew on the sofa and leaned back. Celwyn doubted the man ever really relaxed. He entered Nemo's mind and discovered a myriad of questions about what he'd find in Palermo, a yearning for cherries in sweet cream, and a solid suspicion of Pelaez that demonstrated his common sense and intelligence.

Outside the aquatic window, the water roiled above and around them, but the ship continued forward, sliding through the depths effortlessly, heading east. When the magician remembered why they headed in that direction, he winced and looked for a distraction.

His brother turned his back on the window, displaying his expression, which was as innocent as a snake in tall weeds, watching.

Celwyn glared. Just looking at Pelaez made him angry, as if he knew what the magician felt; Qing emerged from Celwyn's collar and rubbed his ear. Jonas scratched his neck and calmed down—to a point.

When he looked up again, Celwyn encountered Captain Nemo's hooded gaze. "Perhaps we can enjoy a good meal? Please be seated, everyone." The Captain gestured. "Jonas, you must be famished."

"I am, and this will be wonderful." Silently, he sent Nemo a message. *Please be assured I will not abuse your hospitality.*

Captain Nemo started forward and stopped. "Err … thank you."

Jules Verne must have had an inner alarm that went off just before the announcement of dinner. He scampered into the room with a fistful of pens and his notebook, detoured to deposit them on the chess table, and then took his seat at the table beside Celwyn. Pelaez placed himself next to Kang, and Bartholomew occupied the chair at the other end of the table from Nemo.

During times like these, with the anticipation of a long leisurely meal, Celwyn especially missed a feminine presence, such as Annabelle or Elizabeth. Kang must have thought of his wife, too, for he developed a wistful look as the first course of clams arrived, swimming in a fragrant broth of basil and garlic.

"Captain, thank you for everything," the automat said. "Now that the immediate danger to Jonas has passed, may I request that we stop in the nearest port where I may telegraph my wife?"

"Of course. That will occur tomorrow."

Celwyn said, "And after that, as guests, we may have worn out our welcome."

Nemo shook his head. "Your service to me can never be repaid. I can clearly recall the Mizuchi battling against this ship and the flooding of the bridge." He picked apart a clam. "I also remember you removing me from the lake along with Mrs. Kang as the Mizuchi closed in. I am honored to have your company."

Celwyn acknowledged the compliment with a nod.

Verne eyed the magician. "You look much better, Jonas. May I ask how this occurred?"

As he hid a grin behind his water glass, Kang raised an amused brow at Bartholomew. They both enjoyed watching Celwyn sitting on a hot spot.

"It appears to be up to me to update you, Jules." He took another bite and enjoyed it thoroughly. "Do you remember our agreement that you wouldn't publish, or speak of, the fantastic adventures you might see while in our company?"

A tick started above the author's temple. "Yes. After you dangled me over that river. Yes, I do."

"Please consider that request as in force again."

"But Jonas—"

A glare from Celwyn silenced him. Verne finally nodded.

"To answer your question, yes, I am recovered."

Verne had a good recovery system from any disappointment. "That is good news. How?"

"The Professor has informed me that one of the long-standing myths over the ages centers on a descendent of the Greek gods who can heal people who have … unusual constitutions."

Verne glanced across the room at his notebook as if he wished it could fly. Celwyn sent it over Pelaez's head to him.

"Oh, thank you," Verne said and opened it.

"This person healed me." Celwyn turned to his food. "With that out of the way, I am ravenous." A crewman refilled his plate with more clams. "Thank you. I love garlic."

Verne asked, "Is … is…"

"I don't remember much else since I was rather ill, as you know," the magician said.

"Captain, what are your plans?" Bartholomew changed the subject. "You are not obligated, but we must travel to the catacombs, as you know."

Throughout the conversation, Pelaez ate with delicacy, tearing off sections of bread and popping them in his mouth like a pigeon with hands. He also took turns staring at each of the others, except for Celwyn.

While one of the crewmen served the fish course, Captain Nemo nodded at the big man. "I know what you are obliged to do, or at least try to do. However, I have a proposal."

The automat's eyes lit up. "We would love to hear it."

Celwyn continued to eat and savor, wishing he wasn't nearly full. It would take a bit of time to recover the weight he had lost, but thanks to Thales, he had regained his strength. And more. If what he suspected was true, he needed to confide in Kang, Bartholomew, and now Captain Nemo. Above all, they needed to be warned about his dear brother. Nemo had brought the proverbial snake into their midst without knowing it.

"Jonas, because of your illness, you would not know this; we shipped the flying machine by barge to a safe location when we departed for Thales island," Nemo said. "If all goes well, after repaying your debt to Thales, I propose that we go to that location. Once there, Bartholomew and the Professor would advise on the flying machine for a short time. Just long enough to get our efforts on the right track." The Captain sampled his wine and awaited their reaction to his request. "I want to take advantage of your close proximity and beg your indulgence."

Kang looked at Bartholomew, who nodded. When the automat glanced at Celwyn, he smiled.

"Captain, we would be honored to accept your proposal and do more than that if we are able to. Despite your denials, you have done a great deal for us." Celwyn ate a bite, then continued, "Although I can contribute little, I wouldn't miss what you propose for the world." While the magician spoke, Qing jumped up and down on the windowsill and greeted a long scaly fish, much bigger than he, as it wiggled by.

"I hate to intrude, but what do you propose to do about me?" Pelaez's question was a dare.

Celwyn felt the food in his stomach churn, and the glassware on the table vibrated. Kang grabbed his wrist and said, "You are still recovering, as far as I am concerned." He turned to Pelaez. "You were there and heard what Jonas said he would do. It included you."

"Yes." Pelaez stared at them with intenseness designed to make everyone uncomfortable. "Even *he* knows he can't go after our father without me."

Celwyn waved a hand, blocking what Verne could hear. He glared at his brother. "Now that Jules can't listen, let us be forthright. I agree that you will be needed. But I do not trust you."

"Why should you help us?" Kang demanded of Pelaez. "What do you get out of it?"

"I could say that my motives are none of your business and that you should be thankful that I am assisting you." Pelaez cut into his fish, dissecting it like he would an enemy with sharp cuts at strategic points. "Have you even seen Father since the spectacle at Fotheringhay?"

Celwyn breathed deeply, trying to stay calm, trying not to shudder as he remembered his father knocking him down and what had happened afterward. The fork in his hand snapped in two.

"No." It was a whisper.

Pelaez laughed. "Interesting."

"Sir," Celwyn addressed Nemo. "I have lost my appetite and need to lie down for a short time." He carefully deposited his napkin on the table. "Please excuse me."

Chapter 11

NEAR MIDNIGHT, CELWYN returned to the study, bathed, refreshed, and armed with a solid plan of things he needed to do. Over the head of his seemingly occupied brother, he silently sent Bartholomew a message, then turned and went back into the hallway, waiting in front of the map room. The big man obeyed the summons, bringing the Professor with him. Celwyn pointed to the bridge. Bartholomew mouthed, *"Captain?"* Celwyn nodded and added silently, *"bring him to the engine room."*

Without a word, Kang followed him down the corridor and below deck. The noise from the engines met them, growing louder the further toward the stern they went. Even though the *Nautilus* was powered by batteries, the inner workings of the ship were not silent. After a moment more, Captain Nemo and Bartholomew joined them in the farthest corner of the engine room. Courtesy of the magician, a cluster of chairs appeared.

Celwyn leaned forward and lowered his voice. "My brother has extraordinary hearing, as you know. And even at distances, there is a chance he can hear anything said on this ship. However..." he pointed to the engines, "...in addition to that, I have a block around us. We should be able to converse for a while in confidence."

Bartholomew frowned as he also hunched forward and spoke. "I do not like that man."

Celwyn nodded in agreement. "We won't have too much time before he penetrates this area. Allow me to give you some information, and then we will talk of other things."

The Captain's lips were so tight he didn't look capable of speech. This kind of intrigue was not normal or wanted on his ship.

Celwyn held up a finger. "One, we cannot trust my brother, but we will need him in Palermo. Two, he will try as many tricks as he can to cause trouble. It entertains him. He can impersonate any of us. If you are in doubt of who you are addressing, begin talking about Annabelle. Discuss how many children she plans to have. If it is truly one of us, we will respond with "three." If that is not the answer you hear, it is probably Pelaez you are speaking with."

"This is going to be difficult." Bartholomew sighed.

The magician couldn't agree more. "Next, if you encounter one of his impersonations, call him on it. Do *not* say how you knew." Celwyn said, "He will laugh and stop whatever he is doing for the moment. This is all a game to him. Everything is."

The shadows in the far corner brightened. Celwyn frowned and glanced at the engine room door. "Don't worry about Jules; I'll brief him, but our time to confer is urgent. Damn it."

"The lights in the corner, they are ... changing." Bartholomew sounded more angry than worried.

"Pelaez is pushing his way in." Celwyn growled in his throat. "You should know that my brother has certain abilities and weaknesses. That pig you saw is how he manifests and refines his magic."

"Like you do with music." Kang nodded.

Bartholomew gulped and whispered, "The pig wasn't real?"

"No. There is more." Celwyn reached into his pocket for a peyote button. "Thales not only restored my health, but gave me much more strength than before. Probably to help us when we ask for my father's cooperation."

"Interesting," Captain Nemo said. "Did he give you anything else?"

"I think so, but I need to verify my suspicions, to be sure. I hope whatever he did will fade away when we are done in Palermo."

The room lit up as bright as day. Pelaez sauntered in, yawning wide, eyes alight with mischief.

"Oh, hell," Bartholomew said.

They stood and faced him. Along the starboard wall, the crew discreetly kept busy checking the turbines.

Captain Nemo sighed in annoyance. "May we help you?"

As Pelaez drew closer, he patted another yawn. "It seems my invitation to your party was misplaced."

"We do not include you when we talk business." Kang snapped out each word. The automat was well on his way to losing his patience with the intruder.

Pelaez walked to the nearest turbine, and it stopped turning. With a growl, Celwyn restarted it.

His brother clapped, sarcasm slowing the action. "You still have your magic. Congratulations."

Bartholomew demanded, "What do you want?"

"To be a part of whatever you are doing. You do expect me to help with Father, do you not?"

"Yes," Kang told him. "Since you are here, we'll ask again. Why are you helping us?"

Pelaez smirked and turned to Celwyn. "It really bothers you, does it not? To have to see Father again?" His laugh was a low taunt. "Are you still afraid of him?"

Celwyn went for Pelaez, his hands a blur around his brother's throat as he landed on top of him. They rolled across the floor, crashing into the chairs. Pelaez threw Celwyn against the turbines, fifteen feet away. When the magician turned back, he found both Kang and Bartholomew blocking him from Pelaez.

"Jonas, you almost died yesterday." Bartholomew spread his arms open to hold him at bay. Celwyn lowered his head and charged forward.

"Stop!" The Professor pushed him back. "You need to rest, not fight."

"Yes, listen to them," Pelaez sang in a falsetto.

Bartholomew whirled and decked him.

Kang bowed to Captain Nemo, who appeared too annoyed to speak. "Please excuse this display, Sir." The automat pulled Celwyn, resisting, out the door, with Bartholomew leading the way.

Chapter 12

AS HE GAZED OUT THE WINDOW IN the study, Celwyn poured his first cup of tea for the new day; he was accompanied by Qing and a cascading clicking noise as the bird sat on the magician's shoulder and fluffed his wings.

"If ever a bird looked self-satisfied, Qing does." The automat arrived and put his book on the table between them. "He missed you as much as we did over the last few weeks." After he sat, he aimed a speculative look at the magician.

Celwyn patted the mechanical bird's back. "I am glad to be back."

"You need to take time to recover, you know."

The Captain walked in. The magician stood, feeling much stronger than yesterday. If only he grew more intelligent each day as well. He bowed. "Captain, please excuse my behavior last night. It will not happen again while I am aboard your ship."

Celwyn didn't add that he wouldn't be bound by any rules off the ship and intended that Pelaez would get the worst of it.

Captain Nemo regarded him a moment. "Discipline aboard a ship is paramount, Mr. Celwyn." He poured coffee and added a dash of cream. "However, I understand your provocation more than you realize."

"I certainly do." Kang asked Nemo, "Would you care to hear about my own dastardly brother while we await breakfast? We encountered him aboard the ship called the *Zelda* last year."

The magician held up a hand. "Before that tale, Captain, can you tell us about our next stop? I believe we need to send a telegram to Annabelle, and everyone else at Tellyhouse, to let them know that I am alive and reasonably well."

Nemo pursed his lips. "I had planned to stop in Dakar this afternoon to send mail and telegrams and to obtain a few supplies. A message could be sent from there."

"Excellent."

"I am also most appreciative of your other message."

Kang began, "All right. When the *Zelda* set sail from San Francisco…"

⌣

The message Nemo referred to had provided Celwyn with confidence in their endeavors as he wrote it. Late last night, after penning his letters to everyone at Tellyhouse, Celwyn had composed three more missives. He delivered them to Kang and Bartholomew under their closed cabin doors located on each side of his own and then found Captain Nemo in the map room. With a finger to his lips, he sat across from Nemo and laid the third identical message in front of him.

Bartholomew, Xiau, and Captain:

> *As I've said, my brother has acute hearing. Please destroy this message when you are done reading it. He would not hesitate to steal it or take it by force.*
>
> *I mentioned earlier that while Thales repaired what was killing me, he also made me much stronger. Not wiser or more patient, as Xiau would wish. For the last few hours, I have been trying to determine what else Thales did, and I can now report the results.*
>
> *My eyesight has become extraordinary.*
>
> *There is more. Unlike my brother, I still cannot predict the future, but now I can sometimes anticipate actions by those who are immediately in front of me. This may prove useful.*
>
> *I've saved the most disturbing ... and ironic ... change for last; Thales resides*

in my mind like an unwanted guest with fleas. I see glimpses of him and occasionally hear him speak in that guttural voice that sends chills up my spine every time I hear it. Perhaps he uses me to see what is in front of us. I do not know.

So far, he has limited his intrusions and does not appear to be doing more than monitoring things. I will tell you more of Thales if and when my god-damned brother isn't listening.

Please ponder this; I haven't seen my father in hundreds of years and do not know what to expect when we meet him again. I am worried that fulfilling the request from Thales is not only dangerous but could be fatal to any of you or the Nautilus.

This is your moment to bow out, and I completely understand if you wish to do so.

Jonas

As Captain Nemo finished reading, he lost his look of irritation. A determined set of his jaw replaced it. With speed, he wrote on the note.

We are all in this together, Mr. Celwyn. I,
and my crew, will not bow out.

They shook hands, and Celwyn left him to
find Bartholomew and Xiau and discover if they
thought the same.

Chapter 13

A STROLL THROUGH CASABLANCA did not remind Celwyn of a promenade through the leafy streets of Paris or being immersed in the grandeur inside the Seville Cathedral. Far from it. His companions did not appear smitten with the streets they passed through, either. Although serviceable, the plank sidewalks were not designed for show, while the buildings that had been there a hundred years more had not received any attention. They marched on. A rat raced over the magician's boot and scampered into a dim alley.

Verne, the Professor, and Bartholomew walked beside him, and it felt strange to have several of the crew from the *Nautilus* with them. Pelaez strolled along beside Verne as if this were an everyday occurrence. Nemo's lieutenant, Granger, who spoke English with an American accent, directed them toward Bukina Street, a busy thoroughfare that ran perpendicular to the docks. A few blocks later, Granger addressed them, saying he would meet them back on the ship. With a bow, he pivoted and entered a medieval building next to the Banco de Portugal.

The remaining crewmen took over, leading them forward into a thickening throng. Various derelicts, vendors, and tourists crowded the street. When one of the pickpockets, a skinny, bald man in a dapper suit, encountered Pelaez face-to-face, he paled and staggered backwards before scuttling away. The clatter from hooves and wheels on the cobblestones added to the cacophony.

As they went along, Pelaez maintained a position at the rear of their party, keeping step with Verne and listening to the author's detailed recitation of his latest plot. Celwyn had no doubt at the same time his brother also listened to everyone else's conversation just as closely.

"Are we stopping at the bookstore today?" the magician asked innocently.

Kang laughed.

"I want to buy Zander and Otto some books. Perhaps I'll peek at the shop's poetry section."

Bartholomew's steps slowed. "I had no idea you enjoyed poetry, Jonas."

"I do. Much of it I've reread over the years, and it has lost its appeal. For a long time, John Dryden was a favorite."

"Interesting. What changed?" Kang asked. They turned a corner, and the buildings became much more elaborate with well-maintained facades and trimmed shrubbery. Prosperous patrons, or at least important ones, judging by the bows and greetings they received, entered the establishments.

"Dryden did. We used to enjoy the theatre occasionally, or we'd row the River Cherwell in Oxford to entertain women we had enticed out for an afternoon picnic." The magician liked reliving those afternoons, up to a point. "But it became a full-time occupation to keep the man from killing himself. He had developed highly inventive methods, and his efforts exhibited the persistency of a terrier with a bone."

"I had no idea," Bartholomew said. "Did he eventually succeed?"

They stopped under an ornate sign that announced, "Dorphino's Ices, Wine, and Post."

"No, he found inspiration in his poetry and prose again, thank God. Then, he finished *Albion and Albanius,* his opera."

"And you went back to rowing on the River Cherwell?" Verne asked as he examined the scrollwork on the wall in front of them.

"Yes. Here we are..." Celwyn fished out several envelopes from his coat and patted Qing, who'd been chewing on his collar since they left the ship. "I managed to write another letter to Annabelle, Patrick, and the boys last night." The magician eyed the Professor. "Our telegram has just enough information to make them want to know more and will arrive at least a week before my letter. It won't tell them details about our activities."

Verne said, "I have several missives for my wife, including one explaining why I did not come home to Amiens as promised. She will understand."

"You are fortunate, Jules." The magician turned to the automat. "I assume you have a letter for Elizabeth?" He happened to know that Kang's wife would not understand if she did not hear from her husband, nor be content if he did not return on the day he promised.

"More than one." Kang patted his pocket. "Actually, one for each day since we left Odessa."

With a wistful look drawing his mouth into a frown, Bartholomew said, "I have written to Otto and Zander too. We will buy them many toys today."

"In my letter to the boys, I mentioned that you were bringing them some shark teeth." Celwyn twisted his mustache and teased the big man.

Kang laughed. "I do believe you are back to normal, Jonas."

"Nearly." The magician dodged a rotund woman leading a white poodle, both with a haughty attitude. He wiggled his hips like the woman had. Kang had to smother his laughter, and even Pelaez's lips twitched.

"I think so, also." Bartholomew pretended grumpiness. "But where am I going to find shark teeth for them?"

As they mounted the stone steps leading to the telegraph office, on a hunch, Celwyn glanced behind them. The same ornate carriage with twin white and black Arabian horses that had passed them more than once in their short walk from the docks pulled to the curb down the street. He noted the coach's curtains were not quite closed. *How interesting.* He felt a certain satisfaction in confirming his guess that they had picked up an admirer, and Kang and Bartholomew would certainly have a reaction to the news.

Who was following them?

When they emerged again to the street, Bartholomew used perfect Italian to ask one of their guards where they could find an outdoor café known for their pastries. The muscular crewman, who greatly resembled the one Celwyn had chased out of the gardens of the Empress Hotel in Singapore a few months ago, pointed down the street to Ben Slimane Boulevard. As they made their way there, Celwyn darted into a tobacconist to obtain another peace offering for the Captain. When he emerged again, he directed a sneer at his brother, thinking what he would like to present him with.

His sneer evaporated as they entered the courtyard of the de Bapaume Cafe. Ornamental orange trees shaded most of the tables, and a profusion of sweet plumeria perfumed the air, along with hints of other flowers and native spices. Masses of red, pink, and white roses lined short stucco walls separating the patrons from the people riding and walking by, and in the center of the courtyard, an enormous, tiled fountain rose in tiers from the ground, burbling musically. Celwyn couldn't help himself and added a light passage of harp music that weaved in and out of the water.

As they sat down, Professor Kang pointedly didn't look at the fountain, but his words recalled his first encounter with Pelaez. "No additions, such as pigs, or fish, please. I find them highly disturbing."

In reply, Pelaez developed the kind of smile that made Celwyn look away. Out of curiosity, he entered his brother's mind.

As children, and later until he lost contact with his brother in the 1500s, Celwyn had been somewhat successful when exploring Pelaez's mind and only occasionally would find a solid wall he couldn't penetrate. Now, he entered a world of color that swirled like a hurricane, and from within it, hundreds of voices shouted, including his brother's. Celwyn backed out before he got a headache.

After a glance at Pelaez, Bartholomew must have also found him difficult to look at and turned to stare at the street as the waiter took their order.

"What do you see?" Verne asked, peering around the big man's shoulder.

Bartholomew frowned and maintained his study of the entrance. "We have been followed ever since we walked into town..." he pointed with his chin, "... by that carriage."

The ornate carriage with the yin and yang horses clopped to a stop in front of the café, and, in seconds, the driver climbed down and opened the cab door.

Celwyn had expected a mysterious mustachioed villain—in fact, he would have put money on it—but instead, a graceful form emerged, quite petite, in pale blue silk and lace. Even more of a surprise, another woman emerged. Also in silk, but much taller. The smaller woman wore a hat that shaded her face, but not the mass of artfully arranged black curls that cascaded down her back. The other woman's intricately braided hair seemed nearly white by comparison.

"Heavens, your pursuers appear so … dangerous," Pelaez drawled.

Kang shot him a dark look. "How do we know that you aren't one of our pursuers?"

Pelaez laughed.

As the women crossed the courtyard, a fat fish arose out of the fountain beside them, pirouetted on its tail and posed, ready to be noticed or jump on their hats. Celwyn growled a curse and dissolved it. The women skirted the other tables, passed by the fountain, and headed directly toward them.

"Ah. We seem to be the object of interest." His brother snickered and stood with the others. When the women arrived at their table, Verne licked his lips and sidled closer to Celwyn, who patted him on the shoulder.

"Vampires," the automat murmured under his breath.

"It appears so." Celwyn glanced at the guards from the *Nautilus*. They remained in front of the café, watching their table and on alert. He bet Nemo would not be pleased if something happened to anyone here—with the exception of his brother.

Bartholomew sucked in his breath but didn't back down. Pelaez seemed to enjoy the moment, a pregnant one full of anticipation, as he leaned against his chair and maintained his disconcerting rictus smile. Celwyn doubted these strangers would be as easily frightened as Verne, but it didn't stop his brother from trying.

This close, Celwyn had no trouble enjoying the smaller woman's golden-green eyes, firm chin, and lovely face. The sight took his breath away. Her gaze, direct and riding an invisible string just from her to him, submerged him in a wonderful sensation so rare he couldn't speak or move—until Kang elbowed him.

The magician shook himself and said, "Good afternoon, Miss?"

In the kind of contralto Celwyn couldn't resist, she addressed them.

"Mr. Celwyn, Mr. Bartholomew, Professor Kang, Mr. Verne, and Herr Pelaez, I am Miss Tara McFein." She turned to her companion. "This is Miss Simone Redifer."

The other vampire appeared just as stunning in a Nordic way, with her high-cheek bones and eyes chipped from the fjords. As she nodded to each of them, her nostrils flared, and her attention seemed to linger on Bartholomew. Celwyn inhaled as deeply as he could. The fog of his instant attraction to Miss McFein was gradually replaced by his normal reaction to vampires—caution.

"What the hell," he murmured under his breath, just as the automat had.

Kang heard him yet still pulled out the empty chairs at their table.

"Please be seated."

Chapter 14

WITH BARTHOLOMEW AND KANG flanking him, the magician sat again with Verne and Pelaez just to his right. From directly across the table, he encountered a knowing and amused regard from Miss McFein. He sighed; she fascinated him to no end, and he had to consciously remember what she was. To make things more difficult, she studied him like she peeled an onion, layer by layer, taking her time to see what was hidden inside. He reminded himself of his history with vampires—which usually ended violently. When she finished her inspection, she sat still, regarding him from under her lashes. When the sky did not fall, he went back to enjoying her attentions, oblique and proper as they were.

It had to be his brother who broke the spell, of course.

"To what do we owe this pleasure?"

Pelaez's voice sounded how thirsty ghouls wallowing in a dank crypt would—scratchy, unsettling, and garbled. "Is it our outstanding sense of fashion?" He regarded their guests long enough to be rude.

Ever the gentleman, Bartholomew slid into the conversation. "I am surprised that you know our names, Ladies."

Celwyn liked the big man's logic, which was so similar to Kang's, knowing his statement should reward them with information while stifling his brother.

As Bartholomew spoke, Miss Redifer accepted a coffee and addressed the table. "We were asked to offer our assistance to you."

Kang cocked his head to the side. "To do what, if I may ask?"

Celwyn felt Miss McFein's gaze as clearly as if she touched him. When he looked up, he encountered it head-on, and reveled in it, until he felt himself begin to blush. He had to look away and hope no one else saw him.

"A good question." As detached as if she was ordering a pair of gloves, Miss Redifer said, "We are here to help you with Thales's request."

"Really?" Kang gasped his surprise.

Celwyn flung an arm in front of Bartholomew when he would have risen from his chair and bolted.

"Please, do not be alarmed." With equal parts seriousness and sincerity, Miss McFein added, "We want to help."

Celwyn frowned. *Was his attraction to this woman also part of Thales's plan?*

"I won't ask how you know of our intentions. However, I must inquire as to how you would be able to help with my father?" The magician made the request with respect and hoped it was received as such.

It wasn't often he was surprised, but in the next second, he was floored.

"Many years ago, I met him," Miss McFein said.

"Close your mouth, Jonas," Kang murmured.

"We are able to fight as needed," Miss Redifer told them.

"Excuse me, but in our experience, vampires are destructive and dangerous. Not someone who helps us." While Celwyn spoke, he had no trouble remembering Telly's death as vividly as if it had happened yesterday.

With a graceful hand, Miss McFein gestured at the patrons in the courtyard. "Everyone knows of vampires. There are multitudes of stories; however, not everyone is aware of the strong ties within the vampire families, which are no different from anyone else. They do not know that civilized vampires exist in harmony with everyday citizens. We even marry and enjoy normal lives." Her earnest appeal held their attention. "There are good vampires, not just evil ones."

Somewhat mollified, Celwyn took the opportunity to study the way her hair curled around her ears and the graceful slenderness of her fingers. Of course, the others might assume he studied her for good or evil tendencies. He said, "That was the only kind that I have ever met ... before now."

Miss McFein's lips twitched in amusement. "Only because of your unusual activities. You and your companions are attractive to evil."

The automat and Celwyn exchanged a look. Bartholomew stared at them and nodded; they had discussed this many times before. Celwyn noted that although Miss McFein seemed to find the phenomena amusing, she didn't speculate on what caused it.

"Not all of us are like Delgado," Miss McFein said with care, fully expecting a reaction to the name.

Bartholomew's eyes bulged as if someone had poked him with a stick. Kang knocked over his coffee as he jumped to his feet. In seconds, a pall of sadness enveloped them.

"I thought I killed him in Paris." Celwyn could hardly get the words out as a pair of wine glasses on the table next to them shattered, scattering the couple sitting there.

The blonde vampire raised a brow at the mess, but didn't appear surprised. "You tried. There are those of us who are not affected by direct sunlight, such as Delgado." With ice in her voice, she added, "We are aware of what Delgado did to your family, and we deplore what happened and regret we were not close enough to stop it." She nodded at each of them. "Years ago, Delgado was expelled by our Congregation, as were Mrs. Karras and her followers."

Miss McFein held out her hands, appealing to them. "They do not represent the rest of us."

"This is too much to suddenly understand or accept." Bartholomew's voice wobbled just enough for Celwyn to detect it.

Celwyn agreed. "May I suggest that we halt this conversation for now and discuss it with our partner in this enterprise? And then, perhaps, meet again?"

"Yes," Miss Redifer said. "But, of course."

"Where can we reach you?" Kang asked as he pulled out her chair.

"The Hotel Mezzagno." Miss Redifer pointed along the boulevard. "It isn't far."

"Allow us to escort you to your carriage." Celwyn stood and bowed. "You will hear from us before sundown this evening."

The magician couldn't help himself. Perhaps it still was his reaction to being alive again, or the aura of Miss McFein, but he caused a love ballad, the music itself a soft caress, to accompany the women as they boarded their carriage. With a faint blush, Miss McFein cast a shy smile over her shoulder.

From beside Celwyn, Kang heard the ballad and his tight-lipped glance at the magician held worry, not words.

Chapter 15

To say that Captain Nemo also had concerns about the two women did not explain his reaction enough. He said little all through lunch, contrary to his usual social banter as they ate. After everyone adjourned from the table, he stood at the aquatic window, his back to the other occupants of the room. When he finally spoke, everyone gave him their full attention.

"Anything we do will be dangerous at this point. I am reconsidering our enterprise."

"That is understandable," the Professor said. "If I may? We..." he gestured to Bartholomew and the magician, "...discussed the situation on the way back here. We relieve you of your obligation to us and extend our gratitude. We will travel to you and the flying machine after we fulfill Thales's request."

"If you prefer to leave us here, we will take other transport to the catacombs." Bartholomew shuddered as he said the word. "We understand that you wouldn't want to endanger this ship."

"I assumed all of that and appreciate your intent." Captain Nemo shook his head. "But my point is that the enterprise itself is troubling."

Pelaez watched the exchange from his position by the bar, and his eyes tracked each of them with the intensity of a snake watching a mouse take a bath.

With a glare at Pelaez, Celwyn produced a tea tray and wished his brother would leave, finding his presence distracting. Major discussions required tea—several pots or more. He sent a sample to Captain Nemo, who stared at the cup as it floated in front of him and then accepted it.

"We could meet the women at the catacombs." Bartholomew thought more and frowned, then eyed the whiskey bottle as if it held all their answers. "Though do we accept their help in the first place?" A cigar arrived to hover in front of him. When a lit match arrived right behind it, the big man waved it away and lit it himself.

"I would be more comfortable if they were not on my ship." Irritation clipped Captain Nemo's voice. "It is not just superstition of women aboard ships; I do not like vampires, no matter their claim of peaceful natures."

"Do we need their help, Brother?" Celwyn asked Pelaez, breaking his reluctance to speak to him.

As if he had been waiting for his cue to walk on stage, Pelaez sauntered across the room and deposited himself on the sofa next to Kang. He took his time, crossed his ankles, and studied them a moment before speaking.

"Wolfgang Augustus Griffin can only have gotten more unpredictable over the years. Who knows the state of his mind? I would accept help from anyone at this point."

"I find it interesting that Miss McFein has met him," Bartholomew said. "Under what circumstances, I wonder."

The silence in the room lasted until the magician addressed Nemo. "Sir, we appreciate everything you have done for us. It is beyond what we should ask of you. We owe you much more than assisting with the flying machine or fixing a leak on your ship." With concurring nods from Kang and Bartholomew, he continued, "We recommend that we meet the women at the catacombs, as Bartholomew stated, and that once our mission is accomplished, we travel to you and the flying machine. Or you could pick us up near the catacombs." He wished this would be an easy operation, but doubted it. "We do not want to endanger you."

As he spoke, a flurry of blue and yellow striped fish crowded the window, causing Qing to bounce up and down with so much excitement he fell off the ledge. The magician enjoyed the fish as much as Qing; bird happiness is important.

"I agree. These particular vampires do not appear to represent what vampire lore is made of." Captain Nemo hesitated. "However..."

"We should *all* be cautious." Kang shot Celwyn another worried look that had nothing to do with their enterprise.

"Let us proceed as you suggest," Captain Nemo told them, not catching the automat's oblique warning to Celwyn. He stood decisively, with his hands behind his back. "We will travel at a leisurely pace to the catacombs to allow the vampires time to meet us there. I will keep the *Nautilus* offshore until you are ready to leave again."

He turned to Pelaez, and his voice changed. "If you are to continue to enjoy my hospitality, I need your assurance you will follow my orders. If there is anything done to my ship or the people on it, our association will end. Abruptly."

Celwyn looked his brother in the eye. "Anything you disrupt with your magic, I can undo. If anyone is hurt or threatened, I will retaliate."

"Such distrust." Pelaez executed another yawn and crossed his legs negligently. "Am I that threatening?"

"Yes," Celwyn retorted.

"Do you agree?" Captain Nemo barked at him.

Pelaez stood and bowed. "But of course." He waved a hand. "Such silliness."

Captain Nemo's fist clenched, and he took a step away from Pelaez to maintain control.

Kang moved closer. "While we're discussing the subject, tell us more of your father's background."

"How old is he? Or how dangerous?" Pelaez asked. "I think he was born around the fifth century. His father, and father's father, descended from the early Greek gods, as you've heard. Of course, intermingling with assorted human women along the way. Again, I cannot confirm any of this."

Qing left the curious fish at the window to fly the short distance to Celwyn's shoulder. The magician patted his back and opened his collar, inviting the bird to nest inside, then addressed the others.

"Like others, I believe that every time someone in my lineage fathered a child with a mortal, the inherited god-like traits were watered down in their children. By the time my brother and I were born, both from different mortal mothers, we had limited abilities compared to the originals. Even compared to our father."

The automat regarded Celwyn. "You are saying that he would be much stronger than you."

"Oh, yes. Even now with Thales's enhancements."

"I wonder about the other children he fathered before us or after us." Pelaez's eyes took on a faraway, introspective gaze.

Bartholomew had been very subdued, and now he gazed at them with what bravery he could summon. Of all of them, the big man found the idea of magic and immortality hard to swallow.

"Continue," Kang said.

"As you wish." Pelaez closed his eyes in remembrance. "In the beginning, our father's days were spent as an alchemist to the Queen. In 1342, we retreated to his new wife's ancestral castle in Scotland, where Jonas was born. Everything appeared to be blissful. Five years later, Mrs. Mary Griffin drowned in the lake by the castle."

Celwyn had been expecting this part of the story, but he still swallowed hard and wished his brother would just finish the tale. When he did not, Celwyn helped it along.

"Between her death and our father's sampling of his own alchemy, he became volatile and reclusive, finally abandoning us to be raised by servants in the castle. The rumors at the time reported that he left for the land of the Pharaohs."

Pelaez said, "I heard the same, and I tried to find him here and there for the next 200 years."

"Where did you find him?" The big man stopped wringing his hands and sat heavily on the sofa beside Kang.

"France. At King Louis XIV's court. He had installed himself as the Queen's paramour." Pelaez shook his head. "I've never thought of him as particularly brilliant."

"And here I complain of your flamboyant tendencies." Kang rolled his eyes and looked at Celwyn fondly. "They are directly inherited." Despite the stress of the moment, Celwyn elbowed him just as fondly.

"Bring us up to the last time you saw your father," Captain Nemo said.

Pelaez pursed his lips. "Perhaps Jonas should."

"Seriously?" Celwyn just wanted to get this over with. "Fine. The short and sweet answer is that my father tried to kill me." The magician attempted to control his anger and fear, well-aware of the breakable artifacts on Nemo's shelves only feet away. "While my dear brother stood by and watched."

105

The automat regarded Pelaez without favor.

Pelaez raised an unconcerned brow. "It was a situation where I expected Jonas to prevail."

Celwyn started for him, remembered Captain Nemo, and settled for flexing his fists.

"You coward." Pelaez yawned.

Celwyn lunged. Both Kang and Bartholomew blocked him.

"I suggest you go to your cabin." Captain Nemo leaned into Pelaez's face. "And stay there until we arrive in Palermo."

With a casual shrug, Pelaez got to his feet and sauntered out.

Nearly hidden in the corner by the library shelves, Verne wrote as fast as he could in his notebook.

⸻

Kang composed their response to the women, accepting their help and asking them to rendezvous in Palermo, only a few miles from the Capuchin catacombs. Nemo suggested the Quattro Tril restaurant in the Ficarazzi quarter of the city for their meeting. It attracted a variety of clientele and had an advantage—a busy atmosphere filled with interesting personages. While they dined, that should be distracting if any odd incidents occurred. The automat wrote that they would check the restaurant every night at sundown for their new acquaintances' arrival.

After Kang had given the note to a crewman for delivery, Captain Nemo paced in front of the game table while Bartholomew waited for Verne to take his turn. The magician likened the game of checkers to watching paint dry on the side of a barn—it bored him to no end. Xiau loved it. Bartholomew only played when he had something troublesome to think about; he could worry and play at the same time.

As their game progressed, the magician turned his attention to the fish swimming by until the Professor asked, "How long is it until dinner? This afternoon's controversies have made me quite ravenous."

From beside him, Qing watched the fish also, enthralled by the endless parade of bird theater. Celwyn always wondered how the automat could be hungry since he had metal parts for intestines. An impish mind must have built mechanical sensors for that into him.

"About an hour," Verne said. "I am hoping to learn more about the activities of the last few days while Mr. Pelaez keeps to his room." He jumped several of Bartholomew's pieces. "It will be so nice to have an evening free from drama."

Celwyn grinned at Captain Nemo, who sent a sympathetic glance at the author. The magician had not talked with Verne yet, and needed to. "We'll see. Something you should know; Pelaez can hear long distances and probably hears exactly what we say in here."

Verne paled.

"Do not worry," The magician said. "Of anyone here, I am the most likely target for my brother.

Kang pivoted. "Mr. Verne, you know that we are traveling to Palermo and then on to the catacombs there."

"Err ... yes. Why?" Verne's button nose twitched with interest.

"Is your word still good?" Celwyn asked.

The author chewed on his lips. With a sigh, he said, "Yes."

Taking his checkers in hand, Bartholomew hopped over three sets of Verne's. "When we visited Antigo Island the other day, a descendant of one of the Greek gods healed Jonas."

Verne wiggled in anticipation of a story. "I see."

"In return for saving him, this descendent requested Jonas and Pelaez journey to Palermo. Their father is in the underground catacombs there. They are supposed to convince him to go see the healer."

"Oh ... cadavers." Verne pinched his nose as he thought about decomposition. "Your father is formidable? That is why those women in the café said they would help you?"

"Yes." Bartholomew finished taking the rest of the author's checkers. "It will be a difficult endeavor ... and dangerous."

"Jules, you understand why you must remain on the ship when we reach our destination." Captain Nemo joined them, standing beside the checkerboard, and rubbing his stomach. Celwyn had noticed long ago that his gesture occurred just before their dinner arrived.

Verne appeared ready to argue, even looking to Celwyn for support. The magician told him, "If things go badly, we'll probably flee the area as fast as the *Nautilus* can go." While the author attempted to pry more information from the others, Celwyn left them to their game and approached the oversized organ beside the library shelves. He considered it a handsome instrument with its dark wood, carved legs, and decorated sides. Every time he went near it, the magician felt something unusual emanating from it that he couldn't name. Bewitched musical instruments were not unheard of. He pulled out the bench and sat down.

By the time Celwyn had reached the second stanza of Mozart's *Alla Turca*, Captain Nemo's frown had disappeared, and his face relaxed. He leaned over the organ and watched Celwyn's hands as he played. When the magician added a pair of unseen violins, their tones intertwined with the organ music on an intimate level. The Captain cocked his head to the side, and the tension eased from his brow.

"Sir, you have very little time to enjoy a most basic pleasure." The magician gestured, and a hand-cranked phonograph sat beside the chess table. On the nearby library shelf, a collection of music appeared, also. The ballad finished, and without stopping his efforts, Celwyn ran a tinkling scale to the upper register. "That music is for whenever I cannot provide it for you."

Celwyn brought the *Mephisto Waltz* forward in a minor key, increasing the volume. "Have you heard of Liszt's signature legacy, the *B minor Piano Sonata*, and his *Années de Pèlerinage*?"

Nemo shook his head, lost in the melody.

"I owe you much, Captain. Providing music is the least I can do," Celwyn said as the notes became a discordant clash of sound, as if a battle raged, growing stronger. Then silence before a strong march up the major scale in triumph. "Music tells a story. Like ours."

"It sounds like you expect to prevail in the catacombs," Captain Nemo surmised.

"I do."

Qing chose that moment to walk across the top of the organ and stop before the Captain.

"I have two favors to ask of you, Sir." The magician finished the piece, and they adjourned to the sofa to sit beside Kang as he wrote to Elizabeth. "If, for some reason, we do not survive the catacombs, please take care of Qing. He does like you."

Without stopping what he was writing, Kang made an appeal and went back to his letter. "Please accede to Jonas's request; Annabelle is not fond of Qing." The automat sounded like he didn't expect to survive if Celwyn didn't. *Interesting, but unlikely.* The magician would make sure the big man and Kang were safe no matter what they expected, and the others as well.

Proving Qing understood much more than anyone imagined, the bird edged closer to Captain Nemo's jacket sleeve and stopped. The fact that Qing didn't attack Nemo's golden amulets surprised Bartholomew.

"If that were me, that bird would have already been pecking at what he wanted by now."

The magician smiled. "Qing is on his good behavior." The bird blinked at Celwyn and remained beside the Captain.

"He isn't exactly a normal pet." The automat stopped writing to come up with a description. "More of a good luck charm."

Captain Nemo regarded Qing. "We will see how things go. Despite your brother, I believe you will be successful. The three of you are resourceful." He glanced at them. "And much luckier than most."

Bartholomew laughed. "I hope you are right."

The Captain twisted off a shiny button from his jacket and presented it to Qing. The bird eyed him with his diamond gaze, imprinting Nemo into his memory, probably under "Conquests."

"Mr. Celwyn, what is the second favor you mentioned?"

"I esteem and respect you as a friend, Captain. Please call me Jonas." He stood and bowed. "By the time this is over with, we'll have no time for formalities."

"I agree." The Captain nodded. "We will surface near Le Vagnole tomorrow. Mondragone is nearby, and I hope everyone will take the opportunity to visit Athanasius Kircher's museum while my crew gathers supplies."

"Oh!" Kang's voice held the intense excitement he usually reserved for the flying machine. "I saw some of the exhibits there years ago when it was under construction." The automat rubbed his hands together. "It could only have gotten better since then. Excellent!"

Chapter 16

J UST BEFORE DINNER, CELWYN FIN-
ished a long session with Kang in the map room;
one of them enjoyed it much more than the other.
As he left the room, in front of him, a fog thickened
all the way down the corridor. *Oh ...* Celwyn became
alert, realizing he was not alone. About fifteen feet
toward the bow, a fat and sinuous dragon-like creature faded in and out of the mist near the ceiling.

A door at the end of the corridor opened, and
a crewman emerged. As he took a step into the
hallway, the fog evaporated, taking the scaly green
creature with it.

Celwyn inhaled a moment and thought. *Was
Thales playing some sort of game?* As he entered the
study, the magician decided not to mention the
apparition ... if that was what it was. *Could it just
be his imagination manifesting itself?* The magician
growled in his throat; he didn't know.

That night, Celwyn's dreams featured the creature he'd encountered in the corridor. He found it highly annoying; if he made something with magic, he constructed it by his choice, and for a specific purpose or entertainment. But what he found in the corridor had invaded his dreams without his permission. By two o'clock, he gave up trying to sleep and went to the study.

He perused the books in Nemo's library, finding they contained many interesting things, but nothing specific about what he saw. Then he found Loblaw's *Beasts*. As Celwyn poured a fresh cup of tea, he balanced the book on his knee and pondered the origins of the visitor in the corridor. It could be a capricious present from his brother, yet Pelaez didn't have that kind of innocent imagination; if Pelaez had been the source, he would have had it attack, or spew green vomit on him.

Kang entered the room and approached to examine the book Celwyn held. "I'm usually the only one in here at this hour. Care to share? This isn't your normal reading material."

"Perhaps." The magician eyed him. "I saw something."

The automat raised his brows.

"This afternoon, I discovered something new in the main corridor..." he pointed out the door, "...that shouldn't be there, and didn't belong anywhere. Do you remember the paintings we saw at the museum in Mondragone the other day?"

"Certainly. Many were rather beautiful, and the ones of the Mongols I found rather disturbing because of the memories they brought up."

"Shall we talk about that?"

"Perhaps after we finish this discussion." The automat regarded him. "Before now, I did not consider you much of an art lover."

Celwyn maintained eye contact. "I saw one of the creatures from the paintings yesterday after I left you in the map room. It was green, scaly, and simply odd. It had dead eyes."

"And you think it is a wyvern?"

"Yes, if this book is accurate." The magician held it up.

Kang sat beside him and settled the book in his lap. "Is this something your brother would do to be amusing?"

"Not likely, at least this time. It didn't actually do anything and left as soon as a crewman came along."

"Thales?"

Celwyn frowned. "Possible. Perhaps we shouldn't bother the others about this until we know for sure. It will only needlessly upset the Captain if we tell him and the thing never returned. Agreed?"

Kang glanced at the doorway. "Yes, Bartholomew would be alarmed, and it would make him more nervous. As you know, the Captain finds fantastic phenomena irritating, and this could merely be a product of your mind."

As he spoke, a few of the crew came in to service the bar and dust, their presence effectively stopping the discussion. Celwyn continued thinking about it.

⌣‾‾⌣

Near midnight, a few days later, the submarine surfaced a mile down the coast from Palermo. The city's lights surrounded the crescent-shaped bay, and a pregnant moon hung low over the black water.

Several constellations filled the night sky in complex patterns and appeared as mysterious as could be. From the platform atop the ship, the magician studied them as if seeing the stars for the first time. In the last few weeks, it had become more appropriate to contemplate the heavens than before and to ask questions. He wagered Thales could answer them. The fact that the magician had survived death also encouraged self-introspection. Of course, Celwyn had luck on his side, and this close call just proved it again. The automat would just say, with as much sarcasm as he could summon, that Jonas had dodged Fate because Fate didn't aim properly.

As the others joined him on the platform, he pointed out one of the party boats in the bay meandering about without a care as it made a wide turn and headed toward the docks. Two more boats full of revelers passed them heading further out. Raucous laughter and a melody of guitars and drums reached the *Nautilus*, riding a breeze full of brine and fish.

Bartholomew blew smoke rings and gazed across the water. "Beautiful."

"What is our plan, Sir?" Kang asked as he lit Nemo's cigar and then his own.

"I will keep this ship offshore until we have word that Miss McFein and Miss Redifer have arrived." Captain Nemo contemplated his boots for a moment before raising his gaze to theirs. "This entire operation worries me, but I cannot deny that I am curious."

Shortly after dawn, their party crossed the floating pier of the *Nautilus* and arrived on land. Conversation resumed as they neared the track running parallel to the water, and they turned toward the city.

"We're staying at the Il Bella near the plaza. From there, we can rent a carriage to take us to the catacombs. I suggest we plan an initial survey of the target area this afternoon." Kang watched the magician and Bartholomew gather their bags into a pile under a tree while the crew handed off the rest of them. "I am also worried because I do not know what to expect."

From the moment they left the ship, Pelaez had not spoken. He averted his eyes, and the knowing smile faded to sadness. The magician entered his mind as they walked toward town.

At first, Celwyn didn't know what he had found. Utmost in Pelaez's thoughts was a silent scene set in a glade of brilliant greenery, one typical of their childhood. A second more, and the magician identified it as the familial pond before Thornwell Moor ...

and then he knew; his brother was thinking of where they picnicked with his mother before she died.

As Pelaez's thoughts moved further into the remembered glade, Celwyn followed, fearing something he couldn't face but had to see. When he caught up to his brother, he saw his mother sitting on a blanket, heard her laughter, and spied Pelaez as a ten-year-old boy staying close to her side and staring at her with grief. Even that young, his brother knew the future. In her arms, she held a baby—Jonas.

As he backed out of Pelaez's thoughts, Celwyn's tears poured down his cheeks to where he couldn't see through them, and he stumbled over a rock as he wiped his eyes. Kang touched his arm with a look of concern and elbowed Bartholomew. When they reached a rise in the road, they stopped; below them, the light from the silvery dawn painted a fleet of vessels, and the barking from a lone dog echoed in the distance.

Celwyn turned to Pelaez. "Brother."

It could have been the gruff tone in his voice, but when Pelaez looked up, the sarcastic glint had disappeared from his eyes.

Celwyn took a step toward him and embraced him wordlessly.

Bartholomew's eyes watered; he coughed and looked away. Kang patted Celwyn on the back.

Pelaez gazed at his brother another moment before they began walking side-by-side downhill toward the city of Palermo.

117

Three days passed without incident. In the evening, while they awaited the vampires, they took their dinner al fresco overlooking the harbor. That the magician eagerly anticipated the arrival of the vampires seemed a novel situation, and he could easily recall Miss Tara McFein's fine profile and chin that would fit nicely in the palm of his hand.

Tonight, Pelaez sat across the table from Celwyn, dissecting a broiled lobster with studious precision. On his right, Bartholomew tackled a fine cut of beef while Kang picked apart his chicken piccata. It had taken some discussion to settle on the wine of choice, and they finally ordered both a red and a white.

The magician had just requested another bottle of white when he felt a feather-light brush of sensation from a heady perfume laced with lilacs and musk. Although only a faint whiff, he knew who it belonged to. The scent brushed his cheek again.

Kang saw them first and, in a moment, had attracted the attention of their waiter to request a third bottle of wine. More chairs and additional place settings appeared as the staff reacted.

Another surprise awaited them. Wearing a handsome black jacket, the man they had last seen driving the yin and yang carriage in Casablanca held the elbows of each of the women with the kind of familiarity and solicitousness that seemed like much more than a driver as he escorted their guests across the crowded restaurant.

The newcomer's height equaled Celwyn's—well over six feet. His wavy silver hair bordered on effeminate and grazed the tall collar of the man's coat.

The magician noted the expensiveness of the coat did not disguise the man's broad muscled shoulders, instead accentuating them, and his mustache had been waxed and curled artfully over his full lips. All in all, a most handsome man who knew he presented a striking appearance.

As they drew closer, the automat stared, recording every minute detail about the man in his internal library.

Confidence and haughty aristocracy emanated from the newcomer. Celwyn didn't need Kang to tell him this man was also a vampire, yet most interesting, the magician didn't sense the usual danger from him, instead recognizing a refined threat kept in check. When Celwyn again saw the man's hand on Miss McFein's elbow, his jaw tightened.

After everyone was seated, the magician found himself across from Miss McFein once more. He hadn't noticed exactly how Kang had arranged it since he'd been so busy speculating about the silver-haired man. She smiled at him, and the magician had a bit of trouble meeting those extraordinary eyes.

"Good evening, everyone," Pelaez said. "At last, we meet again."

"Allow me to introduce myself; I am Valentine Leonardo Domenico Soriano." The newcomer's bejeweled fingers tapped the tablecloth, and his eyes sparkled like champagne as he assessed them. "I assist Miss Redifer and Miss McFein, as needed. You have been described to me, *Messieurs*. I am the head of Miss Redifer and Miss McFein's family and have also been asked to provide aid to you while you fulfill Thales' request."

How did they know about it? Celwyn maintained a neutral expression, watching the man and the strong aura of command around him. He stifled speculation as to the man's relationship with Miss McFein. "Family" could mean several things.

"Stop growling," Kang murmured in his ear.

Their table overlooked the water, and as a breeze picked up, it billowed the umbrellas, teased the trees bordering the water, and pushed sailboats across the bay like colorful leaves. There seemed to be many more pleasure craft on the water this evening compared to the afternoon.

The trio declined to order dinner, but accepted glasses of wine. Celwyn tried not to stare when Miss McFein picked up her glass and brought it to her lips. He must not have been too circumspect because Kang kicked his shin and began speaking. "We are hoping to conclude this business quickly and be on our way as soon as possible."

"We are as well." A small smile touched Miss Redifer's lips as she regarded the big man. "We have other obligations." She batted her eyes at Bartholomew. "Though perhaps not as enjoyable."

Celwyn played with the chain on his pocket watch and stole a look at the automat. Xiau rolled his eyes and mouthed, "*Both of you.*"

The magician cleared his throat and ignored him. "Yesterday, we made a short journey out to the catacombs. From a distance, we observed the area but did not descend underground."

"A wise precaution" Miss Redifer nodded.

Pelaez asked them, "Could you enlighten us a bit on your relationship to Thales?"

Valentine's expression darkened. "No."

Pelaez leaned back in his chair with an expression just as forbidding. His eyes narrowed, and his fork rose a few inches above the table. Celwyn saw it and dissolved the fork.

Miss McFein must have spied the fork, also. "This is going to be interesting," she said with an undertone.

Kang leaned toward her and confided, "You have no idea."

The magician hated confrontations, and his brother and Valentine looked ready for battle. Celwyn sent his brother a pointed look. Pelaez shrugged and turned to the others. "Miss McFein, you mentioned you have met our father?"

She waited for the waiter to uncork another bottle of wine and depart before answering.

"It was June 1685. A hot summer full of intrigue and secrets. I had recently been "made" as they say, and my appetites were sometimes unpredictable."

Doing his best to display bravery when faced with the morbidly unusual, Bartholomew squared his shoulders and asked, "Where did this occur?"

"The court of Prince Elector Maximilian II Emanuel." She nodded at Pelaez and Celwyn. "I spotted Mr. Wolfgang Griffin in Vienna and approached him, possibly to feed. When he realized my intention, he tried to seduce *me*." She shuddered.

"He is extraordinarily strong, and I saw the situation was not safe. So, I tricked him and reached safety."

Celwyn felt the flush of anger suffusing his face, and the glassware on the neighboring table shook before the umbrella over it flew upward and away. While everyone reacted, Bartholomew tugged on his sleeve, and Kang steadied the wine bottle.

"For weeks, he pursued me, more politely, in various disguises." Miss McFein shivered as delicately as a butterfly beating its wings. "Eventually, I had to leave the country, and he did not follow me."

Bartholomew frowned in confusion. "Why did you have to leave? Because you are—"

She laughed, and Celwyn made a mental note of duplicating the wonderful sound in his music.

"A vampire? No, at that time, Maximilian II embraced vampires, daemons, and other creatures, usually for a lustful purpose. If you kept out of his reach, there was no problem." She smiled at them. "I left for London on business."

After she finished speaking, Celwyn noticed she gazed directly into his eyes. A subtle challenge of sorts. He thought it interesting the way the setting sun seemed to light the gold in her irises from within. He sighed and broke the contact. Their impending confrontation with his father would be difficult enough without sorting out longing from curiosity, or from something more.

His brother didn't seem to have the same concern. "That sounds fascinating. You must tell us more." He rested his chin on his fist to gaze at her.

Celwyn caused a passing waiter to trip and dump a glass of water in his lap. "Heavens! How unfortunate." Several napkins flew toward Pelaez as the magician turned to the others. "We need to plan our foray into the catacombs. Where are you staying?"

Valentine's lips twitched in amusement as he watched Pelaez. "We have also taken rooms at the Il Bella."

"We have the suite on the top floor," Miss Redifer told them. She smiled at Bartholomew as he refilled her wineglass. "Would tonight be a good time to finalize our plans?"

"Although," Kang answered, "I would rather stay here to discuss things. Yes, it would be better." He gestured to the panoramic bay before them and then to the surrounding tables. "We are already of interest to the other diners."

It was true. A few faces ducked back behind menus, and a few more pretended to study their companions or the view. As the magician thought about giving them something worth their inquisitiveness, Kang elbowed him and whispered, "Don't make it worse."

"I wonder why," Valentine drawled. He stood and helped Miss McFein to her feet as Bartholomew pulled Miss Redifer's chair out. Valentine told them, "Please enjoy your dessert, and we will await you in our suite after sundown."

Chapter 17

As Valentine ushered the women through the arch leading to the restaurant's main room, a container ship in the harbor blew its horn. Another answered, then another, the harmonizing horns echoing. The sunset had reached the point where the pinks darkened to maroons over the brilliant cerulean sea, and in the distance, the outline of several islands shadowed the water before the horizon.

"Such a beautiful setting, complete with a collection of vampires for color." Pelaez added cream to his coffee and stirred.

Bartholomew blurted, "Can we trust them?"

"Probably not," Kang said. "However, whatever incentive Thales has provided will compel them to help us." He thought a bit. "Or the threat he has made will do so."

While Celwyn considered the situation, which was much easier without the intense gaze of Miss McFein upon him, the automat voiced something Celwyn didn't want to believe. "Whatever motivates them is serious; I have a feeling if we got in the way, we'd be as expendable as a cigar butt."

"Is that your delicate way of hinting that it is time for a smoke and stroll along the boardwalk?" Bartholomew asked as he patted his pocket for a cigar.

———— ⌒ ————

The early evening breeze lifted their coattails and played with their hats as they walked, four abreast, dodging other strollers. Kang had opted for his pipe and couldn't keep the damn thing lit. Celwyn lit it for him without touching it and began talking.

"I am hoping your logic prevails, my friends." A beat later, he added, "and brother." It still seemed strange seeing Pelaez after all these years, much less conversing with him.

"Until we know what to expect, I have a feeling logic won't help us," Kang said.

When they reached the end of the promenade and leaned over the rail, they discovered a gaggle of ducks playing in the mud flat below. Bartholomew yelped and jumped back. Kang peered over the rail to see more clearly in the fading light. He stared at Pelaez. "Really."

Celwyn tried not to laugh. What lay below reminded him of his childhood. Along with the ducks and ducklings, a pair of baby piglets wallowed in the mud, but instead of snouts, they had fish faces. When Celwyn spied Bartholomew returning to the rail, he added a fluffy tail to each of the pigs.

"Nice touch." Pelaez puffed on a smelly cigarette and watched the pigs.

Bartholomew told the automat, "This is going to be a very good test of my resolve not to be superstitious."

When Kang opened his mouth to respond, the pigs sat up and sang in harmonizing baritones, like the American barbershop quartets.

"Don't be, don't be, don't be superstitious!"

❧

Miss Redifer opened the door to their suite on the top floor of the hotel and led them into the living room. In front of the panoramic view of the bay, Valentine occupied an upholstered chair, as regal as could be. Twin sofas flanked the windows, and Miss McFein patted the spot beside her with the kind of smile that dared Celwyn to sit with her.

The magician hitched up his trousers and sat, treating himself to her perfume while he did his best to concentrate on the matter at hand. From across the room, Miss Redifer asked what they would like to drink and began filling their glasses. Celwyn added a tray of Earl Grey to the table in front of them. When everyone was seated, Valentine nodded to him to begin.

"I feel a great responsibility to you all because it is I who is in debt to Thales. I do not take that lightly."

126

Celwyn verified Valentine's expression, noting his interest seemed benign for now. After the conversation this afternoon, the magician wondered if the vampire blamed him for his presence in Palermo. It couldn't be helped. Celwyn shrugged and continued. "I have asked my associates if they wish to decline this adventure, but they prefer to participate, as does my brother."

With a nod to the other vampires, Kang asked Miss McFein, "In order to plan, we need to know your motivation. Does Thales hold something over you, or do you expect to gain something if our efforts are successful?"

Without hesitation, she said, "The former."

"I do not think you need to know more," Valentine inserted along with a slight hardening of his eyes.

Bartholomew asked, "What can we expect if we enter into league with you?" He gazed at Valentine. "What are you willing to do? Would you sacrifice one of us?"

Valentine rested his chin on his chest, downed his wine, and held up a hand.

"Allow me to clear this up." He glanced between Pelaez and Celwyn. "What do you know about your father? Past or present? It isn't a great deal. Am I correct?"

Both Celwyn and Pelaez remained silent, each lost in their thoughts.

"Neither of his sons have seen him in over three hundred years," the Professor said.

Valentine frowned, then his face changed, flushing in anger. A muscle in his temple pulsed, keeping time with the clenching and unclenching of his hands. "You have no idea of the trouble he has caused. None." His expression displayed what the vampire looked like when sufficiently annoyed.

"Nothing will surprise us," Pelaez said. "Neither my brother nor I feel any allegiance to him."

"Is it true he tried to kill you the last time you saw him?" Miss Redifer asked Celwyn.

Celwyn wanted to hurry this along. "Yes."

"How did you locate your father?" Valentine probably asked in case this didn't go well and he had to find him again without them.

Pelaez looked at Celwyn, who stared back at him. "After the beheading at Fotheringhay Castle..." Pelaez tapped his lips with a manicured fingernail, "...we found him in a fetid slum near the Bastille. Father was in rags. Raving. Stomping through filth. We had bribed a series of people who thought they knew of him, eventually finding those who did."

"Back to our situation, please." Professor Kang made a face of distaste. "To succeed, we need to develop a level of trust between us all."

Showing her willingness to participate, Miss Redifer moved closer to Bartholomew until their knees almost touched on the sofa. Celwyn assumed the big man could find an excuse to escape if he wanted to.

With a sigh that went all the way to the toes of his highly polished boots, Valentine began talking.

"It is as the Professor intimated. Thales can end our family. Our assistance was a request from him, and here we are." He indicated the women. "My nieces and I will do anything, sacrifice anyone, to that end."

With a matching sigh, Celwyn thought about what Valentine had said. "At least we know."

"We need background and then a plan to move forward." Bartholomew stood and began pacing. "It was preferable to wait for you before making decisions."

Pelaez piped up, "A good idea. However, I know little since I was banished to my cabin for the last few days."

Bartholomew ignored him and raised a brow at the magician. Celwyn's reluctance on the subject knew no bounds. "It is useless to speculate; I no longer know my father." The magician took his time pouring another cup of tea and choosing his words. "Would I even recognize him? I do not know."

Pelaez nodded. "If you want a true sense as to what Father looks like when he isn't employing subterfuge, picture a man even taller and broader than Mr. Bartholomew here, but with my mannerisms and hair color. His features strongly resemble Jonas's—especially his profile."

"I agree," Miss McFein said. "Although I never saw him smile."

The magician sent her his best one, wanting her to know the difference. "Everyone should remember that he is most adept at magic; he can appear as anyone or manipulate objects, the weather, anything, and do so at extreme speed." Celwyn executed another shrug. "I have no idea as to how to persuade him to travel to the lair of Thales. Do any of you?"

"I do not, but wonder why Thales wants your father to go to him at all." Bartholomew frowned at his boots.

Valentine said, "It is a mystery, just as much as how to make this project successful."

Miss Redifer crossed the room to the bar and brought back several bottles. "We have given this much thought, and the three of us have come to the conclusion that we will have to use force to deliver him to Thales."

Bartholomew sank back into the couch. "This is a fine mess."

"Can't we think of a way to trick him? Appeal to his vanity perhaps, or sense of responsibility?" Kang asked.

Pelaez laughed.

"He has a great capacity for vanity but no sense of morality." Celwyn could have given them so many examples. He would have also wagered his father's indiscretions had grown in audacity and violence as the years went by.

With a virulent glare that made him appear as dangerous as he probably was, Valentine told them, "The only thing we know is that he wants my niece, Tara."

Celwyn thought, *so do I,* and carefully avoided her gaze.

Miss Redifer said, "She would be the bait."

Even though Miss McFein nodded in agreement, Celwyn didn't like the idea for several reasons. "You do realize that he is extraordinarily strong? And that he is probably faster than any vampire?"

So swift that Celwyn felt the air move but did not see it, Valentine suddenly sat beside him, his breath cold on Celwyn's cheek. The magician carefully did not react. Everyone else did, especially Bartholomew, as he tried to climb up the back of the sofa. Valentine smiled and returned to his chair.

"Impressive example." Celwyn took his time, straightening his cuffs to show how the display did not frighten him. "However, I stand by my statement. My father is capable of astonishing speed, and what he can't do naturally, he augments with magic. Unlike my brother and I, he doesn't need any time at all for his work. It occurs as soon as he desires it."

"How did you get away from him?" the Professor asked Miss McFein.

"Sorry." She shook her head. "I can't tell all my secrets."

Kang raised his brows in surprise. Celwyn wondered if she teased them, but not urgently, considering the other things of importance to worry about.

With an effort, Bartholomew took his eyes off Valentine and said, "We're back to our original dilemma. What are we going to do?"

"Our only suggestion is to capture him," Miss Redifer repeated without conviction.

"I suggest that we meet him, make Thales' request, and then, if we have to, capture him," Kang said.

The magician didn't have confidence in that option, either. His father would simply laugh at them, and God only knew what he'd do next. While everyone thought about Kang's idea, moments passed when only the faint sounds from the street and the harbor could be heard.

Through the open window, Celwyn watched the few vessels still upon the bay this late at night. A party boat inched into port, raucous laughter bouncing across the water, riding the music like an excitable apparition. A light breeze stirred the drapes in the suite with the scent of roses and the sea. It also brought tiny, colorfully dressed dancers pirouetting and tumbling from within the music. Flute players, horn artists, and drummers settled on the floor between Valentine's boots. The dancers flitted through the air near Bartholomew and ran up his long legs to cavort in a flurry of skirts and high kicks in his lap.

"Oh ... Jonas ...." Bartholomew couldn't decide whether to laugh or run.

With a smile, Miss McFein held out a finger to one of the dancers who walked across it to her wrist. She appeared fascinated, and her smile at Celwyn was one he would remember. As the dancers and music faded away, Valentine clapped his bejeweled hands.

"An extraordinary interlude. But, to finish our business, are we decided *mes amici*?"

The magician wasn't sure they were really Valentine's friends, but refrained from saying so.

"Yes, I believe we are. We will capture Wolfgang if possible. One more question. Do we know why he is in the catacombs?" Kang asked.

No one answered.

"If we did, we could offer him something to entice him or bribe him." Bartholomew brushed at his pants in case anything still twirled there.

Celwyn had forgotten about Thales' visitations to his mind. Of a sudden, he could see the old man's face and hear him as clearly as he did on Antigo Island:

Your father has built a kingdom in the catacombs. He fancies himself a god.

Use this perception.

"What is wrong, Mr. Celwyn?" Miss McFein exclaimed with the kind of concern he would normally have enjoyed very much. "You look ready to faint."

Kang started to rise, fearing the worst, but Celwyn waved him back. He shook himself and brushed off his reaction.

He told the vampires, "You are not aware of it, but Thales stayed with me after our visit to his island." He saw Valentine's brows shoot up. "Just now ... I understand from Thales that my father has, uh ... built his own world in the catacombs, and he says Father considers himself a god down there."

Bartholomew asked him, "Are you sure you are all right?"

Celwyn inhaled as deeply as he could and nodded.

"Extraordinary." Valentine stood and smoothed down his trousers. "We need to make arrangements for our transportation in the morning." He held up a piece of paper and told the Professor. "I have your requirements."

"Excellent." Kang still eyed the magician. "Tonight, I will go over the local maps I have acquired and look for another way into the catacombs, other than what the tourists use."

"If necessary, I, or my brother, can make an opening," Celwyn said.

"We may need it, but I prefer one naturally occurring so we do not call attention to ourselves." The automat tossed off his drink and stood also.

As they prepared to leave, Miss McFein approached Celwyn and studied him up close with concern that brought the lovely corners of her mouth down. "Are you sure you feel well? You looked as if you had seen a ghost."

"Perhaps I did." Celwyn bowed. "I am fine." The worry in her eyes, this near, almost made Celwyn forget what she was. For seconds, he just stared back at her until the automat tugged on his elbow.

"We must go. Thank you for your hospitality." Kang said, "Your uncle has assured me he will have our transportation in hand for tomorrow."

THE
CATACOMBS

The gods, too, are fond of a joke
-Aristotle

Chapter 18

ALTHOUGH EARLY SPRING, THE hills surrounding Palermo glistened a brilliant emerald green. It was late morning, and Valentine drove the rented carriage containing Kang, the women, and Pelaez into the hills. On their heels, Celwyn and Bartholomew rode horses packed with their supplies and gear. Behind them, only a field of weeds lay before the cliffs overlooking the Tyrrhenian Sea.

Before they turned inland, Celwyn squinted against the sun, hoping to glimpse the *Nautilus* near shore. They'd left Captain Nemo a message with the hotel concierge saying not to expect them for a week or more and listed exactly when and where they intended to go underground via the caves north of town. Ideally, after a successful mission, they would very soon find themselves standing on the cliffs, signaling the submarine to pick them up.

As they neared the appointed area Kang had chosen, the magician noted that, although the land looked fertile enough, he saw no crops or farmhouses. Tall grasses and rocks covered a landscape void of any sign of civilization. Then he understood—local superstition flourished here because the farmers knew what lay below.

The dirt road they traveled upon wound under the shade of ancient oak trees that entwined branches overhead like skeletons embracing. Some writhed in agony as they reached downward, scraping the top of the carriage. A glance on Celwyn's right showed the eeriness had not been lost on Bartholomew, and his eyes bounced in all directions while he kept a death grip on his reins.

A mile ahead, the land began to form low hills as they neared their target. When the carriage rolled into an area of low brush under the taller trees, it triggered a memory of the lightning storm on the way to Prague when their party took cover in caves. If a cadaver had joined them in the cave they sheltered in that day, good god, Bartholomew would have never been the same.

The magician couldn't spy any caves now, but trusted Kang had found their access point to go below. Another minute and their procession pulled to a stop under a group of centuries-old banyans. Bartholomew and the magician dismounted to stretch and help the women from the carriage. Celwyn enjoyed it very much.

"Thank you," Miss McFein said as she, too, stretched. She wore a riding outfit and boots, as did

Miss Redifer, all the better for a quick getaway or climbing over rocks and caskets.

Throughout the ride this morning, the big man had explained his fears several times, and in detail. Whether occupied or unoccupied, caskets were the main subject of Bartholomew's worry about what they would find below. The big man's level of unease had been hard to soothe, but the magician did his best.

A breeze flirted with them, lifting the ribbon that held Miss McFein's curls back, and toying with Valentine's fancy hat with its jaunty feather. It also brought a strong, earthy scent that tickled Celwyn's nose, but not in a pleasant way.

"Is the cave entrance close by?" Celwyn studied the terrain, seeing no track for the carriage to travel upon, and ground too uneven for anything except a hike by foot. He could elevate their carriage, but if others had not passed beyond this point, this was probably not the right direction.

The automat nodded and eyed the horses with distaste as he moved away from them. "Just over there." He indicated the brush. "If, for some reason, anyone needs to find this spot by themselves, look for those two trees that seem to be embracing over the triangular pile of rocks."

Valentine stood by him, following where Kang pointed. "Noted, Professor."

"Are we ready to go?" Pelaez asked as he strapped on a pack like the ones Kang, Valentine, and Celwyn wore. The women carried two lanterns each, and Celwyn had another. As needed, magical illumination could be provided by either brother, but not if they were separated from the rest.

"All right. To verify, this is a short trip underground to assess what we are up against. Let's get going." The Professor kicked gravel aside and started off.

With a backward glance to the west, Bartholomew said, "I agree that we shouldn't go too far underground. Who knows about the distance the tides travel inland? I cannot swim."

As they strode toward the hill, Celwyn clapped him on the shoulder. "I assure you that between my brother and myself, we can stop the tides for a short time if need be, my friend."

Valentine and the women walked in front of them, and after a few minutes, Celwyn decided that riding breeches had merit. He caught Kang's cynical expression and decided to provide a distraction before the automat offered a caustic comment.

He called out to Valentine and the women, "Do we have any new ideas on what to say to my father?"

"None from here," Miss Redifer replied. "I do wonder how long it will take to find him." She stared at the hills that extended for miles around them. "Or how extensive the catacombs are."

Kang raised his voice loud enough for everyone to hear. "I have read as much as I could find about what is down there. After the initial area that the tourists are allowed into, there isn't much information available. A cave-in about a hundred years ago blocked access to everything beyond that point." He gestured to the far right.

"Essentially, we're coming in the side door?" Pelaez asked.

"Yes."

Bartholomew sighed. "At least there won't be any freshly buried bodies."

Celwyn would not have placed a wager on that as he added a chorus of trilling sopranos whose song cascaded up and down the minor scales playfully. Perhaps this would lighten their mood. Pelaez raised a brow, and a flock of blue and white birds flittered around them, leading the way into the densest part of the thicket.

"Here we are. There should be an entrance nearby." Kang examined the dirt below and the smooth rock wall that rose fifteen feet above before them. The others fanned out, doing the same, and for minutes they searched, but to no avail.

"Nothing," Valentine grumbled.

"Observe." Pelaez opened a hand and sent a white rabbit into the brush with a salivating wolf bounding after it. They watched for several minutes as the rabbit ran from bush to bush, racing ahead of the wolf. When it reached a cleft in the rock above Miss Redifer's boot, it disappeared.

Pelaez dissolved the wolf as it ran by and knelt in front of the cleft.

"I wouldn't do that," the Professor called out as he removed a small shovel from Bartholomew's backpack and hurried forward. "If we disturb the area, it could cave in."

Bartholomew shuddered and backed up, as did the others.

The automat took his time and, little by little, scraped the cleft until they could see the yawning blackness beyond. A waft of pungent mold and decay drifted out as if a ghost had been released from a tomb. Which it probably had been.

Like a fascinated ghoul, Pelaez drew closer while the others retreated.

Nearly an hour later, they inched their way inside with Pelaez in the lead, then the vampires and Kang, with Bartholomew and Celwyn bringing up the rear. The ceiling just cleared the top of Bartholomew's hat. As they went forward, the passageway enlarged, and they slipped and slid through soft earth for a while before they could walk normally again.

"This looks like foxfire," Miss McFein said as she ran a hand across the shiny green surface of the walls. Just in time, she sidestepped a pool of water. "And things seem to be getting muddier."

"We're still descending, too." Valentine tripped and righted himself as he called back to the others. "Watch your step, please."

Celwyn threw more light over their parade, front to back. "If you'll turn off your lanterns, please? In case we need them later."

As the lanterns darkened, Bartholomew said, "I smell something sweet."

Kang made a face of revulsion. With regret, he said gently, "Decay smells sweet at first."

Bartholomew didn't say a word, just turned and ploughed forward.

As they went along, the only sound was their steps and an occasional curse from Valentine as he tripped or stepped in something. Celwyn paused and listened, as did the others, before they signaled. They heard nothing, either. Both Pelaez and the magician knew that was not a good omen; it was a sign their father was nearby. Once, a bat flew by Miss Redifer before the darkness swallowed it again. The path became a bed of seashells that they crunched underfoot, indicating the nearby tides used to flood this area.

The tunnel they walked through widened further until it was at least ten feet across. Celwyn felt the chilly drafts swirling around them, and in his fancy, he wondered if they were the souls of the dead dancing to unheard music. He knew better than to say so to Bartholomew.

The big man had taken the lead earlier, and now he let out a yelp and tumbled out of sight. As Kang hurried forward, Valentine blocked the women before they also did.

"I'm safe!" the big man called. "I just rolled down … a hill."

From a dozen feet above him, they watched Bartholomew dust himself off and slog his way back up the rise to help the women down. He knew they did not need his assistance, but he was a gracious and polite man, no matter the circumstances. Once they were all together again, the magician fanned light around them and then upward in a great arc, revealing a towering and empty amphitheater that ended a hundred feet above the tunnel opening where they had emerged. He counted at least three other tunnels leading away from the amphitheater.

"We stand at a crossroads." Bartholomew's stage whisper bounced upward.

Using the mud underfoot as glue, Celwyn constructed a cross as big as the automat from the larger shells, propping it against the nearest wall where it could be seen from a distance. "That will remain as a marker to the way out again." He didn't have to say why he didn't make it with magic, but his statement drew a stubborn glare of denial from the automat. The magician let it go—there would come a time when his magic wouldn't be enough, and he would fail. It was not today.

While the magician constructed the marker, Kang had begun to explore the area to their left. He stopped moving. "Oh, my." He looked at his feet.

Everyone did the same, realizing that they no longer stood on a carpet of shells but on a bed of bones embedded in the mud—thousands and thousands of bones bleached white with age. Celwyn turned to Bartholomew just as his eyes rolled back in his head. He and Kang caught the big man as he fell dead away.

Chapter 19

AFTER THE AUTOMAT AND THE magician tilted Bartholomew back upright, and verified he was going to stay that way, Celwyn inspected their surroundings while Kang tried to help the big man recover.

To the north, quartzite ribboned the blackened walls like a bizarre diagram, at times blossoming into an exploding river of gold and traveling in all directions. The face of the walls appeared to be man-made; perfect indentions had been scooped away at regular intervals, and the sections of solid rock ascended beyond what they could see above them. Pelaez threw more light upward, and they discovered a ceiling tiled in an intricate mosaic; the design vaguely Persian. It stretched for fifty feet or more to the east, where the walls became shadowy and glistening water oozed downward like a vertical river. At least, Celwyn assumed it was water.

The ocean of bones underfoot seemed endless, as if every casket from the beginning of civilization had been turned upside down and shaken thoroughly. The magician assumed that since he spied no wooden caskets, only stone, the bones must be much older than this century. He watched Bartholomew vibrate all over and take a deep breath before again leading the way toward the murky corner of the amphitheater that they couldn't see into.

As they went, his brother enlarged and strengthened the field of light around them. Along the path they walked, a row of grimacing skulls escorted them. Pelaez kicked them away and kept walking with the vampires. If things weren't so dangerous, Celwyn would comment on the perception of bravery; Bartholomew displayed great courage to conquer his fears, and in contrast, the vampires seemed to take the situation in stride.

Just as Kang came to a halt next to Bartholomew, a rock ledge above them gave way. Faster than Celwyn could see, Tara and Miss Redifer became colorful streaks that rushed them, pushing them out of the way as the rocks crashed down. Valentine wasn't the only one supremely quick. As Miss Redifer dusted herself off and Bartholomew thanked her, Celwyn enjoyed the automat's courtly bow to the other vampire with the golden gaze.

"Thank you, Miss. That was a close call."

The magician could admit to a twinge of jealousy; he was usually the answer when things went wrong. Yet, the more he thought about it, if they continued their association, there would be more than one occasion for Miss Tara McFein to save him, and he would enjoy it very much.

By silent agreement, they stayed close together as they explored, and each checked on the others. When the Professor spoke, his voice seemed restrained and uncharacteristically uncertain. "We have been down here nearly two hours. I suggest we head back soon." Kang regarded Valentine. "As a reminder, this was just a quick look. We run the risk of not making it back to the surface before dark."

Bartholomew said, "I second that."

Valentine rejoined the others, and they formed a tight circle. This close, Celwyn noted the anxiousness in Miss McFein's eyes. Falling rocks did not frighten her but finding Wolfgang certainly did.

"Do we have any idea of what we will discover if we continue?" she asked.

"Probably only what we can see and what lies ahead without straying too far down rabbit holes." Kang frowned. "This area is too big, and there's too much to explore in one try. There could be dozens of tunnels with disguised entrances and only one leading to our quarry. It is another reason to turn back before we become lost."

"Allow me." Celwyn stepped forward, and with a single gesture, scores of man-size mirrors appeared, each strung on an undulating rope stretching across the landscape.

He'd suspended the mirrors feet above the ground like columns of soldiers that eventually became smaller and indistinct, their surfaces pinpricks of light twinkling in the faraway darkness.

Each mirror reflected a picture of the terrain to the next in the chain. The mirrors also refracted light dozens of times over. Pelaez added more illumination until it seemed that the sun itself bathed the expanse.

"Extraordinary." Miss McFein gazed at the scene and said, "This shows the extent of what we must explore."

Pelaez produced a collection of spy glasses and handed them around. Celwyn waved it off. Thanks to Thales, he could see.

As Kang had said, the perimeter began to narrow from that point on. Under the enhanced light, the quartzite glittered into the distance until it suddenly stopped, and the darkness took over, shadowing mounds of debris and rock formations. With a shudder, Celwyn wondered if the others knew what that meant; it wasn't a natural phenomenon for the light to stop. Pelaez tensed and sent him a glance that assured him, like before, he understood the significance.

From the deepest point of the abyss, they heard a faint crack like a muffled rifle shot lost in the silence, then another, sounding like a mirror had shattered. Dozens more followed as the series of cracks echoed upon each other, growing closer and louder.

One by one, the mirrors furthest away disappeared as Celwyn searched for the source, all the while knowing he wouldn't see it. Before each one shattered, they heard another faint metallic click. Kang hopped back, and the others did the same as the speed of the clicks increased, racing toward them until only the tallest and widest mirror swayed in front of Bartholomew.

As he gazed into the remaining mirror, the hair on Celwyn's neck stood on end, and he felt a deathly chill to his core. The mirror tilted slightly and then swiveled to face each of their party, inspecting them, spending the most time on Pelaez before turning to Celwyn.

The face of Wolfgang Augustus Griffin filled the mirror. Under heavy brows, his eyes glittered much brighter than the sun, and with more malevolence than Celwyn's nightmares had ever created.

The mirror exploded, and his father's hands wrapped around Celwyn's neck. Bartholomew leapt on top of Wolfgang and was flung off. Peleaz went flying next. Each of them tried and was repelled as Celwyn gasped and clawed at his father's hands.

Kang yelled, "*Jonas*—"

Everything faded to black.

Chapter 20

W HEN CELWYN AWOKE, HE FOUND himself lying in Miss McFein's lap while she smoothed the hair off his forehead. He sighed. This must be what heaven would be like. Her eyes were even more lovely this close, her lips kissable too.

"Jonas!"

This time, Bartholomew interrupted his enjoyment. The big man pulled him to his feet and hugged him, and when the automat did the same—Celwyn looked over Kang's shoulder at Miss McFein's highly amused expression. After the automat released him, Celwyn blinked at Pelaez a few feet away. His brother saluted him, and slowly the magician saluted back like they used to do as children. Pelaez leaned against a massive altar of black stone, patted a yawn, and went back to cleaning his nails.

They were surrounded by a herd of oversize tapestry pillows. Miss McFein reclined on one of them, and Celwyn wished he could rejoin her again. Miss Redifer perched on the next one over. Their party occupied a rather small, luxurious, three-sided alcove in front of a cavern so big Celwyn couldn't see the end of it. He touched his neck and felt the bruises. Although he could have stopped the pain, he left it there to remind himself of danger. During his father's attack, their shock had held them all spellbound, and Celwyn had been too stunned to react.

"What is this place?" the magician asked Valentine, who stood beside him, frowning at everything. The vampire looked none the worse for their ordeal, every hair on his perfect mane in place. Out of habit, Celwyn repaired the tiny rip on the vampire's sleeve.

"We're not sure. After you passed out, your father threw you over his shoulder and came here. We picked ourselves up and followed." He pointed to the intricately woven rugs underfoot. "After he dumped you on the floor, he left again without a word."

"From what I can tell, we're about another mile further underground," the Professor murmured as he stared at Celwyn. "I can clearly see your father's fingerprints on your neck."

The magician made a face and pivoted to inspect the walls behind the altar. Row after row of sarcophaguses had been stacked in compartments ascending upward. There had to be hundreds, if not thousands, of them. Some cubbyholes held a body, others a closed coffin; a few of the exposed bodies at one point had sat up, posing in lifelike positions, while others appeared to be asleep. One of the corpses pointed at them, its mouth open in an interrupted scream. The magician sincerely hoped Bartholomew would not turn around—the body nearest to them had diamonds for eyes that caught the light, seeming to animate the skeleton.

Beyond the proliferation of pillows, there was nothing in the alcove besides floor rugs. No jugs of wine or decorations anywhere; the point of the place seemed to be the altar, in size easily as long as a carriage and full set of horses. Its polished sides ascended upward between the rows of sarcophaguses.

"What is that odor?" Celwyn asked. Again, the air smelled sweet, yet this time it wasn't decomposition—more like a touch of excrement mixed with roses. Then he saw the pig at Pelaez's feet. Oh, really?

"We seem to be in the proverbial lair of the lion, Brother," Pelaez drawled as he scratched the pig's ears. "By the way, since Father knows where we are, there is no reason we cannot talk."

"As long as we assume that he could be listening." Bartholomew turned to the magician. "Can Wolfgang read thoughts like you?"

Celwyn said, "No, not that I remember. But his hearing is even better than my brother's."

Pelaez bowed at the compliment. So did the pig. Then it winked at him. The magician sighed and looked away; all of his brother's annoying habits had returned.

The magician found his backpack and tossed a sandwich to Kang and to Bartholomew, aware that the vampires would decline. Kang produced flasks of water, and the vampires opened the wine they'd brought. As he ate, Celwyn asked, "In what direction did my father go?"

Bartholomew pointed with his sandwich to the right. "The shadows just swallowed him. All of a sudden, I couldn't hear his steps or see him anymore."

"If your brother's magic centers on fish and pigs, and yours on music, what does your father use?" Kang inquired as he chewed.

Pelaez and Celwyn exchanged a surprised glance. "We don't know."

You want to do *what*?

Miss Redifer wrote the question on the paper they'd been passing around.

Celwyn scribbled.

> *My brother will leave an audible conver-*
> *sation here that will last long enough to*
> *make Father think we're still here...*

He pointed at the altar.

> *...and not on our way toward him.*

He glanced at the others and wrote.

> *I'm going to ask you a question out*
> *loud, and you will please indicate that*
> *we plan to stay here. It will also serve*
> *as samples for my brother's imitation*

of your voices. Talk as you normally would, please.

After they read it, he waited for their nods, and said aloud, "Should we stay here for now?"

"Yes." Valentine took his cue, making his aristocratic baritone loud enough. "We should."

Each of them responded in kind. Pelaez listened to them with his ear tilted to one side as a mimic would, and as soon as they began to gather their things together, a disembodied commentary, spiced with a discussion of odd subjects, began around them. The magician was impressed. His brother's version of Miss McFein's voice sounded like a fine match for the real thing. Kang wrinkled his nose when he heard the imitation of himself, then shrugged.

As they finished making their preparations to leave, Celwyn entered their thoughts to say, "This effort will be tricky, and there will be dangerous traps laid for us. My father will want to know when we leave here. Do not venture beyond the pillows until my brother and I have checked the immediate area."

Pelaez told Celwyn silently, "He could have made it impossible for us to leave here, to keep us captive along with those." He pointed to the sarcophaguses.

"We'll soon know," the magician responded.

Celwyn and Pelaez moved forward in concert, and when the rugs ended, they kicked small pebbles ahead of their steps. Nothing happened, but the rocks dissolved. With his fingers to his lips, Pelaez pointed to the rock wall to their right. A fine thread of iridescence, like a single strand from a spider web, had been stretched across their path. Celwyn discovered more strands appearing about five feet above them. Pelaez held up a hand and then crab-walked between the strands as Celwyn looked for more traps.

The others watched as Pelaez tossed a handful of pebbles down a small incline. The stones made no noise at all. Pelaez frowned and shook his head. He repeated the process in each direction until they heard the pebbles scatter as they should. He, like Celwyn, would know that their father must have left a path outward that did not disturb his magic.

Celwyn nodded and turned to the others silently. "Now that you've seen a demonstration of my father's strength, we can abandon the idea of capturing him. We'll have to think of something else. From now on, either my brother or I will be at the front or back of our party in case he attacks again—we stand the best chance of at least distracting him while you get away. If you agree, please nod." He waited, seeing agreement. "Do not stray from our footsteps, even slightly. It could be fatal." He pointed. "Do as my brother has done; duck down and step across the area he is indicating. After this point, if you must talk, get my attention, and I will enter your thoughts for a message."

Valentine shook his head like a bee had buzzed up his ear, but nodded. When Celwyn turned to Pelaez, it seemed much easier than usual to enter his thoughts to relay messages. Perhaps his brother allowed it during stressful or dangerous times. In the dead silence, where only the sound of flowing water could be heard, he told the group, "The Professor's make-up does not allow me to enter his thoughts to communicate. Bartholomew will pantomime messages to him. They also know sign language. Feel free to use it also. Stay close together, walk as quietly as you can. I will provide a magical shroud around us, but it may not be enough."

Behind them, the prearranged magical conversation between Valentine and Kang about the merits of vintage wine began, and Celwyn provided illumination for what lay directly in front of them. Pelaez took the lead, sending bursts of bright, concentrated light in different directions. They ducked over and under the iridescent threads, treading across rough gravel, not bones, toward the shadows ahead. Distantly, they could hear the drip, drip, drip of water.

The murmur from the improvised conversation followed them as they descended further, and the ceiling overhead rose higher. From what Celwyn could discern, the walls were rough cut—as if a crazed giant had hacked away at the granite—sometimes cutting deep, other times scraping sections smooth. High above them, the magician caught occasional flickers of sunlight where the ceiling was the highest and thinnest.

Something scurried behind Miss Redifer, and her inner voice alerted Celwyn. He turned and spied a hairy rodent about the size of his hand. Even from fifteen feet away, its teeth appeared sharp. The magician froze the creature, studied it, and courtesy of Thales, he could now see into it as he had not been able to before. The rodent's skeletal frame wasn't that of a mouse or rat, and under its hair, the face looked human. Inside of its paws, he saw the distinct shape of fingers. It did not breathe, and Celwyn doubted it still had a soul. This was a vessel for his father to watch over them. Luckily, it hadn't scurried far enough ahead to see everyone.

He controlled a shiver and dissolved it, leaving behind a pile of ashes and a collection of iridescent teeth.

Celwyn rubbed his face hard, told the others of it, and signaled Pelaez to push ahead again. Kang blinked understanding at him. Each of them would watch for more of the rodents. As they went forward, Bartholomew's eyes bulged, and he stared at the pile of teeth. Kang gave him a gentle shove to close the gap again behind Pelaez.

To their left, the unending rock wall gradually angled toward them, narrowing their path, which still noticeably descended, bringing a dampness to the air and underfoot. Miss Redifer cursed in a muffled whisper and removed her boot from a pool of mud. Within a few minutes, Bartholomew's head barely cleared the rock ceiling, along with his massive shoulders. Water trickled as through a sieve from hundreds of cracks in the rock, and as it splattered them, the magician noticed that the water felt warm. A volcanic presence nearby, perhaps? The automat touched a drop to his lips and mouthed the word "fresh."

As he walked, Celwyn ran his hand along the slick walls. When the surface changed to something scaly and bumpy, he jerked his head to the side and realized he gazed into the dead eyes of the dragon-like creature Kang had called a wyvern. It had embedded itself in the wall at eye-level and blinked at him. Interestingly, this time it measured no more than a few feet long. With slow deliberation and adoration, it flashed its teeth at him and faded away. Celwyn weighed saying something colorful and appropriate, but they needed to concentrate on things more immediate and deadly.

Proving he'd made the right decision, Pelaez stopped so suddenly that the others crashed into each other like a row of tiptoeing dominoes. Celwyn pivoted, on alert.

In Pelaez's mind, Celwyn heard, "Massive cavern around the next corner. At the bottom of it is Father and hundreds of men and women ... mostly dead ... some alive ... not sure."

"What else?" Celwyn asked silently.

"He is sitting on a throne of sorts, drinking and being worshiped by the clusters of women. At his feet ... some old people ... wings ... fur ... can't see details ... large object moving in front of him."

Ahead of them, an organ began to play an echoing and sonorous processional march. It slowed—like time itself had slowed—and the sound reverberated as if the pipes stretched to a great height. A chorus of discordant voices sang with it, sending a cold hand up the magician's back.

Celwyn asked Pelaez, "Is that enough to cover our approach?

"Possibly, or he already knows we're here. I'll increase the protection around us."

To Valentine and then the others, the magician silently related what Pelaez saw. After Bartholomew gestured the details to Kang, the automat gave Celwyn a direct look and pointed to move forward.

Celwyn told Pelaez, "Together, we may be able to control him."

When Pelaez met his gaze, his eyes danced in anticipation, and for the first time in ages, they also danced in fear.

⁓

They crept forward. Celwyn paused, waiting behind Kang as the automat picked his way downward behind a jumble of cart-size boulders. What he saw took his breath away.

To the left, so close he could have touched them, unending rows of coffins filled cubbyholes carved into the wall like a grotesque library of death.

The repository must have gone back thousands of years, not just centuries. Just as before, the spaces ascended upward fifty feet or more. Celwyn thoroughly hoped Bartholomew didn't turn around. If he did, he would see two of the skeletons climbing out of their coffins and down the shelves. Once on the ground, they flailed their arms, stretched, and squatted before walking stiffly across a field of bones. Their destination was the mass of humans and skeletons cavorting in front of his father.

Even obscured by the distance and shadows in front of them, he had no trouble smelling the thousands of animals that slept or roamed everywhere.

Horses, turkeys, wolves, foxes, African gazelles—and other animals that shouldn't exist on this continent—wandered everywhere. Celwyn would need to be much closer to tell if they were real. Did his father animate them?

Two hundred feet or more beyond his father and his deadly kingdom, he spied the beginnings of an opaque lake that stretched a mile or more in every direction; he couldn't see where it ended on the far side. Much closer, above everything, shimmered a domed ceiling remarkably like the one Thales resided under. But before he could study it further, his skin prickled, and he knew Miss McFein would plunge off a rock and tumble downward.

Celwyn stopped her fall just before she struck the rocks below. Knowing of impending actions isn't a bad thing, he decided as he floated her back to a spot beside him.

"Why didn't you just jump down?" Celwyn asked her silently.

"We thought your father would detect the sudden movement." Even her thoughts were in a rich contralto. She touched his hand. "I remembered one thing that might help; he is superstitious of animals. If needed, use the other creatures against him—he is jealous of anything more talented in a supernatural way, and that could help distract him." She gave his cheek a peck and rejoined the others.

Pelaez enjoyed Celwyn's surprise and smirked. The magician shook it off and turned back to the scene in front of them. The large objects Pelaez had seen weren't obelisks or rocks. Worse. Instead, huge, grotesque, and misshapen puppets teetered crazily on stilts as they lumbered between the animals, parading throughout the scene. At the same time, they resembled the animals somewhat, as if they were the animals' mirrored image from the inside out—covered in bloody animal skins. The moon-like eyes on the puppet masks rotated side to side, following the rise and fall of the organ music as it grew louder.

The instrument had to be the largest the magician had ever seen; no church could have held it. As he assumed, the rows of brass pipes—some as big around as a horse—reached upward to the very top of the amphitheater, enhancing the volume. The sound wasn't musical, and the jarring noise made Celwyn's head ache.

He focused on which of the animals moved away from the horrible noise of the organ, which would indicate they were alive. Using Miss McFein's advice, he caused dozens of the bear-like creatures to rush toward his father, running on their hind legs. At the last moment, they veered away with a cascade of nasty laughter and back into the herd of animals. Wolfgang had hesitated at their approach and, with a roar, resumed his attack on the organ when they retreated. Celwyn would use this again if the situation worsened. He thanked Miss McFein silently.

The din segued into an uneven and terrible semblance of Verde's *Il Trovatore*, escalating in disharmony and violence within the animal audience. What happened next caused Bartholomew to grip Kang's shoulder and squeeze his eyes shut. The automat pulled on his arm, and they moved behind a pile of rocks a few feet away.

The skeletons lined up in a score of rows, facing what appeared to be humans in torn and shredded finery. They bowed to each other and began the prescribed steps forward and back in almost three-quarter time, the rhythm off enough to make the dancers stop and start, hesitate, and move like a crazed puppet master yanked on their strings. As the chaos continued, it wouldn't have surprised Celwyn if the picture they saw tilted on end.

"What a spectacle!" Miss Redifer pantomimed the words. Valentine watched, blinking rapidly in alertness, not fear, while Bartholomew just stared. Celwyn checked their thoughts.

When he got to Pelaez, he heard, "It appears Father must miss King Louis XV's court more than he should."

In Valentine's thoughts, the magician heard what he already knew; they couldn't just hover here forever—they'd soon be found out, or sniffed out, by the creatures below...

An inner sense caused Celwyn to look to the right. In the distance, something so small, so minute, glinted out of the darkness over the opaque lake that he wasn't sure he saw it until ... it flashed quickly ... whatever it was, it lay beyond Thales's enhancements to his eyesight. The magician pulled a spyglass out of Pelaez's pocket.

Oh! ... he'd wished for this ... Celwyn tried not to hope until they knew with certainty ... Then he did. He tapped Kang's shoulder, pointed, and mouthed the word 'Nemo.' He gave his brother the spyglass and rapidly and silently relayed a message to the others. "The *Nautilus* is sitting in that lake. They are here to help us." When the impact of the submarine's presence hit him, for the first time in hours, the magician smiled. He had an idea.

A risky one, Celwyn acknowledged, and one best not mentioned to the worrisome automat yet.

He entered Pelaez's thoughts and asked a few questions. Pelaez nodded. To the others, Celwyn sent an urgent request and mimicked it for Kang as the organ music reached a crescendo. Kang shook his head and stamped his foot; Celwyn hissed insistence into his ear. Xiau couldn't have been more worried, but he finally bobbed his head.

While he argued with Kang, the others were already making their way down the backside of the mountain of rubble between them and his father's bizarre court. With the debris and noise to hide them, the vampires jumped the last twenty feet, landing like exotic cats on their feet—Valentine literally flew down, spreading his cape as a bat spreads its wings. Once everyone was on the ground, Bartholomew took the lead and the rest mimicked him, running behind boulder to boulder toward the lake. Soon, they would be out in the open where Wolfgang and his horde of the dead could see them.

Celwyn checked with Pelaez, and when he received a nod back, they threw up a wide and tall screen of invisibility between the lake and their father's court where still he attacked the organ and the skeletons danced. The screen would serve two purposes—hide Bartholomew and the others as they ran and be something to use against his father.

Together, Celwyn and his brother descended the remaining distance to the ground and darted behind the screen. This would be a real test of his magic, and Pelaez's. They would need luck, too. Celwyn repeatedly inhaled, gathering strength with each breath, using the music of the violins as they grew more powerful. The magician glanced at Pelaez and saw his thoughts had turned inward, his eyes closed, and he, too, breathed, concentrating his energy. The pig, odorous and sly, leaned against his calf, seemingly asleep.

Celwyn clenched and unclenched his fists, feeling the intensity build as the violins grew stronger.

It was time.

The brothers raised their hands, and silence fell from the dome, covering the organ, the animals, and their father. Like a blanket of mid-winter snow, it smothered everything with an eerie kind of quiet in the monstrous theatre of the dead.

As Wolfgang Augustus Griffin arose from the organ, Celwyn projected a picture of Thales across the screen, one much larger than life, a disembodied face that seemed to float in the air. The image solidified. It had depth, becoming clearer, substantial, and real. Celwyn cued his brother to begin the show.

In the enormous cavern, Thales's voice boomed, echoing off the walls more forcibly than the organ had, shaking rocks loose as it reverberated from wall to wall and finally to where their father stood underneath the screen with hands on his hips, staring at Thales.

"I demand you return to Antigo Island," Thales's image spoke.

Wolfgang's face turned white, then red with rage.

"Now!" Thales's voice thundered.

Celwyn motioned to Pelaez to run for the lake. The magician raced with him, running for his life as the violin music increased, and he prayed it covered the sound of their flight. Every clue Celwyn remembered from Antigo Island told him music supported and empowered Thales as much as it did for him.

As they ran, he had to use every bit of his magic to maintain the screen between them and the organ, not having anything left to enhance their flight. In seconds, the pig began to fade away, as did the violins. The last of Thales' voice still echoed in the chamber.

When Celwyn glanced back, he saw his father had approached the hologram of Thales and touched it, tears streaming down his face.

As the magician sprinted, he sent everything he had into maintaining the screen and suspected Thales helped him. The ground became muddy, and he followed the steps of the others, gaining the floating pier and pounding it down to the hatch.

Pelaez dove inside. Celwyn followed as the crewman cut their floating pier loose before jumping in after him. The hatch closed before Celwyn swung over the last half of the spiral steps and landed beside his brother. Pelaez's hands were raised, his face red with exertion, and he shook all over. Shoulder to shoulder, they held their magic as high as they could, keeping the screen in place and turning it to completely cover the lake. Veins in their foreheads stood out, and sweat poured off their faces.

The gongs in the belly of the ship resounded as if every alarm possible had been activated, and the *Nautilus* dived.

Chapter 21

"WE DID IT," CELWYN TOLD HIS brother as they lay slumped in a pile on the floor. He started to laugh. Pelaez did, too, as he rolled onto his back, and they roared. "Come on," the magician said as he pulled Pelaez to his feet.

"It took both of us. A brilliant plan." His brother saluted. "How did you know what to do?"

Celwyn saluted back. "Just did. Thales directed some of my actions—a most ghastly experience, I can tell you. When Thales healed me, he also added a rather unique pungent scent, his own, as a type of souvenir."

"How lovely."

"Assuming Father and Thales had met, I blew the stench over Father, making our illusion more believable." As Celwyn spoke, Kang arrived at the foot of the stairs, with Bartholomew right behind him, coming close enough to confirm they were not hurt.

"I didn't know about the scent. I saw the image," Bartholomew said in a rapid staccato, evidence of his still stinging nerves.

"Nice touch, Jonas," Kang growled. "But everything you did was dangerous!"

"Come on," the magician said as Pelaez led the way up the corridor. Celwyn slung an arm over Bartholomew and Kang's shoulders. "We should check with Nemo. Our energies should be directed into getting as far from here as possible."

Bartholomew caught up to Pelaez and asked, "Do you think your father will go to Thales's island?"

After his brother shrugged, Celwyn said, "No idea from here. He appeared stunned and afraid." He pursed his lips. "I've fulfilled my obligation to Thales. In fact, he told me so as I ran for my life to get back here."

With a squawk of joy, Qing careened at full speed down the corridor and into Celwyn. They rubbed noses and beaks. "I haven't been gone that long this time." He staggered down the hall, feeling more than the usual exhaustion after magic.

"If Father tries to stop us, we need to help." Pelaez gestured at the narrow corridor. "This would not be where I want to take my last breath."

Bartholomew said, "I just left Nemo. We are backing out of a four-mile-long river to the sea. It is tricky." He bowed to them. "If you don't mind, I will wait out here."

"We need Nemo's maps!" Kang shouted and darted into the map room.

Celwyn understood—any excuse to play with maps could not be ignored.

⌣

Hours later, Celwyn awoke in his cabin to find Qing on his chest, his diamond eyes inches away from his own. The magician wasn't awake enough, or in the mood, for a squawk in the face, so he produced Qing's favorite toy—a finger-size green snake with ruby eyes. He tossed it in the air, and in seconds, the bird zoomed around the ceiling with it dangling from his beak.

Time for tea. Celwyn knotted his tie and noted he'd regained nearly all the weight from his illness. "Most handsome," he told his mirror and wondered if Miss Tara McFein appreciated neatly trimmed whiskers, a fine physique, and brilliant emerald eyes. Qing hopped on his shoulder, and they headed down the corridor accompanied by the always present gongs and other muffled noises of the submarine.

When he walked through the study door, a panoramic view of thousands of fish scattering into a mass of seaweed met him. From the way the ship pierced the water, and everything parting in front of the submarine, the *Nautilus* sailed through the Adriatic Sea at full speed, each league guaranteeing that they'd escaped his father. Celwyn sighed in relief. Although he hadn't voiced it, he sympathized with Pelaez's earlier fear of being entombed underwater while his father raged overhead.

Qing left him to fly to Kang and Bartholomew at the chess table. They looked happy, debating something scientific, and Celwyn cocked his head to listen. Ah, the flying machine. Probably not the time to interrupt their happiness with news about the return of the wyvern. He purposely stopped thinking about Wolfgang Augustus Griffin.

As Celwyn sat on the sofa and produced a service of steaming Earl Grey, Valentine ushered both women into the room in front of him. They settled into chairs beside the chess players, and Miss McFein vouchsafed the magician a knowing look.

"Greetings, Mr. Celwyn. You missed a most jovial luncheon while you recovered." Valentine's smile caused his luxuriant mustache to curl upward. "Your Captain Nemo also gave us a tour of this ship. I had no idea something such as this was possible."

Miss Redifer stretched like an elegant cat, possibly for Bartholomew's benefit. "A fascinating vessel." She looked at the big man. "Do you agree?"

"But, of course," Bartholomew said and pushed his rook forward.

Captain Nemo marched into the room, saw Celwyn, and detoured to sit opposite him.

"I'm sorry we couldn't talk before on the bridge. Things were ... tense." He sighed. "This has been quite an adventure." He lowered his voice. "I can now understand your reluctance where your father is concerned. With the periscopes, we observed quite a bit of that place before you joined him."

The magician handed him a cup of tea without getting up. "Your assistance was unexpected but most timely, Sir. I do not think we would be here without you."

Kang's hand shook as he set one of his chess pieces down, evidence that he remained on edge. "As I said earlier, we were quite surprised to find the *Nautilus* in the lake."

"I couldn't take a chance on something happening to your party." Nemo crossed his legs and sipped. "I've grown quite fond of all of you since our initial and inauspicious meeting."

Celwyn remembered very well wrapping the Captain in a large python and yelling at him. "I am very glad we have progressed, Sir."

From beside the aquatic window, Miss Redifer called over, "You did not trust that we would succeed, Captain?"

Nemo's glance at the vampires was not a friendly one. "Something like that, madam. My purpose was to get close enough to be of assistance."

Kang turned to face them fully; his eyes as happy as when he discovered a plate of cookies. "I found the map that showed the river that feeds that lake. It did not list depths, Captain. You took a chance, a tremendous one, to help us."

Captain Nemo waved it away as if the adventure were an everyday occurrence. Perhaps it was. "All of us are fortunate." He held up a hand to block further praise. "It was deeper than I expected, but also narrower, and at the rear of the lake, the river continued further underground past where the map had been marked. Therefore, we backed out."

"Not ideal, I'm sure. Your crew is most skilled." The magician poured another cup, thinking all was right again in his world. He could also detect Miss McFein's perfume and private glance from across the room. Indeed, things were wonderful.

"My men are very well-trained," Captain Nemo granted. "By the way, we are heading to Naples."

Celwyn checked his Tissot and saw that he'd slept nearly seven hours after their ordeal.

With a bow, Valentine excused himself and left the women to join the magician on the sofa. "We requested to be taken to Naples. The Captain kindly agreed."

Nemo said, "It isn't far, and the city is one of my usual supply stops. The garlic grown near there is far superior to anywhere in the region."

"Also, the wine selection is superb." The big man developed a dreamy look thinking about it.

Celwyn suspected the Captain really wanted the vampires off his ship as soon as possible. "Is my brother still resting?"

"Yes," Bartholomew told him. A few days ago, he would have growled his answer. Today, things had changed.

Jules Verne bustled into the room, notebook under his arm and holding his usual fistful of fountain pens. He stopped short when he saw the vampires and detoured to mince his way across the room and sit on the other side of the magician.

Bartholomew moved his bishop back two spaces and said, "You remember our acquaintances from Palermo, Mr. Verne?"

The pleasantries were exchanged. All the while, Verne's face registered the same expression as if he'd been asked to shake hands with dangerous snakes.

Valentine rejoined the women and enjoyed the author's discomfort after he invited him to sit with them. He repeated his invitation, "Come, come. Sit with us." Miss Redifer smiled at Verne and treated him to a view of her cleavage. Miss McFein stifled a giggle and turned back to the aquatic world outside the window.

The author flushed, murmured something polite, and gave his attention to Kang and Bartholomew a few feet away. "What happened at the catacombs?"

Kang frowned at the big man who had just captured his bishop. Bartholomew blinked as innocently as a babe. "First, their father attacked Jonas, then we evaded his defenses, and Pelaez and Jonas distracted their father with magic while the rest of us ran to this ship. You didn't see us?"

"No. The Captain asked that I stay in my cabin because of the possible danger." With a raised brow, Verne turned to the magician. "I suspect there is more to the story."

Celwyn caught Miss McFein studying him with unabashed interest. He didn't mind at all.

"Jules," Captain Nemo said, "we're on our way to Naples and should arrive there tomorrow. Mr. Soriano and his nieces will disembark, and after gathering our supplies, we'll be on our way again."

"The story of what happened can wait. We need music." Celwyn clapped Verne on the shoulder as he crossed to the aquatic window. They traveled in deep water, and the speckled fish they passed appeared much larger than the small schools they usually saw.

By the time they approached a wrecked schooner with a gaping hole under its keel, the bigger fish had disappeared. The vessel lay on its side on the sandy bottom. Across the stern of the wreck, he could just make out the appropriately named muse of the seas, the *Urania*, painted in old script. Debris from the ship littered the sand, and a fine layer of silt puffed into the current as the submarine's screw agitated the water. Celwyn stared, and a gathering of harps entered the room, softly at first, waiting to be heard.

The strings sounded as smooth and fluid as the waters they traveled through as the music intensified. Everyone watched the wreck as a deep, sonorous creaking reached them, causing reactions from fascination to fear in the study. Amazement won as Celwyn lifted the *Urania* out of her crypt. She swayed, settling into an upright position. After he repaired the hole in her hull, her broken masts stood tall and fresh again as her canvasses bowed against the pull of the current.

A translucent glow emanated from bow to stern as the ship shifted free of the sand and pointed her nose toward the surface. Sailors in brightly colored shirts scurried across her deck, their hair flowing in the current. In the reflection from the *Nautilus*'s lights, more sailors climbed the masts and pulled on chains to bring her encrusted anchor aboard. When one of the crew waved a broadsword over his head, it reflected the light streaming from the surface above.

"Oh, my," Miss Redifer breathed as the scene changed again.

The music swirled in a strong major key, gaining strength, and pushed the wreck upward, trailing a wide river of bubbles like a wedding veil. The *Urania* broke the surface bow first, then settled on top of the water.

Bartholomew did his best. After a shiver, he managed to say, "What will happen to that ship? The sailors?"

"They aren't real," Pelaez said, downplaying the wonder of what they saw. He had entered the room in time to witness the resurrection of the wreck. "As we travel away, it will begin to fade, perhaps seen by a few lucky sailors traveling by in the next few hours. Then it will sink again."

"Now you know how sea myths begin." Kang treated them to his dry expression and eye roll. "It occurs when magicians have too much time on their hands and vivid imaginations." He slid his queen to the corner of the board and said to Bartholomew, "Checkmate."

Miss McFein had joined Celwyn in front of the window, standing so close they could have rubbed elbows. Qing peeked down at her, spying someone new. When he saw her crystal hair clip, he chirped his approval. Celwyn tapped him on the shoulder and shook his head.

"Why Naples?" he asked.

She had widened her eyes at the sight of Qing, her interest clear. They stared at each other a moment more before she tilted her face up to

175

Celwyn. "Because I must return to London, and my uncle wishes to stay in Naples until the summer sun becomes unbearable."

"And Miss Redifer?"

"She'll stay with me as far as Milan." She brushed her hand against his.

"And then?" Celwyn noticed he enjoyed standing next to her, watching her face change as the light played across it, and imagined kissing her.

"Onward to London."

Celwyn entered her mind, hoping he wouldn't get slapped, but he couldn't resist the intimacy of the gesture.

"What will you do in London?" he asked silently.

She stood on her tiptoes and whispered in his ear, "I can't tell you. I am a spy." When she saw his expression, she laughed. "We're not in danger anymore. You should ask permission before you do that again—you can never tell what you'll encounter."

"I'll remember," the magician said.

She sobered. "I understand that you have met other vampires and usually avoid them."

"That is true. I have had to defend myself, or my friends, against them."

She regarded him with a mix of pity and patience. "I heard what Delgado did to your fiancé in Paris. My condolences."

Celwyn inhaled deeply and did his best to shut down the emotions associated with Suzanne's death. "Thank you."

"I also heard that he died at your hand in Prague a few months ago—after he caused a child's death."

The magician glanced at Bartholomew and Kang. "It was a very difficult time."

"Although unpleasant, it is good to get this conversation out of the way ... if we are to become acquainted."

Celwyn nodded. She was right.

"What do you know about vampire families?"

The magician said, "Nothing about their families. Just the individual ones that I have had to destroy. I still do not know how, or if, Mrs. Karras got away after she attacked me and the Professor in Prague."

With satisfaction in her voice, Tara confided, "She did leave the city. But Valentine took care of her. We're gradually weeding out the vicious, out-of-control vampires." She touched his hand again. "We're becoming more civilized."

Celwyn sighed with pleasure. "You certainly are."

Chapter 22

AFTER DINNER, EVERYONE RELAXED in the study as the crew dismantled the improvised dining table and brought more chairs and the coffee service. The *Nautilus* had been designed for speed, not entertainment. Weeks ago, Celwyn had deduced that she had also been designed for scientific exploration, war-like activities, and subterfuge.

The suggestion of a game of bridge floated around the room, and by popular request, Celwyn found himself banished from the game because no one trusted him not to listen to their thoughts—or see their cards. *Such nonsense.* They needed to be more trusting; he never entered thoughts unless it was urgent. Or romantic. Yet, it was probably for the best anyway since, courtesy of Thales, he could see through the cards and wouldn't need to do more.

Kang partnered with Captain Nemo, and Miss Redifer had been matched with Bartholomew.

Valentine played chess with Pelaez. The magician knew it would be wise to keep an eye on them, fully aware of their volatile personalities. Things could get noisy, or worse, because his brother's ability to cheat at the game had been perfected long ago.

While Verne sat on the sofa scribbling in his notebook and unabashedly listening to the other conversations, he couldn't help gazing at the vampires with wide-eyed fascination. The magician controlled the urge to make what he saw even more interesting.

That left Miss McFein to wander the room and sit beside him at the organ. The silk of her dress rustled as she moved closer on the bench. She didn't quite touch him, which made him want her to. His opinion of vampires seemed to be evolving, along with his worry about her occupation. Most spies he knew of were either shot by other spies or hanged when royal courts discovered them. He sighed. As Kang was fond of saying, nothing for the magician was ever simple.

"Play something," she requested. "With your hands."

"As you wish."

Celwyn gazed out the aquatic window, seeing the last watery streaks of golds and reds from the sunset on the surface above them. If Captain Nemo held true to his usual pattern, they would cease traveling when the darkness became complete.

He struck a low key in A, pure and as blue as the sea. Then he began a ballad, one which he considered as mysterious as Miss McFein herself. His judgement of her character told him she would appreciate music in a minor key that captured her feminine senses.

Over the next few minutes, Celwyn's music rang, and the organ responded with the same internal energy that he'd noted before—releasing feeling and emotion, more than simply notes. The room had gone silent as the magician played, seemingly spellbound.

As the last note resounded, Tara touched the back of his hand. "Thank you," she breathed, the emotion from the music in her eyes and voice.

"Bravo, bravo!" Valentine shouted, on his feet. "I am honored to witness this, Mr. Celwyn!"

Kang and Bartholomew shouted their appreciation.

Pelaez clapped, somewhat sarcastically, but still with vigor. "One of your best. Who wrote it?"

"I did."

The *Nautilus* had stopped moving, and bubbles filled the glass wall as the water darkened.

"Captain, are we near land at the moment?" Celwyn asked.

"A beautiful concert. Thank you." Captain Nemo basked in the last reverberation of sound. "We are near Sorrento, probably twenty miles or more from the Naples coast."

"Thank you." Celwyn took Miss McFein's hand, brought her to her feet, and bowed. "I'd like to get some fresh air topside ... if you would care to accompany me?"

He carefully avoided Kang's sarcastic glance and raised brows as he escorted her out the study door.

The magician helped Miss McFein through the hatch and onto the platform. At the other end of the ship, a lone crewman faced away from them in the cage at the bow. They were alone.

Like a new friend, a light evening breeze greeted them as more of a suggestion than enough to cause discomfort. Yet Celwyn dressed his companion in a fur wrap that went well with her hair. She touched it and regarded him. "Very nice. Did you make it just for me?"

"I did, even though you do not feel the cold."

They gazed across the sea to the east, where the faint flickers of light from Sorrento's harbor decorated the shore. The *Nautilus* floated alone on the water, the only sound the lapping of the waves against the hull. When Tara turned toward him, Celwyn was ready.

She fit into his arms as naturally as if she had been sculpted to do so, tilting her face up to him. With a sigh, he kissed her once, then again more deeply, drowning in the pleasure of her. When he opened his eyes, she looked back once more, intense and serious. Celwyn rubbed a thumb across her brow above the remarkable eyes, enjoying her closeness. For weeks, he had been waiting for this moment.

"We should go back inside," she said. "The Professor is probably worried about us."

Celwyn nodded. "Probably." He continued to smooth her brow.

"He worries because he doesn't approve."

In the distance, a ship's horn blew, echoing across the water.

"Must you leave tomorrow?" he asked.

Her eyes saddened. "I must. But I will find you again."

Celwyn drew her closer.

"Our base is in Prague. Dakaran street, Tellyhouse."

She held his face in her hands and kissed him again.

"I will remember."

———〰———

Near noon, the *Nautilus* passed Naples's harbor, cruising toward the southern headlands. An hour more and the magician had improvised twin carriages to take them into town while Pelaez supplied fat mice as horses. Once within the city limits, the carriages rolled toward the railroad yard, where the vampires planned to purchase tickets.

Celwyn said a formal goodbye to Tara in front of the train station. Their eyes said a more intimate farewell as she handed him a small leather-bound book.

"Mizora's poems," Celwyn murmured. "I hear they are beautiful."

"There is nothing so intimate as a gift of a book from one person to another," she told him. They continued their farewell silently until, with a small wave, she walked away.

Celwyn surrounded her with music just as intimate and tried to shake the heavy hand of fate that said he wouldn't find her again. The last thing he saw was her smile, just from her to him.

As they rode toward the commercial district, Celwyn grew quiet. Kang tried to help in his own fond and annoying way. "We will have an enjoyable lunch to take your mind off a relationship you'd have trouble explaining to Annabelle, Patrick, Elizabeth, and especially to Mrs. Thomas."

Celwyn could imagine their formidable housekeeper's reaction and knew Kang teased him, but it still felt a bit difficult to smile. "I won't have to because I probably won't see her again. The life expectancy of English spies is not great."

The automat blinked his surprise as their carriage hit a pothole square on, and when everything settled again, Bartholomew said, "You don't know that for certain. I, on the other hand, escaped amorous advances by only a thread."

"Oh, you did?" Kang laughed.

Bartholomew leaned forward to confide. "That other woman. She tried to seduce me."

"Oh, my," Verne muttered.

Celwyn asked in an amused undertone, "What did you do?"

"I locked my cabin door and stayed awake all night long, on guard." The big man shuddered.

Celwyn regarded him, seeing the romantic man and widower who'd almost fallen in love with Crazy Mary.[2] That encounter had turned out badly, deadly too, and Bartholomew still felt a bit protective of his heart. The big man also did not appreciate being aggressively pursued. With a private smile, Celwyn thought about Tara again; she had a much different approach that he didn't mind at all.

The Professor sobered and bestowed a skeptical look on the magician. "Would you have locked your door?"

"How do you know I didn't leave it unlocked?" Celwyn twisted the ends of his mustache and smoothed them back.

Verne stopped fussing with his notebook long enough to ask, "What are you talking about?"

Bartholomew whispered in his ear, "Vampires."

---

[2] See *Music Shall Untune the Sky* the second book of the Celwyn series.

Chapter 23

HOURS LATER, LOADED WITH AS many packages of tea, tobacco, pastries, and books as they could carry, they headed across the shopping district to the carriages. Drat. Celwyn frowned at the coaches because Pelaez had based the horses upon rodents and it had been a few hours; already he saw fuzziness around the animals' ears, indicating his magic would begin to fade soon unless he reinforced it. Their "horses" would scatter underneath sheds and houses again.

After they had everything packed inside, Kang lit his pipe and began pacing in front of the carriage. "If we had bought any more, we would have needed a second carriage again," the big man observed to Celwyn.

Both the automat and Bartholomew seemed relaxed, and nothing threatened any of them at the moment. Now seemed as good of a time as any. The magician asked the big man, "Have any of you heard of a wyvern? Xiau has."

After Bartholomew shook his head, he asked Kang, "What you know of them?"

Kang lifted his shoulders and let them fall again. "Various reports describe wyverns as scaly, snake-like dragons. Sometimes they are mistaken for firedrakes, the two-footed type. They're mythical, favorites of the English, and have been reported from nearly everywhere in the civilized world over the years."

Bartholomew rubbed his chin. "Are they frightening?"

"Not that I know of," the automat said. "There were a few paintings of them in the museum in Mondragone, in the middle room with the illuminated manuscripts." He eyed the magician with speculation. "Jonas studied one up close for a while."

"What size would a typical wyvern be?" Celwyn asked.

Kang's shrug came again, along with a raised brow of dawning suspicion. "I do not know, but would guess fairly large if the pictures I've seen in texts and in that museum are to be believed." He studied the magician. "Time to tell us why you ask, Jonas."

"I suppose so. Before you begin to nag me like a fishwife." Celwyn tried to put his annoyance aside. This conversation could become highly amusing at his expense. "I told you of the first time I saw one on the ship. You should know I saw it in the catacombs, too."

The automat asked, "What did it look like?"

"The same—scaly, green, and dead eyes. The first time, it was easily twenty feet long. This time, not more than two feet, and embedded in a rock wall at exactly where I would encounter it."

"Oh ..." Bartholomew's eyes grew wide. "Oh, my word."

Kang continued to stare at Celwyn, determining if the magician was spinning a yarn. "Are you sure of what you saw? I asked before; could it have been Pelaez teasing you? Or an illusion courtesy of Thales?"

The magician shook his head. "Neither. I will let you know if it happens again."

"Please do so, but it is probably just a product of your mind." The automat grinned at him and gazed upward. "Or a wager between you and your brother to see how gullible we are."

"Bah." Celwyn knew Xiau wouldn't believe him.

"Where is your brother?" Kang demanded. "He said he only had one more stop to make. It's going to start raining soon, and the track back to the ship will be a muddy mess." The Professor pointed with his pipe to the dark clouds moving in. Verne saw the clouds and scampered inside the carriage.

Bartholomew stood beside Celwyn, watching the pedestrians and casting nervous glances at their driver a few feet away. The man appeared elderly, with a full gray beard and beady eyes, and sat hunched over the reins. With a nervous twitch of his lips, Bartholomew asked, "Tell me that is a man from town that you hired and not a converted rodent?"

Celwyn laughed. "I will lie to you. It isn't a rodent, and he will bring the carriage back here and leave it. Or, by nightfall, it will revert back to a crate, and the horses—"

Bartholomew held up a hand. "Don't tell me."

"Where is Pelaez?" The Professor asked again. "We need to get going."

Bartholomew suggested, "Why don't you take Mr. Verne and the packages back to the ship? It's only about four miles south of here. Jonas and I will look for him and walk back."

Kang frowned as he scanned the avenue again. "All right. Replace the mice with fresh "horses" please."

———⌣———

As the first drops of rain began, the carriage drove away, and Celwyn and the big man entered the bazaar.

"Damn Pelaez. Where is he?"

The magician agreed. His brother had always had a selfish streak of feminine lateness. As they began checking the stalls, he handed the big man an umbrella and made one for himself. Overhead, the buildings were easily four stories high, and on many of them, baskets tied to long ropes extended off balconies to the street. Just as he decided to ask if Bartholomew knew why—a man stowed several bottles of wine and a loaf of bread in one, and two women on the top floor began pulling it upward. That certainly saved effort climbing stairs with packages.

Although interesting, it didn't help their situation. Celwyn realized this part of the bazaar extended for blocks, and the side streets they hadn't explored the first time offered even more choices in jewelry, candles, rugs, fruit, bread, and fish. Their quick check of the booths produced nothing.

"Where is he?" Bartholomew demanded of the bazaar.

Celwyn yawned. "We've skipped the shops with feminine interests. Maybe we should go back and look at them also."

"Where would he go?"

Celwyn listened to the question while he studied the street, seeing more patrons, more tourists, and a few monks he had ignored before. That was it! To the consternation of an outraged carriage driver, the magician darted into the street to gaze north several blocks and verify what he'd just remembered. Certain things fascinated his brother.

"Come." He gestured to Bartholomew. "There is a medieval church at the end of the street. My brother loves art from that period and may be there. I remember Xiau telling him about it."

Bartholomew ran with him. "It looks more like a castle than a church."

Celwyn concurred as the turrets, ivy-covered keeps, and dark towers of Castella della Vergine came into view. The building had to be a city block long and made of stone. It appeared as forbidding as the medieval jail in Algiers, which the magician had occupied for a short stay before a hasty and colorful departure. This was a church. It was also guarded, which was odd.

When they walked up the wide brick path to the front doors, a pair of uniformed men blocked their way and asked their business. In his best Italian, Celwyn explained he was seeking his brother and a view of the artwork inside.

"He is not here, Senior," the guard replied in perfect English and with a steady gaze.

Out of the corner of his eye, Celwyn caught sight of something that proved Pelaez was indeed there. With a deep bow, he thanked the guard and took Bartholomew's elbow, steering him back down the brick path to the north side of the building. In silence, they headed up a flower-lined walkway toward a side door hidden behind stone columns and again blocked by a humorless guard. Celwyn smiled at him, and the man sank to the ground. He nudged the guard with the toe of his boot and suggested, "You might want to borrow his pistol."

Bartholomew did so and opened the door. "What are you waiting for?" he whispered from just inside the door.

"One moment ... ah, there he is." Celwyn waved Pelaez's pig inside. "Take us to him."

The pig grunted and hurried down one of the darkened hallways off the foyer. They followed, with Celwyn on high alert. Already he could smell something old and evil that nearly overwhelmed the odor of the pig.

Above them, the low ceilings caused Bartholomew to stoop as they went along, and after they crossed under an arch into an even older corridor, Celwyn also had to. The frescos of hunting scenes accompanying them appeared well-preserved considering they would have been from the 8th century. When he noticed they portrayed humans as prey, he hustled Bartholomew forward a bit faster into a trot. As they went, he felt a cold urgency crawling up his spine, one which he rarely knew, perhaps courtesy of Thales? This part of the hallway had twin mullioned windows letting in sparse light, yet the passageway seemed wide enough to drive a coach through.

Silently, Celwyn told Bartholomew that they neared where his brother should be and muted their steps. With that news, the big man withdrew the pistol from his belt and crept forward like a rather large panther would through a jungle. Seconds more, they heard methodical thudding coming from the end of the corridor.

Celwyn concentrated, seeing beyond the door into a shadowed and windowless chamber covered in ornate tapestries, plush rugs, and blood.

Pelaez had been tied to a wooden chair in the middle of the room. Only his eyes moved. Three men surrounded him while another man, nearly as big as Bartholomew, beat him viciously with a pipe. Their thoughts confirmed they were Mafioso. Celwyn wondered why Pelaez didn't get away from them as violently and colorfully as possible. Just as he started to intervene, he recognized a voice he hadn't heard in hundreds of years; no wonder Pelaez had been subdued, despite his magic.

"Tell Senior Gio what you know," Lorimar Mab Duncan croaked and slapped Pelaez hard.

Celwyn shook off his surprise. He sent Pelaez a silent message. "*I am here, Brother. When I come in, use all your concentration to break your bonds. Ten seconds."*

The magician motioned to Bartholomew and sent him a message, also. *"Pelaez is in a chair in the middle of the room. There are four men. Shoot the short red-headed one in the right elbow first. Then shoot the others."*

When Bartholomew nodded, Celwyn squared off next to him and blew open the door. He burst into the room with Bartholomew at his side and knocked Duncan against the wall, hoping to at least break his concentration and make him easy for Bartholomew to see. He heard the first shots as he began undoing the spell of bonds holding his brother. Magic against witchcraft wasn't easy. Bartholomew fired again, right in the bastard's elbow, and then took out the next man. The last man brought up a pistol, and Bartholomew shot it out of his hand.

Celwyn freed Pelaez's left arm and leg. Pelaez jerked his head to the left, and the magician swiveled. He didn't try anything fancy, just knocked Duncan down again and started to choke the life out of him. The warlock bounded up again as if nothing had happened, but Duncan's surprise when he recognized the magician changed the outcome; the warlock hesitated. Bartholomew backhanded the blood-covered pipe into the warlock's head, and he dropped to the floor. The spell on Pelaez lifted. Celwyn pulled his brother up with Bartholomew's help. When the man with the hand-wound tried to run out the door, the magician stopped him.

"Take him out." The magician passed Pelaez to the big man. "I must take care of this one." Celwyn identified Duncan so that the big man understood how delicate the situation had become.

After Bartholomew threw Pelaez over his shoulder and ducked through the door, Celwyn began flexing his hands, bringing a complement of harps forward, the music echoing louder as he turned to Duncan, knowing he had little time; the warlock could best him in combat, and that tap on the head wouldn't do more than enrage him further once he awoke again. The warlock's protection spells would soon make things more difficult.

Celwyn preferred to prepare before a battle occurred.

He bound Duncan in so many ropes he resembled a mummy. Making it as impenetrable as he could, the magician wrapped a force field around him. The warlock moved, and Celwyn smacked him again with the pipe, thinking how appropriate to use the same weapon the warlock had used on his brother. Apparently, pipes weren't covered by warlock protection spells.

I need more, Celwyn told himself. While he thought, he trussed the other men and sent them to the basement of the castle. With his hands on his hips, he faced his old enemy.

Using care, Celwyn wound his own magical bonds backwards—if Duncan tried to remove them with a spell, they would tighten every time he tried. Celwyn knew that the further away from Duncan he went, such as fleeing back to the *Nautilus*, the more the bonds would fade. Nevertheless, this should buy them time.

"You bastard," Celwyn growled. "Now, where to put you..." He ended up depositing Duncan on the roof under an invisibility screen that he hoped would last until the *Nautilus* got away. It wouldn't do for the bastard's confederates to find him.

The magician smiled as he set a magical drip above the warlock, one that would dribble cold water on him and wake him. It would begin as soon as Celwyn left the building. Before the magician made it to the end of the block, Duncan would be awake and trying to escape, thus tightening the bonds before they faded. As the magician reminded himself to tease Xiau with the details of what he'd set up, he chuckled to himself. The automat needed something to complain about.

Celwyn loped back up the corridor, using drops of Pelaez's blood as a guide at the hallway intersections. When he found Bartholomew and his brother waiting in the shadows by the side door, the big man still looked formidable, with the pistol in his belt and fire of battle in his eye.

"We must hurry." Celwyn blocked Pelaez's pain. "Let's take our 'drunken' friend away from here." As he cleaned the blood off his brother, he put an overcoat on him and added a large hat.

He growled, "Let's go!"

Chapter 24

B Y THE TIME THEY BUNDLED PELAEZ into the *Nautilus's* transport boat, a sunset of oranges and pinks painted the horizon for as far as they could see. All the way back to the ship, Celwyn used magic and urgency to propel them while keeping an eye trained behind them. Dread ate at him that Duncan had already freed himself, and it wouldn't go away. With luck and with the little presents the magician had left behind, the bastard might assume Celwyn remained in the city.

As soon as they neared the submarine, the magician sent a silent message to the bridge, asking Nemo to get the ship the hell away from here as soon as they boarded. When they did, the engines came alive with a rumble, and minutes later, Celwyn led the way down the corridor. After Bartholomew laid Pelaez on his bunk, the big man backed out of the cabin, letting Kang and his medical bag inside. The vibrations of the engines underfoot increased.

"Brother, I can help," Celwyn said as a series of muffled gongs resounded in the ship's belly. With force, she dived, and everyone held on.

"Hush while I examine him." Kang asked, "Why are his wounds so clean?"

"We had to get him through the crowds and didn't want anyone stopping us. Or following us. A policeman started—"

"He just winced. Block his pain again. What you did is wearing off."

"Done."

Kang continued to work with a stethoscope hanging off his ears, reminding Celwyn of a circus mouse in an elephant's ears. "Your brother is unconscious. Can he heal himself like you can? Or can you do a better job of healing him?"

Celwyn shrugged. "I don't know. I'll do it."

Minutes went by. Captain Nemo and Bartholomew appeared at the door.

"Per your request, we're traveling at full speed out to sea and due south," the Captain told Celwyn with a twitch of his lips. "I've never had instructions appear in my mind before. It was an experience."

Celwyn managed a sheepish grin. "Thank you. I'll explain as soon as we see how—" he blinked several times. "How my brother is."

Captain Nemo bowed and said gravely, "I understand. From what Bartholomew tells me, it seems we've attracted a new enemy."

As Kang checked under Pelaez's eyelids, he drawled, "Jonas has that tendency."

⌒

The automat worked a few minutes more and asked, "Jonas, can you see his liver?"

"Is that the curved part here?" he pointed to his side.

"Yes. It's been damaged. Severely."

"Let me try."

By the time Celwyn had repaired some of the damage and guessed at some of it, his brother had opened his eyes. "What are you doing?" he whispered.

"Trying to help. Can you repair yourself?" Celwyn asked, frowning at Kang for direction.

Pelaez groaned.

The automat said, "Start with the front side of your liver. Jonas has done what he can."

Another wait, then Pelaez said, "I think that will do."

"Fix your ribs." Kang sat back in his chair. "Everything else will heal." They watched Pelaez's face contort. Kang said, "It will be painful, and you must remain in bed. You have taken several severe blows to the head." With a sardonic eye on the magician, he added, "I suggest you do not make any sudden moves and refrain from the family habit of ignoring my advice."

The gleam in Pelaez's eyes came back.

"I'll leave Qing on guard to be sure he stays in bed," Celwyn said. Bartholomew laughed, saw the automat's expression of disbelief, and laughed again.

Kang reared back and sputtered, "As if you are such a good example! Shoo, you two. You are soaking wet."

He'd forgotten about the rain. With a wave of his hand, Celwyn dried both of them. The big man led the way down the corridor, and when they entered the study, they found Verne on the sofa, holding a whiskey glass against his chest and staring, but not seeing, the fish outside the window.

When the author heard them, he scrambled up. "How is he?"

"The Professor believes he will be all right." The big man paced, still on guard after their adventure.

Xiau arrived and downed the whiskey Celwyn handed him. "He will live, and he will heal over a period of time." After everyone sat down, Kang faced Bartholomew and the magician. He demanded, "What happened? Where did you find him?"

The magician finished pouring a second collection of whiskies as Nemo walked in, and Bartholomew began the tale.

"After we left you, we looked everywhere, finally heading to that castle beyond the bazaar. Jonas deduced we'd find him there because Pelaez enjoys medieval art." He sipped and rolled his shoulders, reliving their afternoon excitement. "Jonas had to knock out one of the police guards to get into the building."

"Another reason why we needed to get away from Naples speedily," Kang surmised.

Celwyn sank onto the sofa next to Captain Nemo. "Where are we at the moment?" he asked.

"About thirty miles off the Ustica coast."

Celwyn sighed in relief. "Then we should be safe again, but we need to ask my brother what he told his attackers. From what I heard, the attack was an attempt to locate the flying machine."

"My Italian is good, and that is what I also heard," Bartholomew contributed.

Captain Nemo sighed, but it turned into a growl. "Every criminal organization in this hemisphere is looking for it." Then an unamused smile crossed his face, and he appeared calmer than one would expect. "They think the flying machine was taken to Morocco." An amused glint entered his eyes.

"It isn't there, is it?" Bartholomew guessed.

"No. It is near the Cappadocia Mountains of Turkey."

Celwyn finished his drink as he thought. "This news allows us to settle down for the night. We are already out of danger. Our pursuers will be on their way to Morocco." He addressed Nemo. "You are probably wondering about my request to leave in such haste. It was because an old enemy had part-nered with local hooligans to beat the information out of my brother."

Bartholomew rested his chin on his chest. "Something like this is cancerous. People talk and talk eventually reaches where the evil lives."

Captain Nemo crossed to the intercom, issued the order to slow to normal speed, and returned to the sofa. He lifted his glass.

"To the flying machine. Finally."

They toasted.

"You have been most patient, Captain," Celwyn said. "This has been a difficult journey and we owe you whatever assistance we can to build and protect this project."

"I agree," Bartholomew said. "We owe you more than our knowledge."

Nemo waved it away. "Once more, you forget those enormous monsters fighting in the lake last year and endangering my ship."

"I agree," Verne spoke. "It has been a long journey. Please tell us what happened this afternoon after you arrived at the castle. I do not understand."

"As Bartholomew said, we entered the Castella della Vergine looking for my brother and found him tied up in the bowels of the castle. He was being beaten by members of the Mafioso—the criminal family of Naples. You might wonder why he didn't protect himself with magic. He couldn't."

"Why?" Verne asked.

"Because the fourth villain in the room was Lorimar Duncan, a malicious warlock from Ireland that I know very well. He is much stronger than my brother. Before my time with Thales, Duncan was stronger than I. Now, I stand a chance to best him if I prepare ahead of time."

The automat patted a sarcastic yawn. "Things are never dull with you, Jonas."

"Pfft. Anyhow, knowing the danger to my brother, we had to act."

"Is this when Bartholomew shot them? I can smell the gunpowder on him," Kang said.

The big man lifted his coat and removed the pistol from his waistband. Captain Nemo looked it over and handed it back.

"Bartholomew is an excellent marksman. By request, he shot the warlock in the right elbow, where he was most vulnerable." Celwyn smiled a wicked smile. "Then what he did next gave us a chance of success."

The big man performed an innocent shrug, complete with an innocent blinking of his eyes. "It wasn't much. I smashed a pipe on the warlock's head. Then I shot the rest of them while Jonas wrestled with Duncan."

With an eye on the automat, so he wouldn't miss his reaction, Celwyn said, "I smeared a mixture of strong pepper and dung on the warlock's leg and the room where we found him. He will think it is from one of his intruders." Celwyn grinned. "As we fled, I added a bit of it to every hire carriage we passed. It is a unique odor that the warlock will follow when he frees himself."

Kang's mouth dropped open.

"He will search in circles all over town." Bartholomew's wicked smile matched the magician's smile.

As they enjoyed the vision of the warlock's quest for dung, the crew arrived and began setting up the table for dinner.

Kang darted to the hall and sniffed in the direction of the galley. "I am famished."

"So am I," Celwyn said. "Mayhem stimulates my appetite." The magician imitated the automat. "'I think I smell roast beef.'"

"I do, also." Xiau chuckled, enjoying their usual banter.

Verne finished writing in his notebook and eyed them. "Please continue."

Ha. The magician did detect roast beef. It would be a lovely reward after a long day. "I had to meet violence with violence." Celwyn told Verne, "Remembering Duncan for what he is made the act more satisfying."

Chapter 25

A**S THEY ADMIRED THE BEEF ON**
their plates, courtesy of the Professor's nego-
tiation with the butchers of Naples, Bartholomew
sawed off a piece and asked, "May I inquire why you
are not partaking of the roast, Captain?"

"I no longer eat land-based meat such as this
and prefer to eat food only from the sea. However,
I understand your desire to do so." Nemo leaned
back as the crewman served him from the bowl of
seared squash. "This preference does not change
my fondness for fruit and other sweets, however."
He deboned his fish and dipped it in sauce. "I am
satisfied."

After a few minutes of silence, while they savored,
Celwyn asked, "I wonder why everyone is so quiet
this evening?"

As the wine glasses were filled again, Qing's
squawk came from the sofa.

Bartholomew's head jerked up. "I thought that bird was supposed to be in your brother's cabin watching him."

Kang and Celwyn glanced at the sofa. The top of Pelaez's head could be seen.

"Really? I thought I ordered you to rest." Kang's annoyance caused most of them to hide a smile.

"Resting can be done here just as well." Pelaez must have seen their expressions, for he added, "Never fear. I walked here, and I even brought along a blanket." Qing left him to parade in front of the aquatic window and peck at the curious red-and-yellow striped fish bumping their noses on the glass.

Kang glared and went back to his dinner. "To answer your question, Jonas, we're waiting for you to tell us more about Duncan."

As the crewman removed his empty plate, Celwyn wrinkled his nose and said, "Lorimar Duncan is not an immortal or relative of ours. I do not know his lineage. He is just a vicious and lucky warlock."

Pelaez grunted and shifted to a more comfortable position on the sofa. "If I'd known of him, he wouldn't have captured me."

Celwyn doubted it, but said nothing.

"What happened is evidence of interest in the flying machine, as much as the odd characters we seem to attract." Bartholomew pushed his plate away and dabbed his lips with his napkin.

Celwyn had never encountered the Mafioso before, except from afar, and wondered how many of them would be in the area. "If any of you need to recognize Duncan, he is about five feet tall with dirty, red, curly hair. He looks like a mean cherub." A mental picture of the naked warlock came to mind, and he shook it off. "He has a button nose more suited to a fairy, and his teeth are tiny and pointed like a child's."

"His voice is nearly as deep as Bartholomew's," Pelaez told them.

"True." *Why did they have to deal with this, too?* Celwyn made a face. "Duncan hasn't changed at all over the years. He must have a spell for that, too."

"Excellent description. As a warlock, can we assume he disguises himself at will?" Captain Nemo asked.

Celwyn nodded. "Yes, and no. When I knew him, he was much too vain to disguise himself, always saying he wanted his enemies to see his face before they died. You should know that when Duncan kills, they are usually highly unpleasant deaths." Talk of the warlock seemed depressing at dinner. The magician wondered what their dessert would be this evening … something with rich chocolate would be good.

"And this man wants the flying machine," Nemo said under his breath.

"Just as much as his Mafioso partners, from what we heard," Bartholomew said. "At least one of them survived and saw both Jonas and me."

Celwyn tried to decide if he preferred an after-dinner liqueur or a nice cup of Earl Grey. "Yes. From the little I translated from the ruffians' minds, they are paying Duncan for his assistance. My knowledge of the language is usually centered on their food and art." He told Nemo, "I caught bits of Duncan's thoughts as I trussed him up and heard confirmation of this."

"Wonderful," Kang murmured and glared at his dinner plate full of bloody juice from the roast. One of the crewmen removed it, seeming to sense the mood in the room.

Dessert arrived. Not chocolate. Celwyn waited until the crewman's back was turned before sending his spice cake across the room to Pelaez. When the crewman turned back, Celwyn folded his hands demurely and said, "None for me, thank you." The crewman hesitated and glanced at the other plates before retreating.

"Cute, Jonas." The Professor gave him a look and dug into his cake.

The magician's playfulness faded. "To go on, I don't know where or when Duncan joined forces with the Mafioso, but it is a dangerous combination. If it becomes necessary to fight them, my brother will also be needed to defeat them."

Another Captain Nemo appeared next to the real Captain and frowned as he reached for Nemo's water glass and lifted it to his lips. Kang stared at the second Captain Nemo, and when he poked a finger at his jacket, his finger passed through the sleeve. Bartholomew's eyes couldn't have been any larger, but he kept his seat.

Before things got out of hand, Celwyn said, "Please remove your sample, Brother."

As the second Captain Nemo disappeared, Kang drawled, "We could have used your brother's talents last year when we were sneaking off the *Victoria*

Express." While he talked, Bartholomew visibly calmed down. Verne just stared with the fascination of a man making detailed mental notes of what he shouldn't be seeing and who didn't want to call attention to himself.

"I recommend that because of the danger to the Professor and Bartholomew, we avail ourselves of my brother's talents and disguise them both any time they leave the ship."

"Very well," Bartholomew said with as much conviction as he could. "Although it will be highly disconcerting."

Verne asked, "Please explain what benefit Duncan receives from all of this?"

"I don't know." Celwyn thought more as he watched the others finish their desserts. Then he remembered something. "Little do his employers know, but Duncan usually kills his confederates and keeps the spoils for himself."

The Captain said dryly, "After they pay him, I presume."

"The Mafioso is a huge organization with members everywhere. I had encounters with them on my business expeditions before I met all of you." Bartholomew frowned. "That is probably how they found us here. They would have had teams in each port and on all the likely coasts looking for one of us."

"Captain." Kang dabbed at the crumbs on his plate. "We can remain on the ship. If we follow Bartholomew's and Jonas's logic, it will behoove us to have a minimal number of your crew obtaining supplies in the ports we visit on the way to the real location of the flying machine. Please do not have them wear their naval uniforms—that is how we first noticed them in Singapore."

"Noted," Nemo said.

Kang continued, "They will need to be circumspect when returning to the ship, even more so than usual."

Captain Nemo pushed his plate away. "Civilian disguises and instructions for the crew will be provided." He lowered his voice, and his expression turned grave. "I am beginning to be concerned for the safety of the *Nautilus*. If they covet the flying machine, they will want this ship as well."

"I'm afraid you are right." The Professor regarded him for a long moment.

"Perhaps we can move the flying machine to a different location and go there by a circuitous route?" Bartholomew asked.

Nemo rubbed his chin, and after a moment, shook his head.

"I'm sorry we've brought danger to you here." Kang sighed.

The Captain told the automat, "You haven't. The issue originates in the invention of the flying machine and the greed surrounding it. It is an expected risk of the dangerous process that I have undertaken."

"I imagine this isn't the only "dangerous process" that you have encountered." Celwyn speculated and did so without cheating, i.e., entering Nemo's thoughts. Sometimes, a wager with himself was an enjoyable pastime.

Nemo's expression affirmed the guess, but he said nothing.

Bartholomew frowned. "Once we have done everything that we can to engineer a safe flying machine, we will provide you with the written specifications." He checked with Kang and received a nod. "Xiau is excellent with diagrams and documentation, and I intend to become so also."

Captain Nemo stood and straightened his jacket. "Let us adjourn so the crew can clear the table, and Jonas can tell us more about the warlock."

Celwyn smiled broadly. That was the first time Captain Nemo had called him by his given name.

***

Before they settled in front of the aquatic window a few minutes later, the automat pantomimed a request to Celwyn. In seconds, Pelaez began to snore.

Qing looked annoyed as he hopped to each of them with his form of greeting. When he arrived on Bartholomew's knee, the big man covered his watch and said, "Move along."

The mechanical bird fluffed his feathers in disappointment and snuggled into Celwyn's collar. The magician patted his back. "It sounds like we have a plan. When will we arrive in the Anatolian Mountains?"

"Three to four days," Captain Nemo said. "It's been a few years since we've stopped in the area. You may expect high mountains, extensive forests, and plains."

The Professor asked, "What if the location of the flying machine is known to the Mafioso already? It wouldn't be too far-fetched to assume so."

"Our compound is remote and guarded. I doubt it at this point." Despite his words, Nemo's brows lowered as he intercepted one of the floating glasses of whiskey circling around. Bartholomew snagged one too.

The automat wasn't satisfied. "Even though the location is guarded, it could also be observed by them from a distance while they wait for us to arrive."

"If so, they'll know where we are, and attempt to kidnap us." Bartholomew's thoughts colored his face with grim amusement. "I would welcome a chance for more contact with the ruffians. My first shot went wide, and with a bit of practice, they won't fare as well if we meet again."

Silence fell over the study, except for Pelaez's snoring.

"Sir, I respectfully suggest that we approach your retreat from a circumspect direction. It would be a mistake to underestimate Duncan." Celwyn eyed the others. "And I agree that we should assume that they'll be watching the coast anywhere in this hemisphere."

With a growl that matched his mood, Nemo said, "If they were in a vessel, I would sink them."

Remembering the iron horn on the nose of the *Nautilus*, Celwyn could well believe it. "We would cheer while you did so."

Pelaez snored louder. Qing popped out of the magician's collar at the sound and stared at him.

"It is good that he rests," Kang observed with an innocent, blank face.

"Is that your medical opinion," Celwyn asked with a chuckle, "or is it because he irritates you when he is awake?"

"Both."

Collectively, they stared out the window at an opaque sea until Bartholomew grunted.

"Will we enter the area from the south or north?"

"Before Jonas suggested it, I had considered approaching the compound from an unexpected direction. Now, it is imperative that we do so." Captain Nemo regarded them. "Professor, of everyone here, you enjoy traveling on an underground river more than others. We will do so this time."

"I do indeed." Kang rubbed his hands together.

Bartholomew's face developed a fine sheen of perspiration. "How long will we be underground?"

"Assuming the maps are correct and the water tables high enough, it will be about six hours until we reach our destination," Captain Nemo said.

Kang nodded. "If I remember my studies correctly, there will still be a generous amount of snow in those mountains, even this late in the spring. As it melts, the high run-off will bring the water tables up."

Celwyn studied Bartholomew, who feigned calmness and sipped his drink. The magician would do something to help him when the time came.

As an interlude, Qing decided to visit Verne at the chess table. The author had been watching them while taking notes of what he heard. When Verne saw Qing's metallic foot on his page, he licked his lips and waited for the bird to move.

"Yes. The snow has also hampered some preparations for our arrival at the site. However, everything is almost complete." Nemo pursed his lips. "After the events of today, I'm relieved we are at that point in case the Mafioso has bribed any of the local people." Again, his expression darkened; *he wasn't sure.* Celwyn sighed.

"What will we do if the underground river becomes too shallow for the submarine?" Verne asked. Qing pecked at his fountain pen until the author edged it away from him and under the table. The bird dived to the floor and jumped for the pen from underneath the table.

"If that occurs, there is a solution." Nemo's lips twitched. "I have a special treat for you, gentlemen." He smiled outright. "The *Nautilus* is equipped with an individual diving apparatus for each of you."

Bartholomew broke out into a full sweat. He swallowed hard and looked at the magician.

"Let us hope it does not come to that." Celwyn clapped him on the back. "However, I would enjoy a diving adventure under non-emergency conditions. I've always found shipwrecks fascinating."

"I would also," Kang said. "Wouldn't the Great Reef be a marvelous experience?" His eyes glazed over at the thought.

With a shudder that shook the sofa, Bartholomew said, "You are both insane, but I understand the fascination." He stood and scooped Pelaez into his arms as easily as if he were a small child. "I'll put him in his room, and then, perhaps, we can play a few hands of bridge? I could also do without any more talk of underground rivers this evening."

As Bartholomew pivoted and walked out of the room with Pelaez, Nemo said, "I'm not certain I have a diving suit big enough for him, but will request one to be made very soon. There could come a time when we *have* to use them."

"I understand." The automat leaned forward to ask, "On another subject, did you decide if you prefer Jonas and myself to remain as investors in this enterprise? If so, Bartholomew has indicated he wants to invest also."

"For now," Captain Nemo said, "let's leave everything as it is. Thank you. Fogg's heirs will receive his refund anonymously."

Chapter 26

A T MIDNIGHT THREE DAYS LATER, Celwyn and Captain Nemo lounged against the navigator's cage atop the *Nautilus* and smoked cigars. Strong moonlight painted their faces, and a light wind darted around them, skipping across the waves to stir the salty brininess.

"A bit chilly tonight." Celwyn remembered the most enjoyable time he'd spent atop the ship with Miss Tara McFein a few days ago. He removed a peyote button from his inside pocket and chewed.

To the south, a scattering of lights twinkled from miles away, and further down the coast, the sea disappeared before the mountains in the distance. To the north, the reflection from the glowing moon displayed an unending flat expanse of dark water.

In front of them, the village of Fethiye slumbered on the Mediterranean shore. "These villagers have no idea that they live above a river as wide as the Nile," Captain Nemo said.

"I imagine it must be quite deep to be usable for our purposes." Privately, Celwyn sincerely hoped it to be.

"Correct." The Captain relit his cigar before continuing. "We didn't finish talking about Duncan. What should my crew expect from the warlock?"

After a few more puffs, Celwyn said, "My first contact with him was near Zaragoza, about two hundred years ago. It was winter in the mountains, and I came upon him just as he slit the throat of his last partner. There had to be a dozen others bleeding in the snow. There was so much blood the snow had turned red. He saw me and gathered himself up, ready to attack."

"And then? I see your amusement."

Celwyn listened to the sound of a breaching whale in the distance, and with as much modesty as he could, said, "Well, I can be quite the acrobat, and I'd been warned about Duncan. So, I elevated him as high as possible and dropped him. Before he hit the ground, I had attained the cliff above him, expecting him to block his fall and attack. When he stood up, I caused the cliff to fall and bury him. It didn't kill him, but it did give me time to get away."

"Interesting."

"Duncan had assassinated two of my acquaintances, and I would have killed him if I could have. Back then, he was stronger than I, but with Thales' enhancements to my repertoire, we'll see. The other day, I had Bartholomew shoot him in the elbow because of the weakness in it from a long time ago. The elbow isn't enough to kill him; however, it can distract him from his spells."

"And now?" Captain Nemo tossed his cigar into the water, gently lapping against the hull.

"I should succeed in killing him with a little help from my brother." He fiddled with his pocket watch chain and weighed what he knew. "To answer your question, expect Duncan to be exceedingly quick, and only have one thing on his mind—to kill everyone except Bartholomew and Xiau."

"I see."

"He is especially fond of knives. I have had two other bloody encounters with him over the years. Be aware that he tends to wait to make a sudden appearance and then destroy everything he can."

In the distance, something large breached the water. Nemo finally got his cigar relit, puffed, and asked, "Does your brother know how to deal with Duncan?"

Celwyn raised a brow. "Good question. He had never met him ... until Naples. I will talk with him."

The moon emerged again from behind the clouds, and the sea turned a beautiful silver. Just as Celwyn was about to comment on it, Captain Nemo leapt backward and drew his pistol.

"Damnation!"

Celwyn stared and then laughed.

A few feet off the starboard side of the *Nautilus,* a petal-pink pig swam through the water. When it drew level with the Captain, the pig flipped onto its back and blew bubbles at him.

Celwyn was still laughing. "Apparently, my brother is feeling better."

Captain Nemo's lips were pressed together so tight it was surprising he could speak. "All of this magic may be necessary, even amusing. But I do not like the disorder of it."

The magician sobered. "Understood, Sir."

Captain Nemo breathed until he was calm again. "I relate to Bartholomew's point of view about it. Nevertheless, I am honored to have met the three of you and, of course, Mrs. Kang." He hesitated. "I cannot say the same for your brother; however, he did step up when you almost died."

"That is true." Celwyn waited a moment, still thinking the overall situation was highly suspect. "Don't you find it odd that so many immortals are clustered here at one time? And now the warlock. I find it suspicious."

"Perhaps. Though, as the Professor says, the three of you make attractive bait. There is also the novelty and potential of the flying machine."

Below them, the pig swam by again as it circled the ship. This time, it had a lit cigar in its snout, and puffs of smoke accompanied it. When it flipped over and began a flamboyant, but graceful, backstroke, Nemo turned his back on it.

"The flying machine would represent many things to many criminals. But to immortals?" Celwyn searched for a reason. The pig made a wide turn and headed back to them.

Kang emerged from the hatch and offered them fresh cigars. When they were lit, Captain Nemo said,

"Correct, the flying machine represents more—for the future." He pretended he didn't see the pig on its next pass by. "On another subject, during the diversion that you and Pelaez used on your father in the catacombs, was Thales there? We could see some of it with our spy glasses."

Celwyn puffed and enjoyed Kang's reaction to the aquatic swine.

"Yes. Thales even told me when we should run for this ship. Someday, we may find out what happened afterwards."

Kang stared at him for a moment. "What do you think Thales' purpose really was?"

"No idea. After Thales saved me, he never really left me. Even now, I expect to hear his voice in my ear." Celwyn felt a shiver pass over him from head to toe. "Sometimes, I see a glimpse of him in my thoughts."

Kang asked, "Like a nightmare?"

"Yes, but also during the day, especially when I am thinking about or playing music."

"That is odd." Nemo's voice seemed thoughtful. "It must be difficult to endure."

"So far, it is not painful, just surprising. It is as if someone sprang out from a hiding place and startled you." Celwyn hesitated when the pig arrived in front of them, its fat belly floating in the water like a balloon. "You asked about what our father saw that day in the catacombs." The magician still couldn't be certain. "Thales made some of the images and as much of the projected voice as my brother did. All I cared about was shocking my father so that Bartholomew and the others could reach this ship." He voiced his guilt. "It was a mistake to endanger everyone in the first place."

"We will always stand with you, Jonas. Don't argue," Kang said.

"I still regret it. Anyhow, to answer your question, my brother and I could have battled him, probably unsuccessfully. Then I remembered one thing about him; Wolfgang Augustus Griffin was, and apparently still is, highly susceptible to suggestion."

Kang murmured, "Ah. So, you thought of the illusion. From what I could see, Thales' head looked like it floated in the air."

"I saw that, too," Captain Nemo said. "It was one of the strangest things I've ever seen."

"That was the intention. It floated on that screen to block anyone from seeing Xiau and the others running for this ship. I made the image from what I could remember of Thales."

"Interesting." Captain Nemo hesitated and repeated, "Interesting." He pointed. "I'm not talking about that." Three new pigs cavorted in the water, splashing each other. One of them wore a tiny porkpie hat with a chin strap. When the pigs began to sing in falsetto, Nemo turned his back on them again. The magician listened until he identified the piece—Verdi's *Rigoletto.*

The Captain's frown threatened to become explosive. Celwyn hurried to say, "At this point, I had silently told my brother what to project in Thales' voice. After a few seconds…" The magician squared his shoulders. "...after a few seconds, it was Thales himself who spoke."

Kang's mouth was open. "I ... thought it was you who made that."

"No. That was Thales's voice that echoed everywhere. I distinctly heard him speak to my father. He *commanded him* to return, and I do not wish to remember any of that scene ever again." Celwyn shuddered all over as the breeze whipped up. "Sir, Xiau has already heard about this, but when Thales healed me, I also received a sample of his personal scent for some ungodly reason—from Thales himself. It smells like a cross between a dead mouse and a pot of cinnamon." He made a face. "So, to make the projection more believable, I blew a cloud of it over my father. The eeriness of Thales's voice completed the picture."

Captain Nemo chuckled. "I must say, as a fellow recipient of your unexpected voice in my thoughts, I understand."

Celwyn smiled with him before telling Kang, "Your patient has been entertaining us for the last half hour," and pointed to the pigs who had begun barking at each other. "He must be feeling better."

"Humph." Kang tossed his cigar butt over the side and growled, "Just what I've always wanted—another patient who doesn't listen to me."

"Do you think your father will go to Thales?" Nemo asked, his gaze set, but not seeing, a point far away in the water.

Celwyn replied, "I do not know."

Chapter 27

SHORTLY AFTER FIVE IN THE morning, the *Nautilus* entered the underground river below Fethiye. Everyone, including Verne and Pelaez, had gathered in front of the aquatic window as the dark water turned muddy and then green in the ship's lights. Qing sat on Celwyn's shoulder, watching as avidly as everyone else.

Next to them, Verne occupied one of the seats at the chess table with his notebook and a half dozen pens spread across the board. He had adopted a quiet demeanor since their visit to Thales's island and spent much of his time writing in his cabin. A few times, he'd cornered Bartholomew to ask questions about the catacombs, which caused the magician to wonder what Verne would have done if he'd seen Thales's roaring vortex of skeletons and birds.

Pelaez left them to recline on the sofa, honoring his promise to rest under Kang's watchful eye. To

Celwyn, his brother appeared much better. And colorful. His bruises were coming along nicely in a rainbow of blues and greens. Once again, his hands moved constantly, as if they were independent of his body with minds of their own.

The Professor said, "Captain Nemo reports that they went up this river a few years ago, but for only a mile. Today, we'll go much further."

"O' comrades o' mine, exactly where are we going?" Pelaez called over in a sarcastic brogue.

The automat snorted at the idea of Pelaez as a friend. "North, before the foothills of the mountains. I'm not sure of exactly where."

For minutes they watched walls of mud go by until Bartholomew stammered, "Does the Captain expect this river will be deep enough for the *Nautilus* all the way?" A sheen of sweat covered his cheeks as he watched the passageway narrow.

Hoping to calm the big man, Celwyn said, "Captain Nemo reports it will be deep enough. Above all, he won't endanger his ship. There is good news; we're entering the river at its yearly high from the spring melt." He turned to Kang. "Correct?"

"Yes. If we stop along the way, it is to allow the crew to verify conditions. The Captain is hoping for a lake, or an extremely wide section of the river, when we reach our destination so that the ship can turn around."

"Remind me why we're approaching things from this direction?" Bartholomew asked with faint hope there wouldn't be a reason. The earthen passage seemed to narrow further with his question. With a sigh, the magician decided this wasn't the time to add a few caricatures in the water, such as aquatic mascots to escort the ship. He'd already imagined a fat crab with the whiskers of a catfish. Next time.

"Because our enemies will most likely be watching the Black Sea ports near those mountains," Kang said with gentle patience, "this will be over soon."

Bartholomew took several deep breaths to calm himself, then asked, "How far upriver will we travel?"

Kang stared at Celwyn. The message was clear—his turn to be the bad guy.

The magician said, "Forty miles."

"Oh ..." Bartholomew gripped his chair arms and held on while his knuckles turned white.

"However, most likely we'll be able to turn around when we reach the appointed spot." The automat gazed at the big man and asked Celwyn in an aside, "Should I give him a sedative, I wonder?"

Bartholomew's eyes remained tightly shut, and he breathed in quick breaths.

"No. We may need him if anything goes wrong," Celwyn said. "If it gets worse, I'll do something that I can remove in a hurry."

"There is more." Verne regarded Bartholomew and tried to lighten his statement for the big man's benefit. "The Captain told me that he hopes to pinpoint the area underneath Mavi Işık şehri. It is a city located inside one of the mountains that hasn't been seen since the early times by the Moors."

Kang patted Bartholomew's shoulder. "As a scholar, this journey is a wonderful opportunity, even without the opportunity to see the flying machine again."

"The occasion calls for a ship full of rabbits' feet and four-leaf clovers," the big man intoned.

⌣

After breakfast and Celwyn's second pot of tea, they remained in the study, continuing to watch the water as the submarine swam against it. Occasionally, a large fish would wiggle by too fast for Qing to attack through the glass. Little pieces of greenery drifted by regularly. Once, a man-sized branch scraped against the side of the ship and continued out to sea. In the *Nautilus's* study, the electric current of adventure did not waver through the hours, but the anxiety stayed with them as strong as the outgoing river.

In Bartholomew's case, his claustrophobia had steadily climbed as he paced from the bookshelves to the glass and back down again. His face dripped with sweat, and he tried to hide his trembling hands. In contrast, Verne's curiosity consumed him as he scribbled what he saw and what he could imagine.

Enough. The magician turned and stared at Bartholomew until he relaxed, and his head lolled to the side.

Kang had allowed Pelaez to sit in one of the armchairs to convalesce, with his promise that he would not do anything strenuous. Celwyn doubted Pelaez ever kept a promise, and he also doubted that any of them would be napping until they reached their destination. If the ship became stuck ... or ran aground ... they might need his brother's help.

Over the next ten minutes, the *Nautilus* passed through increasingly clearer water full of a variety of flora waving healthy tendrils at them as they cruised by. Some of the trout looked familiar to the magician, but he wasn't sure. As he watched the fish, the magician realized the ship no longer moved forward.

In seconds, Celwyn had his nose pressed to the glass. Above them, darkness still reined. Below the ship, the riverbed appeared illuminated, littered with glittery rocks, perhaps pyrite. He didn't see any wood or anything organic, except the infrequent algae-like greenery. The automat stood at his left, and even Pelaez made it to the window to stand beside him.

Celwyn indicated the rocks. "Is the glittery light from foxfire or pyrite?"

"Foxfire is a fungus," the Professor shook his head, "that wouldn't survive in ice-cold water."

"Is that really true?" Verne frowned.

Kang said, "Yes. This is not foxfire."

"I should wake Bartholomew soon," the magician told them.

"Agreed." Kang pointed through the window. "Do you see that shadowy area just beyond that ledge? It isn't too big. I think it is a cave."

"It is." No matter how much the magician squinted, he couldn't see into it.

Minutes ticked by. The submarine hovered, buffeted by the currents in the water streaming by her.

Celwyn gazed below the *Nautilus* as best he could from the window.

"I think we still have the same draught below us. The water is so clear I can't tell how deep it is." Kang's annoyance showed in his peeved voice.

"What is the Captain doing? Measuring the distance of what is in front of us?" Pelaez asked.

"Or they actually see something in front of us," Celwyn said. The study lay midway along the starboard side of the ship, which made seeing in front of them difficult. "The Captain has his hands full with whatever is going on."

The silence became acute as the minutes ticked by.

"Perhaps we need whatever you did for Mr. Bartholomew." Verne had an uncharacteristic quaver in his voice. "I no longer even see the friendly fishes."

Pelaez had walked to the stern end of the window and gazed through the glass. The *Nautilus's* external lights flooded the area underneath her, but only revealed more rocks.

"We are still sitting in the same position," Celwyn noted.

"This type of wait—it is a good thing Bartholomew isn't experiencing it." Kang stretched as tall as he could to see beyond the top of the glass. "We will reach a point soon where we'll have to back out if we can't move forward to allow for the incoming tides."

Pelaez drawled, "How encouraging."

Celwyn waited for Kang's eye roll, saw it, and grinned. "What do you think the Captain will do?"

In answer, the ship began to move forward just perceptively. If the magician hadn't been watching a particular rock in the riverbed, one that resembled a melting gnome, he wouldn't have noticed.

A low-pitched gong sounded from deep in the ship's belly. It repeated a few seconds later. Then again, and again.

"When the water is beyond a certain depth, the ship's gauges can't determine how deep it is." As the echoes continued, Kang studied the scene. "The crew is using sound to determine that. They measure how long it takes the sound to return and the timber of it."

Since Bartholomew wasn't listening, Celwyn said, "Similar to an aquatic tuning fork, but with a possible tragic ending." He listened to the gongs for a while and decided against adding his own music since things seemed so tense at the moment.

"Don't let Bartholomew hear you say that," the automat told him.

"I won't."

Captain Nemo strode in, his face set, but not grave. He bowed. "I'm sure you are curious as to our status, gentlemen."

The automat faced him. "Sir, you didn't have to leave the bridge for us..."

"Excuse me, Professor, but I preferred to. You should know that we are nearing our target. The water level is good. Better than I had hoped."

Celwyn exhaled. The others did, also.

"What is wrong with..." Captain Nemo crossed to the sofa and regarded Bartholomew.

"I put him into a more blissful state to counter his nervousness and..." Celwyn gestured, "... claustrophobia."

"Err ... thank you," he said, still eying the big man. "Regardless, I had mentioned a possible diving experience. We'll soon know whether or not it will occur."

———

Over the following half hour, the tones of the gong continued as the *Nautilus* inched forward. It was Pelaez who first noticed a change in their surroundings. "The earthen walls on our side are not as close as they were—" He pointed. "In fact, they are widening."

The others watched and nodded in agreement. Celwyn leaned in as close to the glass as he could to view the bow end of the ship. "We've entered either a very wide part of the river or a lake ... it is still too dark to see anything near the surface." He frowned, noticing the amount of greenery around them had increased also.

"They are still moving slow and careful," the Professor said. "Probably to gauge what is in front of us. I can just see the glow from the ship's lights in front."

Pelaez asked, "Is there a viewing window in the nose of this ship?"

"No," Verne said. "Having armor in front is more important. However, there are pipes the crew can use to see out—like what Jonas used when he fought off the sea monsters. And there are lights around part of the ship."

"Fascinating." The automat continued to gaze out the glass.

He jumped back as an enormous black fish nearly as wide as the room came straight at them, veering away at the last second, its fin beating the water next to the glass.

Qing squawked and flew to Celwyn, who let him hide inside his coat. "It's all right, Qing."

More fish appeared, many of them either without eyes or seemingly blind.

"We have a wonderful example here of the world of nature." The automat's annoyance lifted. "Those are a freshwater species, common to the mountain streams here." He pointed to the schools of trout that had arrived. "These fish that have been here for a very long time without light are now without the ability to see. Simply fascinating."

"Speaking of fascination, Bartholomew would probably prefer to be awake for this." Celwyn waved at the big man. Bartholomew sat up with a start.

The Professor told him, "Welcome back, my friend. We've arrived at what we think is an underground lake. We're not sure, but the good news is that it is very deep, and it is so wide the ship should be able to turn around if she needs to."

Bartholomew licked his lips as the situation came back to him.

"First, we must see if we can get inside the mountain from here," the automat said. "The Captain tells me that we prefer to go over land at this point to our destination."

Celwyn slapped the big man on the back. "Plus, the trip out again will be faster and much smoother. We'll be riding the outgoing river back to the sea. The worst is over."

Bartholomew regarded each of them, wet his lips again, and dared a glance beyond them. With a deep breath, he got to his feet and approached the aquatic window. "I will be all right. Especially when we reach our destination."

Kang said, "I suspect Captain Nemo is looking for a spot where the water is not as high. Have you noticed how clear it is?" The others obediently checked as he went on. "In my estimation, this is the water from the snow melt above us. Other streams must intersect with our "lake.""

Verne had switched to pencil and sketched the scene outside. He encountered Celwyn's gaze and smiled. "For the future, of course."

"Of course."

The gong stopped. If possible, Kang became more alert and pressed his face to the glass. Clouds of bubbles arose from underneath them, surrounding the *Nautilus*.

"We're stopping," Bartholomew said. "Look—there is light over there." The relief in his voice couldn't have been measured.

Faint light streaked the water about fifty feet to the west in a ribbon as wide as the *Nautilus*. The surface remained dark elsewhere. The magician debated whether to announce that the low ceiling over the surface appeared to be descending. Thread-like streaks of metal glittered above them as the ship moved toward the far bank.

The Professor said, "To the flying machine, gentlemen!" The automat trotted out of the room as fast as he could.

The magician followed, not voicing his hunch that they would endure a few surprises before they reunited with the flying machine again.

⌣

As they climbed out of the hatch, a quartet of crewmen dressed in diving costumes, shuddering from the cold water, unstrapped the second boat from the underside of the ship. They scampered up rope ladders as new crewmen arrived and scrambled into the boats.

Celwyn's eyes adjusted to the gloom, and he noted the ceiling above them barely cleared the top of Bartholomew's head, which did nothing to lessen his fears. The big man stared as the water rushed by with a purpose, rippling with the strong current as it moved west. For as far as Celwyn could see, in every direction, the surface spread away from them to infinity. Yes, the ship would be able to turn around.

About forty feet separated rocky walls from the ship. Although he knew it was there, the magician could barely make out the strip of gravel-like rocks that bordered the water before a wider ledge leading into the yawning darkness.

"Where does the light come from, do you think?" Bartholomew asked, his voice almost steady as he pointed to the ceiling. He shivered. "It is very cold here."

"I think through a series of fissures that graduate to the surface." Kang gestured upward. "This is intriguing ... I wonder where that entrance leads to?"

While they talked, Pelaez had been squinting at the opening. "Will we be providing light for our little journey, Brother? It appears we will need it."

Chapter 28

"DAMN, IT IS COLD." CELWYN PULLED his coat closer as their boat made its way toward the shore. For company, a wicked breeze snaked around them, trailing icy fingers.

"Did you leave Qing in your room?" Kang asked.

The magician shivered and huddled in his coat. "Yes. In case things become dangerous." He'd left instructions with one of the crew on dispersing a variety of shiny toys for the bird. If their party was gone too long, Kang would find he had contributed his cufflinks toward Qing's happiness.

Of course, there were other things of more concern. Their earlier discussion in the study had included the possibility they would encounter the Mafioso before they saw the flying machine. Celwyn glanced at the bottom of the boat and the assortment of pistols and rifles at their feet. Between Captain Nemo and everyone else, he had no worries they could defend themselves; however, if the villains brought along Duncan, things would become much more dangerous.

From his seat beside Kang, Captain Nemo nodded. "I share your concern."

Their boat bumped against the rock face, and Bartholomew tossed a rope out, secured it with a peg, and practically leapt onto the rocks a good five feet above them. Sweat poured off his face as he gauged the distance between the top of his head and the rock ceiling. In seconds, he had helped Kang out, then Verne and the others followed. When Nemo ordered the crew to return to the ship and wait four hours, Bartholomew swallowed hard.

"They have to leave with the tide," Nemo told them. "By the time four hours have passed, we would have returned here or should be on our way to the compound. The ship will wait off the coast of Unye."

"Thereby drawing the Mafioso's attention if they're watching the coast," Kang concluded.

"Exactly." Nemo's expression held grim satisfaction. "Once they are spotted or are attacked at sea, Lieutenant Granger will sink anyone working with the Mafioso."

Nemo's second in command was a quiet sort, the magician had discovered, but he had the same self-contained discipline as Nemo. Wordlessly, they shouldered backpacks, strapped on pistols, and prepared to follow Pelaez into the shadowy entrance. Kang trailed Bartholomew, with Captain Nemo, Verne, and Celwyn bringing up the rear. Celwyn thought of his and Pelaez's positions as magical bookends.

An even chillier wind whistled by them as they passed through into the shadows. The entrance could have accommodated four of Bartholomew standing shoulder to shoulder, but it was only tall enough for Kang. Everyone else stooped and went forward in a crabwalk across ground that immediately ascended sharply.

Celwyn sniffed and sniffed again. He'd just caught the scent of smoke. With a frown, he sent Pelaez a silent message to go slower and then informed the others more caution was prudent. As they moved forward again, Bartholomew brought his pistol out and pointed it downward in case he stumbled. Steps more, and the ceiling lowered further until everyone moved forward on hands and knees through silt-like sand.

"Wait," Pelaez whispered.

The odor of smoke was stronger here, and they could see little. Celwyn wiped his eyes and sent another silent message to his brother. *"Where is the smoke coming from?"*

Pelaez held up a hand to the others and crawled forward. When Verne would have spoken, Celwyn hissed a warning. Minutes later, Pelaez backed up again until he was level with Kang and the others. In a whisper, he rasped, "It is very dark for the next thirty to forty feet, then the path ascends dramatically. After that, there is a glow from a fire. The smoke is intense."

Celwyn had been hesitant about having Pelaez leading them, considering the beating he had taken only days ago. He suspected his brother's energy at the moment had a magical base. The magician whispered to Verne, "What is your favorite insect?" When Verne gawked at him, Celwyn said, "We will have a cockroach then." He hated doing this in front of Bartholomew in his nervous state, but they had to know what lay ahead. As a leggy roach, Celwyn scuttled into the tunnel, with Bartholomew's horrified gasp following him.

Celwyn stayed near the walls as much as possible, and by the time he reached the glowing fire Pelaez had reported, Bartholomew could have stood normally.

The passageway ended.

Far above, yellow and red tiles formed a pattern on the ceiling that Celwyn had never seen in all his visits to churches, castles, and mosques. The design appeared geometric and set in distinct rows, but he soon discovered it told a story in crude hieroglyphs. Xiau and Bartholomew would be thrilled. The area in front of him opened into a sort of half-circle and measured about twenty feet long.

Celwyn waited in the far shadows, but the smoke worsened. He coughed, tasting charcoal. Then he spied a thin stream of smoke funneling through a crack in the ceiling. Behind the worst of the smoke, another passage began. The magician scurried back. Before he reached Bartholomew, he appeared as himself.

After the magician related what to expect, Bartholomew led the way, with Pelaez now bringing up the rear of the procession. His face showed his fatigue, and he didn't argue.

As they stole forward, Celwyn searched for clues as well as monitored for danger. He'd always had a fine sense of knowing when others were present. Bartholomew was even better at it. Right now, their party was alone, at least as far as the tiled room. When they reached the fissure where the smoke escaped, the magician elevated himself to see inside the fissure, finding what appeared to be a similar room above, but with much fresher air.

They gathered in front of the next passageway. Celwyn sent Bartholomew a silent message to look the other way. The big man didn't argue, and Celwyn transformed into a roach again and scrambled down the second passageway. Feet more, and he arrived at a gallery of sorts. Dozens of archaic stone sculptures rested on pedestals, and progressed gradually—colors so vibrant they could have been painted yesterday.

Every sculpture appeared alike—children with large eyes full of sorrow.

Celwyn transformed back and signaled the others. As Kang paused to study the art, the Captain did as well with the kind of intensity and nods to himself that confirmed whatever he had heard was true. The scientists traded excited, mystified looks and continued forward as the floor once more ascended.

A chorus of children's voices reached them as they neared the end of the gallery. Even more interesting, a bluish light infused the air as if they stood inside a cloud.

"Put a block around us," Kang requested of Celwyn.

Captain Nemo exchanged a look with the magician and put his pistol away. The others did the same. They approached the end of the passageway and stopped before a flight of stairs leading downward. To their left, a wide arched opening overlooked a courtyard below.

The courtyard had been built on a miniature scale. At least a thousand robed figures kneeled and prayed in the strong sunlight. Beside them, tiny pots of ferns and low benches lined the walls, along with small tables. The hazy blue light blanketed everything, painting the scene with an unreal feeling, especially when Celwyn noticed the group of robed figures who faced one of the intricately decorated walls. Verne pointed beyond the courtyard to where the mountain opened into a wide expanse of air. In the distance, fluffy clouds crowned more mountains.

Kang studied the foothills and barren fields splayed out before them as if he could see to Yozgat.

"Those are children," Bartholomew whispered as he stared at the courtyard.

Verne also gawked, recording each detail in his mind, his fingers itching to hold a pen.

Radiating like beams from the sun, dozens of tiled passageways led from the courtyard back into the mountain, and a stream of clear water burbled in front of the decorated wall before tumbling over the top in a crystalline waterfall. Under it, the robed children drank from the stream. When one of them stood and turned, his hood fell back. Bartholomew called their attention to the child, who appeared about eight years old, hairless, blue-eyed, and his skin a smoky color like olives bleached in the sun. With a shiver, the magician studied the other children; they looked identical.

To the left, hundreds more of them occupied another courtyard. At this point, Celwyn realized there were no adults or animals, just the children and the eerie blue light that filtered across them before billowing out the opening in the mountain and dissipating. He could detect no odors or perfumes. If anything, he thought he smelled the clear water from the underground lake far below.

The chanting from the children became peaceful and hypnotizing, which alerted the magician. Yet, something about the scene seemed familiar.

"This is like the description of Thonis, but the architecture seems similar to Atlantis," Kang whispered. "Ptolume's work concerning this more closely matches the undersea buildings and artwork we passed by a few weeks ago."

"Yes, we saw something just like this." Bartholomew's fear had been replaced by his inner curiosity.

Celwyn remembered their description of the underwater scene on the *Nautilus'* journey to the Cape Verde Islands and once again regretted he had not been in any condition to see it.

"This *is* just like it." Verne licked his lips. "Exactly."

The magician sent a message to each of them saying they must move on before they were discovered, and they'd talk about this later. He whispered it to Kang, who looked ready to pout. Celwyn gestured for them to follow him back to the first passageway. The scholars did not move fast, and the magician received a dirty look from Verne, who had more of an interest in selling books than history. When they arrived at the smoky room, Kang blurted, "This *is* the lost city of Mavi Işık şehri. It must be! It was modeled after Atlantis from everything I've read. *Everything!*" His eyes shone with wild academic fervor that the magician hated to stymy, but they were in a precarious position here.

"They appear to speak Greek or something similar," Bartholomew said and tapped his lips, so deep in thought he forgot his claustrophobia. "It reminds me of Attica, the language of the Trabzon empire..."

"Please, we need to..." Celwyn started to herd the automat toward the exit.

"Did you see that they all had blue eyes and no hair?" Kang sighed with excitement and dug in his heels.

Captain Nemo held up a hand of authority. "This can wait." He nodded at Celwyn.

"We need to get beyond this city and be on our way. Hopefully, without bloodshed or disturbing the inhabitants." The magician kept his voice down and waited as the others gradually settled back to normal. Verne still hadn't returned to the present, judging from his unfocused eyes. Celwyn would transport him one way or another.

"What do you suggest?" Nemo asked.

The magician said, "We could quietly return to watch them from that room and remain there until they notice us. Then let them approach us."

Bartholomew frowned. "That could change their peaceful world."

"Or even infect them." Kang's frown matched the big man's.

Celwyn said, "Or..." He smiled encouragement at Bartholomew, "My brother and I could utilize a spot of magic to get us out of here." When he presented alternatives to a magical solution, he heard less complaining.

"What do you have in mind?" Bartholomew asked and covered a cough from the smoke that still clogged the room.

Pelaez's eyes held a special kind of mischief, and when Bartholomew saw him, he sent Celwyn a pleading look.

"My brother and I can make us all look like the children." Pelaez approached the big man, moving closer to study his ears. "You wouldn't be required to speak, but you would look very much like them."

Celwyn noted Bartholomew's discomfort as he tried to smile. He clapped the big man on the back. "Enough teasing. There is a simpler way."

With a wave of his hand, he swept a path about twenty feet long and eight feet high. The floor could no longer be seen, nor the wall opposite.

"Step inside and follow me. My brother will bring up the rear." Celwyn demonstrated, disappearing inside. Kang didn't hesitate and followed him. Captain Nemo pulled Verne in behind him.

241

Bartholomew was the last, with an assist from Pelaez. The magician whispered, "We're invisible. This will last until we're out of the city. *Adiamo*! Let's go."

Chapter 29

THE SKY APPEARED BLUER THAN THE children's eyes as they climbed off the mountain ledge and down granite slabs bigger than the automat to more rocks nestled amid snow drifts. A dry wind buffeted them and threatened to take Kang's hat. The magician saw Pelaez's amusement and shook his head—*leave the hat alone.*

Bartholomew lost his worried look, and with an effort, he smiled. "Look at the view! There are times when I am very grateful for your magic, Jonas. Otherwise, we may not have seen this."

The magician bowed. "We mustn't forget the Captain's expertise to get us here."

"Here, here!" everyone agreed.

Pelaez beamed at them, his expression full of sarcasm at their display of camaraderie. "We are finally on our way again." He eyed the snowdrift behind Verne, and it started moving closer to him.

Celwyn moved it back and glared as the Professor turned to Nemo. "Sir, how far is it to where the flying machine is located?"

"One moment, please." Nemo scrambled part of the way back up the rocks they'd just descended. He gazed north. All Celwyn could see were miles of gradually descending rocky terrain, spotty snow, and stunted trees. As the sun glinted down on them, the magician patted the thermos of water in his backpack.

The Captain brought up a spyglass and trained it across the inhospitable land to the east. Minutes later, Nemo landed at their feet again and said, "It is about twenty miles, maybe more, to our destination."

Gazing much further away than that, Celwyn tried for a glimpse of the sea to the north. He certainly hoped the *Nautilus* would be swimming through it again.

"What about your ship, Captain?" Verne asked.

Nemo re-strapped his backpack and said, "They had instructions to head back to the Baltic Sea if we did not return." He waited while the others readied themselves. "They'll turn around, or back out, and go to the Mare Nostrum."

He led the way as they trudged downward through less and less snow and circled around oversized rock formations. Clumps of greenery gradually decorated the path, becoming more plentiful the further they went. After they had walked more than a mile from the city of children, Celwyn dissolved the block around them.

"It is a beautiful day for a hike in the snow, even if it only lasted a few miles," Bartholomew said as they tramped along.

They hadn't gone a few feet more before Verne slipped and would have tumbled if the big man hadn't grabbed his arm. The author retrieved his hat from the slush at his feet. "That was close. Thank you."

Another half hour and they left the rocks and the last of the snow behind. The automat skipped ahead and skirted the remaining boulders. As he waited for the others, he gazed at the desolation around them and smiled, including Celwyn in his joy.

"I cannot wait to research more of the city of children we just saw, but even more, I cannot wait until we see the flying machine again." He looked at Captain Nemo. "Sir, we have you to thank for that."

The magician bowed. "For many things, Captain. Including my life."

As Nemo began to deny the compliment, Celwyn squinted above his shoulder at something he hadn't expected.

"We're about to have company." He pointed.

"Ah! That is the crew from the compound." Captain Nemo turned and waved. He inhaled in satisfaction. "I didn't want to mention it unless they were able to find us."

Two large canopied carts with oversized wheels bounced across the terrain, dodging between the stunted trees and rock formations. Celwyn hadn't seen a Turkomen horse in many years and marveled at how they stomped through the uneven terrain as easily as across cobblestones. Nemo waved again.

"What is the second cart for? The one with the white horses?" Bartholomew asked.

"Those are Arabians. Most handsome animals. That cart has more guards, our luncheon, refreshments, and chairs." Nemo bowed. "I believe in civilized dining."

"Very nice." Celwyn's stomach rumbled. "Thank you, Captain."

As they hiked toward the approaching carts, Celwyn glanced back at the mountain. Little puffs of blue mist decorated it about halfway to the top, but no curious faces looked over the edge.

The carts arrived in a clatter of hooves and sprays of dirt. Celwyn added a personal cloud of warmth. Even without the snow, it still felt cold enough here, and in the clean air, he could smell nothing at all.

"You are correct." Bartholomew patted the back of one of the Arabians, and Celwyn added clean water in front of both sets of horses. "Simply beautiful animals."

By the time they sat down to a luncheon of cold chicken and salad, the wind had picked up again. Pelaez growled a profanity and waved a hand. The gusts no longer blew up their pant legs, but around them. Although appreciative of nature, the wind reminded Celwyn of the warlock; he could easily have corrupted it to use a spell to spy on them.

"Sir, would you have your men monitor the area for anything unusual, please?" he asked Nemo.

The Captain spied his expression and gestured to his men. "What do you suspect?"

"Nothing. More of a precaution, or perhaps a premonition."

Chapter 30

IT DIDN'T TAKE LONG FOR THEM TO finish eating; Kang and Bartholomew couldn't stop talking about the flying machine and couldn't sit still. They dismantled the table while the crew attended to the horses, and soon everyone climbed onto the wooden benches inside the first cart. By agreement, Kang and Bartholomew kept to the shadows furthest from the edge of the awning where the canvas overhang concealed them, leaving the others more visible to anyone watching.

Celwyn, Pelaez, and Nemo pulled their hats lower and faced the center of the cart. "There will be more to worry about when we are closer to the compound. Be assured; if we have spyglasses, our enemies do also." The Captain trained his glass on the mountains to the east. When their cart hit a hole, everything flew upward, and he dropped the glass.

"Allow me." Pelaez stared at the road until the bumpiness disappeared, and soon it seemed as if the cart floated on air as it traveled across the landscape. Quiet, smooth, and comfortable. Their adventure had entered a new phase. The magician distributed cigars to those in the cart following them and the one he rode in.

Bartholomew chanced a look over the side of the cart and swallowed. "We're about a foot off the ground ... the entire cart."

Pelaez gestured, and the cart to the rear floated along with them.

Verne wiggled in his seat and said to Pelaez, "This is much better."

"It will certainly give my crew something to think about," The Captain said caustically.

With a half-smile, Pelaez added a collection of pillows, glasses, and a variety of whiskey bottles. Celwyn decided a road party needed a baroque, a lively one with appropriate exuberance. Soon, the music rang out as the whiskey flowed, and their singing sent rabbits and other small vermin running off the track. Bartholomew's baritone contrasted with Pelaez's rasp while they refilled glasses and sang as loudly as they could.

The magician couldn't tell if Captain Nemo was enjoying, or tolerating, the off-key singing. He shouted over the commotion to him, "How much further, Sir?"

"Eight miles." Nemo huddled into his coat, muffling the noise to an extent.

Celwyn studied the terrain. It would change in about another five miles or so, the track becoming flatter. As he brought up the spyglass, he noted trees and a smattering of buildings at one end of the little valley ahead. He swung the glass to the north, where the thicker brush bordered the beginning of a forest. An answering glint from another spyglass reflected the setting sun.

"Well, well."

Kang asked, "What do you see?"

"At least one watcher."

Captain Nemo followed his gaze and murmured to the crewman sitting beside him over Bartholomew and Pelaez's duet. The crewman nodded and saluted.

"We'll be at our camp in a few minutes. My men will take a look."

The trees thickened, and the land seemed less barren as they descended into a long valley. To the north, a smattering of farms and a single road led toward the forested mountains between them and the Black Sea.

"How did your men know where to find us?" Verne asked.

The Captain studied at the countryside. "I gave them our coordinates for the underground lake and a map. The trip up the river went so well; we arrived a bit early. My lieutenant reported that we emerged about three miles south of the targeted area. It could have been much worse."

"I see."

"If we need to, how will we find that fissure between the rocks again? Or the opening in the mountain where we emerged?" Bartholomew asked.

"I've noted the location of both, and suspect I'm not the only one." Nemo raised a brow at Celwyn.

The magician nodded. "In case you should return without me or the Captain's coordinates, you will find distinct markings on the rocks below where we emerged. They can be seen from a distance with a glass."

"A nice solution," Bartholomew hiccupped and said. "But you shouldn't think you won't be with us."

"I second that sentiment," Kang said as sternly as he could with a silly grin.

Next to the road they traveled on, a fence patrolled by a score of guards came into view, and soon, to the right, a series of whitewashed wooden buildings appeared under a stand of trees. In the opposite direction, Celwyn spied the expected wind flags of the landing field and a flat expanse of ground before them.

"Where is the flying machine?" The automat stared at the buildings.

"Inside the last building, the one with the large rolling doors." Nemo pointed it out. "It is under guard at all times."

The automat checked on Bartholomew and his excitement. "I believe we have at least two hours of sunlight left."

Captain Nemo played ignorant. "And what do you propose to do with it?"

Bartholomew's grin stretched to each ear. "I had hoped for this, so..." he reached inside his coat, "...I brought along some notes to get us started." He tapped his backpack. "The rest are in here. And the Professor brought some also."

"I'm feeling so left out," Celwyn complained and patted a yawn. "Perhaps I'll try some new magic to entertain myself."

The automat rolled his eyes and pretended he didn't hear anything.

❲ ❳

As the cart continued to the last building, all along the perimeter, a line of guards stood at attention, their firearms at their sides. One guard, with his cap shading his features, seemed especially interested in who sat inside their cart. The magician noted his interest and continued his inspection of the largest structure. One end of the building opened to the compound, most likely for wheeling the flying machine in and out.

"Captain, I am placing a block out here while the Professor and Bartholomew are working inside. And," he checked with his brother and received a nod. "My brother will build a more secure but invisible fence around the building."

Nemo appeared a bit confused. He frowned, "Thank you, but..."

"It is just a precaution in case any of your guards have been compromised. I'm assuming some are from local sources?"

Nemo sighed as he listened to the magician's concern, and they jumped to the ground. "Some are men I've been able to depend on from Constantinople. Some are new."

As they walked inside the building's massive opening, the magician addressed Kang and Bartholomew. "When you come and go from here, take one of us with you for added protection whenever possible, please. The magic will allow us, and Nemo's men, in and out, but no one else."

Nemo's frown deepened. "What do you suspect?"

"Duncan would take a more direct approach to get what he wants. He would attack and destroy things." Celwyn gestured at the rows of equipment and tools piled in the corners of the hangar. "But if the Mafioso are here, at first, they are more likely to bribe your guards to watch us."

Captain Nemo sighed and turned in a slow circle, looking out the door at the rest of the complex while he rubbed his head and then replaced his cap. "I will discreetly inquire about the guards. And agreed, we need extra precautions."

Pelaez approached the flying machine parked dead center in the hangar. Various boxes and tools surrounded it. He didn't say a word as he walked around it.

"Did you see this in the air in Odessa?" Bartholomew asked.

Pelaez shrugged.

Celwyn eyed the bright yellow machine. "Bartholomew chose this color?"

"Yes," Captain Nemo said. "It fits."

From beside him, Kang spun the propeller. "Plus, it helps us spot it when it is in the air."

Several ladders and platforms on wheels had been pushed to one side, and the automat trotted to one of the ladders. Soon, he sat in the cockpit. While Bartholomew crawled under the tail fin, two crewmen in coveralls stepped forward.

"These are my men." With a gesture, the Captain introduced them as Kirk and Martin. "There is no question of their loyalty."

Pelaez picked through the pile of backpacks and selected Bartholomew's and Kang's. After he delivered them in front of the flying machine, he added a table with writing instruments, and new tools appeared on top of the platforms.

"At least he waited until the new assistants were looking the other way. Let's leave them to it," Celwyn suggested. "I am curious about dinner and, of course, a nice pot of tea."

Like the others, the main building had been built of wood with a tiled roof and painted a dirty white that mimicked the landscape. Someone had planted boxes of rosemary, peppers, and herbs next to the front door. The magician remarked that boded well for the sauces accompanying their food.

Captain Nemo led the way up the walk and through the entrance into a spacious room lined with windows and comfortable sofas. A limited library with reading tables filled the west wall, along with a chess table and a much smaller globe than the one on the *Nautilus*. On the east wall, a rough-hewn dining table awaited them, topped with a large bowl of oranges that perfumed the air. Straight ahead, Celwyn spied a full bar, then a hallway.

Even before they passed through the front door, the magician had detected the aroma of lamb roasting. Off to the left, a set of doors led to the kitchen and the murmur of voices. Inhaling the scent of the roast would be torturous until dinner, which was probably many hours away.

Thoughts of dinner reminded him of past pleasant and congenial evenings. Celwyn sighed, missing Qing. He chuckled, thinking of what the mechanical bird could have destroyed by now. His thoughts softened as he remembered how Tara had looked that night as they stood on top of the ship in the moonlight. Vampire or not, he very much enjoyed the way she looked at him. He didn't dwell on the future more than several times a day, but he knew he wouldn't see her again.

The Captain bowed them toward the hallway door. "Follow my crewman, please. He will show you to your rooms. You'll find each has its own lavatory and bathing facilities, and I've provided your wardrobe ... since most of your things are on the ship."

"Thank you." As they trailed the crewman, Celwyn asked, "You had this built for us?"

Nemo shook his head. "No. This ranch belonged to a local shah, and he kept his harem out here, away from his wife."

Chapter 31

AFTER A REFRESHING BATH THAT did nothing to keep his mind off the roast lamb, Celwyn reentered the main room and found the others, except Verne, already there. He hitched up the pants of the serviceable clothes he'd found in his closet and sat. There were drawbacks to leaving his things behind on the ship, but he doubted they would have a formal evening here.

Nemo had made a most comfortable hideaway for them. Behind the sofas and across the walls, tapestries of battle scenes and tasteful depictions of unclothed women bathing in mountain streams predominated. Soft lights lit the room. This wasn't the study of the *Nautilus*, but it would do nicely.

Celwyn ignored the bar and bypassed the whiskies the others enjoyed and stopped himself from producing his own tea. "Captain? How does the household staff feel about magic?"

"I'll leave it up to you." Captain Nemo did smile this time. "None of them have experienced it before. They are local people I've known for years. Though..." he glanced at the kitchen door, "...I would tread carefully around Fatima, our cook. She is far more superstitious than Bartholomew and would not handle it well. Not at all."

The magician nodded and produced his tea service with an eye on the kitchen door. "You'll notice I made the cups resemble those beside the coffee service." He pointed to the unused cart beside them. "This should do, I think."

"Yes, it will, but my staff would be pleased to bring tea upon request." He lowered his voice and nodded at Pelaez as he explored the library books at the other end of the room. "If you can control his imagination while we're here, it will be less stressful."

"And noisy."

As if he could hear them—and probably did— Pelaez turned. His eyes gleamed with amusement when his pig appeared and started across the room toward the kitchen. Celwyn dissolved it.

"It will only be a few weeks, Brother."

The Captain watched Pelaez saunter back to them with an annoyed frown. Before more irritation could occur, a pleasant-looking middle-aged couple entered the room from the kitchen and began setting the table. Like many married couples, they appeared very much alike— medium-sized, with curly gray hair, spectacles, and square chins.

"Mr. Sogun and Mrs. Sogun, these are a few of our guests." Captain Nemo stood and performed the introductions. "I'll go retrieve our scientists. Dinner is imminent."

❲ ⌣ ❳

Although Celwyn had trouble remembering some of the spices in the keşkek, and he couldn't recognize the yellow vegetable laced with tarragon, he enjoyed his dinner very much. He found the lamb as good as it smelled, though he wasn't as sure about the reactions from the Professor and Bartholomew. They barely tasted their food as they chattered about the flying machine. Much of the dinner talk sounded too technical to understand, except for their enthusiasm.

Kang set his water glass off to the side and laid a pencil and paper next to his plate. "Bartholomew's design changes are marvelous." The automat scribbled and held up the paper. "See here? He fixed the problem with the yaw." More scribbles and a quick bite of bread. "We must work on the engine, though."

Captain Nemo basked in their discussion, his face alive, and his dream finally coming true.

Bartholomew said, "I agree. Captain, we are perfecting the design first and then fine-tuning everything." He stopped talking long enough to pop a bite of the yellow vegetable into his mouth. "We'll work on the specs as we go to an extent, but..." He glanced at Kang and received a nod as Kang caught up on his dinner, realizing his food had begun cooling off. "...when the time comes, you will have to employ a different type of engineer to determine how to efficiently manufacture more machines."

Kang took up the narrative. "So far, we have made a start on the new type of parts needed. And we're designing some of the tools that will be required. That is Bartholomew's specialty."

"It sounds promising." Pelaez finished his wine and signaled for more.

Celwyn had to admit the enterprise sounded exciting and that he knew little about it. Nemo seemed to know more.

"I realize this will take time, too. I had already begun a search for the engineer that you've described."

Verne asked, "What does the aeroplane use for fuel?" The author had his notebook out. From over his shoulder, Mrs. Sogun served him a scoop of fluffy rice while she aimed a frown at the automat; dinner wasn't the time for pencils, notebooks, and drawings.

"A blend of rich fuel," Bartholomew murmured and stared at a bite of lamb as if he wondered how it climbed onto his fork.

Kang faced Nemo. "Sir, we need the crew to pace off the landing field tomorrow. I want to know the distances for the take-offs and landing requirements and probably add footage to them. So far, we've been lucky with no mishaps."

"I will arrange it. What else?" Nemo said.

Instead of scientific fervor, Celwyn felt relief. The Captain was finally getting his reward for everything he had done and for occasionally rescuing them. Even if he didn't know a yaw from a hammer, the magician intended to provide security and anything else he could to be sure everything went well and that they made it back to the ship.

Kang eyed Bartholomew and saw his nod. "From what I could tell, the next field over is fairly flat."

Bartholomew nodded in agreement as he finished his dinner. The magician noticed he had begun eating faster, probably so that they could return to the flying machine.

"Do you wish for that field to be cleared also?" Captain Nemo asked.

"Please." Kang gazed over the top of Celwyn's head, probably adding up distances. "The one at the end. We need an extraordinarily long field to get the machine safely off the ground. There needs to be enough distance for the machine to make a run for it. And land again."

"I do not understand," Verne said.

Bartholomew told him, "That is how we leave the ground. The speed and lift from the flaps."

"I can't wait to get into the air." The automat rubbed his hands together.

Celwyn compressed his lips and thought it fortunate that Elizabeth wasn't here to witness the Professor's enthusiasm. She would be horrified and expect Celwyn to stop him.

"What else do you need?" Captain Nemo asked.

Bartholomew leaned back in his chair, thinking. "When I took off and landed by Odessa, I became very aware of each dip and hole in the field. The smoother the ground, the better, please. We could damage a tire if not. Or even flip and crash."

"That should do for summarizing our first day." Kang smiled at the Captain. "After dinner,

Bartholomew and I must confer and organize our notes."

With another sniff of disapproval concerning non-dining activities, Mrs. Sogun deposited plates of glazed cake in front of them, and Mr. Sogun pushed the coffee service into the room.

Nemo said to the Soguns, "I am sorry I did not introduce the rest of our guests sooner. This is Professor Xiau Kang and Bartholomew of Jubal." He turned to them. "And this is Mr. and Mrs. Sogun, who take care of this house."

After they exchanged formal greetings, Bartholomew said, "We assure you we will not be late for dinner again." A winning smile came with the promise. "Will we meet our chef this evening?"

"No, sir. She is very busy right now. Tomorrow." Mrs. Sogun sounded a bit gruff as she moved one of the rulers out of her way and removed dishes.

Celwyn hid a smile at the automat's expense and turned to Verne. "That means you will be my partner for bridge this evening, Jules." If Nemo and his brother partnered for the game, it might contribute to the new comradery, which was much needed for their enterprise to succeed. At least, he hoped so.

After they adjourned from the table, Kang and Bartholomew hurried off to Bartholomew's room while Nemo excused himself, saying he would return shortly. As the front door closed behind him, Celwyn poured whiskies and handed Pelaez one. They settled at the game table.

"For security, what do you suggest?" he asked his brother. That subject reminded him—without getting up, Celwyn lowered the shades over the windows to block the glare from the setting sun and prying eyes. Before they closed, he spotted several pairs of guards in the yard.

"I don't know yet." Pelaez patted his stomach. "A very nice dinner. In the middle of nowhere, no less." He yawned. "The Captain must have an incredibly vast operation and an excellent set of contacts."

Verne bustled back into the room again and arrived at the game table, clutching his pipe. He stopped short before sitting. "I assume we can smoke here?"

Celwyn shrugged. He didn't feel nervous, but he didn't feel settled either. He tapped a nail on the table and still couldn't relax ... music would help. A soft waltz entered the room, meandering through the air like the scent of fine perfume.

Verne lit his pipe. As he got it going, the Captain returned from the courtyard, paused, and approached where they sat under the windows. Verne shuffled the cards.

"Mrs. Sogun may, or may not, know that I do not have a phonograph in here." Nemo eyed the magician. "They are a fairly new invention."

Celwyn nodded. "You have just received one, although, at the moment, it is not in use." He pointed to the bottom shelf of the bookcase.

"That will do," the Captain agreed.

With his characteristically intense gaze, Pelaez said, "Captain, under the assumption that Duncan will attack us here, my brother and I have made some plans. For the Mafioso, I suppose you have enough guards to repel them if needed?"

"Yes, and you'll remember when we entered the compound, we passed through a wire fence." His eyes danced a jig. "There are batteries wired to it."

"Ah, fried rodents." Pelaez approved.

"Correct." Captain Nemo gestured out the windows. "We'll close the gate at night. If a large man touched the fence, it wouldn't kill him, but it will deter access."

Pelaez stared at the windows, seeing beyond them. "I'll add a complete block on the building where the flying machine sits. There will be less to worry about."

After a spot of quiet, while everyone considered the situation, Celwyn said, "I will do the same for these buildings since Xiau and Bartholomew are just as tempting as our invention. Do the rest of your staff sleep here, Captain?"

"Yes. The cook, the Soguns, and the cook's helpers all sleep on the south side of this building, opposite our rooms. The next building over is the barracks for the guards and crew." He frowned. "Do you think there is still a threat, despite the number of guards? There are more than twenty-five of them."

"Yes." Celwyn said, "The Mafioso is a large and vicious group of hooligans."

"Very well." Nemo sighed. "I will accept your opinion and hope it will not occur."

"There is more," the magician said. "If you add Duncan to the problem, I believe we could be in serious danger—if we don't take precautions."

"It is at times like this that I appreciate your magic and that of your brother. But it is distressing." Nemo's brows drew together in exasperation. "I am out of my element on land. This is not controllable." He rubbed his chin and his gaze turned inward. "If it weren't for the flying machine, I would be on my ship now."

"You had no way of predicting we'd attract Duncan's attention." Celwyn followed Nemo's lead and moved to the game table. "We're happy to assist, sir, and my past with Duncan should prove useful." He hoped he hid his enough from Nemo and the others. "Maintaining magic all night means that we will sleep during the day in staggered shifts. If you haven't already posted guards with spyglasses on the roof of the tallest building, please do so. Also, it would be best to have a runner stationed below to alert us if they see anything."

The Captain said, "It will be done."

"I have hopeful news." Celwyn tried to look confident, but knew it depended on the listener's point of view.

"Such as?" Pelaez regarded his brother. "Ah, I know. You think our enemies won't try anything until the work on the flying machine is done? They may even wait until we leave the compound."

"Correct."

"That was my initial assumption, yes, and I hope it is true. But, no matter." Captain Nemo stood and straightened his jacket. "I'll arrange for men up top beginning at first light tomorrow." To Verne, he said, "Please deal the cards. I'll be right back."

As he strode out, Verne piped up, "The Captain is fond of arat, the Turkish liqueur. Would any of you care to try it?" He headed toward the bar.

Chapter 32

T HE NEXT DAY PASSED PEACEFULLY with Kang and Bartholomew too involved at the hangar to luncheon with the others. Nemo dispatched a picnic basket with Mrs. Sogun and then decided to join them.

It had been a long night; Celwyn yawned wide and approached the sofa, prepared to nap. Pelaez remained at the window with a book about African birds and an eye trained on the courtyard. "Please refrain from snoring, Brother."

Celwyn growled something appropriate and stretched out, noting he was just as comfortable as in his bed. As he relaxed, his thoughts drifted to Tara. Of course, he also missed Qing, his napping partner.

"How many more days until they are done with the flying machine?" the magician wondered. He had an excellent view out the window and spied an eagle swooping across the far field and into the trees.

Pelaez pursed his lips. "From what Bartholomew reported, they had several technical issues to resolve. Then they must go back and correct anything connected to them."

Celwyn's yawns took over. "And then write everything down."

"Yes. They call that the specs."

Celwyn felt his eyes getting heavier. "We should talk with everyone about our return to the *Nautilus*."

"You are fighting sleep," Pelaez told him as he yawned, too, staring at the courtyard. The day had turned cloudy, and the first raindrops began to fall as a pair of armed guards walked by the window. "We will talk about it."

"Do you know what is behind this building?" Celwyn asked. Although he could have put some effort into seeing through the back wall, he wasn't in the mood.

"I have walked the entire complex," Pelaez answered. "The back of this building abuts a solid rock face before a steep drop. The rest of the complex does not. Therefore, those buildings have the regular attention of the guards." He raised his voice. "Pay attention, please. How will Duncan attack?"

That woke Celwyn up. "I fear he is cooking up something. We need to prepare."

Music would help him think. The magician sat up, and a handful of violins and a harmonizing oboe in a major key filled the room. Upon every surface, he caused dozens of abacuses and metronomes to appear, clicking and clacking their accompaniment. With each second, they moved faster, and the commotion built tenfold. With a flick of his wrist, compliments of drums entered, keeping time with the clacking.

Pelaez lifted his chin, and streaks of iridescent lights crisscrossed the room, becoming a swirling and shimmering cornucopia over their heads. As it grew, a low rumbling came from the middle of the iridescent funnel. With one last click, the cacophony of the metronomes and abacuses blossomed into a rainbow of fat parakeets that rose upward, gathering into a pulsating storm above them.

One by one, they broke free to swerve high and dive into the cornucopia. When the birds had all disappeared, the cornucopia shimmered violently and dissolved in a rain of tinkling bells.

A wine glass sailed by the magician's ear and crashed into the wall behind the sofa. Others followed. As Celwyn turned, he saw a flash of a raised arm and the fiery eyes of an extraordinarily fat woman draped in scarves and shrieking curses at them. Quicker than he could decide what to do, non-lethally, she threw more glasses from her position by the bar.

"Dethils!"

Celwyn blinked. Then understood. Being almost toothless, "devils" sounded like "dethils."

As graceful as a ballerina, she advanced on tiny feet encased in gold slippers. Atop waves of her silvery hair sat a chef's toque. The magician brought forth his most charming smile and scrambled to his feet.

"Good afternoon. You must be Fatima." He bowed. "I am Jonas Celwyn, one of the guests." He hoped mentioning he was a guest would calm her down. "This is my brother, Pelaez."

With an eye trained on the woman, Pelaez arose and bowed also. "Pleased to meet you, Madam. Both you and the Captain have been extraordinarily busy since our arrival, or he would have introduced us."

Celwyn stepped around the broken glass at his feet while resisting the urge to use magic to clean it up. Nemo had said Fatima was superstitious. Her widened eyes and panting supported that observation.

"Would you like to sit down and have..." he stopped himself from offering tea that didn't exist. "...and have a conversation?" He pulled out a chair from the nearby dining table.

Pelaez took his cue and unobtrusively moved to the other end of the table. When she hesitated, Celwyn extended an open hand and added, "Captain Nemo is a good friend of mine, and he would want us to talk. Please?"

She didn't take her eyes off them. The magician detected a strong whiff of cinnamon as she sidled by him to settle in the chair. As he sat, he bestowed another smile upon her.

"The Captain said he would take us on a tour of the compound and your kitchen later this afternoon. I hope that is acceptable?" At her slight nod, he continued, "Have you been with the Captain long?"

While the magician talked, Fatima had initially watched him from under a pair of bushy brows, but now her attention centered on Pelaez. She stared at him with her bottom lip extended as far as possible, more fascinated than afraid.

"This is the Captain's first visit." She spoke in careful English and studied Pelaez like she would a child she had caught with the roosters. "You remind me of my son, Hakim."

Celwyn covered a snort while Pelaez decided what to say.

"Thank you, Madam."

Fatima shook herself all over, causing a minor symphony from the bells hanging from her earrings and wrists. Then she addressed them with more force.

"I am a religious woman!" She slapped the table. "What I saw is not ... natural. Not at all." She fingered a token around her neck and regarded them with a modicum of suspicion, but not hostility.

"We apologize," Celwyn said.

She hesitated and glanced at the floor of broken glass. "It is me who should apologize."

"No, that it is not required. We should not have been doing, err ... what we were doing." Celwyn couldn't bring himself to use the word "magic" in front of her for fear of setting off another explosion.

"They were just parlor tricks," Pelaez put in as smoothly as he could. "We should have warned you."

Fatima's voice grew calmer. "No. You are guests. It is I who apologize for my behavior."

"No, Madam." Celwyn waved it away. "You do not owe an apology. We have a few somewhat odd questions for you, if that is acceptable?" Talking about her work would be calming. Hearing about how the compound was maintained would be helpful in their defense of it.

"Certainly."

"Thank you. Do you have supplies delivered on a regular basis?"

"Oh, yes! Nearly every day." She bobbed her head, and the torque bobbed also. The question reminded her of solid, normal activities. "They bring all the newspapers on Fridays also. Even from Ankara."

"How do you keep the food cold? Yesterday, it was a very warm day," Pelaez asked the question as the rain increased, pattering the roof so loudly they had to raise their voices.

"A big box and batteries from Captain. I do not know how it works." She waved a hand toward the outside. "We get water from our spring in the other building." She stopped talking to again stare at Pelaez, this time with a measure of sadness. "You look like my son," she repeated. "I miss him."

Celwyn noticed their chef had lost her fear of them, and thanks to Pelaez's resemblance to her offspring, she seemed much friendlier. He asked, "Have you been told how much we enjoyed last night's dinner?" He pursed his lips at the memory. "Exotic and unusual."

Fatima blushed. "I am pleased you enjoyed it." She pushed herself up. "I must see to tonight's dinner." With an awkward curtsy, she bustled to the kitchen door.

"Would you ask Mrs. Sogun to bring us a tea service, please?"

As soon as she left, Celwyn dissolved the mess of broken glass.

"Shall we make a wager?" Pelaez picked up his book and resumed his seat by the windows. "I say Fatima will accept our magic by this coming Sunday. Three days hence."

"Sooner. What is the wager?"

"The loser takes an extra round of maintaining the magic at night."

They shook. "It is a bet. By midnight tonight," the magician said as innocently as he could.

Pelaez laughed. "Oh? What did you have in mind?"

Chapter 33

BY SIX THAT EVENING, EVERYONE had gathered in the main room of the house. Some of them were more willing than others to be there; Celwyn had tricked Bartholomew and Kang into returning to the main house by saying Captain Nemo requested their presence.

The Professor still glowered at Celwyn, but after he relaxed on the sofa, his countenance smoothed out, and he smiled at Verne as he peppered them with questions.

"No, we're not done, but we're making good progress. Captain?"

"Yes?" Nemo called from the chess table, his attention on whatever move Bartholomew had just made.

Kang looked down his nose at Celwyn. "I think we should hurry our efforts before the magicians become bored."

As Verne poured whiskies, he said, "Odd. We seem to be short quite a few tumblers. But, I have enough, I think."

From his position sprawled on the sofa, Pelaez murmured, "We had an incident earlier."

Captain Nemo hesitated as he picked up his knight, frowned at him, but didn't say anything.

"All is well." Celwyn jumped into the conversation before things became more fanciful, courtesy of his brother. "And after an explanation, we became friends with Fatima."

The Professor enjoyed Captain Nemo's raised brows of doubt before saying, "Again, I think we should hurry our efforts before the magicians become bored."

"Excellent suggestion." Captain Nemo deposited a sliver of glass on the neighboring table.

Bartholomew pushed his pawn forward. "We made great progress today. The flaps are finally as we like them. If all goes well, we will be performing a test flight Saturday that should confirm our changes."

"And verifying the field length required for take-offs and landings." Kang said, "So far, we've been lucky."

Captain Nemo sipped his liqueur and regarded them. "I've given this some thought and recommend that we begin the test at first light. It would be impractical to light a field of that size and would also highlight what we're doing to anyone watching."

"Most logical," the automat said. "Can you tell me about your staff? Who should I talk with about setting up the test?"

"Alistair Hobbs oversees the guards and their schedules. He appreciated the suggestion of the spyglasses on the roof." Captain Nemo picked up another shard of glass and tossed it on the table.

Celwyn asked, "How does Mr. Hobbs feel about magical displays?" He added a point to Bartholomew's nose. Each time he blinked, it lit up.

Kang coughed and tried not to react. "It will take some finessing to be certain that any fear or confusion in the guards doesn't compromise our tests, such as unwanted visits from Duncan."

"If we put blocks around the complex," Celwyn said, "it would be less likely that the staff would have to grapple with accepting odd occurrences."

"But if we're attacked, things could become quite lively." Pelaez shrugged.

Captain Nemo regarded Bartholomew's blinking nose as he finally moved his queen but said nothing. Nemo played the part of a neutral country during magical demonstrations; he wouldn't say anything or side with anyone's point of view. Oblivious to his performing nose, the big man picked up his bishop. "I recommend saying nothing to the guards, but take Mr. Hobbs into our confidence, along with the crew that attends to the flying machine." His face cleared as he finished thinking it through. "If of a sudden, Jonas caused it to turn a different color and disappear, they need to be expecting it."

Celwyn giggled into his sleeve and covered it with a cough.

As an appropriate example, Mrs. Sogun bustled into the room and began to set the table. Celwyn removed the enhancement of Bartholomew's nose before asking Nemo silently, *should we tell Mrs. Sogun?*

Captain Nemo shook his head violently.

"I say..." Verne had pushed up another chair to the chess table to sort through a fresh pile of newspapers.

"Yes, Jules?" Captain Nemo asked.

Verne shook the paper to straighten it. "This story says war has broken out between the Prussians and Austrians."

"Neither have many warships," Nemo said. "It will probably be decided on land."

"Or someday in the air?" Bartholomew raised a brow.

Pelaez crushed his glass in his hand, spraying whiskey everywhere. "War is war!" His look was as dark as Celwyn had ever seen it. In a voice so angry the magician expected the furniture to explode and lamps to fall, his brother said, "Many more men will die. *Don't you understand?*"

Verne sputtered, "You don't know for certain..."

Pelaez left them in a string of curses. As the door slammed shut again, they could see him stalking down the pathway, away from the main building, toward the perimeter fence. Small explosions in the dirt and flying gravel surrounded him all the way. Celwyn started to go after him, then thought better of it.

Verne held up the newspaper. "What I didn't finish reading aloud was the summary at the end of the report. It states both countries have agreed to peace talks."

"Excellent." The Professor's mood lifted, and he asked, "Would you like Bartholomew to tell us what he discovered about the fuel-to-air mixture? We have at least an hour until dinner."

Talk of the flying machine lasted through the first course and into the salad. Pelaez had returned in time to wash up and join them with his mood changed, so much so that he joked with Kang and Bartholomew over their efforts. Celwyn kept busy with his dinner of fresh trout, but did wonder why his brother's attitude had so radically changed. It could be because of the excellent food.

The magician savored a bite of flavorful bulgur laced with hints of garlic and said, "When we met Fatima this afternoon, she seemed to warm up to us and our peculiarities. In particular, she thought my brother resembled her son. Could that be the reason this meal is so wonderful?"

Everyone smiled, including Captain Nemo. "I met her son a long time ago." He studied Pelaez. "I suppose there is some likeness."

Kang enjoyed another bite of the fish. "Whatever it is, I recommend that we do not disparage it. This trout is superb."

"I concur," Bartholomew said. "It is the sauce."

Interestingly, Verne was the one to bring up a most worrisome topic.

"Captain, how will we get back to the *Nautilus*? If the Mafioso know we're here, it may not be easy to do."

With a sigh that went past his satisfied belly to the tips of his fingers, Nemo hesitated. A long moment passed, broken only by the sound of forks and crystal, before he spoke. "Let's assume that we are able to avoid an attack here at the compound. We have a few options for what happens next. Eventually, we would meet the *Nautilus* on the coast of the Black Sea."

Verne sipped water and watched Nemo.

Bartholomew reminded them, "Annabelle's wedding. If we're not there..."

"I'd be blamed for that." Celwyn had no doubt.

Kang sent him a smirk devoid of sympathy. "To go on, there are some things that we need to consider." The automat held up a finger. "First, the biggest risk is not knowing what could befall us on our way to the coast."

Captain Nemo said, "This is true. I've already considered a scouting party to Trabzon."

"That could be a most dangerous endeavor, but it is probably necessary." Celwyn stared at his plate and wished he could finish it while listening to something pleasant. Instead, he nodded at Pelaez. "We should both be here to repel an attack from the Mafioso and Duncan. There's no guarantee our enemies will wait until we leave the compound to strike."

The author had been watching the exchange with nervous glances that bounced to each of them. "How many days is it until we leave here?"

Bartholomew added something in his head and said, "If this weekend's flight test goes well, we'll need another two or three tests in the air to confirm our changes. A fortnight should do it."

"That will help us with our exit plans." The automat rubbed his hands together, thoughts of finishing his trout abandoned. "All right." He looked at Captain Nemo. "Sir, my suggestion is to immediately send your scouting party overland to the north coast. When they return, we should be about four to six days away from completion here."

Celwyn thought about what Kang had said, thought more, and began to laugh. The Professor was not amused because he knew him so well.

"Whatever is so entertaining, I don't like it," Kang told him.

Bartholomew chuckled and tried not to.

"We may not have a choice." The magician grew serious. "We cannot afford to lose you two to those villains."

The Professor glared. "Now, I know it is dangerous."

"I know what you are thinking, Brother." Pelaez's eyes had lit up with his special kind of mischief.

Captain Nemo matched Kang's glare. "What *is* it?"

Celwyn searched his plan for flaws and found none. He leaned back. "I propose that we entice the Mafioso and Duncan out into the open and into attacking us. Once they are no longer a threat, we go forward, as Xiau has outlined. It is our only logical path to success."

"Why were you laughing?" Verne asked.

Kang drawled, "Because it will be an insane plan full of magic, music, and danger—all of the elements Jonas enjoys. God help us." He ended his speech with an eye roll.

Pelaez said, "I think it is a marvelous idea!"

"We could..."

The exasperation in Xiau's voice rose to a squeak. "I don't want to know, Jonas. I do *not* want to know!"

Despite the enjoyment of teasing Xiau, Celwyn had only decided how to entice the Mafioso out in the open, to where he could get at them. What to do about Duncan? He didn't have a clue. Yet.

He made himself comfortable next to the phonograph with a tea service handy for cognitive purposes. Across from Pelaez, Verne leaned over the chessboard with a perplexed frown. Considering his brother was cheating, Celwyn assumed the author would soon tire of losing.

As the wall clock chimed midnight, Captain Nemo returned from his conference with his man Hobbs. He poured a drink and joined Celwyn on the sofa.

"The scouting party for Trabzon leaves early tomorrow."

Celwyn felt a trill of excitement; they were finally going home.

As he took Verne's rook, Pelaez asked, "I assume they will look for areas where we are likely to be attacked?"

"Yes."

Celwyn watched Pelaez's knight move back onto the chessboard. Verne peered at the board with his mouth open and slowly moved his queen forward. When he let go of it, the pig sleeping on Pelaez's boot grunted. Minutes more went by, and everyone was lost in his thoughts. "The Soguns retired about an hour ago," Pelaez stated without looking up.

Captain Nemo spied the pig, and his brows drew together with annoyance. "It's funny how some of this..." he indicated to the pig, "...seems a tad normal now. Did the others retire also?"

"I believe so. They are going to be out at dawn measuring wind velocity and other things." Celwyn sent Pelaez a sympathetic grin. "My dear brother drew the short straw and will go with them. I will be taking a nap since I am on duty during the night."

Captain Nemo frowned. "If you prefer, I can ask..."

"No, thank you." Celwyn tamped the air. "This is a special situation where normal precautions aren't enough. The minute we relax our vigilance, they will attack. It is the unspoken law of rogues." The magician crossed to the library shelves and table of maps. After a short perusal, he said, "I have a question."

"Certainly," Captain Nemo said.

"From these maps ... to the north is a low mountain range, then a fertile valley just before the sea. Is this correct?"

"Yes, there are some populated towns, but mostly farmland."

Celwyn rubbed his chin. "Indeed."

Pelaez removed Verne's bishop, tossed it in the air, and caught it again, then looked at Celwyn. "Do you intend on sharing your thoughts, or just expect me to perform miracles when our enemies attack?"

"Neither. I want to wait until the others are with us so that they can provide their perspective." He shrugged. "As you know, Xiau worries like an old woman. Sometimes with reason."

Pelaez asked, "What does Bartholomew do?"

"He becomes nervous and then provides insight." The Captain balanced his empty glass on his knee. "After that, he prays in his native language. It is quite beautiful to hear."

Pelaez said again, "The Soguns have only been in bed an hour or so..."

The Captain shook his head. "Tomorrow, after the tests and luncheon, we will confer."

"When we meet, I'll supply more background on Duncan that might help." As Celwyn spoke, Nemo's face relaxed again. The magician didn't mention that a germ of an idea had formed in his mind. Thankfully, it had occurred without any help from Thales. The last few days had been more pleasant without that experience, and the longer it continued, the more Celwyn predicted that he was free of Thales.

Chapter 34

BREAKFAST THE NEXT MORNING WAS a miserable event; that it was al fresco, in a cold, robust wind complete with blowing dust, did not provide a delightful epicurean experience. Bartholomew and Kang seemed oblivious to it, while Pelaez appeared amused at Celwyn's discomfort. The magician had planned to sleep after being on guard for hours, but this morning, he'd decided the danger would be even greater with the flying machine out in the open.

Earlier, Mrs. Sogun and her husband had brought a hamper of food to them as Celwyn sipped his tea and gazed back at the compound and distances between the buildings. Occasionally, specks of light reflected from the guards' spyglasses on the roof. The magician hoped they were the only ones watching the operation.

The Captain and Verne had joined them in an open-ended tent that the wind laughed at and whistled through. The tent did have the advantage of being located next to the field where Kang and his helpers trotted back and forth with clipboards and measuring devices. It also gave Celwyn a view to the south without having to stand outside.

Everyone awaited the moment when Bartholomew would return with the flying machine.

The magician left his camp chair and shivered. He had to control the urge to use magic on the confounded wind without either frightening the Soguns, the nearby guards, or, most importantly, changing the conditions of Kang's test. He'd been specifically—and peevishly—asked by Xiau not to interfere with the atmospheric conditions.

Probably ten miles or more to the west lay a range of low mountains under a mantle of mist that hung like a garland around the higher peaks. He turned to the south, to the undulating hills leading to the forests before the Mediterranean, which appeared much further away than the Black Sea and the *Nautilus*.

Captain Nemo and his team had chosen the landing location well. It was so flat Celwyn could have skated on it in winter. Next to it, and only feet away, the buildings stopped at a wall of rock, just as his brother said. No enemy could come at them from that direction. That only left the territory east of the complex from which an attack could occur.

The magician yawned and turned his attention to the new landing field, which began where the original field ended. The low brush had been cleared for a half mile beyond where the gravel gradually took over, framed on each side by a few of the stunted trees. The magician squinted beyond the immediate area, spying nothing alive except wolves and a few curious and furtive rabbits. The thought occurred to him that any of the animals could have been spellbound by Duncan. After a moment's scrutiny, he relaxed; he didn't detect the tell-tale glowing eyes that indicated they were more than simple animals.

Celwyn sat again and accepted a pastry from Mrs. Sogun. As he ate, he kept an eye on the Professor, who paced in front of the tent, oblivious to everything except his calculations. The automat tripped and got up again, still writing in his notebook. Beyond him, Captain Nemo had walked nearly halfway down the field with his hand shading his eyes against the dawn as he scanned the horizon for the flying machine. Just as Celwyn decided not to let Nemo walk any further away and possibly into the grasp of their enemies, he started back.

The magician glanced at the pleasant countenance of Mrs. Sogun and her husband, Franco, standing at attention by the entrance to the tent.

He asked Verne, "How do you say, 'please bring more tea' in Turkish?"

"*Lütfen daha fazla çay getir.*"

"Thank you. And 'take your husband with you.'"

Verne's brows went up, and he said, "*Lütfen kocanı da yanına al.*"

Silently, the magician sent those messages to Mrs. Sogun. When nothing happened, he sent them again, louder. She jumped.

"Come," she touched her husband's shoulder and waddled out of the tent toward the main house. Franco trailed her, grumbling, and passed by Captain Nemo re-entering the tent.

"Sir, do not be alarmed. In a moment, I will leave you for a short while," the magician warned him in a low voice. "You'll hear a short distraction for the guards."

Captain Nemo nodded, not quite understanding.

As if the wind had caused it, Celwyn knocked over the trash bins next to the house, and when everyone looked at the commotion, he transformed into a gray dove and flew out of the tent toward the field. He swooped over the Professor's shoulder and laughed in his own voice before turning toward the end of the field where the gravel began.

"Subtle," Kang called after him and resumed what he was doing.

Ten minutes later, once again, the trash bins went flying, and Celwyn landed, converting back as he settled into his camp chair again.

Nemo looked as if he'd just eaten a lemon, but didn't say a word. Pelaez waited with his hands dancing a jig on his knee, and Verne continued to sip coffee and make notes in his little notebook. Nothing phased him anymore. The door to the house opened, and the Soguns approached bearing trays of coffee and tea.

Before they reached the tent, Celwyn said, "We're clear. No unfriendly parties are out there. Right now."

Captain Nemo said dryly, "I trust you enjoyed your flight."

"Yes." He accepted a fresh cup of Earl Grey. "How much longer..."

A low hum reached them; then Captain Nemo shot to his feet. Everyone ran to the edge of the field.

The bright yellow flying machine crested the hills in the distance and made a wide arc upward before flying lower and leveling off as it neared the far end of the field. Seconds later, it flew so low it seemed to skim the top of the stunted trees.

With a roar of the engine, Bartholomew throttled down. The aeroplane bounced twice, landing and rolling toward them as it swerved and bobbed across the ground. Kang and his helpers rushed down the field. They stopped short until Bartholomew had turned the machine in a sharp circle, spraying gravel and coming to a full stop. Celwyn assumed brakes were a soon-to-be-developed feature.

The Captain began to clap, and the others joined in. The automat climbed onto the running board and opened the big man's door. Celwyn called his congratulations to them and stopped; a tingle down his spine told him to look at something he didn't want to see. He turned toward the trees.

Hell, and damnation. A mile away to the west, the tell-tale vapor trail of the warlock drifted upward.

Curses!

Celwyn's flight had been in vain.

As they sat down to luncheon, Kang and Bartholomew came through the door jabbering about wind ratios and riding high atop a cloud of celebration. The big man's laughter shook the windows, startling Mrs. Sogun as she placed the soup tureen on the table.

After the successful dawn landing, Captain Nemo's obvious relief made the magician sigh with the same. It would be years before the flying machine became common, but the first attainable step of the Captain's vision had come to fruition.

Nemo supervised as the wine was poured and admired. "A toast," he said as they touched glasses. "It has been a long and difficult journey, my friends. I cannot thank you enough." Their glasses clinked again. "You have accomplished the impossible."

"Here, here," Celwyn toasted them and smiled with fondness at his friends. He had no clue what they were doing to get the craft into the air, but felt their happiness as well.

Xiau picked up his spoon, then set it down again. "We had a wealth of knowledge to draw upon, and with Bartholomew's fine mind, we improved the theories until we were successful." The automat tried the soup and tilted his head to the side, trying to determine what was in it. "Mrs. Sogun, please let Fatima know this is one of the finest soups I have ever tasted."

"Perhaps it is because of the cumin in the broth?" Bartholomew suggested.

Pelaez shook his head. "I disagree. It is because of the lemon. The local ones here are just as fine as the ones from Seville."

From beside him, Verne ate as quietly as a nun, but his impish eyes missed nothing.

This was a historical event and a private one. Celwyn sent the author a silent message. *Remember our agreement, Jules. Everything that happens here is not for publication.*

The author dropped his spoon and shot Celwyn a hunted look. After reading the magician's expression, he nodded.

That taken care of, Celwyn asked, "Do you still need another week of tests?"

Bartholomew pursed his lips. "About that. Sir..." he turned to Captain Nemo, "...when will your new scientist arrive? Will he build the next prototype? We'll need a few days to go over our findings with him before we go."

"And answer his questions after he reviews the specs," the Professor added.

"Doctor Maeler will arrive in Unye by the ides of March next week."

Celwyn said, "May I suggest that when they meet him, to disguise him as a woman before bringing him here? The more feminine and flamboyant he appears, the better."

Verne stuttered, "A-a *woman*?"

"Yes. To fool the Mafioso, or Duncan, if they are still a problem."

Pelaez laughed. "Is that how we're sneaking our scientists out?" He looked over Bartholomew's muscular arms as offensively as he could. "I'm not sure what style will look best."

Celwyn shook his head. "Brother, use your imagination. We won't be limited in our plans." He saw Kang's raised skeptical brow. "Remember when I said Thales added something to my magical repertoire?"

Xiau's brows lowered again, and his expression indicated he didn't really want to know. "He certainly didn't instill any sense of caution in you, Jonas."

After the automat finished his complaining, with a smile Celwyn waved it away. "I am now much more adept at form changing. Things went well when I scouted the area beyond the field this morning. Doves are beautiful and most graceful."

"Humph. I've been too busy since then to talk to you about that," Kang said.

Talk of magic ceased as Mr. Sogun bustled through the kitchen doors, pushing the serving cart with their main course. Celwyn waited until he left again before saying, "I am planning to practice my new skill between now and the time we decamp. Or before we're attacked." He blinked at them as innocently as he could.

Bartholomew started to laugh, knowing the magician well.

Celwyn decided to begin his personal tutorial with Pelaez for two reasons. One, Bartholomew would probably enjoy it. Two, so would his brother. After Mr. Sogun had removed their plates, the magician caused the kitchen door to stick shut behind her and the crewmen in the room to fall asleep. Verne saw them and licked his lips.

The air surrounding Pelaez grew fuzzy. When it cleared, across the floor lay a long primitive tail attached to a fat belly covered in scales. Above that were tiny, set-in ears above a nearly three-foot-long jaw full of teeth. The thing had Pelaez's eyes, and its tail swished from side to side against the furniture. When Pelaez turned to face them, the toothy smile of the crocodile became a souvenir that none of them would forget. Bartholomew's eyes displayed a new level of superstitious alarm, and his glances at the front door measured if he could run there before the thing caught him. Kang patted him on the shoulder, saying it would be over soon.

What to do with Verne wasn't a mystery. In seconds, the author wiggled the nose of a fluffy gray rabbit, and his ever-busy ears appeared much taller than before. Satisfied, Celwyn turned his attention to Kang. When Xiau should have become a compact and intelligent cat, nothing happened, except his chin seemed more pointed. *Damn.* The magician had hoped Thales's enhancements could handle the mechanical aspects. "Hmmn. It seems my subjects must have a complete nervous system. I'll have to practice on beings who have one."

The automat smirked. "As you should."

Celwyn looked down his nose at him. "I will perfect it."

"This is quite—unsettling." Captain Nemo studied Pelaez and Verne with a somber frown. "But I cannot deny the artistry. Or the usefulness to our enterprise."

Celwyn added a set of emerald earrings to the crocodile. They tinkled against the rough scales of Pelaez's jaw when he moved his head. "This type of illusion will become part of our exit plans."

While he watched the rabbit and crocodile, Bartholomew tried his best to accept what frightened him. "You will have to explain to me how you do this, Jonas."

"I will." The magician considered it incongruous that the big man thought nothing of taking on a room full of ruffians but found magic hard to swallow.

The door to the kitchen creaked as someone pushed on it.

With a wave of Celwyn's hand, once again Pelaez relaxed in his chair, perfectly groomed and wearing a supremely sarcastic expression. Verne had just discovered his new paw before Celwyn changed him back. When he noticed his hand once again appeared as usual, he glanced at the others to see if they saw it, too.

Celwyn sniffed the air and sighed in happiness; a wonderful distraction had arrived.

"Baklava!" Kang cheered.

As Mrs. Sogun pushed the dessert cart forward, she gave the kitchen door a kick with her foot.

"That looks very good. Thank you." Bartholomew sat back as the housekeeper deposited a plate in front of him. "I'm very happy you and Fatima are friends, Jonas."

Pelaez's sarcasm surfaced. "That is his way of saying he is pleased you haven't scared the cook."

Chapter 35

A S THE BROTHERS WALKED ACROSS the courtyard to the barn-like building that housed the flying machine, Celwyn decided to spend the rest of the afternoon practicing his new skill. His brother would enjoy the session and could provide suggestions.

Bartholomew and the Professor had already returned to the hangar and now crawled over and under the yellow machine. The big man giggled over something Kang said and handed him a long-handled tool. Celwyn asked his brother to put the nighttime block on, even though it was only mid-afternoon. "And please make sure no one can see in here, spyglass or not." After Pelaez nodded, he turned to the scientists.

Bartholomew had taken to wearing white coveralls like Kang's and sported a matching collection of mechanical pencils in his breast pocket, along with a ruler. Celwyn realized he had never seen the big man's face so alive and so pleased. For the first time, the magician worried. "Are you planning on staying here, my friend?"

Bartholomew's head whipped around, and he stared. "No, but I thought about it."

Kang leapt out of the cockpit and landed in front of them. "He is more worried about keeping Annabelle and Patrick waiting for their wedding. And explaining to Zander and Otto why we've been gone so long." He smacked one of the machine's propellers, and it spun. "Nice. It has been oiled properly."

As Pelaez strolled to the oversized rolling doors and back, he smoked a cigar and blew rings high into the air. When he arrived under the doors, he swiveled and began a promenade toward the others again. He, too, seemed inordinately happy. The magician shrugged. It was odd—his brother usually seemed as grumpy as a bear.

Bartholomew tapped his clipboard. "I would like to return here again next year when our replacements have the next test machine built and where there are more questions and challenges to resolve."

"Someday, you will fly into the skies, then to the moon."

Bartholomew didn't laugh at Celwyn's prediction, instead nodding his agreement, much to the magician's surprise. He couldn't help asking Kang as he scooted out from under the wheel well, "Do you feel the same?"

"Hell, no. My wife would shoot me."

Celwyn laughed.

The automat sobered. "As it is, we had better hope those scouts heading to Trabzon send our telegrams when they arrive. Elizabeth is a patient woman, but there are limits."

One of their assistants approached Bartholomew with a clipboard. After they conferred, he returned to a pile of metal parts where he squatted and began to sort through them. When Celwyn glanced back, he found the automat eyeing him as if he'd grown another nose.

"Your assistants cannot see anything I do," Celwyn told them.

Bartholomew murmured, "That is good," as he twisted the bolt on one of the wheels. "They are very helpful, and I do not want them upset or nervous."

"Also, how difficult is it to change the composition of something that already exists? For instance, when you became a dove this morning?" The automat raised his voice over a strong downpour of rain that beat like an insane percussionist sitting on the metal roof overhead.

Celwyn glanced outside. The rain came down so hard he couldn't spy the end of the airfield, making it the kind of weather suitable for an attack. He nodded at Pelaez, who sauntered across the floor and stepped outside.

"Actually, creating the bird this morning had to be the easiest thing I've attempted in a long time." Celwyn had promised himself he wouldn't practice on Bartholomew, and Kang was too much of a challenge with his mechanical parts. A functioning illusion had challenges. That left only his brother.

When Pelaez returned inside, he strutted toward them as a fat baby bull with big ears and plump hooves. He heard the noise of his hooves and stopped walking long enough to slap his rear with his tail.

Celwyn suggested, "Turn your head normally."

Pelaez shrugged. "Like this?" He dipped his head and shook his ears.

"Are you sure our assistants can't see him?" Kang inquired in a low voice.

"Yes. Don't fuss." The magician studied his brother for a moment. "Do you feel as though you could trot as a bull would?"

Pelaez clopped forward at a bouncing gait, turned, and came back.

Celwyn told Kang, "I would say it is fairly easy, to answer your question. The problem is the energy needed to maintain it."

Over the next few hours, the scientists worked on the flying machine, and the magicians played. During a lull in the activity, Bartholomew stopped measuring something in the engine and stared at the peach tree the magician had made. He wet his lips and looked at Celwyn. "This doesn't bother me as much as it used to."

Celwyn clapped his shoulder. "Is that a good thing?"

The big man nodded. "I think so."

Two more guards arrived with Verne in tow, shaking off the rain and lowering their umbrellas. Kang called out from the machine's cockpit, "It appears you have some fresh subjects, Jonas."

296

After dinner, everyone relaxed by the game table and sofa. Captain Nemo excused the Soguns early, telling them that the guests would find anything they needed themselves. He didn't mention that Celwyn would do so without getting out of his chair.

The clock on the wall above the automat chimed.

"If we were on the *Nautilus* at this moment, we would hear the bells announcing the eight o'clock hour." Captain Nemo's voice contained a certain amount of melancholy. "We would just be finishing our dinner."

"And Qing would be pecking at the aquatic window," Celwyn said.

"And I would be looking for a bridge partner." Bartholomew stood over the chess table, frowning at the pieces.

Pelaez asked, "How many guards are there at night, Captain?"

"Ten, plus another four come on at midnight. The fence is fully armed also."

Bartholomew checked each corner of the room, looking into the shadows and the crisscrossed beams above them. "It is so quiet. It makes me nervous."

While the big man talked about his nervous premonition, Verne began a chess game with Pelaez. Apparently, he didn't mind some recreational cheating by his opponent.

Celwyn agreed with Bartholomew, and as he thought about their waiting game, he turned Verne into a pudgy duck, specifically resembling a spotted whistling he once had as a pet. He admired his work for a moment and changed him back. Pelaez cooperated by not pointing out the change to the author. Nemo watched the reversal with some effort before speaking.

"As you requested, I dismissed the staff so we could speak privately." The Captain asked, "What are we to talk about?"

"Our plans for when we're ready to decamp, Sir," the magician said. "Jules, would you and my brother join us here for a moment, please?" He pulled out the dining chair beside him.

As Verne arose, he stared at the chessboard. His queen had grown a snout and bulging eyes that stared back at him, seeming to accuse him of something. She had also acquired enormous breasts.

"Your queen is asking why you are endangering her," Pelaez drawled as he pushed his chair in.

"That wasn't me," Celwyn called. "Come, sit with us. We have a story to tell you."

When fresh drinks had been poured, and everyone had settled down, the magician took the floor. "As many of you know, I grew up in Scotland." Several of them nodded. "My brother and I heard stories from my father when we were young. One of them was about the ravens of the Tower of London."

Verne's eyes widened in interest. "That is…"

"It is truth. However, there is more to the story."

Pelaez took over. "Celtic myth maintained that the ravens were present in the Tower when Lady Jane Grey was hanged. By the way, someone should lose their head for botching that proceeding. Did you know they had to actually cut off her head? Anyhow, the birds also had a reputation for getting in the way of the king's astronomer, Brownlee."

"Interesting." Verne uncapped his pen without taking his eyes off Pelaez.

"However, it was considered highly unlucky to kill a raven, so the king moved the astronomer to a different castle," Celwyn told them.

Verne scribbled in his notebook. "This information was from your father?"

"He just confirmed it." Pelaez cleared his throat. "Did you know that the Welsh word for 'raven' is brǎn? At the time, Brǎn was the king of the land and resided in Castle Glamorgan."

"This is fascinating, but how does it apply to us?" the Captain asked.

"You will know very soon," Pelaez said. "The legend that maintains that as long as the ravens are in the Tower, England will not fall is true. Because of this prophecy, the six ravens of the Tower had their wings clipped to keep them there."

He recited a poem in a sing-song dialect straight from the ancient moors.

"*Noddais I 'myrd yn addwyn*
Er yu feb yr Awem fwyn
Yn ids ire r naws eirian
Fy myd I gyd oedd y Gan
Un o'm Ceraint ni'm carai"

Pelaez glanced around, expecting a compliment from his audience. "That is a poem from the 1790s about the ravens by Iolo Moranwg. He was known for his translations at that time."

"What does it mean?" Bartholomew asked.

Pelaez smirked. "I have no earthly idea. I just memorized it a long time ago."

"Really?" The Professor was exasperated, and Nemo wasn't far behind, judging from his glower at Pelaez.

"I apologize for my brother. We have more serious matters." Celwyn turned to the Captain. "Sir, the ravens in the Tower are the connection to us. Remember, Duncan is a warlock who has been around for hundreds of years. In Palermo, during our rescue of my brother, I asked Bartholomew to shoot Duncan in the elbow. That elbow has always been his weakness." He waited until the automat's eyes widened in understanding. The magician said, "*It is the clipped wing of a raven that never properly healed.*"

Kang's mouth fell open. "Duncan is one of the ravens of the Tower?"

"Oh, my!" Bartholomew said under his breath.

The automat glared at Celwyn. "Why didn't you tell us this?"

"Because you, the Captain, and Bartholomew were, and are, busy with the flying machine and do not need the distraction." The magician inhaled. "Until now, when we have to discuss it."

They all thought about what had been said for a moment, then Bartholomew murmured, "Duncan would be more than three hundred years old."

"If it was Charles II who clipped his wings, then Duncan is immortal also?" Captain Nemo asked.

"No." Celwyn shook his head. "Just lucky and clever, with plenty of spells to keep him alive. I intend to kill him."

"He isn't descended from gods, and he will die, I promise you." In contrast to the lethal look in his eyes, Pelaez's voice sounded pleasant.

"Warlocks are tricky. However, his tricks are the only thing protecting him." Celwyn envisioned several ways designed for the warlock's demise.

"Describe them?" The Professor requested as he opened a box of wood and unwrapped the tools that he'd brought with him. "What can he do compared to you and your brother?"

Pelaez grinned, not quite as disturbingly as when he was a crocodile. "That is like asking about the difference between a tiger and a snake."

The magician said, "Duncan's witchcraft is dark, based on elements of the earth, and his spells strong and ancient. He can protect himself from anything or appear literally out of thin air and everything in between. It is said he traveled across the Continent, found many other powerful warlocks, killed them, and stole their spells."

Kang scraped and shaped a chunk of the wood. It looked like another wooden replica of the flying machine.

Verne asked, "He casts spells? Doesn't that take time?"

"No." Celwyn rubbed his face, aware Kang would notice his aggravation growing. The automat saw everything. "He is as swift in his actions as any vampire. Victims and observers sometimes only see a blur before he arrives or attacks." The magician gestured at Bartholomew as if he held a weapon. "If he wants to run someone through with a sword, it happens faster than an opponent can react."

"How does he usually kill?" Kang asked.

Celwyn made sure he had all their attention before saying, "Usually, he is very close to his victim. He is fond of knives."

"Anything else to tell us about him?" The Captain's eyes ignited, accepting the challenge. He was not afraid of Duncan. Irritated, yes, but not afraid.

"From what I have seen and heard, he relishes the ritual of terror he can inflict on his victims before he attacks. He enjoys it as much as the kill itself." When Celwyn saw their faces, he decided it was time to refill their drinks and did so, leaving the bottles suspended in the air within everyone's reach as he produced another pot of tea for himself. "You now know what we know about Duncan."

Captain Nemo murmured through tightened lips, "This won't be easy."

"Nothing worthwhile is. Only this time the reward is our safety," Bartholomew said.

"Do you wish to finish the evening working on your paperwork for the flying machine or help us plot the demise of Duncan?" Celwyn asked Bartholomew and the Professor. The big man didn't move, and the automat just glowered at the magician as if this were another fine mess that he had gotten them into. Celwyn shrugged and smiled at him. Xiau didn't want to, but he smiled back and rolled his eyes.

"Capturing him wouldn't be an option to us?" the Captain asked.

Celwyn poured more tea and sipped. "No. He would eventually escape and hunt us."

"There's more, isn't there?" Bartholomew guessed.

Celwyn nodded at the big man's intuition. "The Captain has heard some of this already; Duncan usually kills his confederates in any nefarious games he is playing, and if he were successful in stealing Bartholomew, or the Professor, or the flying machine, he would eliminate the Mafioso working with him."

"That rather sounds like an additional benefit," Pelaez said.

Celwyn shrugged. "Perhaps." The magician preferred to eliminate his enemies himself.

"What else?" Kang asked. By now, he had the body of the first plane nearly done and had started on the cockpit.

For a moment, the magician debated. "His worst crime, in my opinion, was the murder of the children of St. Almster on the Jersey Islands. This happened during the Napoleonic War." Celwyn breathed deeply as tears filled his eyes. "He deserves to die. What I did to him back in Palermo was improvised with what was nearby, knowing it would only buy us time to get away. We need an intricate and very well thought out plan to truly rid the world of him."

With a certain amount of reluctance, the Captain asked the magician, "What do you propose?"

Before Celwyn could answer, his brother asked, "Do you plan to continue operations here after we leave?"

"If there is anything worthwhile left after a battle, yes." Nemo sighed. "I plan to finish the flying machine and build several prototypes."

The magician poured and shook the pot. It was empty.

"You go right ahead," Kang grinned at him.

The magician did so, and a freshly brewed pot appeared at his elbow. "In that case, we will need to draw our enemies away from here." He produced a smile that boded ill for their enemies. "Or arrange for them to think there is nothing to find here. I assume that when your new scientist arrives, things will be hectic. In two days, you say?"

Captain Nemo nodded.

Bartholomew asked, "Are you still planning on dressing him as a woman when he comes here?"

"Yes." The magician said, "Every time he walks among these buildings, or anywhere else, he will have to be disguised. The Mafioso, and probably Duncan, will be watching, even if we can't see them."

Bartholomew asked, "Captain, do the Soguns know of the *Nautilus*?"

"No one does." Nemo shook his head. "We keep our activities private."

Kang tapped the block of wood with a finger. "I'm betting a few governments know of the *Nautilus*."

"Correct. There are a few countries who suspect we exist and search for us. Such as the United States and their blasted Navy." With a wistful look, Captain Nemo enjoyed whatever thought ran through his mind. "They will be curious for a long time."

"Although an educating discussion, we still have an ordeal ahead of us," Bartholomew said. "It is good we have diverse skills among us."

"I appreciate that also." Verne nodded. "Especially in dangerous moments."

A comfortable silence surrounded them for minutes.

"It is at times like this that I am aware how fortunate I am to know all of you." Captain Nemo studied the shaded windows along the wall facing the courtyard. His gaze continued as if he could see all the way to the Black Sea, where the *Nautilus* awaited them. "And how tenuous knowing you is."

"Things are dangerous. However, it is all of us who are fortunate to have met you, Captain," Bartholomew said.

From the murmurings, they all agreed and would have brought out a bottle of champagne to toast the moment if it hadn't been so late.

"I wonder how the new scientist will react to all of this," Verne said.

"Would he fit in Fatima's or Mrs. Sogun's clothes?" Kang asked as he admired his carving, blowing the shavings into the air and causing the author to sneeze.

"There won't be a problem," Celwyn said. "When Doctor Maeler arrives in Trabzon, I will be there with a bag of clothes for the occasion, and I will adjust them as needed."

The automat drawled, "I'm sure he will appreciate the opportunity to dress himself."

"I thought you wanted to remain here to repel an attack." Bartholomew frowned.

The magician shrugged. "I should be, but safely transporting the scientist here is imperative, and it may take just as much effort to protect him. My brother will remain here, and we'll enhance our protections before I depart."

Kang eyed him. "By the way, Annabelle says you always make the shoes too small."

"Noted."

"What if those ruffians know you left?" Verne asked.

"I'll be in disguise when I leave the compound, and we won't be gone long."

Chapter 36

IT STILL LACKED A FEW MINUTES before two in the afternoon when dust clouds billowed beyond the gates, and the daily supply cart came to a stop in front of the main building. The horses pawed the ground and snorted. The cart's arrival from Tokat, and its regular assortment of newspapers, had been expected.

As usual, Celwyn and his brother approached the cart to observe the delivery, partly out of curiosity and because of the need for constant vigilance. The magician enjoyed exploring the variety of foodstuffs and scrutinizing the wine choices. As he replaced a bottle of Chablis in the case with the others, he felt a tickle of awareness slither across his face.

When he straightened again, he saw what he expected to see; a few feet away, Mr. Sogun watched the guards as they walked more boxes into the main building while the rest of the guards handed off crates into the storage building. The sensation of awareness intensified. When Celwyn glanced at the cart driver, the man's attention on the activity around him seemed casual, but his gaze kept returning to the building at the end of the compound containing the flying machine.

The magician passed behind two of the larger guards, and when he came out from behind them again, he flew upward, beating the translucent wings of a small fly. In an instant, he landed on the driver's rather dirty collar.

Half of the supplies remained to be unloaded. The driver slipped out of his raised seat, sauntered away from the cart, and toward the end of the compound. Celwyn entered his mind and heard grumbling in Italian—"*pistole*" and "*bastardi*," guns and bastards, the only words he recognized.

The driver neared the building containing the flying machine and, more importantly, Bartholomew and Kang. The guards in front turned toward him.

"Stop—Fermare!"

When the driver pulled a pistol from his pants, Celwyn bit his ear. The driver yelped and raised the weapon just as Kang opened the hangar door. The pistol went flying, and the automat dove behind some crates. Celwyn enlarged himself until he appeared as a ten-foot-tall fly with an even wider wingspan and his eyes burning like the sun. When the man saw him, the magician caressed his cheek with a long feeler.

"*Merda, oh Merda!*" The driver started to run. The magician picked him up, flying away with him across the field.

"Subtle again, Jonas," Kang called after him.

As he gained altitude, Celwyn could hear the shouts of Nemo's guards and spied Kang with his hands on his hips. The higher he flew, the louder his passenger screamed until he suddenly drooped. Celwyn tightened his grip and shrugged internally; there would be many more fantastic displays than this in the next few days.

Mist caressed the magician's cheeks with a delicate touch. As he flew, he realized this newfound ability to change appearances so readily opened a wonderful world of sensations—of perspectives and freedom. The short flight yesterday morning in semi-darkness had a serious purpose in mind. In contrast, today's breeze teased him, and he felt the welcome heat of the sun each time the clouds parted.

The ground became hilly, and the brush and trees denser as he flew. Like a silver snake, a sinuous river ran through it, occasionally glinting in response to the sun's rays. The magician shook his captive; he should be awake to appreciate the panoramic view. The ruffian groaned and went limp again.

Playing a hunch, the magician assumed the Mafioso camped in these low hills. They needed to hide and yet be near a source of water, and they wouldn't find that in the brush near Nemo's camp. Minutes more, he nodded in satisfaction as dozens of tents came into view nestled between the hills.

Thick trees concealed more tents and some of the heavily armed men who patrolled the camp.

Celwyn circled until he found the largest tent and made a slow pass overhead, dropping the driver on top of it. He flew a second pass, even lower, to ensure the rogues saw his gorgeous wings.

As he traveled back, the magician inhaled a measure of pleasure; in one afternoon, he had located the Mafioso and enjoyed hearing their outraged yells. A few of them chose to express themselves by dropping to their knees to pray.

＊　＊　＊

Over dinner, Celwyn related the details of his recent flight.

"You do have a block on what the Soguns can hear?" Kang asked, and Celwyn nodded.

"Ah. Now, I know what happened to the driver." Captain Nemo glanced at the kitchen door. "Fatima complained to the others, loudly, that the devil had taken the driver away."

"Of course, that is so much better than telling her a giant fly kidnapped him," Kang observed as he cut into his trout.

Bartholomew laughed, somewhat cautiously, as if that kind of luck would befall him if he found it amusing.

"Sir, what were your guards' reactions to what they saw?" Pelaez asked.

Captain Nemo rubbed his face, a frequent sign of annoyance, and downed his wine without tasting it. "I sat them down with the crew I brought from the ship. They are used to these, ah, activities. I instructed them to explain it to the others. Since we'll be leaving soon, that should be enough to keep the unease under control."

Celwyn waited for Mr. Sogun to serve more of the scalloped potatoes before saying, "Captain, we will arrange the confrontation with our enemies to occur elsewhere. That should help." After Mr. Sogun retreated to the kitchen, he added, "I can wipe what the guards saw from their memories, if you prefer, but the attack also served to highlight how dangerous things are right now. It might inspire their vigilance instead."

"I will consider it." Nemo eyed him. "Taking the danger elsewhere is much appreciated. Do you want to tell us the details? Or do I want to be surprised?" His eyes gleamed. He enjoyed a confrontation as much as Bartholomew.

Kang spoke, sounding as dry as possible, a sure sign he was trying to be amusing. "Sir, you do want to know. Jonas has no sense of self-preservation, much less common sense." Xiau patted a pretend yawn. "Thankfully, Bartholomew and I are here to help him." By the time he finished speaking, Bartholomew was snickering into his sleeve.

When he could, the big man said, "Today's incident proves that our enemies either tracked us here or they bribed enough people to find us."

"But, not necessarily Duncan." Pelaez paused to chew. "Today was a test by the Mafioso to see what we'd do."

Celwyn held up a hand. "I saw evidence of Duncan at their camp and bits of his luminescence outside *our* landing field."

"Any of it inside the compound?" Pelaez asked.

"Not that I could see." The magician asked Nemo, "Sir, what time does Dr. Maeler arrive tomorrow?"

"Noon. I understand your brother will place an unpassable field around us until you return."

Pelaez nodded.

"I will need a letter of introduction from you asking for his cooperation while we disguise him." Celwyn savored a last bite of cheese and watched Mrs. Sogun as she returned with the coffee service. That caused him to wonder what their dessert would be when it arrived. "As discussed, I will also be in disguise so that no one realizes I have left the compound."

Kang asked, "Could Duncan detect that?"

"Only if he gets close enough," Pelaez said. "I'll be watching to be sure he doesn't."

Captain Nemo sampled his potatoes, approved, and ate more before saying, "Then, I believe we are ready for Doctor Tavros Maeler."

In his form of celebration, Pelaez lifted a hand, and his pig started across the room. Celwyn stopped it before the Captain discovered it. Bartholomew saw the pig dissolve and chewed faster.

A volley of shots peppered the courtyard like firecrackers. Pelaez and Celwyn bolted for the front door, with Bartholomew in close pursuit.

Celwyn darted out and crouched behind the perimeter wall, with the others doing the same while the big man tried to shoo the automat back inside. More shots erupted in front of the hangar, and their guards fired back at two score or more attackers. Another pack of armed hooligans ran toward them from across the field.

Pelaez leaned close to his brother. "Cover me." Celwyn did so as his brother inhaled, flexing his hands and standing tall. Then he brought his hands forward as if lifting a great weight.

With a roar, a great wind arose, blowing the attackers backward, tumbling them head-over-heels across the field. With raised arms, Pelaez and Celwyn walked toward them, and the magician added more wind, tossing them into the air like toys. Nemo's guards backed up, amazed and frightened.

Kang thudded to a stop behind the brothers.

"You plan to scare them, not kill all of them, correct?" he asked. "To send a message back to their leader?"

Celwyn had just driven most of them into the air again and then sighed. "I suppose." He didn't block their fall to the ground. He bowed to Pelaez. "After you."

With the malevolent smile Celwyn expected, Pelaez left them and strolled toward the field in a ball of fire that grew bigger the further he went.

In a deep and sonorous voice, Pelaez intoned, "*Dio ti maledice*! God curses you!"

The fireball flared, and thunder boomed over-head, shaking the ground as the attackers ran for their lives across the field and into the brush.

Bartholomew and Kang clapped. "Bravo!"

313

Celwyn slapped Pelaez on the back as he rejoined them. "We won't have any trouble the rest of the night."

"I agree," the automat murmured. He peered through a spyglass, watching the intruders' retreat as they reached the trees. They wasted no time mounting the collection of horses waiting for them and whipping them into a retreat.

With a raised fist, Captain Nemo shouted, "Bastards!" as the horses disappeared into the trees. He took off at a jog. "Excuse me while I see to my men."

The magician caught up to him by the hangar, finding two of the guards on the ground and bleeding. Celwyn gestured at the remaining men. "If you would distract them for a moment, the Professor and I will see to the wounded."

As Kang and Bartholomew ran up to them, Nemo motioned the remainder of the guards through the hangar doors.

Pelaez caught Celwyn's nod and blocked the area where the bleeding guards lay; they needed privacy from anyone else who might be looking, either friend or foe. The magician caused the wounded guards to lose consciousness as he knelt beside them, and after a moment, he handed Kang a bullet from the first man. He pointed to where he removed it. "A serious shoulder injury. It appears to be good now. Do you agree?" He produced the medical contraption Kang used to listen to patients breathe and handed it to a very surprised automat.

"Err … thank you." Kang squatted beside him and checked the man's shoulder first, then the rest of him. "Yes. Very neatly done. You would have made an excellent surgeon instead of a provocateur."

"Pffft." Celwyn had moved to the other man, noting the wound in his thigh bleeding profusely. In minutes, he'd stemmed the flow and handed over another bullet. "He was lucky. This could have been worse."

Kang verified all was well and nodded. "I need to clean the wounds properly and make sure they are bandaged so they do not cause problems. Remove your block so they can see me." He gestured to another set of guards waiting in the hangar with a stretcher. "I'll follow you to the barracks in a moment."

The magician stood, stretched, and sent Captain Nemo a silent message that they were done. He asked Pelaez, "Do you have any changes to our nighttime protection based on this attack?"

Pelaez stared at the scene. "No. I usually don't apply our protection until dark to conserve my energy. But now, it will be in place much more of the time."

"I'll do the same for the rest of the buildings and main house." Celwyn gazed beyond the fields. "It will mean an extra nap or two."

The big man didn't smile at the magician's joking. "Do we need more guards?" he asked. Increased concern painted his face, and he jumped onto the parapet to see further beyond the compound. The attack had cracked open the warm cocoon of science protecting his world.

As Captain Nemo joined them, he heard the question. "I hope not. It would take a week to find more men and vet them." He gestured to his guards, and they took the wounded away. "I assume that we will be on our way to the coast by then?" He eyed the scientists.

"Yes," Bartholomew and Kang said at the same time.

"Going forward, perhaps the gate should be locked during the day, not just at night. And the batteries turned on." Nemo waved the rest of his guards back to their stations and switched to the scientists. "I'll also add a few more men from the day shift for tonight's patrols, just in case." As they walked back to the main building, he added, "After we finish our dessert, I propose we have a rousing game of bridge to distract us from this unpleasantness. We only have a few more days here, and I'll be busy once we're on the ship again."

"Why didn't the guards on the roof see them coming?" Bartholomew asked.

With surprised looks, they gazed upward, seeing no one.

It wasn't often the magician heard Nemo curse, but he did then, virulently, as he waved a pair of his men to the roof. Minutes later, they heard that both guards had rifle wounds but were alive. Celwyn and the automat climbed up to the roof while Nemo sent for more stretchers.

Verne had been waiting for them at the front door, with the Soguns close behind him, wearing worried faces. When Fatima saw everyone approaching the house again in good health, she whirled and, in a flurry of skirts and scarves, retreated to her kitchen.

"I'm so glad that is over with." The author trailed them inside, saying, "I wish to be Bartholomew's partner for bridge."

Celwyn understood. Apparently, Pelaez's cheating was not to be borne while playing bridge. Chess, yes, bridge no.

Chapter 37

MOZART PLAYED SOFTLY FROM THE phonograph, putting Celwyn into a contemplative mood as he watched the bridge players begin their game. *Why had the Mafioso attacked now? Retaliation for the ostentatious return of their infiltrator?* The magician had a feeling there were scores more of them out there; there had been time to send out for more of the villains. Perhaps the point had been to discover what Nemo's defenses were capable of or at what point the magician took over. He enjoyed speculating on what they thought of Pelaez's windstorm.

The bridge game progressed, with Pelaez partnered with Captain Nemo. From nearby, Celwyn could study the Captain's hand while he willed the automat to make a move. Kang's caution at chess stemmed from his intellect—and from knowing Celwyn couldn't read his thoughts. He also won a bit more than his share of the games. The magician waved at the phonograph for another recording, choosing Thaddeus Baylor's parlor guitar. An unseen hand operated the hand crank, and soon they heard a sweet melody.

"Sir, if you were to attach one of your batteries to the phonograph and to a connection with a regulator that Xiau and I could devise, that should provide automatic turning of the crank for the music after we leave. The Soguns and Fatima might enjoy it. We could do the same for when we're on the ship. Do you agree?" Bartholomew asked Kang, who nodded.

"That is much appreciated. You'll have several weeks for that while we travel to Prague." Nemo and the others watched the automat squat in front of the phonograph and examine the workings.

"Jonas, when you and the Soguns pick up Dr. Maeler tomorrow..." Bartholomew sorted his cards, "...do you still plan to be in disguise?" He sent Verne a straight look and said pointedly, "Six hearts." Verne licked his lips nervously and tried to smile at him. Bartholomew sighed.

"Yes. I do not want our enemies to know that I have left the compound. Also..." Celwyn moved his knight, "...I love to dress up."

Kang feigned surprise. "We know you do."

"Bartholomew, you and Mr. Verne can have the bid." Pelaez chuckled and turned to Nemo. "Captain, do you think the habits and abilities of our merry little party will scare Maeler?"

Bartholomew took a trick and smiled at Verne's surprise. "I have several other hearts, too."

While they played, the magician leaned back and studied the chessboard. He should have been paying more attention; Kang had his bishop pinned.

Captain Nemo won the next trick. "I have never met Doctor Maeler and know little about him except his scientific background. My agent in Cairo reports he is supposed to be of medium height."

Bartholomew asked, "Is he married?"

"I have no idea." Another trick went by, and Nemo glared at Pelaez. "I thought you had hearts."

Pelaez blinked at him. Celwyn sent him a silent message to behave.

Bartholomew gathered up the final trick. "Well, we are removed from civilization out here. I hope he brought books and other entertainments."

⌣

By noon the next day, Celwyn remembered Bartholomew's hope for Doctor Maeler's entertainment and smiled; Maeler had indeed brought along his own entertainment.

The early hours of the morning had passed peacefully, with Bartholomew and Kang holed up with their clipboards and the flying machine while the others perused books and newspapers. Celwyn spent the time perfecting his disguise for the day. When the magician walked into the main room of the house, Pelaez stopped trying to light a cigar and stared.

Captain Nemo found his voice first. "I would not recognize you in that, Jonas."

Celwyn bowed. "A compliment, thank you."

From his white, bushy brows to his bent stature, cane, gnarled hands, and thick horn-rimmed glasses, Celwyn had transformed into an elderly academic. Walking stooped over disguised his height, and he'd perfected an unsteady shuffle as he hummed nonsense to himself.

"That voice." From across the room, Verne stopped writing in his notebook and marveled. "It is unlike anything I expected. It is so ... so..."

"High-pitched and squeaky," Celwyn supplied. "I hope it is distracting, too." In his normal voice, he said, "Captain, how did you explain my disguise to the Soguns?"

"They know it is you, as a Mr. Wynn, who is traveling with them to pick up my new employee. That is all."

Verne approached and felt Celwyn's whiskers. "They are so soft!"

⌒‿⌒

As Celwyn tottered down the walkway to the waiting coach, he made a point of exaggerating his infirmity and avoided looking at the terrain beyond the fence. His boat hat shaded the top of his face above the fluffy mutton-chop whiskers Verne had admired.

In moments, Celwyn had climbed into the carriage beside Mrs. Sogun and greeted her. Although she started at the sight of him, she did her best. "Welcome aboard, Mr. Wynn." Her greeting sounded loud enough for anyone nearby to hear. "Mr.

Sogun is staying behind, but we will have several guards with us."

The magician responded just as loudly. "That sounds wonderful, Madam." Celwyn lowered his voice to ask, "Are you aware that we'll disguise Doctor Maeler before returning?"

She lifted her brows in moderate disapproval. "Yes."

It only took three hours to reach Unye after leaving Tokat. According to Kang's personal written tour guide he'd pressed upon the magician; the city had been founded 700 years before Christ.

Unye appeared much larger than Celwyn had expected, with hundreds of houses and a park lined with historical statues dedicated to the various invaders from over the years. Mrs. Sogun informed him that the city had been a part of the infamous Silk Road, the trading route that linked the East and West. It surprised Celwyn to learn that the city was originally Greek, not Turkish. The only thing the magician really knew about it was its reputation for first-class wines.

As they clopped down a dusty street toward the center of town, their carriage passed a stable and various storefronts. Before long, they disembarked in front of a linen seller, and the magician waited while the housekeeper bought enough cloth for new curtains and something more ornate for a tablecloth. Twenty minutes later, they approached the rail yard.

Celwyn had grown used to enormous train yards and found the Unye's terminal so small he searched until he verified that it indeed had tracks. Two locomotives sat in the yard, one with eight cars and another with twelve cars and an engine that still seeped steam as it cooled. Neither were of the *Elizabeth's* class but appeared sturdy and popular. He counted at least two-score more passengers either disembarking or standing by as they watched their luggage loaded aboard the second train. Workers shoveled coal into the coal bins, and the memories of traveling by rail reminded him of how much of it he'd done in the last year.

Although he knew, the magician asked Mrs. Sogun, "Where is the telegraph office?"

Her attention had been centered on the herd of passengers, but shifted toward him.

"There, sir." She pointed.

As they entered the terminal, Celwyn maintained his disguise and sang a ditty to himself, keeping time with his cane as he shuffled from side to side. It would be satisfying to add a little jig, but not wise. What if others joined in? Instead, he leaned on Mrs. Sogun's shoulder as they crossed the wooden floor toward the telegraph counters. Her expression reminded him of the automat's when he had used up all his tolerance.

While in Palermo, Kang had sent several tele-grams letting Annabelle know that Celwyn had survived and asking her to make sure the boys heard the news as soon as possible. The telegrams did not describe the journey ordered by Thales. Here it was weeks later, and Bartholomew and Kang had helped craft a careful telegram to Tellyhouse that did not convey the danger surrounding them with the flying machine but would read just as informatively. Kang's message to Elizabeth contained a remarkably similar message, and they had no doubt the two missives would be compared.

The magician had just finished sending the telegrams when he heard Mrs. Sogun's intake of breath in a disgusted hiss. Her lips were set, and brows lowered as she stared at the terminal entrance.

"Mrs. Sogun?"

Her voice matched her reaction. "That man looks like the description of Doctor Maeler. Yes, that is the man."

Celwyn studied the stranger's tiny ears and face as round as a cantaloupe. From his hair to his shoes, the man appeared brown all over. The magician mentally measured Maeler and knew he'd have to shorten the dress he'd made for him and let it out at the waist. The scientist's little pot belly must be at least fifty inches around. However, it wasn't the pot belly that caused the housekeeper's reaction.

As he scrutinized the new scientist's companion, and object of Mrs. Sogun's ire, Celwyn decided he wouldn't have to depend on her to apply cosmetics to Maeler or to artfully arrange the ribbons and jewelry he would wear.

A woman, taller and broader than Dr. Maeler, rested her fingers on his arm in a proprietary manner. It appeared their new scientist had brought along his own entertainment, and one that did not resemble a collection of Darwin's Essays. The woman's brassy blonde hair had been piled precariously high, and her decollate left on display in an indecently bright red dress more common in the saloons of the American wild west. The curve of her painted lips could be seen from twenty paces away, and in her other hand, she held a long cigarette holder.

No doubt about it, she reminded the magician of the prostitutes he had observed in Carson City, and he wasn't the only one with that impression.

"Floozy," Mrs. Sogun muttered.

A close look at the woman verified their observation; her eyes were avarice-fueled and bright blue under a canopy of darkened lashes. They hunted and hungered and hardly blinked. When the woman spied Mrs. Sogun and Celwyn, a sly smile curled her lips, and she murmured in Maeler's ear.

As the pair began walking toward them, Celwyn informed Mrs. Sogun that he would handle the situation. Her response sounded like something between a growl and a spit.

They met in the middle of the terminal.

Celwyn laid a restraining hand on the housekeeper's arm and bowed, which wasn't too far considering his character's stooped position. "Doctor Maeler? I am Mr. Wynn, representing Captain Nemo."

Maeler bowed in return. "Pleased to meet you." He ushered the woman forward, along with a cloud of perfume. "This is Virginia May Ford, my fiancée."

The woman stood much too close to Celwyn, dipped her cleavage lower, curtsied, and purred, "Pleased to meet you, Honey."

Before the housekeeper could react, Celwyn said, "And this is Mrs. Sogun. She and her husband oversee the household at the Captain's compound." After Mrs. Sogun pried her lips open in a grimace at them, he added, "We must speak in private. Please come this way."

The magician shuffled forward, steering everyone to an unoccupied corner of the terminal, and for added measure, provided a block around them.

"Did the Captain mention in his telegrams that there are competing interests for the project you will be working on?"

Maeler eyed him. "Yes, he did."

"Good. Now that you are here, you should know that there are dangerous forces afoot and that we must take precautions." Celwyn held up his cane, blocking the man's retreat. "There is no need for alarm. There are things that you will soon learn that will ease your fears. However, first, we must get you out of this terminal."

"We can't just walk out?" he asked.

The magician handed him the bag containing the clothes, shoes, and a wig. The good doctor would have to get used to his new costume; Celwyn didn't plan to dress him every day. "Please take Miss Ford with you into the women's lavatory over there." Celwyn pointed to the corner near the exit. "When you emerge again, you will be wearing a costume to mask your identity."

Miss Ford peeked in the bag and started to laugh as Maeler sputtered, "*Excuse* me?"

The woman announced with a broad smile, "You'll be dressed as a woman, darling!"

"No, I won't!"

Celwyn murmured in his ear, "Yes, you will." He showed him Captain Nemo's letter asking for his cooperation.

"I cannot go into the women's lavatory!" Maeler whined.

Celwyn gave them a gentle push toward it. "I can assure you no one will notice."

Chapter 38

WHEN MAELER AND MISS FORD emerged from the terminal, two of Nemo's guards escorted them as they minced their way with surprising ease across the uneven ground to the carriage. Celwyn decided the scientist must have been coached by his fiancée on how to walk in a long dress and high-heeled boots.

Under a hat Annabelle would have approved of, he wore the full fluffy wig and a liberal amount of rouge that gave his sallow cheeks a bit of life. Yet, it was the thick layer of lip paint that drew the eye. Well aware of prying eyes all around them, Celwyn encouraged the couple into the carriage and clambered in after them. Mrs. Sogun had already boarded and glared from the corner seat like a highly annoyed cat.

After everyone had settled in, Celwyn closed the drapes in the cab and sighed. The coach lurched forward, and they were on their way.

In his own voice, he said, "Miss Ford, my compliments. Your companions' disguise and cosmetics are perfect."

Maeler stared. "Your voice is different."

Celwyn shrugged. "I am also in costume."

The woman regarded him with renewed, non-prurient interest. "Call me Ginnie; everyone does. Don't they, Pookie?" She snuggled into Maeler. He allowed her to peck his cheek as he fussed with the gloves that he'd been forced to wear.

"These are tight," he growled.

While Celwyn hesitated, deciding if magic would or wouldn't make things worse for the man, Ginnie laughed. The sound wasn't musical but instead reminiscent of a backroom bordello Mrs. Sogun would do more than sniff at.

"I'm afraid the bloomers you gave Pookie weren't big enough, so we made do without them!" She winked.

Mrs. Sogun's mouth fell open, and before she could say anything, the magician plunged ahead, saying, "It will take us about three hours to arrive at the compound, and we have armed guards on horseback with us. It will appear to anyone watching that Mrs. Sogun and I are escorting two women." Celwyn thought it best not to mention yet that Maeler would have to be similarly dressed for the next week. "I'm hoping there won't be an incident along the way, but if so, I am also armed." He didn't say how.

"Your voice is so deep and so different. So delightful," Ginnie purred. "I rather like it."

Celwyn ignored her and focused on the scientist. "Did the Captain's agent explain what you will do at the compound?"

Maeler shrugged lace-covered shoulders, and the oversized flower on his hat bobbed. "Somewhat. He has a prototype for a flying machine, and he wishes to build several more."

"Correct. My associates, Professor Xiau Kang and Bartholomew, will tell you of the details of the prototype and the handover of work, which will take about three to five days or more. At that point, most of us will be on our way, leaving you in charge. The Professor and Bartholomew will be in communication with you if you should have further questions." He checked Ginnie's expression out of the corner of his eye and noted she listened to each word as carefully as if she had memorized them. "When we leave, the danger from the competitors will also disappear."

Maeler peeked out the back curtain. "Did you get all of our luggage? My texts are in them."

"And my fancy drawers!" Ginnie gushed, "You'll have to borrow some of them, Pookie." She guffawed and elbowed him. Mrs. Sogun was too shocked to speak.

"We have most of your luggage strapped to the top of this carriage," the magician said. "The guards have the rest." They rode in silence for several minutes. "Permit me to tell you about the compound and what to expect—"

"—I would prefer to hear about the prototype," Maeler said through his rouged lips.

Celwyn sighed. "Other than it is painted a bright yellow, I know nothing. I am not a scientist or engineer."

"What do you do?" Ginnie asked.

Celwyn didn't hesitate. "One might say that I provide harmony."

⁓

Hours later, they drove through the gate of the compound, and Celwyn reminded Doctor Maeler to leave his wig on and stay in character until he was inside the house. In his disguised voice, he requested that Maeler "walk like a woman, Dearie."

After they rolled to a stop, the magician helped Mrs. Sogun to the ground and then Ginnie, who held his hand a bit too long. As soon as their coachman helped Maeler down, Celwyn grabbed his cane and hobbled as fast as his disguise allowed toward the front door.

Everyone came out of the house to greet them, and the magician informed the Captain, "We have a second guest, courtesy of Maeler."

Nemo's brows lowered, and he frowned at the woman. Bartholomew stared. As they listened to Ginnie's loud exclamations about their journey filled with American colloquialisms, they approached the carriage. The magician watched the scene from a few feet away, safely out of Ginnie's reach. When he read her thoughts, he found them lewd, speculative, and directed at the Captain. He also thought it wise not to repeat them to Nemo.

Basking in the full brightness of the late afternoon sun, the scientist did appear a bit gaudy, and his wig slightly askew. Celwyn fixed it without touching him. When Nemo reached the carriage, he eyed Ginnie without favor; at least she wasn't aboard the *Nautilus*.

Celwyn had a good view of the Professor and Bartholomew when they stopped in front of the newcomers. Amusement tugged on Kang's lips at the sight of an eminent man in a low-cut dress holding a lace handkerchief. Still enjoying himself and trying not to giggle, the Professor suggested, "It would be best if we went inside."

Bartholomew controlled his reaction at the sight of Dr. Maeler's wiggling walk but couldn't help saying, "It is a mite warm this afternoon, and our guests are beginning to perspire."

When they neared the front of the house, Maeler spied the guards on the roof and tripped over his dress. Bartholomew steadied him and held open the door. "They are there for our protection."

With a final glower of disapproval at Ginnie, Mrs. Sogun left them as fast as she could and passed through the swinging doors and into the kitchen. Celwyn sighed. As far as he was concerned, his responsibility to manage the new guests had ended as soon as they stepped inside. His whiskers itched, and he debated whether to change out of his disguise in front of everyone, or more privately. When he saw Maeler drop the glass of water Verne had procured for him, the magician excused himself and headed down the hallway to the guest quarters. It wouldn't do to upset Captain Nemo's new scientist needlessly.

There would soon be plenty of that occurring without his help.

Over a late luncheon, Celwyn observed the relief in Captain Nemo and the hope in Verne's face that they would soon be on their journey home. As everyone began eating, the author stole a glance to his left, seeming to find Ginnie amusing, somewhat in the way he would a garish monkey that had learned to talk.

"Where is Mr. Wynn?" Maeler asked. "I wanted to thank him for his assistance."

Celwyn raised a brow at Captain Nemo. He hesitated, then shrugged an affirmative answer.

"I am right here, Sir," the magician said in Wynn's voice.

"But … you were introduced as Mr. Celwyn."

Ginnie's reaction was based on other criteria. "You are so much younger and most handsome." She leaned toward him.

The magician cringed and stole a look at Kang, who started to laugh. Celwyn kicked him on the shin.

"We are one and the same, Madam," Celwyn said in his own voice before pinning Maeler with the same look he used to make Verne squirm. "As I indicated earlier, until we depart for the coast, you must be in disguise every time you leave the house to visit the prototype or for any other purpose. We are being watched."

"By whom?" Maeler managed.

Pelaez said, "The Mafioso."

Ginnie paled and would have toppled into her soup if Bartholomew hadn't stopped her.

Dr. Maeler demonstrated the kind of logic Professor Xiau Kang was known for. "What do they have to do with me?"

Captain Nemo finished his soup and replaced his spoon. "They are criminals who will try to kidnap whoever built, or can build, more of the flying machines. However, as Mr. Celwyn has stated to you, when we leave, they will follow us. Their prime targets are Professor Kang and Bartholomew. If you follow our instructions and maintain your disguise, they will assume you are just a female guest here and won't bother with you."

"I see." Maeler ran a lingering gaze over Bartholomew and then Kang, as if they might sprout wings. Little did he know.

Ginnie fanned herself and put a hand on top of Maeler's. "It is only for a few days, Pookie."

Captain Nemo recoiled, despite himself, at hearing the endearment. Celwyn smiled privately, wondering if the well-behaved vampires were beginning to seem preferable to Nemo at this point.

"As soon as we're done here," Bartholomew said, "the Professor and I will be honored to show you the flying machine and begin transferring our knowledge to you."

Like a field of short black grass in a field of snow, Maeler's beard had begun to show, and his teeth appeared yellower because of the liberal amount of powder on his face. The man smiled a superior smile and said, "I have a doctorate from Berlin University and may not need schooling from you."

The magician bet Kang wished he could perform a bit of magic to answer their new guest.

With their early dinner over, Celwyn opted to visit the flying machine with everyone else, especially after Ginnie announced she would stay behind at the house. Bartholomew sent him a knowing smile, and Xiau said loudly, "Are you sure? You usually take an afternoon nap on the sofa."

The magician added a lively mouse to the automat's pocket as he closed the front door and followed him and the others toward the hanger. Maeler asked a few questions that Nemo answered, including one about the pairs of armed guards in the yard.

"Where is Verne?" Bartholomew asked as he watched the automat jump and fling the mouse out of his pocket. The magician chuckled.

After Kang glared at Celwyn, he said, "Writing in his room and hoping things stay quiet so that he can do so."

While they walked, the magician half-heard the technical chatter from Bartholomew and the Professor. He again felt a vague feeling of unease that fluttered like a drunken butterfly from side to side in his gut. He discounted the source of worry as coming from one of the newcomers; they did not pose an imminent threat compared to Duncan and the Mafioso. Moreover, he could easily restrain them if they misbehaved. With little provocation, he could give Maeler a few feminine adjustments that would remain with him for a while.

The next few days passed peacefully and pleasantly as Kang and the big man worked with the new scientist in his fluffy wig. When it reached the hottest part of the afternoon, Maeler tossed the wig off. And the pearls, too. His superior attitude had also been discarded as he fell in love with the flying machine, marveling over the design with Kang and Bartholomew. They would huddle together for an hour over a particular detail and finally decide to add it to the list of things to do.

Because of the humid afternoon air, the dress Doctor Maeler wore had started to look the worse for wear by the second day, as did his stockings, which bagged around his knees and ankles. When it was time to go back to the house, Celwyn tidied him while he wasn't looking, and Bartholomew held a mirror up so that the wig could be planted on Maeler's head again.

As they came through the front door of the main house, the temperature immediately dropped to a more manageable coolness. Celwyn left a clean dress in Maeler's room; perhaps he would be just as alluring in blue taffeta.

After everyone patronized the bar, they settled on the sofas with sighs reflecting on a long day. Celwyn noted that the Professor seemed fussier and jumpier than usual this afternoon, evidenced by his inability to sit still and his reaction when Pelaez dropped a book behind him off the top library shelf. It could have been on purpose. Bartholomew eyed the automat also before he presented Captain Nemo with a list. "Sir, this is the personnel and materials we need going forward."

A short discussion of the list followed, and then Ginnie excused herself to freshen up. As soon as she closed the hallway door behind her, the magician blocked what Maeler could hear.

Pelaez leaned against the mantel next to the wooden flying machines that Kang had carved. Although the models looked to be no bigger than a man's hand, one of the cockpits contained a replica of the Professor himself, with Bartholomew recognizable as the pilot in the second. The third pilot greatly resembled the original carving of the otherworldly visitor with the odd, flat face.

"Captain, Doctor Maeler cannot hear us. I know everyone has been busy, but could you all..." the magician nodded at the others, "...please tell us approximately when we will decamp from here now that you are acquainted with him?"

Several surprised looks passed between the group. Finally, Bartholomew said, "Today is Thursday. If we continue as we are now, we could leave on Sunday."

Pelaez finished off his drink and said, "Thank you. Very soon, we need to confer at greater length without our be-wigged friend here and his paramour. Perhaps," he turned to Kang and Bartholomew, "You could give him a task tomorrow during the day? Either Jonas or I would distract the woman. We do not want them to talk of our departure or be nervous because of it."

Celwyn twisted his mustaches and blinked at them. "Or after dinner tonight, I can guarantee they will retire early. Will that suffice?"

With a highly amused and alternately suspicious look, Captain Nemo said, "Let's talk now. Before that woman returns."

"As you wish." The magician caused Maeler to fall asleep, and they immediately heard his gentle snore, somewhat like a noise a stuffed-up parrot would make.

"Is your ship waiting for us off the coast of Trabzon?" Pelaez asked.

Captain Nemo nodded at him. "Yes."

Verne asked, "Why Trabzon instead of Unye?"

"Because the Mafioso will be watching for us there. Trabzon is hours north of Unye," Nemo told him.

"Not all of us are traveling in the direction of Trabzon initially." Celwyn inhaled with satisfaction. His plan came together as he talked. He chuckled; Xiau would faint if he knew how often that happened. Pelaez eyed him and nodded slightly.

To the others, he said, "Please stop us if any of this doesn't make sense or you see a better way. Doctor Maeler and his, err ... paramour, won't be told of our actual departure until we're gone. Neither will the guards left behind, except for Hobbs, their superior officer." Celwyn locked the door leading to the hallway and their rooms in case Ginnie decided to return. "We will travel lightly. Most of us only brought knapsacks, and that is all we'll leave with."

Captain Nemo rested his chin on his chest and regarded him. "Please describe how you intend to draw the Mafioso away from here."

"We're planning on leading them in the opposite direction of where you and the others will go." Pelaez shrugged as if his news was boring to him if not for the others listening. "We'll make sure the Mafioso follows us to the area by the mountain where we initially arrived, the one by the city of children."

"They will be led into a trap." Celwyn produced tea and poured it. Their imminent departure will be exciting, and it was time to celebrate the plan. "I believe we will be successful in tricking the Mafioso. However, I cannot predict the outcome with Duncan." The magician regarded the automat and the others. "You'll be on horseback heading across the mountains toward the *Nautilus.*" He sipped tea. "You will bring along two horses for my brother and myself, and we'll meet you near there."

"But..." Bartholomew licked his lips, already knowing the answer to his question, "...why can't you use the horses you will use when you lead the Mafioso away from here?"

Celwyn gentled his voice. "We won't be using actual horses."

Bartholomew hesitated. "Oh."

Kang waved at Celwyn to continue.

"The Captain will share with you the location where we expect to rendezvous with everyone. It would occur about midday. In case there are complications from the Mafioso, we've agreed that you will only wait at the meeting place at a set time and then continue to the coast without us."

Bartholomew's brows drew together. "I don't like for us to be separated."

"I understand, but we have two enemies, and it is preferable to deal with them separately. There is a chance Duncan will also follow us and leave you alone." As a kindness that he didn't believe himself, the magician added something to provide a bit of hope. "You'll be safe once aboard the *Nautilus*. If we miss you, the ship will look for us west of there in Gerze."

Kang popped up and started to pace. "What if Duncan isn't fooled?" When the Professor saw the secretive and mischievous smiles the brothers exchanged, he stopped pacing. "Oh?"

Pelaez said, "We have a surprise planned for Duncan. An irresistible one." His brother's pig wandered by them on its way to the kitchen door. Celwyn turned it around and sent it back to Pelaez.

Kang stifled a laugh. "From the look on your faces, I almost feel sorry for that warlock."

Since they sat down, Verne had been quiet. A tic started in his right temple, keeping time with the clock on the wall above him. "How far is it to where we will meet you?" On his other side, Maeler blew bubbles through his painted lips as he snored, oblivious to the discussion bouncing around him.

Captain Nemo withdrew a map from the desk next to the bookshelves and spread it across the dining table. "The terrain will be hilly and rocky before the forests. And if Duncan does find us, nimble horses will be a better choice."

"What did the scouts have to say when they returned from Trabzon?" Verne asked. With a fingertip, he smoothed out the tick on his temple.

The pig rolled over onto its back and began to snore louder than Maeler. Pelaez patted its head before saying, "We asked them to look at two promising areas for our rendezvous and identify where the ambush points along the journey could be."

Captain Nemo frowned at the globe beside them without seeing it. "We will leave all the guards in place here. Only my original crew from the ship will be going back with us."

"That doesn't sound like enough men to defend us," Verne blurted. His tic started again, beating faster.

Pelaez told him, "For the kind of defense that is needed against Duncan, only my brother and I can supply it."

"Oh." The author seemed to shrink in his clothes.

"There will be less of us for our enemies to notice, too. And they'll assume the flying machine is still here and that we are coming back here because the guards will still be visible," Nemo said. "No one will be taking traveling bags or trunks as if leaving for good."

Before he removed the block on what Maeler could hear, Celwyn raised his eyes upward as a chorus of violins entered the room, moving swiftly, rising, and falling like deer leaping through tall grass. When it ended, Dr. Maeler shook himself and looked around at them.

"I must have dozed off. I say, have you heard about the Prussian war? Perhaps they could use a flying machine to drop explosives on the Austrians."

Pelaez started up from his seat, the fire in his eyes more dangerous than an exploding bomb.

Celwyn blocked him and wrapped him up with invisible bonds. *Calm down, Brother.* Thales' enhancements to his strength proved most helpful at times.

It took nearly a minute before Pelaez nodded at him, and Celwyn unwrapped him.

Chapter 39

EARLY SUNDAY MORNING, THE HOUSE buzzed with last-minute activities. The aroma of coffee filled the air as Bartholomew rushed from room to room, looking for one of his notes. Verne dodged by him, clutching the bag with his fountain pens like it contained golden nuggets.

The main room seemed cozier because the curtains had been drawn across the windows to keep the departure preparations secret. Everyone spent a few moments thanking the Soguns and carefully telling Fatima of their admiration. After they set out a cold breakfast, Nemo asked the Soguns to remain in the kitchen with Fatima. Before leaving them, Mrs. Sogun laid packages of ham sandwiches next to the backpacks stacked by the front door.

As they gathered around the dining table, eating and talking, Verne spoke up. "Where is Doctor Maeler?"

Captain Nemo responded. "Both he and Ginnie have been given a long-acting sedative. They won't awaken until noon, long after we have left. When they do..." he held up an envelope, "...this contains an explanation and instructions to carry on."

"Give us five minutes, please." Celwyn stood and hooked a finger at Pelaez. He followed the magician down the hallway toward their quarters, and once inside Celwyn's room, they transformed into what the magician considered their most inventive and intricate disguises. "I'll maintain our façade..." he gestured to himself and Pelaez, "...while you make the horses. We shouldn't need anything else for now."

Pelaez's pig snorted at him.

"Why you like pigs is unfathomable."

A knock at the door brought a smile of anticipation to his brother's face.

With a flourish, Pelaez opened the door to Captain Nemo and the automat. He imitated the speechless expression on Kang's face and bowed. "Come in. Come in." From the fussy tie and tiny spectacles hooked over his elfin ears, to the well-shined dress shoes, as an exact copy of Professor Xiau Kang, he ushered them inside the room. Captain Nemo appeared more than speechless, seeming astounded as he tripped over the edge of the table. Kang approached Pelaez and touched his leathery face, studying his profile and examining one of his elfin ears.

"Are those my clothes, too?" he asked.

"Yes. Jonas thought it best to be as authentic as possible." Pelaez walked with short steps like Kang to the window, pivoted, and came back. "Warlocks have a highly educated sense of smell. If Duncan approaches us, the clothes will smell enough like you to perhaps buy us some time."

As Pelaez talked, Captain Nemo wetted his lips and studied Celwyn, ultimately nodding. "I think that I finally have developed a complete appreciation for your magic, Jonas," Nemo told him. "You make a most excellent Bartholomew." He scrutinized him more. "The color of your skin is perfect. Can you walk as he does?"

"But of course." Celwyn demonstrated by striding to the far side of the room and back. "I do not think there will be an opportunity for a close-up comparison. But, if so, my brother will supply the voices. As you know, he is better at it than I am."

After examining Celwyn's version of the big man, the automat moved around the bed until he was eye-to-eye with Pelaez. He tilted his head to one side and then the other, like Qing liked to do. Pelaez did the same, mimicking him exactly.

"What the Captain said is true—you have outdone yourselves," the Professor at last murmured. "Just amazing."

"If you are to leave before us, it is probably the time to do so," Nemo told them. "As you requested, there are several horses saddled and waiting outside the front door."

When the automat raised a brow, Celwyn said, "We want to be sure our enemies know we are leaving." The magician was enjoying himself. "They are decoys for the horses my brother will make for us,

and you'll use them when we rejoin you later today."
He picked up a knapsack stuffed with paper and
tossed another one to Pelaez. With a serious look,
he told Kang, "There is one remaining chore."

"Bartholomew himself. It is very difficult hearing
your voice coming from his face. I hope you realize
that, Jonas," Kang complained.

"Yes, I know." Celwyn strapped on the knapsack.
"There is no reason to upset him. Would you take
him into the kitchen on a pretext and keep him
there until we've left? You can tell him about us after
we're gone."

When he saw Nemo's confused glance, Celwyn
said, "I made a version of Xiau once before, and if
Bartholomew sees us, his superstitions will cause
him extreme consternation."

"All right." The automat headed toward the door.
"I'll do it now. How long after you leave should we
wait to depart?"

Captain Nemo and Celwyn exchanged a look.
"My recommendation is two hours," Nemo told him.
"Our enemies should have followed our red her-
rings..." he nodded to Pelaez and Celwyn, "...west-
ward by then."

Pelaez and Celwyn didn't speak as they rode
away from the compound. To imitate Kang and
Bartholomew's voices would require more magic,
and until they reached the area near the city of children, they needed to conserve their energy. It was

enough to maintain the illusion of themselves and the twin guards on horseback behind them for the expected distance.

The uneven path through the low hills reminded Celwyn of when they had taken the same route as they arrived in the country, celebrating their enterprise. Kang, Bartholomew, and the Captain had hardly been able to contain their enthusiasm over seeing the flying machine again.

They rode by a lumpy berm covered in fuzzy weeds, reminiscent of Dr. Maeler in his wig. The weeds increased, becoming fields of grass before low hills as the sun rose higher, burning off the dawn mist.

Silently, Celwyn sent his brother a message.

"It will take us less than a half hour to reach Mavi Işık şehri *from here. Look for the depression in the rocks about half-a-mile west of where we emerged from the mountain. You'll know we've reached it by the irregular ridge of granite hundreds of feet long—this is per Captain Nemo's maps."*

Pelaez glanced back and nodded.

They kept their "horses" moving fast. If they were being followed by the Mafioso, their pursuers would soon be out in the open and visible, especially as they raced to keep up. Celwyn's horse picked his way upward to a low precipice. He squinted to the west and smiled; Pelaez followed his attention and developed his own smile; the scheme had worked.

Traveling even faster, they covered miles and miles of brush, and the magician kept an eye on their followers. Judging from the clouds of dust they kicked up, there had to be a score or more of the villains. As bait, Kang and Bartholomew couldn't be matched. If Duncan had also taken the bait, they would have to adjust their "greeting" for them all at their destination. If not, things became simpler now, but more complicated when they rejoined Kang and the others.

Captain Nemo's description proved accurate—the ridges of granite stood out. Pelaez took the lead as they raced toward them. Celwyn estimated the distance between the highest ridges and pointed to the spot he hoped was correct.

By prior arrangement, Pelaez gathered a magical stand of trees around them for camouflage while they dismounted. Celwyn paced off the distance between the ridges to the lowest depression in the shale-like ground.

"We only have a few minutes. Cover me." The magician moved a few paces north, then lay flat on the ground and listened. "Ah, here we are."

With precision, Celwyn gestured, and a ragged man-sized hole appeared on the surface. Fresh outcroppings for handholds and footholds led downward through the rock. Again, the magician lay on the ground, listening. Yes, he could hear the underground river. This would do nicely. He unwound Bartholomew's red scarf from his neck and tossed it down the hole.

With a wave of his hand, Pelaez changed their horses and guards back to field mice, which wasted no time scurrying into the brush. The pounding of the Mafioso's horses grew louder, vibrating the ground.

The brothers looked at each other.

"Now!" Celwyn said.

The music of the violins whispered around them as Pelaez nodded, and they split apart, leaving the effigies of Kang and Bartholomew behind while they sprinted into the trees. The ruffians must be a bit closer for the next step in their plan.

Celwyn stared at the effigies until the one that looked like Kang turned and led the way down into the ragged hole.

The last of the Mafioso arrived as the top of Bartholomew's head slipped inside the opening. They dismounted in a flurry of curses and dust, and their oaths grew louder as they ran forward and gathered around the fissure. Duncan did not appear to be with them. *Damn.*

Pelaez's eyes danced a jig as he elbowed his brother. The magician could faintly hear him projecting Bartholomew's voice under their feet. It sounded like a normal conversation.

That did it. One by one, the Mafioso scurried down the hole like so many filthy rats, pushing and shoving the other rogues in front of them. When the last one disappeared inside, Celwyn said, "I counted eighteen of them. None were Duncan."

"Seventeen."

"Whatever." Celwyn waved a hand, and the debris beside the crevice shifted over the hole, filling it so fast that soon it didn't exist at all. Once again, the ground appeared to be just a flat bed of dirt.

His brother didn't waste any time. He jumped out of the tree before it dissolved, and Celwyn joined him. "I need to rest a few moments."

"We have to get going soon." Pelaez sat on a nearby rock and laughed. "Nemo would love to see this. Do you hear that?"

Faintly, voices could be heard from deep underground.

"There's no evidence of where they went in." The magician pointed at their feet. "They will find that it is a rock ceiling, especially if they shoot at it."

"And all they'll see is the underground river." Pelaez yawned. "Which is nearly half a mile wide of freezing water they can't cross."

"Exactly," the magician sighed, more in exhaustion than satisfaction. "They won't kill anyone again or bother us."

A few feet away, the Mafioso's horses milled about, panting and snorting from the hard ride. Pelaez flipped a hand, and a large pool of water appeared at their feet.

"The town of Delafan is not too far from here, to the west. Would you care to make the suggestion?" Celwyn asked.

Pelaez bowed. "As you wish." He approached the horse with the most elaborate saddle blankets and whispered in its ear. The horse stopped drinking, neighed, wiggled its head at him, and went back to drinking.

Pelaez told Celwyn, "We can leave when you're ready."

Celwyn sat on the ground and crossed his legs. "I need to rest a moment more. The next step will be all on me." He looked at the sun as it rose and hoped for clear skies. "As we go, I'll be looking for specific landmarks to lead the way to Bartholomew and the others. Let's pray Nemo's maps are correct."

Chapter 40

A S HE STOOD TO THE SIDE OF THE living room windows, Kang shaded his eyes, gazing into the rising sun, seeing Celwyn and his brother ride out of the compound gates. They appeared to anyone watching to be a seven-foot-tall black man and a medium-sized Asian academic. Kang still couldn't comprehend how Celwyn had perfected the exact color of his eyes. Even his wife struggled to describe them exactly.

"It is all right. You can come out now," Kang called over his shoulder to the actual Bartholomew, who hovered just inside the kitchen door.

The big man approached the windows with the kind of caution a man would display to a coiled snake. "Have they gone?" The white around Bartholomew's eyes seemed twice their normal size. "I'm trying to be braver about this."

Kang elbowed him. "I know you are." He poured two coffees, and they sat at the chess table. "Let's have a game while we wait. The Captain says we will leave soon."

"You know, I was actually getting used to Pelaez and his pig." Bartholomew started setting up the board. "I hope Jonas and Pelaez are successful."

"They will be," Kang said, and brought his rook out. "Tonight, we will be playing chess on board the *Nautilus*."

❖

After two chess games, and a long discussion about what the day would bring, a pair of Captain Nemo's guards on matching black Arabians led the way out of the compound. With their hats pulled low, Verne and Bartholomew rode together, and the automat and Captain Nemo came next in front of four more guards. They passed through the gates and trotted north as a light rain began to fall. Kang drew his coat closer.

Charlie, the horse that Kang had been assigned, wasn't as bad as the automat had expected. The beast had held still while Kang scrambled up. As they went along, Charlie displayed a lively gait and cheerful attitude, which made the ride bouncier. Kang withheld a pointed remark the situation deserved—he did not like horseback riding.

Each of the riders carried one or more rifles, plenty of ammunition, and water for themselves and the horses, but little else. They expected to cross several streams where the horses could be watered. According to Nemo, if all went well, they'd reach the designated meeting point with the magicians an hour or so after noon and Trabzon by sundown. The Professor pulled the brim of his hat down and glanced to the south to where the Mafioso's camp should be. He saw nothing. For some reason, he considered that a good sign, one indicating *all* the thieving rogues had followed the decoys.

As they rode along, there appeared to be few travelers and none at all heading northeast. The automat wished they would encounter farmers or someone along the way as a distinct sense of loneliness settled over him. As he gazed to the west, Kang stared at the barren landscape and wondered how successful Jonas and his brother would be in their masquerade. Would they be able to draw the Mafioso away?

Captain Nemo said, "We should reach the beginning of the trees in about two hours. Consider it our first danger point."

"Could you explain more of what we're doing, please?" Verne asked. "You said we aren't going to the city where we receive our supplies from, but further away?"

"Yes, the Mafioso could be watching for us there. The ship is waiting offshore for us northeast of the city," Nemo said.

While holding on to his reins, Bartholomew brought up a spyglass and scanned each direction. Kang doubted he would be able to do the same without falling off this confounded beast.

"It is at times like this that I especially miss Jonas," the big man said.

The automat tightened his lips and his grip on his reins. He felt the same, facing what he'd successfully ignored until now; no matter the planning, Duncan would not easily be fooled, nor give up his pursuit. Jonas had thought he was being kind to keep them from worrying, but at the moment, Kang worried.

Verne asked, "Will they try to steal the aeroplane after we leave?"

"It is useless to them without the specifications." Captain Nemo urged his mount forward around a cluster of rocks. "We have copies, and the copy Dr. Maeler will use is well-hidden and will be until he receives a telegram from me saying the danger has passed. The telegram will tell him where his copy is located."

Now the automat understood why Nemo had approached the logistics of their departure as he had; the Captain hadn't vetted Ginnie yet, and he wasn't alone in his caution.

Kang had also sent a telegraphed query to his contacts asking about her. The request had gone with the supply cart the day after she arrived. If the Captain had received replies to his inquiries, he would have told them; Nemo wouldn't have hesitated to tell Maeler the location of the specs otherwise. Kang chuckled, picturing the woman searching for the drawings like a fluffy poodle rooting around after a treat. He and Bartholomew happened to know exactly where Captain Nemo had hidden them as added insurance.

The rain stopped, and for the next hour, they rode through grassy brush, bumpily and peacefully, their progress punctuated by Bartholomew's sneezing as they passed clumps of yellow flowers decorated with buzzing bees and other insects. In the distance, dark clouds wreathed the low mountains before the sea. It was a lonely place, void of farmhouses and other voices. Kang's sense of nervous loneliness increased. Occasionally, the plaintive howl of a wolf could be heard, which only made it worse.

They rested and watered the horses, but too soon, Kang again rubbed his rear and eyed Charlie and his saddle with misgiving. As the last to mount up, the automat told himself the quicker he did so, the sooner this ordeal would be over with.

High noon and they slowed as they entered deep shadows under a canopy of older fir trees that probably dated from the Crusades. Captain Nemo gestured, tightening the distance between the riders and the guards. and it must have been a prearranged signal, for every guard unstrapped his rifle and rested it across his lap. Bartholomew did so, also. Kang brought his spyglass up and tried scanning the shadows beyond the trees. On cue, the rain returned, drenching them and making seeing anything impractical.

Miles more, and they splashed across a shallow stream that brought the runoff from the mountains. Once they reached the other side, they paused to let the horses drink.

"How far is it to where Jonas will meet us?" Verne asked as he checked the trees beside them. "Like

Mr. Bartholomew, I would also feel better in his presence."

As if they had been waiting for him to finish speaking, a pair of wild boars roared out of the brush and charged straight at the author. He squealed as Captain Nemo raised his pistol and dropped the first boar with a bullet between its eyes. But when a guard behind Kang shot the second boar in the shoulder, it kept coming, reaching Verne's rearing horse. Another guard shot it in the neck, the blast nearly severing the boar's head.

The damage had been done. Verne's horse twisted away and screamed. its leg shredded open.

———

"I suppose it had to be put down," Verne murmured as they passed by the body of his horse. He rode with Kang, being both the smallest of the riders and most inexperienced. Charlie hadn't seemed to mind, especially after Nemo fed him a fresh carrot.

"Those animals did not resemble Pelaez's pig at all. Did you see the size of their tusks?"

The Professor nodded at Verne. "I did, and the look in their eyes. I prefer not to dwell on them." He urged Charlie forward until they were so close to Bartholomew's horse that it could have swatted flies off Charlie's nose with his tail. The forest seemed thicker now, and the road was still wide and clear. Large boulders occasionally abutted the track, and the distant, muted rumble of thunder reached them.

Kang shuddered; he couldn't wait to reach the safety of the *Nautilus*. As a pleasant distraction, he recalled the messages he had already composed for Elizabeth and just thinking about her helped. There were telegrams for Annabelle, the boys, and Patrick, too; it had been an exciting several months, but he wanted to go home.

Though he teased him whenever possible, the automat had also missed Jonas's silliness and friendship. Perhaps even more so while the flying machine occupied his attention. At this point, they had made their design as advanced as it could be, and the three of them could once again spend hours enjoying each other's company. For a while, Captain Nemo and Verne would join them. If all went well, he and Bartholomew would soon hear Celwyn's stories and relish them and his friendship.

The trail ascended slightly, becoming rockier with rivulets of rain threading through the mud as they clopped by. Bartholomew dismounted and took his spyglass to the top of a granite outcropping much taller than he. After a moment, he called, "I see the ocean!"

"Excellent!" Nemo's face brightened with hope. In hours, he would be reunited with his ship. "How far?"

"It is only about twenty miles or fewer, as the crow flies." Bartholomew continued to study the northern mountains. "However, we have more heavy forest to go through."

Within minutes, they reached a flat area where the trail widened and everyone dismounted. The guards watered the horses while Bartholomew reconnoitered from atop various rocks and a few sturdier trees. The guards refilled the water cans from the stream. One of them whispered in Captain Nemo's ear, and everyone remounted their steeds.

"Unless we cross another stream, what we take from here is the last of the water for the horses until we reach the rendezvous point." The Captain bowed, saying, "Let us resume our journey."

Another mile and the track narrowed as it descended to a small vale before widening again between grassy hills. With a strangled cry, Bartholomew's horse reared and would have thrown him if the big man hadn't jumped off. He backed away as the horse bucked and screamed, pawing the ground wildly.

"Look! Foam—in its mouth!" Verne pointed.

Bartholomew sidled closer to Captain Nemo and lowered his voice. "It has been poisoned."

With a curse, Nemo drew his weapon and shot the horse.

As he watched the horse die, a frisson of unease wiggled its way up the Professor's spine. Beside him, sweat covered the big man's forehead, and his expression was far beyond a reaction to an effigy of himself.

Captain Nemo squared his shoulders. "Let's move." He pointed to two of the rear guards, who nodded and prepared to double up. One of them handed their reins to Bartholomew while the others unloaded parcels and knapsacks off the dead horse.

"Leave the rest!" Nemo barked, "Move!"

They resumed at a quicker pace, pistols in hand and on alert. When a squirrel scurried up a tree next to Kang, he jumped and didn't try to hide it. They'd traveled not five minutes more before one of the lead horses froze and began foaming at the mouth. As the horse pawed the ground, the guard leapt off and out of the way.

"*God damn it!*" Captain Nemo yelled.

In a voice he hoped the others wouldn't hear, the automat whispered to himself, "I do not believe we're alone anymore." Kang couldn't control another shudder. He not only missed Celwyn's ability to protect them, but right now, he even missed Pelaez and his confounded pig.

Captain Nemo cursed again. "Shoot it. Double up and fall in." He signaled for the other guards to move, and once more, they rode by a horse who'd died in agony.

Kang was reminded of Celwyn's words about Duncan; *he loves terror and torture.*

When they reached a wide clearing surrounded by oak trees, the lead horse bearing the guards slowed and then stopped. Kang swallowed, afraid to look, yet he couldn't help it. Bartholomew dismounted and reached the guards, just as Captain Nemo did.

The automat told Verne, "Stay here." He slid off Charlie's back, and by the time he arrived next to the big man, he could hear a gurgling sound and saw the horses. Their throats had split open, and foam bubbled up through the gashes; their breath rippled through the blood.

The automat felt queasy. He asked Bartholomew, "How...?"

Bartholomew stammered, "When I got here, they were like this—no one was next to them. No one!"

The automat pivoted and checked the area. The shadows between the trees grew menacing, and the clouds obstructing the sun thickened and thinned, the effect ribboning spectrums across the landscape and heightening the unsettled feeling. The unease wrapped Kang in cold arms. Something compelled the automat to turn to look at the pair of guards behind him.

They lay on their sides, eyes glassy in death, faces frozen in horror. As the automat watched, the same foam oozed out of their mouths to the ground and slowly approached his feet, even though he stood slightly uphill. Bartholomew drew him back with a trembling hand.

"Captain?" Bartholomew asked.

Nemo stared at the dead men, and just as he began to speak, a shuddering noise came from behind them. They turned in time to see the remaining horses crumple to their knees and keel over, each of their neighs a chilling and final agony. Verne rolled off Charlie, clutching his pen pouch to his chest. Kang started forward and stopped. He couldn't help looking into the horse's eyes as its life drained away. What Kang felt ... he couldn't describe.

Captain Nemo shook himself and squared his shoulders. "Bartholomew and Professor, you are what Duncan wants. He won't hurt you. Stay close."

He faced everyone who remained. "Gather what is essential. Leave the rest."

As he watched the scene, Kang spied thin threads and loops of iridescent mist rising from the corpses of beasts and men. At first, it seemed only that—just a wisp—but it grew thicker, gathering into a fog that lay over everything. A shrieking wind whipped by them. When Kang focused again, the dead horses and men were gone.

"Oh!" Bartholomew wheezed and staggered back. "I wish Jonas was here!"

"Steady." Kang grabbed his arm.

The big man inhaled and inhaled again until he could speak. "How far are we ... from the rendezvous?"

"A few miles." In a defensive stance, Captain Nemo pivoted from side to side, his gun extended. "We need to signal them where we are."

Bartholomew didn't hesitate. He grabbed the nearest knapsack; the Professor did the same. Soon, they were ablaze. "Even if we don't flap something over this to signal—they should see the smoke," the big man said.

But, as he spoke, the shrieking wind returned, driving the survivors into a tight huddle. The knapsacks blew straight up through the glistening rain surrounding them, yet no rain clouds hovered overhead. Bartholomew shivered and dropped to his knees, praying quietly. Verne practically stood on Captain Nemo's toes and trembled. As the minutes ticked by, Kang remembered the terrified waiting was part of Duncan's plan. It infuriated the automat.

"*God damn it!*" Kang cursed. "Let's go. The sun is starting to set, and I don't want to be out here in the dark with this fiend." He gave Nemo a look. "We can't just stand here."

"Agreed." Captain Nemo marched ahead.

The clouds cleared, and the wind rose to a gale, trying to knock them over and bringing a blinding cloud of dust. The whirlwind suddenly stopped, and when the automat opened his eyes, he wasn't surprised.

The warlock stood in front of them.

This close, Kang noticed Duncan's rotten teeth and pock-marked face first, then the dull red curls and unnaturally blue eyes. The warlock appeared taller than a dwarf, only by a little, and he smelled like rotting flesh. It could have been the filthy rags he wore.

One of the two remaining guards raised his rifle.

Duncan twirled and skipped to the side, his laugh deep and guttural.

"My, my. What do we have here?" He advanced, and as a group, the automat and the others retreated. "Did you really think I would believe a trick from your magician?" He growled. "The Italians were stupid enough." With the last word, he tore the nearest guard away from them, brought him close, and licked his face. "Nice and salty." The guard fainted. Duncan broke the guard's arm and yanked his forearm bone free, cackling and waving it above his head like a prize. When the other guard raised his rifle, the warlock flipped the weapon and shot him in the throat.

"Enough!" Captain Nemo shouted, and pushed Kang behind him as he took aim with his pistol.

Faster than they could see, the warlock began dancing in a circle as Nemo tried to aim. "*Stop him!*" Kang saw what Duncan was doing and tackled him. Then Nemo saw it, too, and they both rolled across the pentagram in the dirt. Kang realized he no longer held Duncan. When he looked up, the warlock hovered feet above them like a malignant fairy. Verne shrieked and rolled into a ball to hide; the warlock spat at Verne and laughed again.

"That won't help you," he pointed to the smeared pentagram in the dirt and, in his other hand, extended a thin black wand toward Captain Nemo, causing his pistol to fall slowly to the ground. He raised Nemo into the air above them. Too late, Bartholomew jumped for his ankles but couldn't reach him. The big man lunged for the warlock, who danced up and away. As he hovered, he removed a knife from his vest and displayed it to Nemo, running it under his chin.

"Ah, Captain. Your usefulness has ended. Coddling and pampering your pets. For what? For a machine that you will never see again."

As Duncan put the knife to the Captain's throat, Nemo tried to knock it away. Blood spurted from his hand. The warlock ripped the knife across his chest, slicing deeply. In the next second, two things happened at once.

Pelaez's pig nudged Kang's leg and did the same to Bartholomew just as something blocked the sun, turning the scene dark under an echoing explosion of violins.

A raven, black as the night and of tremendous size, dove toward them, beating massive wings spread wide.

Kang grinned. *At last*!

With a flick of the raven's wings, Captain Nemo fell into Bartholomew's arms, and Duncan tumbled down a short hill. By the time he reached the bottom, the warlock charged up again, bellowing and red-faced.

From above, a deep and sonorous voice surrounded them.

"*Bastaird*!"

The warlock froze. He lowered his wand. "Braň?"

"*Bastaird*! Ar do ghlúine!" *On your knees!*

"Braň? My lord!" Duncan bowed and lowered to one knee. "My lord." Yet, as Kang watched, suspicion twisted his face. "I smell…"

Chapter 41

CELWYN MOVED FAST, WRAPPING the warlock in his wings and tightening them. As the magic flexed, the wings pulsated in a web of red membranes, straining to keep the warlock trapped inside. Pelaez joined him, employing every ounce of his strength. The veins in his head bulged, and his arms shook as the brothers enveloped the warlock.

"Make a fire!" Celwyn shouted, and turned to Nemo, staring until the blood stopped flowing from his chest, then turning his attention back to squeezing the warlock tighter.

"He's breaking free. Hurry!"

Pelaez lit the mounds of brush Bartholomew threw to them, and the others scrambled to add more.

"It must ... be ... hotter!!" Celwyn yelled. "*More!*"

Pelaez rooted around in the dirt and held up the warlock's wand. "Got it." He broke it on his knee and tossed it into the fire, causing an eruption of silver and gold sparks that flew everywhere. Bartholomew leaped back and forth over the unconscious form of the Captain as he tossed a dozen more branches into the fire before running back for more.

"Bring more!"

Celwyn tightened his wings even further. "Ready, Brother?"

Pelaez nodded, his eyes on the wings.

The music roared as they threw Duncan into the pyre, and when the flames exploded, Pelaez and Celwyn stood shoulder to shoulder, flexing their hands at the fire, strengthening the magic over it as the flames roared and the conflagration grew taller and hotter. Pelaez nodded at him. Celwyn sank to the ground, no longer able to stand, and crawled to Nemo. Pelaez remained in front of the fire, throwing more magic at it.

Kang and Verne brought as much fuel as they could and went back for more, passing Bartholomew, who hauled a tree larger than himself to the pyre.

"It needs to burn … Brother," Celwyn said as he inhaled and used the last of his strength to put his hands over Nemo's wound, healing it and finally laying his head on top of him and closing his eyes.

Time passed, and when the magician raised his head again, from a few inches away, Nemo blinked back at him.

"Captain." Celwyn felt a little silly as he sat up. Again, he put his hands over the wound, checking. It looked horrible, but closed and not bleeding.

"You fixed it," Nemo croaked.

"Yes. You'll be fine. Especially after Xiau says so."

Kang slid into the dirt next to them and took over, taking Nemo's pulse and other signs after he cleaned the wound on his hand and bandaged it.

Nemo managed, "...saw the raven ... you?"

"Yes." Celwyn patted his shoulder as he got to his feet. "You will ache for a while." He turned. "I repaired all the damage, Xiau." With a half-smile at his friend, he told Nemo in a singsong voice, "Xiau would prefer you lie still for a while, though."

Kang was too busy to do more than roll his eyes. The big man and Verne gathered around them, Bartholomew's expression a study in relief, terror, and worry. Verne clung to Bartholomew's arm and tried to breathe.

"It is all right. He will live," Celwyn told them. "Bring the other wounded, and we'll see what can be done with the Professor's help."

❡

Verne, Pelaez, and Bartholomew gathered around as Celwyn worked on the remaining guard's arm. The big man had retrieved his arm bone, and the magician sanitized it. A few feet away, Kang finished with Nemo and told him to lie still, adding something about not being like the magicians at following instructions. He draped his coat over Nemo before joining the others. Above them, the sun waned, and a breeze blew across the trail, chilling them.

Pelaez said, "My brother flew us all the way here."

They sat in a circle in the dirt next to Celwyn as he reset the tendons in the guard's arm, and

Kang positioned it. "Nice of you to make this." The automat pointed to a transparent coin-size disk placed over the guard's arm that showed through to the arteries and bones just under the skin. "Hook up that artery nearest you, please. See it?" When the magician complied, the automat checked the guard's wrist. "His pulse is weak. Did you make him unconscious, or...?" he asked.

"I did, so he wouldn't have pain." Celwyn leaned back on his elbows, breathing heavily, and scanned the area. He waved, bringing more wood from the trees across the grass, and dropped it into the fire. "Please finish his arm. I've done what I can do."

"You look tired." Bartholomew eyed Pelaez. "You, too."

Celwyn yawned. "Do you smell that? The aroma of burning warlock. There's nothing better."

"You should rest, Jonas. I am serious." As Kang checked under the guard's eyelids, Nemo got to his feet with Verne's help. He stared long and hard at Celwyn, finally saluting him gravely.

Celwyn staggered to his feet and returned the salute. He told the group, "We should get going before it gets any darker."

"Who is Bràn?" Verne inquired.

Pelaez rested his hands on his knees, breathing deeply, appearing nearly as exhausted as Celwyn. He said, "The Gaelic king we talked about. And one of the other ravens at the Tower of London." He smiled his usual humorless smile. "Duncan's superior, so to speak."

"That is why he knelt," Verne surmised.

Kang looked up at the magician with a frown. "I'd rather you rested, Jonas ... before we travel."

Celwyn smiled broadly and patted his shoulder. "Yes, dear," he said in his best imitation of Elizabeth's voice as he leaned against the first tree he found, slid to the ground, and closed his eyes.

⁓

Night had surrounded them by the time Celwyn awoke. The first thing he saw was Nemo sitting on a rock nearby, watching him with the intensity of someone concerned but still confident in what he saw. Where the warlock had slashed him, the magician repaired Nemo's torn jacket. Already he felt the chill in the air, and the Captain would have even more so with shredded clothes. Celwyn finished fixing the rips in his trousers as Nemo helped him to his feet. He thanked Kang for the use of his coat as he handed it back and added a heavier one to the Captain.

In front of them, Duncan's fire still glowed, but nothing moved from within it.

"Tell me what you did, please?" Captain Nemo asked. "They said you flew here. I saw a huge raven." He glanced through the gloom behind them, only seeing Pelaez wedged into a crevice and snoring audibly. His pig lay beside him, watching them.

"I appeared to Duncan as the raven Braň from the Tower and the only thing he would respect. Then, with everyone's help, we roasted the bastard."

Celwyn was proud they had prevailed but knew things had almost turned out badly.

"He knocked you out of Duncan's grip," Bartholomew told Nemo, then asked the magician, "Was that you or your brother who talked to Duncan?"

"It was my brother."

Verne had noticed Celwyn standing upright again and trotted up to them. "You *flew* here? From where?"

"Perhaps fifty miles southwest, near the city of children. We trapped the Mafioso underground." At Verne's confused expression, he said, "Remember on our arrival where we emerged from the mountain by the river? That is where they are. If the *Nautilus* visits there again, they'll have to avoid the pile of bones and guns from the villains." Celwyn grinned at the memory. "For some reason, the rogues believed we were you two." He gazed at the automat and the big man with feigned surprise.

Bartholomew gulped and said, "I am so grateful I did not see that." He clenched his hands together to keep them from shaking.

Kang patted his back and laughed with relief that their ordeal was over.

"I am gratified they are dead. One of my men that they shot died before we left. Plus, many more today from this encounter." Nemo clicked his heels together, and with a grave face, bowed. "I am again in your debt, Jonas."

Just having Nemo's regard was enough for the magician. He straightened Nemo's tie without touching it and shook his head. "No, and no. If I'd been faster, that..." he pointed to Nemo's chest, "...

would not have occurred. It shouldn't have." Captain Nemo's hand was still wrapped in a rag made from Kang's shirt. That wouldn't do. The bandage unwound and flew away into the night. "The least I can do is fix this."

Seconds later, Nemo flexed his fingers and admired the unblemished pink skin on his palm.

Celwyn added, "Don't use it for a bit. It will be well again. I am just speeding up how you would normally heal."

Again, in wonder, Captain Nemo flexed his fingers. "Like I said..." he used the hand to wave to them all, "...I am in your debt."

Bartholomew pointed at Pelaez and said, "We should wake him up."

"If you must." Kang sighed.

Celwyn nodded at his brother's pig, who waddled closer to him. In a moment, Pelaez sat up and stretched before joining them.

Kang slapped at the first drops of cold rain on his forehead. "Oh, hell."

With a shrug, Pelaez brought over scores of leafy branches and spread them over the pyre. "To keep the embers warm a while longer." He bowed to Kang. "Allow me." He pointed a finger, and an oversized umbrella the color of the raven floated above the automat.

"We should get going." Celwyn leaned on Bartholomew to hide his tiredness from Kang. "How much further is it to the *Nautilus*?"

Bartholomew and the Captain exchanged a glance. The big man said, "Probably about fifteen miles, none of it flat ground."

"Thank you. Our transport." Celwyn opened a hand and a covered cart, similar to the one they had ridden in when they arrived, appeared on the trail beside them. Pelaez spied a pair of squirrels, and they soon had a pair of snorting chestnut horses. In the distance, a wolf howled. Another answered.

"I think we're ready, Brother."

"How can we see without light?" Verne worried as he swiveled on one heel and gazed into the dark and mysterious forest around them.

Pelaez flicked his fingers and lit up the trail for about a hundred feet. "There we are. Just like the Champs-Élysées."

As Kang headed toward the cart, he advised, "When we near Trabzon, you'll want to douse the light, or the residents will think we're possessed." He rolled his eyes with fondness at Celwyn. "Not that we are, of course."

Verne scrambled into the cart, still clutching his pen pouch, and Pelaez and Kang followed, sitting next to him on one of the benches. Celwyn threw the remaining backpacks inside and boarded next, lounging on the opposite bench with Nemo and the surviving guard. He added more pain relief to the guard and Nemo and watched their faces relax. It wouldn't make them forget Duncan, but at least they would be comfortable.

"Where is your book, Jules?" the magician asked him.

Verne lifted his shirt to reveal a fat envelope taped to his stomach and another in back. "I took no chances."

"Nice." The magician added a canopy above the driver's seat. "Should I make a driver?"

"No!" Bartholomew called as he took the reins and shook them. "I'm ravenous. I hope the *Nautilus's* cook is expecting us!"

Chapter 42

Near midnight, Celwyn led the way into the study of the *Nautilus*. Qing squawked and flew across the room. As they nuzzled, Kang said dryly, "You spoil him as much as he spoils you, Jonas."

They continued to snuggle. Celwyn told him, "I missed you too, Qing." He realized it had been nearly a month since he saw him as he patted the bird's back and looked at the others. "I am so glad we survived all of that. So very grateful we're all together again."

"Here, here," Bartholomew said and headed to the bar. "Anyone else?"

"Where is the Captain?" Pelaez asked.

"With his crew." Kang called over to Bartholomew, "Whiskey, please." Verne and Pelaez nodded.

"I've waited for this all day," Celwyn said as he produced a teapot and inhaled the strong aroma of perfectly brewed leaves. "Ahhhh." He positioned himself to where he could sprawl across one of the sofas and see out the aquatic window.

As the others settled onto the other sofas, the crew arrived and began setting up the dinner table.

"I am so hungry I could eat raw oysters!" Bartholomew tossed back his drink and smiled broadly.

They laughed, knowing his aversion to them. Kang announced, "I want eggs. I want shrimp. I want bread!"

Celwyn shook his head. "No, you really want cookies."

"Well, of course," Kang agreed and sipped. "But they wouldn't go as well with whiskey."

Verne trembled and sank onto the sofa next to the magician. "I am just happy we survived. That ordeal was simply horrible." He pointed to his muddy trousers. "And look at that mess."

"We all are a bit disheveled." The automat grinned at him. "Are you going to change before we dine?" The crew pushed a cart laden with soup bowls into the room.

Verne shook his head. "I'm too hungry too."

"Fortune saved us," Celwyn said. "It is good that we are together again."

They toasted. Pelaez said little, but joined in the toast with the others. His eyes confirmed his amusement, and the magician wondered if he took surviving danger much less seriously than everyone else did.

Captain Nemo rushed in, arriving just before the crewman pushing the cart with the soup tureen. He stood behind his chair at the head of the table and echoed them. "It is good to be here. Let us dine."

As the soup bowls were filled, they held their wine glasses high. Celwyn admired the rich rose color in the light; little things, like crystal, colors, and the sea outside the window, made this a very appealing place to be. If it weren't for the inhabitants of Tellyhouse, he would stay here as long as he and Qing were welcome. God knows adventure would find him here and, of course, make Captain Nemo's life exciting.

Kang eyed him like he knew exactly what Celwyn had just thought and shook his head perceptively. The magician cemented his spoon to the table.

"To survival and a successful venture." Captain Nemo touched glasses with each of them. "You all have my gratitude and appreciation."

"To our safe return," Verne said. "'All is well, that ends well,' as the Bard says."

"'Better three hours too soon than a minute too late.'" Bartholomew added, "I do not know who said that."

Celwyn intoned with feigned seriousness, "'I bear a charmed life.'"

Kang laughed. "You certainly do." As he spoke, the automat seemed to have trouble picking up his spoon.

Verne said, "'Words, words, mere words no matter from the heart.' You are not just lucky, Jonas."

"'It is not the stars to hold our destiny but in ourselves,'" Captain Nemo said. "I think we proved that today."

"I love Shakespeare, but danger exhausts me. I will sleep well tonight." Bartholomew pointed to his plate. "What is this? It is very flavorful."

Captain Nemo's lips twitched just enough to warn the others. "Octopus in a garlic crème sauce."

The big man's smile stayed in place. He speared another bite. "I am doing my best to accept new things." He raised a brow at the magician. "And things that I shouldn't ever see."

Behind them, Qing pecked the aquatic window at a school of silvery fish who had drawn closer to inspect him.

Verne asked, "Will we be leaving the area tomorrow?"

"Yes." The Captain began cutting his fish into bite-size pieces and dipping them in what Celwyn had discovered was a spicy sauce. "I need to finish mapping our route this evening." He regarded Kang, who had abandoned trying to pick up his spoon and tried his fork. "You also have a stack of telegrams that my crew retrieved for us in town."

"Here, try this one," Celwyn said and sent a new fork to the automat. Xiau mouthed a two-word colorful and ageless curse at him and began eating.

When they had finished dinner, the magician popped a peyote button in his mouth and stretched out in front of the window again to observe the fish and mysteries of the inky water. Qing sat on his shoulder and watched with him. The magician must have fallen asleep. For the next thing Celwyn knew, Bartholomew was shaking his shoulder, and the others stood beside him, except for Kang, who paced to the window and back.

"Jonas! We have a problem." Bartholomew stopped shaking him and waited.

With a sardonic eye, Pelaez watched them from his position in front of the chess table. Celwyn found nothing helpful there and switched to Kang as he began speaking.

"As soon as Ginnie arrived at the compound, I asked the guards who delivered our supplies to send a telegram to my sources. I wanted to check on her." He waved a green slip in the air. "We have a response." He shot an anxiety-filled glance at Celwyn and read aloud.

> *"Virginia Le Vianne is a known*
> *disciple of the warlock Duncan.*
> *She is believed to be one of the*
> *notorious witches of west London,*
> *and is wanted in many countries*
> *for various crimes, including*
> *murder. She is adept at many*
> *languages and disguises. Be warned—she*
> *is considered highly dangerous."*

Kang repeated with disgust, "'A disciple of Duncan.'"

"All this time!" Bartholomew's voice grew louder with each word.

Celwyn sat up with a string of curses, exploding the chess pieces in all directions. "Dr. Maeler and the flying machine are in danger," he growled.

"Please." Although attired in a fresh uniform, Captain Nemo looked exhausted, barely able to stand at attention. "It is late night. We're tired from our ordeal." He regarded the magician, and his sigh went deep. "We must recover from what happened today. As much as we have invested in this project, this discussion will wait until tomorrow."

Celwyn swung his legs to the floor to allow the others to sit beside him. He still felt dead-dog-tired but very much awake.

"An excellent idea. Let us think about our next move before we act," Kang said as he stooped and picked up the white king, twirling it between his fingers. "Sending regular guards, or someone without extraordinary abilities, would not be enough to control a strong witch. Ginnie may kill everyone there, including any guards that are sent. As Duncan's agent, she may even kill Maeler if he doesn't give her the specs to the flying machine."

Bartholomew's lips parted, and he hesitated. "I agree. She is biding her time. Perhaps instead, she is waiting for Maeler to acquire the specs before she acts."

"I guess we are to discuss this now." Captain Nemo nearly smiled, knowing the adventurers well. "I had planned to send a written note to Maeler with the scheduled supply cart from Tokat, telling him where the specs are located." He regarded them with a determined frown. "I could refrain from doing so."

The Professor picked up a white rook and bent over to pick up the black queen. "I suggest that either Jonas or his brother go."

The proposal caused everyone to think for a moment. Pelaez asked Nemo, "Sir, how far is Tokat from here?"

"About two hours southwest, perhaps a bit less if your horse is healthy. The supply depot is called Josephine's, and telegraphs can be sent or received from there."

From behind the sofa, the pig appeared and wandered up to them where they sat. Pelaez scratched its ear and said, "I propose that I go. For several reasons."

Celwyn turned to him, his hands on his hips. "Oh?"

"The decision is elementary." His brother's voice took on a cold, detached tone along with the arrogance that Celwyn remembered well. "I am the best choice." Pelaez smoothed his cuffs. "I'll arrive in Tokat before the supply cart departs and show the letter from the Captain. It will instruct the guard to take me back with him."

Bartholomew retrieved a fistful of chess pieces and tossed them on the table. "And then?"

The pig snorted and eyed the big man before Pelaez answered. "Once at the compound, I will present a letter from the Captain telling Maeler where the specs are *while Ginnie watches.*"

The big man said, "To force her hand."

"I could do all of this," Celwyn told him with controlled annoyance.

"Not all." Pelaez sneered a challenge at his brother.

Celwyn started toward him, and Verne pulled him back again.

"Why, you wonder?" Pelaez's smirk did nothing to calm Celwyn. "Because I will have no problem dealing with Ginnie. Permanently. You, my dear brother, have never been able to kill a woman unless under direct attack. *You can't do it.*"

Despite his resolve not to, Celwyn immediately thought of the attack from Mary Giovanna and Mrs. Karras and how that turned out. He hadn't killed either of them, and instead had been severely wounded.

Kang had been there and must have recalled the scene, too, for he sent Celwyn a straight look before saying, "I agree with your brother."

"Really?"

"Yes." The automat didn't retreat. "You held back when they attacked. Your reaction was more defense than offense."

Celwyn threw up his hands. "This morning, I killed more than two score of the Mafioso in a blink of an eye."

"It isn't the same thing," Kang replied, his voice just as obstinate and sure.

"They were evil *men*, Jonas," Bartholomew reminded him. He sent a nervous glance to Kang, most likely wishing he were elsewhere right now.

Captain Nemo had been watching the exchange. He shot a dark look at Pelaez and stood.

"It is decided then. Pelaez will go. I'll get the letter ready."

Chapter 43

THE NEXT MORNING, PELAEZ climbed the spiral metal steps leading to the hatch. He turned and shouldered a bulging knapsack. With his usual puckish expression, he waved goodbye to Bartholomew and Celwyn as they watched him from the study door.

"It is barely dawn, and we were up most of the night. Doesn't he sleep?" Bartholomew mumbled around a yawn. "I don't know how long he will be gone, but he is taking enough clothes for a week."

"He dresses like an old man." Celwyn yawned even wider as they headed back inside the study. "He will be in Tokat before mid-morning, long before the supply cart arrives."

"Are you still angry about what he said last night?" the big man asked.

"That I cannot kill a woman unless my life depends on it? And maybe not even then?" Celwyn growled his opinion as they entered the study. "Angry, yes. But not at him."

"I hope it isn't at Xiau."

Celwyn sighed and told him, "No, not anymore. At the time, I wanted to do something rude to his ears, though." He yawned again.

Bartholomew poured coffee and asked, "How will your brother get to Tokat?"

"Probably make a horse from a rat or similar." When Celwyn saw the big man's expression, he said, "You did ask the question. Regardless, that way, he won't have to explain who he is or why he wants to buy a horse."

They sat across from each other on the sofas while Celwyn poured tea. "My brother's creations, such as horses, are serviceable but not as realistic as mine. Thales's enhancements to my talents included that change. Pelaez's also do not last as long without him having to maintain them."

Bartholomew laughed. "Do you mean that the horse could disappear from under him?"

"Possibly, if he isn't paying attention or is tired." Celwyn chuckled at the thought. "When we were children, I used to interfere in his magic at every opportunity." The magician enjoyed the memory. "He would make a bird, and I would make it disappear or change it to have one eye or no legs." He saw the big man's expression. "Please keep in mind that none of it is real."

"I will try to."

"Back then, my brother's reactions were memorable. As I became better at magic, I would cause

what he made to multiply a thousand-fold and anything else I could think of." He relived a few more
scenes in his mind he hadn't thought of for years.
"Those were my fondest memories as we grew up."

Bartholomew raised an eyebrow at him. "If you
say so. We just liked *kubada cagta*. Football."

The magician finished his tea and poured another
cup as Verne bustled into the room in one of his little
gray suits. Celwyn added a fresh pink carnation to
his vest. "How are you this fine morning, Jules?"

The author looked the worse for wear, his face
lined and unevenly shaved. He said, "Yesterday with
Duncan and the dead horses was terrible. I dreamt
about it all last night." He eyed Celwyn and added,
"Thank god you showed up." He caught sight of the
carnation, licked his lips, and said, "Errr … thank you."

Bartholomew said, "Jonas. I agree. A few minutes
more and we would have…"

The magician held up a hand. "I just wish I had
arrived sooner. Pelaez is heavier than he looks."

"He rode on your back?"

"Yes. I had to arrive here as a raven to impress
Duncan. Make him hesitate. My brother couldn't
have made a second raven of that size, and if he
did, he wouldn't have been able to fly it fifty miles."
The magician made a face. "Having him on my back
making unpleasant pig noises was part of the ordeal."

As he spoke, the automat arrived in the study.
"But couldn't your magic account for minor things
like that?"

"It might have, but speed became necessary. I concentrated on that." Celwyn shrugged. "As it was, I arrived almost too late to save the Captain."

"Why did the pig reach us before you?" Kang asked as he poured coffee and tried to conceal how he checked behind the cups for anything magical.

The magician put something entertaining in his coffee and smiled. "I dumped my brother off a hundred feet before you so he could alert everyone and so he could project Bran's voice for Duncan's benefit."

Kang went on, "From your expression, I imagine Pelaez did not land softly." The magician chuckled. "And it all originated from a tale your father told you as a child." The automat stared at Celwyn. "Amazing."

The magician suspected the compliment was Kang's way of making up after last night. He said, "It happened to be true. Duncan was one of the young ravens of the Tower and in awe of Bran. Yesterday, I just needed him on his knees between my brother and myself, so we could trap him." Celwyn relived the confrontation, its outcome again, and then grimaced. "Like the malignant curse on humanity that he was."

Verne asked, "Why didn't you use magic to make the fire you put him in? I do not understand."

"Because it had to be natural, of the earth, like his witchcraft. And it had to be a huge fire."

They all thought about that and remembered what the sparking conflagration looked like until Bartholomew said, "I had never seen a sight like that before. And when I first looked up, the raven had to be three times the size of the flying machine. Or more!"

"I agree," Verne dropped his cup back in its saucer and tried to steady it.

Kang asked the magician, "Did you know you fainted after you saved Nemo?"

"I'd prefer to call it exhaustion." Celwyn eyed Kang with a fond smile. However, he wasn't about to admit he agreed with what the automat said last night.

"You passed out on Nemo." Bartholomew laughed. "You should have seen his face when he woke up and found you two inches from his nose."

The automat laughed as well, possibly from belated relief. "I wager he thought he'd died and was in magical hell."

Verne piped up, "I knew the raven was you, Jonas."

"How?" Bartholomew asked.

"The bright green eyes. Ravens' eyes are black." The author rubbed his little belly, a habit he'd picked up from Nemo and a sure signal he wanted breakfast.

"King Brăn was known for his green eyes, which were probably not as fine as mine." Celwyn shrugged. "I thought it an appropriate choice."

After raising a teasing brow, Kang said, "I wonder if he was as modest as you." He sobered. "The pyre you built was a sight and one I hope to never see again. Or smell. Even before you roasted him, Duncan stunk like he'd been consorting with rotten corpses."

"Very true." Verne's nervous tic in his temple returned. "Yet, what was most distressing was Duncan himself. This was the worst thing to befall me since I have known the Captain."

Gongs resounded in the belly of the ship, and they felt the perceptive change as she descended; the water darkened, and the wall sconces brightened. Qing pecked at the glass, seeing fewer fish the lower they went.

"I'm glad you were finally able to rid the world of him." Kang shuddered in empathy and told the magician, "If I were a psychologist, I would say that you have no trouble with killing if someone you love, or respect, is threatened. But for yourself, you hesitate. That is interesting."

"Oh, hush, Xiau," Celwyn said dotingly and tried to think of something to change the subject with.

"Did you see the signal we made for you?" Bartholomew asked him. "We burned knapsacks so you could find us."

Verne shuddered. "Duncan removed it."

"As high up as I flew, I saw the whole area, and yes, I spied the smoke." Celwyn's stomach rumbled as the crew entered the room to set up the breakfast table. "I will regret for a long time not arriving before Duncan attacked the Captain."

As if Fate listened, Captain Nemo marched into the room, again hearing Celwyn's guilt. "My wounds are fine, Jonas." A rare smile crossed his face. "And it is I who owe you again." He sidestepped one of his crew and sat beside Verne.

"But, Captain..." the magician began.

Nemo held up a hand. "It is true. May I sample some of your tea while we await breakfast?"

"But of course." Celwyn poured.

As they clambered out of the *Nautilus'* punter and onto the shore near Trabzon, Bartholomew climbed the rocky promontory and gazed along the southern coast. "It is an interesting town," he called down. "However, we have a two-mile walk to get there."

Kang helped Verne onto shore and thanked Nemo's crew. "We will return as close as possible to five this afternoon." The crewman saluted and pushed away from shore. When the automat joined the others, he said, "What if the Captain's crew thinks we are unlucky? We've been responsible for several of them dying."

"A good question," Bartholomew said. "I'm sure Nemo tells them of the dangers when they sign on. And most likely pays them to match the risks."

"Why didn't he join us today?" Verne gazed at the sea, reflecting the sunlight under fluffy clouds. "It should be a fine outing."

Opposite the shore, a grove of healthy trees lined the beach before a choice of trails. "The Captain said he needed to attend to his ship." Celwyn scanned the coast and far into the trees; seeing nothing untoward, he fell into step with Bartholomew.

"Nemo will map our journey home. He was interrupted doing that last night with the news about Ginnie." The Professor trotted a bit faster to keep pace with the longer legs of his companions. Verne did the same.

Bartholomew said, "I suggested to him that we could wire Prague and have the *Elizabeth* pick us up in Constantinople or a similar city. By now, Conductor Smith will be anxious to be riding the rails again."

They reached a short rise on the trail and looked down upon the city. Trabzon supported a mosque and what appeared to be an orthodox monastery. The red roofs of the houses appeared the identical and surrounded a circular bay full of fishing boats.

Kang said, "I mentioned that also, but the Captain wants to deliver us as close as possible to Prague. So, I prepared telegrams for everyone at Tellyhouse." He pointed to his pocket and then cast an eye over the city. "I say, where do those trains come from? There are no tracks coming north, toward us, or east."

Bartholomew stretched to his full height. Celwyn elevated him a few feet more. "I ... I..." He looked down and back, "...I think I see tracks heading further south."

The magician lowered him and blinked innocently.

"For pity's sake, Jonas," Kang complained and tried not to smile.

Verne said, "Did you know there is a trans-sea cable for telegraph service from Trabzon to Tunis, to Gibraltar, then Marseilles? Then another to London?"

"No. I'd wondered how that worked." Bartholomew told him as they started forward again.

"What route will Mr. Pelaez travel to Tokat?" Verne asked.

Kang said, "For the first part of the trip, directly south, behind us through the forest."

Verne stared at the trees, remembered yesterday, and wiped his brow.

In another quarter-hour, they reached the outskirts of the city and headed toward the rail station. The Professor had bet Bartholomew that would be the location of the telegraph office, not the center of town. He won the bet.

———

As they left the depot, Celwyn found that the populace, from old men in robes to women bearing baskets and children, and even the men smoking in the doorways, all stared at them with an uncomfortable kind of awareness.

"We are objects of interest." Kang saw it too.

Bartholomew stepped off a curb and onto the cobblestones. "I noticed. About a block to the rear, there are two men who have been following us."

"The shopping district is just up ahead," Verne said.

"As soon as we make some purchases, we will be less conspicuous." Kang stared sarcastically at the magician.

Celwyn laughed, and they headed toward the shops. "A guess—there is a bookseller you wish to patronize? Did Nemo tell you about it?"

"Yes." Kang grinned. "The Captain says Pirinos' Books is worth seeing, and it is located just one street over from here. They are supposed to have an extensive poetry selection also."

Bartholomew clapped Celwyn on the shoulder. "I'm sure we'll also find a tea seller." He side-stepped to allow a man pushing a wheelbarrow of cabbages to pass by. "Perhaps we can locate some pistachios? I saw some in the fields yesterday."

Hours later, they basked under a welcoming sun on a seaside terrace, enjoying the breeze, southern Greek food, and extremely strong coffee. Celwyn blinked as the sun reflected directly across the water, then squinted up the coast to where the *Nautilus* rested near the surface. Because of the forested promontory, the submarine couldn't be seen from where they sat. As usual, Nemo's crew had picked a good place for concealment.

Bartholomew finished his moussaka and patted his stomach. Over his shoulder, a single white sailboat skittered by, dipping low on one side. The rest of the boats displayed booms, winches, and compartments across their decks. At the south end of the docks, more vessels unloaded the morning's catch.

"We should bring back something fresh for dinner," the automat said. "I believe I can make some excellent selections." He pointed to his plate. "This was very good, but I have no idea what it is."

Bartholomew stared at what remained on his plate. "Neither do I exactly, but it certainly was good."

"You should know we're sitting in one of the stops along the infamous Silk Road. Nearly anything is available here." Verne squinted at the street nearest them. "Some of these street signs are from nearly that long ago. You can tell by the hammered metal and lettering."

"Probably." After another moment, Bartholomew said, "We should discuss our situation with Ginnie. I worry that she has done something already." The big man finished off his lager.

Celwyn signaled the waiter for another stein for him.

Kang frowned. "I did at first, too. However, if she was in league with Duncan, she will wait for word from him."

"To no avail," Celwyn said with satisfaction.

"I agree, but for only a day or two before she carries out their plans." Bartholomew played with a cigar he'd taken out of his pocket, a sign he wanted to walk and smoke. His next beer arrived, and he put the cigar away.

The automat said, "The specs for the flying machine are actually more important than the flying machine that we built. They give detailed directions for producing multiple machines and various settings and technical expectations." He asked Bartholomew, "Do you concur?"

"Yes. Nevertheless, that woman worries me. What if she finds the copy we left there?"

The magician tapped his lip with a forefinger. "Perhaps she will not find it. To confuse and dissuade Duncan, I wrapped thistle around the package of specs to block him from sniffing them out. Ginnie won't be able to find them that way either."

"Nice." The big man looked at Celwyn. "How long will it take Pelaez to carry out his assignment?"

The magician finished his salad and put his fork down, thinking it exceptionally good crab and unlike what he had tasted in the Aleutians. "How long? Including the time that he'll spend rubbing his pig's ears? My guess is a minimum of two days to get there and set the trap for Ginnie. Then a day back to Tokat, and then another one to here unless he is rushed."

Verne pursed his lips, adding up the days in his head, and said, "Then we will not begin to worry for four days."

Chapter 44

*There is pleasure in being mad
which none but madmen know.*
-John Dryden

AS THEY GATHERED IN THE *Nautilus*'s study before dinner, Qing pecked at a spotted lamprey on the other side of the glass that seemed just as fascinated by the bird as he was by it. It hovered so close to the ship its lips brushed against the window. Beside him, Verne and Bartholomew played chess, and Kang sat on the sofa admiring his new books.

"Here we have an early volume of Joan of Arc, *Abgarus, King of Edessa* from the Bible, and *Itinerarium* by Jacob Cnoyen." Kang opened the last one with deliberation. The cover looked like tough cow leather that someone had beaten with a stick. "I have always thought I wouldn't be able to find this, and the other two are rare enough that I had nearly lost hope for them." He eyed the magician. "That anatomy book you found will make Otto very happy."

"I hope so. It was a wonderful shop after I finished sneezing from the dust. I also picked up a volume of Varsay's poems. We must do a spot of shopping for everyone before we arrive in Prague ... perhaps at a fancy haberdashery."

Everyone grinned back at him, well aware of who loved hats.

"Here is a bit of background you may not have known. Do you see John Dee's book up there?" Xiau pointed to the bookshelves. "Mercator wrote to John Dee in 1577," he held up the book in his lap, "and used the descriptions from the *Itinerarium's* description of the North Pole."

"*'In the midst of the four countries is a Whirl-pool, into which there empty these four indrawing Seas which divide the North. And the water rushes round and descends into the Earth just as if one were pouring it through a filter funnel. It is four degrees wide on every side of the Pole, that is to say, eight degrees altogether. Except that right under the Pole there, lies a bare Rock in the midst of the Sea. Its circumference is almost 33 French miles, and it is all of magnetic Stone.'*"

The Professor stopped reading.

"I wonder what it means ... Perhaps it accounts for shipwrecks or other disappearances." The big man raised his brow in speculation.

Verne wet his lips. "Oh, my!" He stared at the book the automat held.

"Although interesting, for Zander, we do need to find more than the art book," Celwyn said. "He will be happy."

"As an experiment, I bought some popular fiction also." Kang went on, "Lewis Carroll is an extraordinary writer. Funny ... as I read, I did not remember the English countryside being so odd." He read more, sipped whiskey, and turned a page.

Verne sniffed. "I suppose Carroll is adequate."

Celwyn enjoyed watching Jules green with envy. When he thought about making him green, Kang tapped his shin with his shoe and shook his head. The magician blinked away his disappointment and asked, "What are you trying to tell us, Jules?"

"Humph." Verne shifted position on the sofa. "How did you stop those men from following us back here? I saw them again just as we left the last bookstore."

Celwyn refrained from mentioning Verne's transparent change of subject. "When they trailed us through that park, I decided they needed a nap. After all, it was a warm afternoon."

"Did they happen to stumble off the path and hit their heads?" Bartholomew yawned and pushed a pawn forward.

"How did you know?" Celwyn winked. "If we go back into town before my brother returns, we'll need to take other precautions."

"I'm sure," Kang said dryly.

Bartholomew said, "I wonder if they were interested in robbing us or curious for another reason."

He rubbed his chin and shoved his rook forward. "Perhaps we should find out."

"You two." Kang frowned.

Celwyn batted his eyes innocently. "Whatever do you mean, Xiau?"

"I mean, the both of you will probably do something dangerous, and enjoy it immensely."

Captain Nemo strode into the room, preoccupied but in good humor, judging by the greetings he bestowed on everyone. The magician made him a drink and sent it to him. After a sip, Nemo bent to study some of the titles on the books piled next to the automat. "I see you had a successful shopping trip."

"We did and found an excellent cut of beef, which should hold our carnivorous tendencies at bay until we reach home. We also obtained some plump fresh oysters for you, Sir," the automat said as Verne removed Bartholomew's knight.

"Speaking of that," Nemo said, "I have finished plotting our route to Prague." He regarded the automat with a glint in his eye. "I believe you will be pleased."

"Oh?" The automat's hopeful smile came.

"Yes, we will have some exploring opportunities in unusual locations. Perhaps even a few diving expeditions, such as the Tenchante Valley."

The big man's fearful shudder rattled the chess table and knocked over his knight.

By the morning of the fourth day of waiting for Pelaez, Celwyn and Bartholomew had taken to camping onshore, out of sight, armed with a spyglass, a bottle of wine, and ham sandwiches supplied by the magician. They'd also brought a deck of cards so that whoever didn't have the spyglass to his eye could play solitaire. To ensure they weren't disturbed at their vantage point under the trees, the magician had also put an invisible alert around the area.

"This is a highly boring activity." Bartholomew lowered the glass and yawned. "Do you think Pelaez will return on foot or horseback?"

As the magician shuffled the cards, Bartholomew brought the spyglass up again.

"He will probably be riding his pig." Celwyn felt more than his usual irritation at his brother for making them wait. "It goes everywhere with him." The magician gazed at the verdant dell around them as the brook beside the trail bubbled along, and the lizards on the rocks basked in the heat. He decided to alleviate the tedium, sending the music from a collection of light flutes floating into the glade, hearing the notes bouncing high in the filtered sunlight. "Unlike my music, which is much more pleasant and doesn't smell."

After another series of yawns, Bartholomew poured the last of the wine into their cups and handed Celwyn the spyglass. "Next time, let's try a white wine so I am not so sleepy. Your turn." He stretched flat on the grass, preparing to nap.

It couldn't have been more than another minute before something violated Celwyn's alarm on the perimeter; the fountain pen balanced beside the cards fell over.

"Stay here," the magician said, and crept out of the clearing in the direction of the town. Bartholomew unstrapped his pistol and retreated behind a tree wide enough to hide him.

As Celwyn elevated himself into an even taller tree, he canvassed the area, feeling much more awake. It didn't take long to find the intruders skulking through the shrubbery toward them. It was the same two men, and they even wore the same hats.

While they steadily stole closer toward the promontory, the magician glanced at the water and verified the ship was submerged. Yet, the situation was not ideal—if there were two of them today, tomorrow there could be more. Celwyn descended from the tree and circled behind the intruders, close enough to invade their thoughts. He cursed silently; hearing only Turkish, but he did catch the words for "kidnap" and "money." Celwyn thought for a moment ... *What to do*? He knew of one superstition that the Turks respected, and in seconds, the magician had arranged a surprise for them.

As the men entered the glade, they stopped short and stared. A few feet away lay a dead owl.

The taller of the two nudged it with his foot, and they continued forward, but a few steps more, and they halted in front of another dead owl. The men stared, not saying a word until the taller man pulled his companion off the path and away from the carcass. When they attained the top of a short incline, they froze.

Below them, hundreds and hundreds of dead owls carpeted the glade.

The men backed up, arguing in whispers. When the taller one wanted to run, the shorter one shook his head. They jabbered at each other and gestured at the scene until a low rustling sound traveled across the glade, and the intruders stopped whispering to gawk.

The dead owl in front of them rose to its feet and blinked big eyes. In seconds, hundreds of dead owls stood upright and began to sing.

"*Hoot, hoot, hoot—*"

The sound echoed eerily as more and more owls sang. Their song grew louder.

One of the men bolted, and the other screamed and raced after him as the owls took flight, chasing them into the forest.

Celwyn yawned again and reseated himself at their picnic area. By the time he'd put the spyglass to his eye, Bartholomew rejoined him, remarking, "I highly doubt they will be back."

Late that afternoon, Bartholomew and the magician returned to the ship's study. The Professor frowned a greeting at them and went back to his book. Bartholomew stretched out on the sofa next to him.

"From the way Bartholomew is drumming his fingers, and the nervous glimmer in his eye, I'm betting you scared him again, Jonas," the automat said dryly. "Was it another effigy?"

Celwyn sat and pointed to the table between them, producing a plate of Kang's favorite cookies—chocolate. It took only a second for Kang's attention to center on the plate and unwillingly shoot the magician a questioning glance.

"But, of course, I could be wrong, and you are innocent," Kang said and reached for a cookie. The plate moved away from his hand. He reached for it again, with the same result.

"Yes, we had a moment out there. The men who followed us yesterday came back."

Without any problem, Bartholomew picked up a cookie and bit into it. "They will not be doing so again." He eyed Celwyn. "These are very good. I can taste the pistachios."

The plate moved until it was in front of Kang. He grabbed one and said, "Then I stand corrected." As the plate moved back to the table, the automat added, "But I wouldn't be surprised."

Bartholomew cooed, "*Hoot, hoot.*"

"What are you two smiling about?" Kang demanded.

Celwyn said as solemnly as if they sat in church, "You probably know that the Turks are highly superstitious of owls that sing."

Bartholomew cooed again, "*Hoot, hoot. Hoot, hoot.*"

"Oh." Kang regarded the big man, who laughed somewhat therapeutically. "At least you were entertained."

"What is Alice doing now?" Bartholomew asked him and pointed to Kang's new book.

"Dealing with a rabbit," the Professor said.

"That reminds me. Where is Jules?" Celwyn asked.

Kang said, "In his cabin, writing. You know," he faced Celwyn, "one of us should search his things to verify that we do not appear in whatever he is writing."

Bartholomew spoke up, "I will do it. Perhaps you can engage him in something after breakfast tomorrow to be sure that I am not disturbed."

On the morning of the fifth day since Pelaez left, Celwyn became seriously worried about his brother. They'd only been reunited for a short while, and he looked forward to knowing him again for a long time—assuming he was successful in eliminating Ginnie if she attacked him.

By two in the afternoon, they'd finished their luncheon of soup and vegetables and still sat at the table. Talk had gradually died away as their thoughts took over.

As if he could hear what they were thinking, Captain Nemo said, "It has been five days."

"It has," the magician agreed.

The Captain said, "Either something has delayed your brother, or something went wrong when he confronted that woman."

Bartholomew growled, "That witch."

"Since Ginnie is an associate of Duncan and up to no good, she makes Francesca, our witch in Prague, seem outright angelic," the Professor said.

Celwyn pushed his chair back and stood. "All the more reason we should go after Pelaez. He may need our help."

Nemo raised a hand to stop him. "I sent someone last night."

"Ah—" Kang said.

Celwyn sighed. "That will do nicely. Thank you, Sir."

Bartholomew chuckled. "You just want to be a part of the excitement, Jonas."

"Bah—" Celwyn stretched. "Let's play bridge. That is one thing that will go well."

By late afternoon the next day, Captain Nemo and Kang had joined Bartholomew and the magician at their vantage point ashore. Again, they had spyglasses, a larger picnic basket, Celwyn-made wicker chairs, and plenty of wine in a peaceful setting. Kang spent the time carving a new collection of flying machines. He had been a bit grumpy about having to leave the others at the compound in favor of taking his papers with him. The magician noted that this time the details on the wood were more pronounced, and the pilot of the first plane looked like himself. Celwyn huffed; *that* was not likely to happen.

Captain Nemo stayed with them until a bit after five in the afternoon, then announced he had to visit the bridge. "We'll surface and send the boat back for you about eight for dinner, if that will suffice?" He started toward the shore. "After that, it may be too dark for you to see anything with the glass."

As they watched him walk out of sight, Bartholomew remarked, "The moon will be out tonight. On a limited basis, we can watch for your brother throughout the evening, enjoying the fresh air, not just until sundown."

"I'm considering a magical surprise for my brother for being gone so long."

The magician had not decided on what yet.

Chapter 45

Only the dead have seen the end of war –Plato

DINNER CONVERSATION THAT EVE-
ning seemed as sparse and distracted as possible; the platter of roasted squabs couldn't even
hold their attention. As soon as Captain Nemo left
for his map room, the others went topside to the
platform. Kang muttered that there was a drawback
to this new location—no room to pace. The magician agreed; the ability to walk aimlessly had a certain attraction. The tension between them ran high
and had been growing all day.

Around the ship, the water lay calm, and the pre-
dictable winds they'd enjoyed for days had died to
nothing. An analogy of a frustrating day. At the bow
of the *Nautilus*, one of the crew remained on guard.
The rhythmic lapping of the tide against the ship's
hull was the only sound besides the snick of a match.

After Kang lit Bartholomew's cigar, the big man said, "In my opinion, Pelaez is not easily fooled."

"I agree." Celwyn nodded.

Bartholomew said, "Yet, why didn't any of us notice Ginnie was a witch?"

Celwyn said, "Blocking spell." He puffed on his pipe in annoyance. "They are fairly common. The telltale scent of the witch was camouflaged. Every time I entered her thoughts, I heard personal observations of every man in sight. Nothing more."

Along the western coast, the lights of Trabzon still twinkled, and faint music from the town's bawdy houses rode a freshening breeze to them. Far out to sea, across miles of black water, came a plaintive keening, then nothing.

"What was that?" Kang demanded.

"I do not know. One of the harpies? A whale?" Celwyn guessed. Although the moon had deserted them for the last few days, a million stars sparkled in the clear night sky.

"It is beautiful and peaceful here," Bartholomew said. "Yet, I feel nervous. Something bad is about to happen." The big man tossed his cigar butt into the water.

Celwyn considered the situation. "If something went wrong, then the man the Captain sent to the compound will meet the same fate. I propose that we go back there tomorrow. If Ginnie did manage to subdue my brother, I am the only one nearby who will be able to best her."

Kang growled, "I do not like it. At all."

"Neither do I," Bartholomew agreed. "Let us go inside, where it is warmer to talk. It is unlikely Nemo's man will return this late."

Minutes later, they entered the comfort and warmth of the study. Kang stopped and signaled them to halt. As if they'd been best friends for years, Qing sat on Captain Nemo's knee, happy and content with a gold button in his beak. The Captain rubbed the back of his mechanical neck.

"Amazing," Bartholomew said, his voice amused and surprised.

Celwyn continued into the room with the others close behind, and they gathered around the sofas. Qing fluffed his feathers and played with his button.

"From your serious expressions, it appears you have reached the end of your patience," the Captain noted. Qing dropped his button, and Nemo retrieved it for him.

"Yes, Sir." Celwyn told him, "Today is the fifth day. We do not want you to sacrifice any more men. We leave for the compound tomorrow."

Bartholomew said, "We will."

A commotion in the corridor drew their attention, and then a hatless crewman in torn and dirty clothes stumbled into the room.

"Ah, Valdez." Nemo arose to greet him. "It is good that you have returned."

The man inhaled deeply, swayed, and would have fallen if Captain Nemo hadn't caught his arm and guided him to a chair. In a voice they could barely hear, Valdez began talking fast, as if he would lose his nerve if he slowed down. Even before he spoke, the magician felt a cold hand of dread weighing upon him.

"Everyone dead—all of them. Even Mrs. Sogun." Valdez inhaled again. "Their necks were broken."

Kang handed Captain Nemo a whiskey, and he gave it to the man. "Drink that."

It was an order. When the crewman began speaking again, his voice sounded stronger, but no less frightened.

"It looked like a tremendous fight—the blonde woman was gone and—Dr. Maeler ... he died differently. His throat cut." Valdez slashed a hand across his own throat. As he finished his drink and Nemo handed him another. "Then, I heard a scream. I ran to the last building. The big one." Valdez started shaking.

"I ran in. The man," he hesitated and looked at Celwyn, "who was with us ..."

"My brother," Celwyn said gently and nodded at him to continue.

Valdez dropped his glass and shook his head when offered more. With another look at Celwyn, he said, "Mr. Pelaez, he ... he pointed at the big yellow machine, and flames burned all over it. Then he laughed. And ... and laughed." Sweat poured off the crewman's pale cheeks. "He saw me when I tried to run, and then I couldn't." He pleaded with them. "I couldn't move."

Captain Nemo patted his shoulder. "It's all right." He motioned to the guard by the door.

Valdez shot a tortured glance at the magician, "Your brother, he walked right up to me and said I was "late." Valdez switched to Captain Nemo. "H-he said to give this to you, Sir, when I came back." He fished in his jacket and produced an envelope. As he passed it over, he said, "There was a pig there, a big pig, staring at me." The crewman trembled. "Then he put me in a closet ... with a body. It was Mr. Sogun—his head was turned backward." Valdez waved away Kang's hand as he tried to comfort him. "I was tied up—with so many ropes. The man, Pelaez, he left me a knife—he put it under—the body. Made sure I saw it."

"So, it would take you a while to free yourself?" Bartholomew asked. The others nodded in agreement.

"When I finally got out, my horse and the rest of the horses were gone."

Bartholomew said, "And you walked all the way back here."

"Yes."

"Pelaez has several days' head start. Damn!" Kang stamped his foot.

Captain Nemo ripped the envelope open and read aloud.

"*Captain Nemo:*

> *As I write this, you should know that I enjoyed your hospitality very much.*

> *You may think I have abused your goodwill, and I apologize, but the greater good must prevail. The "flying machine" as you call it, must not succeed.*

It will be used for war.

The horrors of war envelop the air we breathe. Each new invention of war bloodies our souls. It must be stopped. I could have destroyed the flying machine a long time ago, but for two reasons:

I felt an obligation to stay and keep you and those in my brother's party from harm. Also, with the specifications that Bartholomew and the Professor made, you would have just built another one. So, I waited until the time was ripe.

I have destroyed both the machine and the specifications of how to build it again."

As Kang ran by him, and out of the room, Celwyn buried his face in his hands.

Captain Nemo continued reading.

"To my brother, you should know that I enjoyed our reunion at times and found your supercilious attitude trying at others. However, I tolerated it to obtain my goals.

Did you know that Miss McFein is not only a vampire, but also a witch? I doubt it. You are so besotted with her that you barely notice anything.

Perhaps we may meet again, hundreds of years from now, when you have forgiven me."

Pelaez

"That is all," Captain Nemo said, and folded the paper as carefully as possible to keep from crushing it. Unfathomable anger darkened his eyes. Then his proud shoulders slumped as profound disappointment overlaid his anger.

"Pelaez killed them all?" Bartholomew demanded as he stalked to the window and back. "*Why?*"

The emptiness and betrayal Celwyn felt went so deep he physically hurt. The glasses by the bar didn't shake or shatter—instead, they began to fall, one by one, turning to liquid like his tears and melting like rain.

Celwyn couldn't speak.

"Or ... it was the witch, perhaps..." Captain Nemo speculated.

Kang returned, and before he sat down, his face told them what he'd confirmed—Pelaez had indeed stolen the specs from his room. Celwyn remembered his brother's overstuffed knapsack the morning he left. More tears streamed down his face as intense sorrow enveloped him and wouldn't let go. After all these years, Celwyn had found his brother once more and lost him again in the worst way.

Captain Nemo regarded the magician for a long moment, and with uncharacteristic pity, said, "I'm sorry, Jonas." He turned and instructed the remaining guard, "Valdez needs food. Have someone stay with him." The guard saluted and ushered Valdez out of the room.

Kang asked the magician, "Would Pelaez really kill them all?"

"Yes," Celwyn heard the certainty in his voice. "I have no doubt of it."

"Or, the wi ... Ginnie did it," Bartholomew suggested as Nemo had.

The Professor said, "We just don't know."

Celwyn raised a tortured face to Nemo. "Take the Professor to Prague and his wife." He glanced at the big man who stood beside him. "Bartholomew and I will hunt Pelaez down."

"What is the point?" Nemo shouted and threw his glass across the room. "Revenge will do no good!"

"But—"

"Stop, Jonas." Kang patted his shoulder and then pushed down when the magician tried to get up. "Revenge is another place, another time." The automat made sure he had Nemo's attention as he said, "Bartholomew and I will recreate the specs on the way to Prague, and we will build another flying machine. Near Prague, if that is acceptable? We can devote all of our time to it."

Morose horns entered the room, exploding with anger and bleeding with the pain of treachery. Qing

413

flew to the magician and nudged his chin. Celwyn's tears fell on his feathers as the ornate organ began to play, joining the music of the horns, soaring high and resounding sorrowfully around the room.

Book Club Questions

1. Which character in the book would you most like to meet? Why?
2. Did you race to the end, or did you savor the pace of the story?
3. Which scene has stuck with you the most? Why?
4. Did Nemo's encounter with Duncan turn out like you expected?
5. When you read another book by this author, would you want more mystery or more adventure?
6. Is there a character you want to see more of in future books?
7. How do you feel about how the group manages their decisions? Should they have one leader or continue like they are?

Author Bio

EARLY WORK WAS HORROR AND SUS-
pense; later work morphed into a combination
of magical realism, mystery, and adventure painted
with a horrific element as needed.

I'm one of those writers who doesn't plan ahead—
no outlines, no clue, and I sometimes write myself
into a corner. Atmospheric music in the background
helps. Black by Pearl Jam especially.

More information is available at LouKemp.com.
I'd love to hear from you and what you think of
Celwyn, Bartholomew, and Professor Xiau Kang.

Milestones:

2009 The anthology story Sherlock's Opera appeared
in Seattle Noir, edited by Curt Colbert, Akashic
Books. Available through Amazon or Barnes and

Noble online. Booklist published a favorable review of my contribution to the anthology.

2010 My story, In Memory of the Sibylline, was accepted into the best-selling MWA anthology Crimes by Moonlight, edited by Charlaine Harris. The immortal magician Celwyn makes his first appearance in print.

2018 The story, The Violins Played before Junstan is published in the MWA anthology Odd Partners, edited by Anne Perry. The Celwyn series begins.

PAIGE LAVOIE
I'm in Love with Mothman

ROBERT J. LEWIS
Shadow Guardian and the
Three Bears

T.S. SIMONS
Antipodes
The Liminal Space
Ouroboros
Caim
Sessrúmnir
The 45th Parallel

VALERIE WILLIS
Cedric: The Demonic Knight
Romasanta: Father of
Werewolves
The Oracle: Keeper of the
Gaea's Gate
Artemis: Eye of Gaea
King Incubus: A New Reign

V.C. WILLIS
The Prince's Priest
The Priest's Assassin
The Assassin's Saint

COZY MYSTERIES

ANN SHEPPHIRD
Destination: Maui
Destination: Monterey

CRIME, DETECTIVE, AND NOIR

A.K. RAMIREZ
Secrets & Photographs

JOE DAVISON
Journey to Hell

MARK ATLEY
Too Late to Say Goodbye
Trouble Weighs a Ton

FANTASY

D. LAMBERT
To Walk into the Sands
Rydan
Celebrant
Northlander
Esparan
King
Traitor
His Last Name

DANIELLE ORSINO
Locked Out of Heaven
Thine Eyes of Mercy
From the Ashes
Kingdom Come
Fire, Ice, Acid, & Heart
A Fae is Done

J.M. PAQUETTE
Klauden's Ring
Solyn's Body
The Inbetween
Hannah's Heart

LOU KEMP
The Violins Played
Before Junstan
Music Shall Untune the Sky

R.J. YOUNG
Challenges of Tawa

VALERIE WILLIS
Cedric: The Demonic Knight
Romasanta: Father of
Werewolves
The Oracle: Keeper of the
Gaea's Gate
Artemis: Eye of Gaea
King Incubus: A New Reign

DISCOVER MORE AT
4HorsemenPublications.com